HIDDEN PIECES

ALSO BY PAULA STOKES

The Art of Lainey

Infinite Repeat (ebook only)

Liars, Inc.

Girl Against the Universe

This Is How It Happened

HIDDEN PIECES

PAULA STOKES

An Imprint of HarperCollinsPublishers

To David, Jenn, April, Molly, and all of the faculty and staff
of the 2010 Oregon Coast Children's Book Writers Workshop.
You changed everything.

HarperTeen is an imprint of HarperCollins Publishers.

Library of Congress Cataloging-in-Publication Data

Names: Stokes, Paula, author.

Title: Hidden pieces / Paula Stokes.

Description: First edition. | New York, NY : HarperTeen, an imprint of
HarpercollinsPublishers, [2018] | Summary: After saving a man's life, Embry Woods,
seventeen, is considered a hero but someone begins blackmailing her for causing his
near-death, forcing her to make choices that endanger her loved ones.

Identifiers: LCCN 2017034544 | ISBN 978-0-06-267362-6 (hardcover)

Subjects: | CYAC: Extortion--Fiction. | Heroes--Fiction. | Dating (Social customs)--
Fiction. | Conduct of life--Fiction. | Mystery and detective stories.

Classification: LCC PZ7.S8752 Hid 2018 | DDC [Fic]--dc23 LC record available at
https://lccn.loc.gov/2017034544

Typography by Erin Fitzsimmons

18 19 20 21 22 PC/LSCH 10 9 8 7 6 5 4 3 2 1

First Edition

ONE

December 11

THERE HAS ALWAYS BEEN THIS gap between the person I am and the person people think I am. It's not that I'm fake—I don't mislead people and I don't lie (too often). But I keep a lot of secrets. I hold back parts of me so you can see the outline of the puzzle and make a guess about the picture, but that's all it is—a guess. My inner pieces? I don't show those to hardly anyone.

One of those pieces is Holden Hassler. Holden is why I'm out in the frigid air right now, trudging up the winding road that leads to the top of Puffin Hill, icy gravel slick beneath the soles of my hiking boots. No one knows I'm meeting Holden tonight. No one knows I've been meeting him for months. Well, except for Betsy. She's the eight-year-old golden retriever by my side. I've had her since she was a puppy. Right now she's tugging at her leash with at least half of her considerable strength. I give her some slack, and she trots over to the nearest mailbox and sniffs around the base of it.

"Smell someone you know, girl?" I bend down to run my fingers through Betsy's soft fur.

Movement on my left startles me. A door opens across the street and a woman exits onto the porch, a broom in her hand. Mrs. Roche. Her husband is a plastic surgeon in Tillamook, the nearest town big enough to have specialized medical services. Mrs. Roche sweeps bits of dead leaves and debris out into her yard. Our eyes meet for a moment. I force a half smile that is not returned. As she disappears back into her house, I wonder if she wants to sweep me away too. I'm one of the few poor kids lucky enough to live in this town.

My mom and I live in Three Rocks, a small town along the Oregon Coast. There are only about three hundred residents who live here year-round. The rest of the people own fancy beach bungalows they use as summer homes or rent out to tourists. Many of the houses on this street sit empty right now, because almost no one wants to hang out at the beach in December. It doesn't snow much in Three Rocks, but the damp air cuts you to the bone, and the wind sometimes blows strong enough to uproot bushes and shatter windows.

"Come on, Bets." I tug the dog away from the mailbox and she trots up the hill at a steady pace, passing by the next few houses with no interest in stopping. This block appears to be deserted. It's a little like being the only person on a movie set after all the crew has gone home. There are signs of life—frosted-over flower gardens, walls of trimmed ivy, wind chimes clanking out an angry music—but no people.

The steady crunch of gravel under my boots is punctuated by the occasional whistling cry of a seagull. A gust of wind rustles through the trees, chilling my face. Pulling my scarf up to cover my nose and mouth, I pause in a clearing to look out toward the Pacific Ocean. It's too dark to see anything except a wide swath of black, a yawning nothingness on the horizon. But I know what's out there—I can practically feel the relentless push and pull of the waves.

My phone buzzes in my purse. It's probably Holden wondering where I am. Right now he's waiting for me in the lobby of the Sea Cliff Inn, a quaint, three-story hotel located at the top of Puffin Hill. The Sea Cliff is one of the town's most famous historic buildings, and up until the end of summer it was *the* place to stay for visitors to Three Rocks. But then Mr. Murray, the elderly man who owned it, passed away, and his adult children who live in different states haven't decided whether they want to sell the property or run the hotel themselves. So right now it's a really nice place that's for all purposes abandoned. Holden and I meet there on nights when he doesn't have to work at the gas station.

My phone keeps buzzing and I realize it's a call, not a text. Definitely not Holden—he's a texting kind of guy. When I pull my phone out of my purse, I'm surprised to see Luke's number on the display. Luke and I broke up—well, we agreed to "take a break"—when his army unit got deployed to Afghanistan a few months ago. We email a lot, though, and I know he's hoping we'll get back together someday.

Winding Betsy's leash around my palm a couple of times, I veer to the side of the road so I can take the call without having to worry about dodging any cars. "Stay," I tell her, my voice muffled by my scarf.

She cocks her head to the side and then smiles at me as if to acknowledge the absurdity of the request. Betsy is great at "fetch" and "roll over," but she responds to "stay" much like a two-year-old responds to "no."

I tug the scarf back down under my chin. "I mean it."

Slowing in front of a bright turquoise bungalow with windows that have been boarded over to protect the glass, I swipe at the screen of my phone. "Luke," I say, trying my hardest to sound excited. "This is a surprise."

"Hey, Embry." Luke sounds happy. He *always* sounds happy. Well, unless one of his sports teams loses. "I'm glad I caught you. Can you talk for a few minutes?"

"Sure. I'm just out walking the dog. Hang on a second." Glancing around, I find a place to sit at the bottom of a wooden staircase that leads up to a house on stilts. Betsy angles her head again, surprised by my deviation from our normal routine, but eventually she lies down on her belly next to my feet.

"What's up? How are you?" I ask.

"I'm good," Luke says. "Great, even."

"Are you still in Kandahar?"

"Yeah. I tried to get leave for Christmas, but we've got more senior guys who requested it, so I won't be home again until after the first."

"That sucks. I mean, I'm sure your family is really going to miss you." I lift my free hand to my face and blow on it. The tips of my fingers are freezing. I arrange my wispy blond hair over my ears, which also feel like ice. I should have dressed warmer for this walk, but I hate the way hats and gloves feel, all tight and constricting.

"Yeah, I already talked to them and they're bummed, but they know how it is." Luke pauses for a moment, then blurts out, "Hey, so I had a crazy idea and I wanted to run it by you."

"Okay." I tighten my coat around my body, blow on my fingers again. "Shoot."

"Assuming I can get leave in January . . . what do you think about the two of us getting married?"

I snort. "Funny."

Betsy looks up at me, curious at the noise I made. I reach down and pat her on the head.

"No, I'm serious," Luke says. "I was thinking—"

"Luke, come on. We agreed to take a break while you're overseas."

The break was my idea, and at the time I really thought I was doing it for Luke's benefit. He had no idea how long he might end up in Afghanistan. His commander or whoever said they were scheduled for six months, but that their tour could be extended if needed. I don't know much about war, but I know a lot of soldiers come home with PTSD, with traumatic memories that I'll never be able to relate to. We'd already been apart for several months while Luke did his basic training and specialized medic school. The last thing I wanted to do was heap additional stress on him by forcing him to remain faithful to a long-distance relationship if it turned out he needed comfort from someone there with him, someone who could understand everything he was going through. What happens in Afghanistan stays in Afghanistan—that was pretty much what I told him.

But given how things have turned out, now I wonder if maybe my benevolent gesture wasn't so benevolent, if I was trying to free *myself* from the stress of a long-distance relationship but just spin it to make it seem that it was for Luke's benefit.

It's possible I'm not a very good person.

"I know what we decided, Embry. But just hear me out."

"Okay." I lean forward and rest my elbows on my knees. Strands of hair blow in front of my eyes. The night seems alien and strange through the hazy blond filter. Dead leaves whisper to each other as they tumble across the gravel road. Naked tree branches tap at the windows of the bungalow across the street.

Luke is saying something about how we could have a small wedding with just our friends and family. Betsy fidgets, and I wonder if her paws are freezing on the cold ground. I jiggle her leash as I rise to my feet again. She lifts herself up and stretches her furry legs. The two of us turn back to the road as Luke keeps talking.

"I know you and your mom are struggling financially, and if you were my wife you'd qualify for housing assistance plus a monthly stipend. It would help you guys a lot," he continues.

My wife. The idea of being someone's wife feels completely detached from reality, like becoming an astronaut or winning a million dollars on a game show. I glance up at the top of the hill, at the Sea Cliff Inn, where Holden waits. If Luke only knew.

I blink hard. In a lot of ways, I wish he did know. Then he'd leave me. Then I wouldn't have to figure out how to permanently break up with a guy who's everything a girl could ever want. Okay, that's a bit of an exaggeration—in addition to the aforementioned obsession with watching sports, he's also a proud hunter with a rifle collection and prone to occasional road rage, two things that have always bothered me a little.

But other than that, he's basically perfect—smart, respectful, selfless, brave. I used to joke that he'd turn out to be a serial killer because no one could be so wholly decent and good. I've known him since we were kids because our families run Fintastic and the Oregon Coast Café, two of the four restaurants in town. We started dating when I was in tenth grade and he was a senior. He had to ask me out three times before I finally said yes, because I thought he was way out of my league.

My phone buzzes with a text alert. *That's* probably Holden, wondering where I am. I clear my throat. "Luke. The fact that you would offer something so huge just to help out Mom and me is . . . surreal. I don't even know what to say."

"Say yes."

I sigh. "I can't."

"Why not?" Luke's voice rises in pitch. Disappointment. Pain. Two feelings I am extremely familiar with.

"I—I don't know. I don't want to marry you for money from the government. It feels . . . gross." It feels like prostitution, but I know he means well, so I'm not going to tell him that.

Betsy continues to pull me up the hill. My fingers have gone from cold to numb. I tuck the hand holding her leash into my pocket and make an attempt to hold my cell phone with my neck so I can warm my other hand as well.

"I know, but it's *free money*. Like a thousand dollars a month. And we can get married again for real someday after I'm out and you've graduated. Bigger ceremony. We can invite the whole town. Honeymoon anywhere you want."

A thousand dollars a month would cut down on our struggling . . . a lot. Mom tells me that we're doing fine, but we were barely scraping by before she was diagnosed with breast cancer this summer. Now she's recovered from the chemo and surgery, but even with insurance I know she's got thousands in medical bills to deal with. I'm pretty sure her definition of "fine" is dire financial straits for most people.

Struggling financially is just as exhausting as struggling emotionally, something else my mom is no stranger to. She was nineteen when she found out she was pregnant with me. My father was—is—married to another woman. He's some sort of tech investor who met my mom at our family coffee shop where she was a cook and barista. They struck up a friendship of sorts and one thing led to another. And then that thing led to me, and a giant scandal. He and his family moved two and a half hours away to Yachats, an even fancier coastal town, before I was born. But small towns never forget, you know? Gram said for almost two years afterward, the business at the coffee shop dwindled down to nothing. Once my mom started showing, Gram wouldn't even let her pick up shifts anymore. Even today there are people in town who give my mom dirty looks when they pass her on the street, as if she were solely to blame for what happened, even though my father was thirty-one at the time.

"Why are you even bringing this up right now?" I ask. "I mean, where is this coming from?"

"I don't know. I miss you. I miss home." Luke's voice gets soft. "I guess Thanksgiving got me thinking about the things I'm grateful for. Plus, one of the guys on my team just married a platonic friend of his so the two of them can split the money. They have no plans to stay together and they're going to get a divorce or an annulment or whatever after he gets out."

I gnaw on my lower lip. "That sounds like fraud."

"Maybe," he says. "But it doesn't apply to us, because we love each other."

Yeah. If only love were enough.

I look up the hill again, to the hotel where Holden is waiting.

"I've always dreamed of marrying you someday, Embry," Luke continues. "So why not do it now if it means that I can help out both you and your mom?"

I don't know how to respond to this. The first few months Luke and I were together, I had this same fantasy. Somehow the intoxicating rush of physical affection was enough to bridge that gap—the one between the person I am and the person people think I am. I knew Luke assumed the two of us wanted the same things, and I didn't care that he was wrong. Kids, family, future, whatever. We'd figure it out later. Just shut up and kiss me already.

Intimacy is like a drug. It messes with the chemicals in your brain or something. That explains why I was all in on Luke until he moved away and I didn't have the constant physical highs to keep me distracted from reality.

The reality is, Luke's world is completely different from mine. He has a sister, Frannie, who is a year younger than me, and three older brothers in their twenties and thirties, two of whom work as bartenders at Fintastic here in town and one who is trying to open a second restaurant up north in Astoria. They are focused, they are driven, and they are an extremely tight clan. Anytime one of them has a problem, the whole family usually ends up pitching in. So many different people relying on so many other different people. I've never been part of a group like that. Since Gram died, it's been just my mom and me. We trade off taking care of each other, depending on who's struggling more. Just this small agreement is sometimes more than I can handle.

I know Luke wants to be part of the family business someday, and I know he wants lots of kids—he's never made a secret of this. But I don't know how I feel about either of those things. And I'm not sure if I want to get married ever, let alone right now. It all feels like so much pressure. After Luke left town, his emails went from "I miss you" to "Here's where I think we should live after you graduate" in the span of a couple months. While he was talking about us moving in together, all I could think about was the inevitable day I would fail to live up to his expectations. He would discover that gap between who I am and who I pretend to be, and then he would leave me—not for three months or six months for a deployment, but for good.

"Embry? Are you still there?" he asks.

I've been walking this whole time, and Betsy and I are almost to the Sea Cliff. "Mom and I will survive," I say stiffly.

"I know. I didn't mean to imply you guys needed help. Just that you deserve more than you're getting. Why not let the government hook you up?"

It's tempting, but if I get married someday, I want it to be for love, not for housing assistance or monthly stipends or whatever else Luke is talking about. So as much as Mom and

I could use the money, I know what my answer is going to be.

But it's not an answer that I want to give him over the phone, especially while he's living in a combat zone.

"We're still good, right?" he asks. "You haven't . . . changed your mind about us?"

I wince. "We're good," I say, unable to lie about the second part of his question but also unwilling to tell him the truth.

"So then just think about it," Luke says. "Until I see you again."

"Okay. I'll think about it." I would prefer not to think about it, but chances are I'm not going to be able to forget it now.

"Awesome. If you don't hear from me again before Christmas, don't worry. We're supposed to be heading out on a mission soon, and I won't have web access until we get back. But I'll email you when I can, okay?"

"Mission where?"

"I'm not even sure yet," Luke says. "But if I was, I wouldn't be able to tell you."

"Right," I say. "The whole classified info thing." My phone buzzes again.

"Exactly," Luke says. There's an awkward pause, and then he adds, "Well, have a good night. Love you."

"You too." Shaking my head, I switch over to my messages and find two texts from Holden:

Holden: You coming?

Holden: Everything ok?

Just seeing Holden's words sends a rush of relief coursing through me. With Holden there are no expectations, no lies, no pressure to be someone I'm not. I feel safe with him in a way I never have with any other guy. It's probably horrible that I can hang up the phone with Luke and be comforted by thoughts of Holden five seconds later, but it is what it is. Sometimes horrible things are true.

I slide my phone back into my purse without answering the texts. The Sea Cliff Inn stands in front of me. It's a Victorian-style three-story building with a lobby, dining area, kitchen, and eight rooms for rent. I know this because Holden used to do landscaping for the place before Mr. Murray died. No one knows that Holden made himself a copy of the key before turning everything over to the Murray family's lawyer. Holden's mom is a cop with the Tillamook County Sheriff's Department, so he's always on the lookout for places he can go to escape her watchful eye.

I let Betsy tug me through the frozen grass and around to the back of the hotel. There's a small clearing with a gardening shed off to the side. Beyond it there's a sheer drop-off of about five hundred feet. I look out at the dark ocean for a few seconds, resisting its siren call.

I've thought about jumping from this cliff once or twice. The idea of the ocean swallowing me up is strangely comforting. Maybe a little too comforting.

I turn to the back door, which I know will be unlocked the way it always is when Holden is waiting for me. I pause for a second, my hand on the tarnished door handle. I think about Luke calling me his wife. Maybe I shouldn't be here. Maybe I shouldn't do this. I could turn back the way I came, go home and do my homework. I could try to be a better person.

But the pull of what I want is too strong. Not just comfort. Freedom. The chance to let someone see me. For some reason, I don't hide those inner pieces from Holden. And that is its own kind of intoxicating.

Besides, what good is being a better person if you still lose? If you look back throughout history, when has the better person ever been rewarded? Better people are exiled. Better people are executed. Better people throw themselves into the ocean because they've spent their whole lives denying who they are and what they really want.

For better or worse, this is who I am, and what I really want is Holden.

TWO

I PUSH OPEN THE BACK DOOR to the hotel and step into the darkness, frowning at the vaguely musty smell. Betsy and I have been here so many times that we can navigate around the furniture in the faint light provided by the moon and stars. We know where the stairs are. We know where the hallway that leads into the lobby is. We know where the sofa is. Most of all, we know where Holden is—on the floor in the corner, his back up against the wall next to the stone fireplace, a sketch pad splayed on his lap.

"Hey," he says. He has the thick and throaty voice of a habitual smoker, even though he's never done more than try marijuana a couple of times.

"Hey. Sorry I'm late."

"No worries." There's the flick of a lighter and then a soft yellow glow appears in front of Holden. He sets a candle on one of the wooden end tables. He's wearing dark jeans and a hunter-green thermal shirt with a heavy flannel open over it. His black peacoat is tossed over one edge of the love seat.

He shakes his shaggy brown hair out of his eyes as he lights a second candle. He sets it on the coffee table in front of the sofa. Betsy follows him from place to place.

"Thanks," I say.

Holden likes the dark, says he feels more protected there. I'm the opposite. Darkness terrifies me—just the not knowing of what might be lurking. Holden *likes* not knowing. He returns to where he was sitting and kneels down to tuck his sketch pad into his backpack.

"I still don't see how you can draw without light."

"I can see enough." He shrugs. "Plus, it frees me up, you know? Sketching isn't about getting it perfect. It's about putting your feelings on paper."

I wish I could do that, turn all the fear and uncertainty I have into a drawing. I imagine a blank paper turned completely black—black sky, black sea, black sand, one girl standing in the foreground wearing all black.

"Were you drawing another tree?" I ask.

Holden chuckles. "Maybe."

Here in Three Rocks, the trees tend to grow in thick,

feathery clusters. Ponderosa pines blanket the areas between houses on Puffin Hill, and Western larches line the road leading out to Cape Azure. But Holden has a thing for lone trees growing in unusual spots—a single sapling sprouting from a crack in a city sidewalk, a solitary pine standing tall at the edge of a cliff.

Sometimes I wonder if it's how he sees himself—alone, out of place.

I go to him and wrap my arms around his waist, press my cheek against his chest. I catch the woodsy scent of his deodorant layered on top of something softer—laundry detergent probably. There's a speck of paint on his shirt. I'm pretty sure everything Holden owns ends up with paint on it.

"What's all this about?" He twines one arm around my back, his free hand gently stroking the ends of my hair.

"I just needed a hug."

"Sure." He squeezes me tightly, lifting me a couple of inches off the floor for a few seconds. "Is everything okay?"

He means is my mom okay. As far as I know, her post-op PET scans have all come back clear, but I've read enough about cancer to know that if it made it into the lymph nodes, it could pop up in another area of her body months later. I'm so terrified of her relapsing that she's stopped telling me when she's going to the doctor so I won't make myself sick worrying about it.

"Yeah. Everything is fine. It's just been a weird day."

"Well, you're with me now, so I promise it'll only get weirder." Holden brushes his lips against my cheek. He slips his hands up under the bottom of my jacket and rubs my back for a few seconds.

I cling to him, fighting a strange urge to cry.

"I can feel your ribs, girl," he says. "When's the last time you ate?"

I pull back to look him in the eye. "I had lunch at school. Mexican pizza."

"Yeah, no. You should sue for false advertising. That slop was neither Mexican nor pizza." He tucks a wayward strand of hair behind my ear. "Why didn't you eat at work?"

I shrug. "I overheard my mom lecturing the cooks about food cost the other day, so I'm not going to make myself stuff if they can't do the same."

Betsy bumps her head into Holden's knee and makes a soft whining sound. She puts her paws up on his leg.

"Oh, hello." Holden looks down at Betsy's hopeful face. "Do I know you?"

Her pink tongue falls out of the corner of her mouth as she pants with excitement. Holden spends a few minutes lavishing affection on her—scratching her behind the ears and patting her all over. She rolls over on her back so he can rub her belly.

"You spoil her," I say.

"She deserves it." Holden pauses in his scratching for a second, and Betsy waves her front paws in the air as if to say, "More, please." He laughs lightly and gives her a second rubdown. Satisfied, she rolls over onto her belly, stretching her long legs out in front of her.

Holden turns his attention back to me. "So. Weird day, huh? You want to talk about it?"

"No, not really," I say. And then after a few seconds, "My father sent me a Christmas card."

"Oh?" Holden waits for me to say more.

I flop down on the sofa and unzip the front of my jacket. "The first one he ever sent. It had five hundred dollars in it. In cash. Who does that? Who sends that much cash?" I don't tell Holden that when my mom gave it to me she suggested maybe I write him a letter in return, that it might be time for the two of us to get to know each other. *Sorry, Mom. That time was seventeen years ago.*

Holden whistles under his breath. "Who cares? What are you gonna buy?"

"I don't know. Maybe nothing. I don't want his . . . charity."

"People can change, you know?" Holden sits next to me.

"Yeah, for the worse."

"At least he's trying."

"Please." I scoff. "With money?"

"It's not like you'd give him the time of day if he showed up in person, right?" Holden nudges me with his elbow. "He probably figures money is a safer bet. You should blow it all on something you've been wanting. Maybe a real camera?"

I've been interested in photography since Mom gave me her old cell phone a few years ago. It's the only camera I have, and it's not very good—five megapixels, which is nothing—but I still manage to get some amazing shots with it. I want a real camera, though, so I can make the most of the photography class I signed up for next semester.

"I don't want to buy a camera with his money. If I did, every time I used it I would think of him," I say. "I wish I could just send the money back, but I know my mom could use it." It sucks to take handouts from someone who's hurt me so badly, but it would suck worse to punish Mom by turning away money that we need. Sometimes being poor means having to choose between your principles and your survival.

"Our heat has been messed up forever," I continue. "Maybe it's enough to fix the furnace."

Holden nods. "Heat is good too."

"Actually, that was only the second-weirdest thing that

happened today," I say. "Luke called me when I was walking up the hill."

"How's Captain America?" Holden stretches his arms over his head. He swallows back a yawn.

"He's fine," I say, ignoring the hint of sarcasm. "He asked me to marry him."

"Whoa. Seriously?"

"Right? Thank you. I didn't understand it either, but apparently the government pays good benefits to military spouses, and Luke thought Mom and I could use the extra cash."

"Ah, I get it." Holden kicks his feet up onto the wooden coffee table. "So then are congratulations in order?"

"Holden," I say sharply. "I didn't say yes."

He coughs. "Did you say no?"

"He wouldn't let me. He told me just to think about it." I look down at my hands. "Plus, I didn't want to say anything that might upset him while he's overseas."

"Right." Holden nods slowly. "So kind of like with Julia."

I wince. Holden is my best friend Julia's ex-boyfriend. She wants to be a political strategist someday, so she spent all summer in Washington, DC, interning for a think tank. Holden and I gravitated toward each other in her absence, especially after my mom got sick. We kept things friendly at first, but then one night we both realized our feelings were mutual. It's not an excuse for what we did, but it *is* a reason.

Holden called Julia in DC the day after we first slept together. He apologized for cheating on her, and they decided to break up. She seemed okay with it at the time, and she and Holden are still friends, but she doesn't know I'm the girl he was with that night. And she definitely doesn't know Holden and I are still hooking up.

"You know I'm going to tell her," I say. "I just don't want to do it right before Christmas."

"Like you didn't want to do it right before Thanksgiving, and you didn't want to do it right before she had to retake the SATs, and you didn't want to do it while she was out of town." He clears his throat. "We both know she was never really that into me, Embry. I wish you had just told her back when I did."

"Me too, but I didn't. So unless you have a time machine ..."

It's not that I *want* to keep Holden and me a secret. Somewhere along the way it just became one of those pieces I hold back. I never even told Julia I was having second thoughts about Luke until recently, mostly because I knew she wouldn't get it. She probably thinks Luke is too good for me too.

But I *am* going to tell her everything after the holidays, I swear. I'm not expecting her to forgive me for stealing away her boyfriend, but hopefully Holden is right about her not liking him that much. She never seemed that upset about the breakup, but Julia believes strongly in "projecting a powerful persona," to quote one of her dad's corporate success self-help books. Even if she was devastated, she might have felt the need to hide her pain from everyone, including me.

Holden bumps his knee against mine. "So are you *gonna* say yes?"

"What?" It takes me a moment to realize he's talking about Luke's proposal. I rest my head in my hands. "No. But I have no idea how I'm going to say no."

Holden bends the fingers of his right hand backward until his knuckles crack. "If you tell him you're screwing the 'salad-eating pansy guy,' that'll probably take care of it."

I cringe. Luke graduated before Holden moved here, and then he left for basic training a few months later, so they don't know each other very well. The four of us have hung out only a couple of times when Luke was home on leave—the last time was for my junior prom. We all went to Fintastic, where Luke teased Holden about being vegan and Holden responded with some sharp words about the way the US military thinks it runs the whole world. A heated argument about politics ensued, with Julia chiming in. I chugged a half a goblet of water and cut my scallops into smaller and smaller pieces, trying not to notice how the whole restaurant was looking at us. Luke's mom had to come out of the back and tell us all to shush.

I narrow my eyes at Holden. "A. He was just joking around and you tried to start World War Three at dinner. And B. You're supposed to make me feel better, not remind me that I'm a terrible person."

Holden smirks. "You always take his side."

"No I don't. I just . . ." My words fall away as Holden reaches up to brush a lock of hair back from my face, his fingertips lingering on my jawbone. I suddenly remember why I came here, and it wasn't to think about Luke. In the dim light, Holden's blue eyes are as dark as storm clouds. I imagine pouring rain, crashing waves, whitecaps. *I want to drown in you*, I think.

But Holden has other ideas. "A. I'm just messing with you," he says. "And B. You're not a terrible person, Embry. You're just a person, like everyone else. And you know that."

I do, sort of. But guilt is basically one of my superpowers. It's been programmed into me from the moment I was old enough to know what it was.

Holden bends down and pulls a half-empty bottle of Absolut vodka out of his backpack. "Now as far as feeling better goes . . ." He unscrews the bottle and hands it over to me.

"Fancy." I run my thumb across the raised lettering. "I

think you might be a bad influence. I only drink when I'm with you."

"That's because I'm the only one providing you with free booze."

"Where'd you get this?"

"Oh, you know. Friend-of-a-friend type thing."

"Right. So you stole it from your mom, then?" I elbow him in the ribs.

Holden laughs. "I don't *steal*. I reallocate resources to needier parties."

I snort. "You're just a regular alcohol Robin Hood, huh?"

He pulls out a small silver flask. "Well, I know you don't like the shit I drink."

"That's because the shit you drink tastes like lighter fluid." I take a long swig from the vodka bottle. The bitter alcohol burns my throat and makes my sinuses tingle.

"And the shit you drink tastes like cleaning fluid. What's your point?"

"That maybe we need better hobbies?" I suggest.

Holden actually has a lot of interests. He draws, he paints, he tinkers around with the motorcycle he fixed up with his grandfather, and he reads for fun the kind of thick, boring books our teachers assign us in English class. I'm the one who needs better hobbies. I used to be on the swim team, but I quit junior year so that I could pick up more shifts at the coffee shop. Now when I'm not working, I mostly take Betsy to the beach or hang out with Julia. Oh, and I worry about my mom. I'm kind of a professional when it comes to that.

Holden reaches out and traces a fraying thread on my jeans. "I can think of more fun things we could do right about now." He arches his eyebrows playfully.

Just the pressure of his hand on my thigh is enough to cause a rush of heat to move through me. It's always like this with him—we start out just talking, but the instant he says or does something remotely sexual, it's all I can think about.

But then I hear Luke's voice in my ear—sweet, loyal Luke offering to marry me so that the army would give my mom and me money. Part of me feels like I should take him up on his offer, just for her. It would have been so much easier for her not to have me. It's one thing to grow up knowing you were an accident, but something altogether different to grow up knowing you're living proof of your mom's biggest mistake.

I turn and press my lips to Holden's cheek. "Is it okay if we just hang out tonight?"

"It's okay if we just hang out every night. You know that." He pats me on the leg.

I lean my head against his shoulder. Across the room, Betsy has fallen into a deep sleep. Her body twitches as she dreams. I wonder what dogs dream about, if she thinks she's chasing cats or eating a big steak right now. Her mouth is curled into what I like to think of as her doggie smile.

"Will I ever be happy?" I blurt out.

"Yes," Holden says, without hesitation.

Betsy twitches again and makes a soft snoring noise. Her tail wags slightly.

"Will I ever be as happy as Betsy?"

He turns to the dog and watches her for a few seconds. "I hope not."

I slug him in the arm. "Ass. Why would you say that?"

"You don't want to be that happy. It's just a longer, harder fall."

"Are you speaking from experience?"

"Nah. My parents were really happy when I was a kid."

"Ah." Holden doesn't talk much about his childhood. His parents split up a couple of years ago, and his mom moved back here to be close to his grandparents, just in time for the start of junior year. I know he spends every other weekend with his dad in Portland, but he doesn't talk much about that either.

Betsy's eyes flick open. She lifts up from the spot in front of the registration desk and pads across the carpeted floor to the sofa. She gives me a hopeful look, and I shake my head at her. "You can't come up here," I say. Ever the obedient dog, she puts her paws on my leg and makes an attempt to clamber up onto my lap. "No," I tell her again. She wags her tail, knocking over the open bottle of vodka. It rolls off the table and onto the floor before I can grab it.

"Shit." I reach down and grab the bottle, standing it upright and capping it, but not before half of what's left has leaked out onto the lobby's threadbare carpet.

"It's no big deal. It'll dry," Holden says. "At least vodka is clear."

"Yeah, but your mom is going to wonder why half the bottle is missing."

"I'll water it down a little. She only drinks a few times a year. She probably won't notice."

"Bad dog," I say to Betsy, who is now attempting to clamber up onto Holden's lap.

He strokes her soft fur. "You're not a bad dog," he says. "You're a good dog."

She leans her neck on Holden's thigh and looks up at him with her big brown eyes. He pulls her up from the floor so she's sitting on his lap, her tail hanging over the edge of the sofa.

"You two make a cute couple," I say.

"As do you and Luke."

I frown. "Very funny. You know we're not together."

Holden snickers. "And yet he just proposed."

"It wasn't, like, an official proposal or anything. He was

just asking me what I thought."

"Which is totally what someone would do with a girl he's not together with." Holden lifts the flap of Betsy's ear and pretends to whisper something to her.

"You jealous?" I ask.

"Would you like it if I was?" That low, throaty voice again.

My insides go tight, and I have to squeeze out my one-word response. "Maybe."

Honestly, I'm not sure how I would feel. Holden is not my boyfriend, and I'm fine with that. We're both here because we want to be here. No one is obligated. No one owes anyone anything. My life belongs to me and Holden's belongs to him. Still, when I think about the future, Holden is always there.

The corners of his lips turn up ever so slightly. "Come here." He lifts Betsy from the sofa and helps her back onto the floor. She lumbers across the room and lies down in front of the registration counter. He pulls me into his lap, adjusting my body so my head is against his chest. "Your turn to keep me warm."

I laugh at the idea of my spindly body keeping anyone warm, but I rest my head against Holden's chest, comforted by his heat, his calm breathing, by the steady thudding of his heart in my ear. For a while we just sit there, and it's everything that I need.

Then he reaches for one of my hands, twining our fingers together. We're both pale, but he's got a bit more color than I do, probably left over from his summer job doing landscaping. He lifts my hand to his lips and kisses my wrist gently. Another rush of heat courses through my body, causing me to shudder visibly.

"What was that?" he asks, his blue eyes dancing with amusement.

"Just what you do to me."

"I make you convulse? That seems bad."

"It's a good kind of convulsing," I say, unable to keep a smile from creeping onto my face.

I don't know if it's the alcohol, or Holden, or the fact that I talked to him about both Luke and my dad, but I've finally achieved the closest feeling I ever get to peace anymore. I turn and adjust my body so I'm straddling Holden's lap. *I'm falling for you*, I think, as we kiss. But I don't say it, because those are words that change things, and I like the way things are.

I guess there are some pieces I don't even show Holden.

I curl my hands around the back of his neck. Our noses bump gently as I lean in to kiss him again. He tastes my bottom lip with his tongue and then uses it to coax open my mouth. I slide my hands up under his shirt, amazed by how his slender frame can manage to be so warm when it's so cold in here. I trace my fingertips down the curves of his ribs and then reach higher to gently rake my nails across his chest. His turn to convulse.

"I want you," I whisper.

"You sure?" he asks.

Instead of answering, I slide off Holden and kneel in the narrow space between the coffee table and the sofa. I undo the button of his jeans and tug them down over his hips. Moonlight reflects off his pale legs. He shivers in the thin fabric of his boxers. Leaning forward, I massage his thighs while I press my lips to his flat stomach.

"Embry," Holden whispers.

"Shh." My hand slips beneath the fabric of his boxers.

He groans softly. His eyelids fall shut as he relaxes back into the cushions. His shoulders drop. I can feel the tension leaving his body as my mouth trails lower. He supports my head with one hand, stroking my hair with the other. I like the effect I have on him. I like that I can help him escape the same way he does for me.

"Come here," Holden says after a couple of minutes. He lifts me back to the sofa. I unbutton my jeans and slide them and my underwear down over my hips.

Holden pulls a condom out of one of his coat pockets. I watch him put it on and then position myself on top of him, letting out a deep breath I didn't even know I was holding. I cradle his face in both of my hands and close the gap between our mouths again.

He wraps one hand around my lower back for support while the other gets lost in my hair.

"You feel so good," I tell him.

He laughs under his breath. "I know."

I slap him playfully on the arm. "You're such an ass."

"I know," he says again, pulling my smile toward his.

Our grins meet and our lips relax. I focus on the feel of him, the way our bodies connect, the way every single touch lights up dark parts inside me.

The first few times Holden and I were together, it was sweaty and fumbling and we both rushed through it. Now we're getting more comfortable with each other and learning to slow things down.

I lean back just far enough to watch the series of expressions flit across his face—concentration, followed by pleasure, followed by restraint, followed by more concentration. His long eyelashes are feathered closed, his mouth open just wide enough to expel little gasps of air. I trace one of his high cheekbones with my fingertips.

His eyes flick open. "What?"

I shake my head, a smile playing at my lips. "I just like watching you."

"Oh yeah?" He locks his gaze onto mine. It's a struggle not

to look away from his blue, blue eyes.

His hands caress my back. Part of me wants to speed things up and part of me wants this moment to never end. Eventually speed wins. As all the heat and tension inside me start to coalesce, my knee slips on the sofa cushion and my foot hits the edge of the coffee table. Vaguely I see a flicker of light in my peripheral vision.

"Shit," Holden says.

Betsy barks, but I'm in no position to be distracted. Whatever is bothering her can wait a few more seconds.

"Hold on," Holden says. "Embry, stop."

"What? Why?" I blink rapidly. Is that smoke I smell? I lift my body off his and turn around. Apparently when I kicked the table, I knocked a candle onto the floor. The carpet of the Sea Cliff Inn is burning.

THREE

I GET DRESSED IN LIKE three seconds. Grabbing Betsy, I drag her toward the back door. Holden starts opening drawers and cabinets behind the registration counter, probably looking for a fire extinguisher. I put the dog outside. "Stay," I tell her. She's smart enough to stay away from the edge of the cliff.

I turn back to where Holden is now in the lobby again, trying to beat out the flames with his black wool coat. The fire has spread across the floor, possibly due to the spilled vodka, and he's just making things worse. I cough from the smoke that's starting to fill the room.

"I can't find an extinguisher," he says. "Can you look?"

I check the dining area and the kitchen and do a quick

skim of the little office behind it, but I don't see anything. The flames have moved from the carpet to the base of the coffee table. Holden has his shirt up covering his nose and mouth.

I grab a sofa cushion and beat at the fire, sending bits of ash swirling through the air. The bottom of the cushion starts to smolder. "Fuck." I drop it back onto the frame.

Holden grabs my arm. "We need to get out of here and call 911."

"We can't." I take a step back from the heat. "If this place burns down, they're going to blame us. We'll get arrested, or sued for a crapload of money, or—" A glowing ember arcs through the smoky air and lands dangerously close to my foot. I take another step back. The flames start to overtake the coffee table.

"No one needs to know we were in here," he says. "Let's just call it in like we were going for a walk and saw the place burning."

I suddenly remember I left Betsy outside off her leash. I nod grimly and head for the back door.

Holden braves the flames long enough to grab the bottle of vodka and tuck it into his backpack. The two of us escape out into the night, the brisk air a welcome relief from the heat.

Betsy is pacing back and forth, barking and whining.

I put her back on her leash. "Shh, girl," I say. "Everything is fine."

I dial 911 as we hurry around to the front of the hotel. "There's a fire," I say. "At the Sea Cliff Inn." I tell them my name and where I'm located.

The dispatcher advises me to move back from the building but not to leave the scene. "Fire and police rescue are en route," he adds.

"Okay." I hang up the phone and turn to Holden. "Cavalry is on its way. You should go. We both don't need to be here."

"No way. I'm not going to leave you to deal with this."

"Holden. They just need me to stay so I can give a statement. I'll tell the cops I was walking Betsy and saw the smoke. Like you said, they don't need to know either one of us was inside."

I glance down at the ground. With a twinge of guilt I remember my words to Luke: *I think that might be fraud.* What Holden and I are doing is different, though. We're not trying to scam money from the federal government via a sham marriage. We're just trying to protect our families from having to pay out money we don't have because I knocked over a candle. Hopefully the fire department will get here quickly and the damage won't be too bad. Either way, insurance companies are always in the news for ripping people off and being generally evil, aren't they? And they all make millions in profits. What's a little extra to one of them? It's basically a victimless crime.

But I still feel like shit about it. Mostly because I know how disappointed my mom would be if she found out.

I turn my attention back to Holden. "If your mom finds you here, she might put two and two together and realize you made yourself a key. That could be bad for both of us."

"Good point," Holden says reluctantly. "Okay, I'll go . . . if you're sure." He reaches out and gives my hand a quick squeeze, his eyes locking onto mine with unasked questions.

"I'll be fine," I say firmly.

Holden turns and jogs away from the Sea Cliff, bits of charred ash fluttering to the ground from his burned winter coat as he heads down the hill. He disappears between two currently unoccupied hillside mansions, making use of a set of stairs that leads down to Three Rocks Beach. From there he'll have to cut over to the main road that goes through the center of town and cross the highway to get back to our neighborhood.

Betsy barks once and tugs hard on the leash, pulling me toward the burning building.

"No, girl." I pull back. "We have to stay here."

The flames are lighting up the night now. Smoke pours

from the roof, gray against the black of the sky. Tongues of fire dance behind the glass of the lobby's big bay windows. For a moment, I'm mesmerized by the twisting and swirling of the bright orange flames. It seems wrong that destruction can be so beautiful. I pull out my phone, switch to the camera function, and snap a couple of pictures.

Betsy barks again, and again. "What is it?" I ask. And then I catch a glimpse of the second picture on my phone, and I realize what she's been barking at. I look from my phone to the hotel. There's a shadow in one of the third-floor windows. Someone else is inside.

FOUR

"SHIT," I SAY. "SHIT, SHIT, SHIT." It's probably a homeless person, or a hiker making his way down the Oregon Coast Trail. Three Rocks gets hundreds of people passing through each year, many of whom choose to camp out on the beach for free accommodations. The lure of an abandoned hotel in the bitter cold might have been impossible to resist.

The shadow disappears, and for a second I wonder if I dreamed it. I zoom in on my phone screen—nope, there is definitely a human form at the window.

I glance down the hill. Still no sign of the fire department. I look back at the Sea Cliff. The fire has spread, but it isn't completely out of control.

Without warning, smoke pours from the window, completely obscuring my view. Whoever is inside probably opened it to try to escape.

"Hey!" I wave my arms over my head. "Don't jump from there. You might break your neck. Go down the stairs and out the back. It's unlocked."

There's no response. I can't tell if the person inside even heard me. Exhaling deeply, I swear under my breath again. There's no way I'm letting someone die because I started a literal fire while I was having sex. Tying the end of Betsy's leash around the mailbox pole, I turn and run toward the back door of the hotel.

I wrap my scarf around my nose and mouth and then duck back into the building. Inside, the smoke is thick and I have to feel my way to the stairs. "Hang on!" I shout. "I'm coming!"

Staying low, I crawl my way to the third floor and into the front bedroom, but the smoke is stinging my eyes now and I can't see anything. Through the open window, I think I hear the beginnings of sirens, but it's going to be slow going for the fire department up the icy, winding curves of Puffin Drive.

I should turn back, but I can't. I've done some dumb things lately, but none of them have resulted in someone's death, and I'd like to keep it that way. *Dear God. Get me and whoever*

else is in here out of this alive, and I promise I'll be a better person,
I think. I haven't been to church since Easter and I'm not
sure if God even hears the prayers of Holiday Christians like
me, but at this point I'll try anything.

"Is anyone here? Call out!" I yell. Everything I know about
fires I learned from watching my mom's favorite TV show,
911 Fire Rescue, the one where the characters look more like
models than firefighters but every episode features at least
three dramatic rescues.

"Over here." The voice is weak. It's coming from the far
corner of the room.

I shimmy on my belly, flailing out with one arm until I
make contact with what I think is a leg. Squinting, I make
out the form of a boy about my age, or perhaps a little older.
He's thin, with brown hair and pale skin. His boots and the
cuffs of his camouflage pants are crusted with mud. He's got
the neckline of a black fleece hoodie pulled up over his nose
and mouth.

"What's your name?" I ask.

"Sam." He's clutching his stomach with one hand.

"Come on, Sam," I say. "The fire is still downstairs. We can
get out of here, but we've got to go quickly before the smoke
gets us. Can you crawl?"

"Yeah." He coughs violently before choking out a muffled
"I think so."

We inch our way back to the doorway of the room, but crawling down stairs is trickier than crawling up them. "Sit on your butt and go down them one at a time," I say. "Stay low. We're almost there."

Sam grunts but doesn't say anything else. Halfway down the stairs, he stops and mutters something under his breath. His hands frantically pat the ground around him. "I can't find Beau," he says.

"Who's Beau?" I ask, cursing under my breath. What if there's someone else in here? What if the whole damned place is full of squatters?

Then you'll be a killer.

Sam doesn't answer. I try again. "Is someone else living here? Is Beau your friend?"

"He was here a minute ago," Sam says. "He can't have gone far."

My heart pounds double-time at the thought of someone else passed out in the building, but I have to get Sam out before the fire spreads and traps us both inside. "Keep going," I say.

"Beau's been with me since Elvis died," Sam mutters.

I don't know jack about Elvis, but I know he's been dead longer than this kid has been alive. Maybe Sam is drunk, or delirious from the smoke inhalation.

"Keep moving. You're doing great," I say. By the time we

make it back to the first floor, Sam is keeling over to one side, his eyelids drooping low like he's about to pass out.

"Stay with me," I choke out. "I'm not strong enough to drag you."

He doesn't respond, but lets me push him toward the open back door. The front part of the lobby is now engulfed in flames, thick black smoke rising from tongues of red fire. "Fucking vodka," I mumble.

Flashing lights dance across the bay windows. I half drag Sam the last few feet through the back door and out into the cold night just as three firefighters—a man and two women—in full gear round the corner of the building.

They rush up to us. The male firefighter takes one look at Sam and shouts, "I need a stretcher back here right away!" He turns to me. "Are you okay?"

I cough. "I think so."

Sam has collapsed to the ground, his eyes closed, his face smudged with black soot. The firefighter drops to a squat. He reaches two fingers toward Sam's neck as the two women head inside the back door. "Are you the one who called it in?"

I nod. "Yeah. I was walking my dog when I saw the smoke."

"What's your name?" The firefighter tilts his hat back on his head. I can't help but notice he's got dark hair and impossibly blue eyes, almost like Holden.

"I'm Embry." I gesture at the guy lying on the ground. "And

this is Sam. He said something about Beau when I found him in there." I pause. "He also said something about Elvis. He might just be out of it, but it's possible he wasn't alone."

"Roger that." The firefighter unclips a radio from his waistband. "Be advised there might be more people inside. Check each floor carefully." He reaches up and unsnaps the oxygen tank attached to his back. He sets it on the ground and kneels over Sam again. "My name is Kyle. So you know this guy, Embry?"

"No, I just asked him his name when I was trying to help him escape."

"You know you could've died going into a burning building, right?" Kyle's voice is soft but stern.

"Yeah. It was after I called 911 that I saw Sam inside. He looked like he was going to jump out the window. I was afraid he might be drunk or something—I didn't want him to break his neck."

"How'd you even get in?" Kyle asks.

Shit. Good question. "I went in the back," I say. "I knew this place was closed right now and figured if he was in there, maybe one of the doors was unlocked. I got lucky."

"Lucky, indeed," Kyle says.

Two paramedics round the corner, pushing a stretcher over the grass. They lower it to the ground next to Sam, roll him onto it, and start checking his vitals. Sam's eyes flutter open as he turns onto his side to hack a mouthful of black gunk onto the ground. He lifts a hand to his chest, and one of the medics bends low to say something in his ear.

"Come on. Let's give them space to work."

Kyle leads me back to the front of the Sea Cliff, where the fire chief has set up a command center with the Tillamook County Sheriff's Department. A second team of firefighters heads inside the front door, hoses unspooling behind them. I give the police a quick statement about how I was walking Betsy when I saw the fire and the guy trapped in the building. Then I decline an offer for medical care myself. My throat burns a little from the smoke inhalation, but I'm sure anyone who gets too close to me will also be able to smell the alcohol on my breath. I don't want to give the cops any reason to doubt my story, and most people probably don't throw back a few drinks before walking their dogs.

"We might need to talk to you again after our investigation," the fire chief says. "I'll have someone call you if anything comes up."

"Okay." I nod. I just want to get the hell out of here.

The medics roll Sam on the gurney from the back of the Sea Cliff out to the street where their ambulance is parked. He's got a plastic oxygen mask over his nose and mouth.

"Do you think he'll be all right?" I ask the cops and fire chief.

"Hopefully," the chief says. "Too soon to tell."

"Did you find anyone else? He said something about a guy named Beau."

"No, but we're still looking," the chief says. "You realize you could have died in there, right?"

"I know it was stupid to go in," I admit. "It was just . . . instinct, I guess."

"Pretty brave instincts. Most people would have run away."

I nod, but I don't feel brave. I feel like my recklessness and stupidity just burned down one of the most famous buildings in Three Rocks and nearly killed someone at the same time. Holden might have brought the vodka, but I can't blame him for this. It's me—my secrets, my lying.

I turn back once more to look at the burning hotel. The firefighters are inside with their hoses, but smoke is still pouring from the building. If I were normal, I would be at home right now, dreaming of Luke and our wedding. Instead, this is what I do—I hide things, I hurt people.

I burn up everything I touch.

FIVE

December 12

THE NEXT DAY IS a surreal mix of people whispering about me at school and reporters calling me at home. I got interviewed for the school newspaper and the *Tillamook Headlight Herald*, as well as featured on the Three Rocks Chamber of Commerce website. I didn't even know Three Rocks had a website before getting an email from the mayor's assistant with a link to the feature.

My mom freaked out when I told her what happened and screamed at me for like ten straight minutes about how foolish I was to go inside a burning building. Then she told me I was really brave and a hero.

I wish I could tell her the truth—that I'm stupid and self-destructive and responsible for what happened to the Sea Cliff Inn. The newspapers said the damage to the place was a couple hundred thousand dollars minimum. They suspected the Murray family would tear it down and sell the land to someone else. We'll probably end up with another private mansion at the top of Puffin Hill.

I haven't talked to Holden much today. He came by my locker this morning just to find out what I told the police, but other than that I think we're both kind of freaked out about our close call. Holden's mom gets child support, plus good benefits from Tillamook County, so they're a little better off than my mom and me. But still, they couldn't afford having to pay for the damage to the Sea Cliff either.

December 14

By Friday, things have started to go back to normal. Apparently there was a fight after our latest swim meet where our school's number one asshole, Lowell Price, called varsity swimmer Misty Whitehawk a squaw and she laid him out with one punch. Lowell tumbled down an entire set of bleachers but wasn't seriously hurt, except for his pride. Misty is the new hero of Tillamook High and my role in the Sea Cliff fire is already old news.

I meet up with Julia at lunchtime. We both go through the cafeteria line, where I get a buffalo chicken sandwich and fries and she gets a salad and fruit cup. She's almost always on a diet, but she's kicked it into high gear lately because of some dress she's trying to fit into by New Year's Eve. She frowns at my tray as we wait for the cashier to swipe our ID cards. I know she doesn't understand why I don't eat healthier since I get free lunches, but dinner isn't always a guarantee at my house, so I'm not turning down a fairly tasty sandwich and crispy fries in exchange for a bowl of iceberg lettuce sprinkled with turkey and cheese, even if it is cheese from our local dairy farm, which is basically the best cheese in the world.

"God, you would not believe the stuff I have to do for this Harvard app," Julia says, as we head for our usual table. "All these essay questions, like am I supposed to know everything before I even *start* college?" She pulls her water bottle out of her backpack. It's got slices of lemon and lime floating in it. Unscrewing the cover, she adds in an envelope of some kind of weight-loss powder and gives the bottle a good shake. "And Dr. Zimmer said she'd write me a recommendation letter, but she forgot about it and now she's saying she doesn't have time."

My eyes scan the room while I listen to Julia. Across the cafeteria, Holden sets his tray next to a guy named Zak who works at the gas station with him. Zak angles the screen of his phone toward Holden to show him something, and both boys laugh.

"And so now she says I have to find someone else for my second recommendation. Isn't that unfair?" Julia stabs violently at her salad with her plastic fork.

"Yeah, totally," I say, even though I kind of zoned out on the exact details of what Julia is mad about. I haven't applied to any colleges or taken the SAT or ACT, because I'm planning on going to Tillamook Bay Community College, and they don't require students to apply by any certain date. Holden isn't sure what he's going to do yet. His grandparents own the gas station at the edge of town where he works, and where his granddad does basic car repair and maintenance for locals and people passing through. Holden likes fixing cars and has considered getting a job at an auto repair shop in Tillamook and working his way up as an apprentice, but his mom hates that idea because she says he's too smart not to go to college. He says just because he's good at school doesn't mean he should have to spend four (or more) years bored out of his mind to qualify for some fancy job he doesn't want.

He could probably get paid for his drawings and paintings— I've seen his stuff in art class and it's amazing—but he always says art is just a hobby for him.

A fist pounds the table so hard my milk carton almost hops off the edge. A girl named Katrina Jensen smirks as she saunters by. "Embryo. Our famous fire rescue queen. No paparazzi today?"

My eyes flick from her ripped jeans to the T-shirt she's wearing. It's black, emblazoned with the words "NO GODS NO MASTERS." Katrina lives in Tillamook but spends a lot of time in Three Rocks because she works at Fintastic. She actually started there as a hostess when she was fifteen. According to rumors, she lost her virginity to Luke at some restaurant party down on the beach that summer. This was back before I was allowed to go to parties and several months before Luke and I started dating. I never asked him if the story was true because I don't really want to know. But it might explain why Katrina has always acted like she hates me.

"Your lipstick is smeared," Julia says sweetly.

"Shut it, rich bitch," Katrina replies, tossing her blue-and-turquoise hair back from her face. She smacks her gum. "Nice purse, by the way."

I've been around Julia for so long that I don't really notice the fancy things she has unless someone points them out. Her purse is heart-shaped, made out of purple leather, with several chunky black zippers sewn into the front of it. It's cute, but unless you follow fashion and accessories, you probably wouldn't know it's the latest design from last year's winner of *Project Runway*, or that it sells for three hundred dollars.

"Better a rich bitch than a poor one," Julia tells her.

I flinch. I know Julia's not talking about me, but it's still hard not to take comments like that personally.

"You would know." Katrina's lips curl into a sneer as she glances between us.

"Nice boots," I point out. Katrina is wearing a pair of fur-lined Rendon hiking boots. The whole line is waterproof, and I know they run for about two hundred dollars a pair.

"I got them at the thrift store." Katrina stares at me for a second, as if daring me to challenge her. Then she adds, "Better eat fast, Embryo. I heard Coach Holland is running a mile with his gym class. He might need some CPR or something."

Coach Holland is like three hundred pounds and seventy years old. "I'll save you the mouth-to-mouth part," I tell her.

"I'll go first. You can have seconds." She smacks her gum again. "It'll be like old times."

I bite back a sarcastic response. She's never brought up Luke with me directly, and I refuse to be baited into hearing about whatever went down with them. I take a leisurely bite of my sandwich and flip her off with my free hand. She spins on her heel and heads across the cafeteria toward a table of kids who all live in one of the poorer areas of Tillamook.

"What is her problem?" Julia asks.

"Life," I say. "Same as everybody else's." Katrina and I actually got into it this summer over Holden too, but that's another piece I haven't shared with Julia.

"Whatever." Julia pulls a tube of shimmery lip gloss out of her purse and applies a fresh coat. She checks her work using the camera on her phone. "Sounds like she's just jealous because you're a big hero now."

"Yeah, no." I snort. "I'm just . . . lacking in survival instinct."

"I still can't believe you risked your life to save a homeless guy." Julia says "homeless" in a way that makes it sound like she'd be okay with it if I'd gone in to save an investment banker.

"I can." Luke's younger sister, Frannie, appears from behind me. She tosses her strawberry-blond braids back over her shoulders. "I would've done the same thing. Luke is going to be so proud when he finds out."

I smile weakly at Frannie. I doubt Luke would be proud if he knew the whole story.

She looks at the empty seat next to me. "Do you guys care if I sit with you? Mona and Patrice are on a field trip today and I don't want to sit alone."

"You can sit with us anytime you want," I say, my eyes

flicking to Julia with a look that I hope conveys: *Be nice.*
Frannie O'Riley is a junior and one of the sweetest people I
know. Julia finds her kind of annoying, but I think that has
more to do with the fact that Frannie is one of the only kids
at school who out-Julias Julia. They're both in student government, but Frannie holds a higher office. They're both on
the swim team, but Frannie has the faster times. Frannie
also got a higher score on her SATs, but I'm not sure if Julia
knows that or not because Frannie isn't the bragging type.
The only reason I know is because her mom told my mom at
some local food service meeting.

Julia stares as Frannie sets her sack lunch on the table
and unpacks a can of soda, a container of pasta salad, a
Granny Smith apple, and a triple-layer peanut butter fudge
brownie—one of the dessert options on the Fintastic menu.
A lot of the kids from Tillamook qualify for free lunches,
and most of the Three Rocks kids are rich enough to buy
school lunch every day, so a packed lunch is kind of a rarity
around here.

"That brownie looks amazing," I say.

"Want a bite?" Frannie pushes the container with the
brownie into the center of the table where we can all reach it.

"Hell no," Julia says. "I'm allergic to peanuts, remember?"
She takes a sip of her diet drink.

"I remember," I say. "I'm still traumatized from watching

you EpiPen yourself at the sophomore conference tournament."

"That's right!" Frannie says. "What was it you ate again?"

Julia shudders. "Rice Krispies Treats. What kind of sadist puts peanut butter in those?"

Frannie starts to drag the container with the brownie back to her side of the table.

I grab the edge of it. "I'll take a little bite." I shoot Julia an apologetic look as I break off a corner of the brownie.

She wrinkles up her nose as I pop the brownie into my mouth. "That thing probably has two thousand calories, Fran. You're going to have to swim like a hundred laps to burn it off."

"Challenge accepted," Frannie says, flexing her biceps.

Julia flares her nostrils as she digs through her purse. She pulls out her phone. As she glances down at the screen, her lips quirk into a smile.

"Good news?" I ask.

She shakes her head. "Ness just sent me something funny off Twitter."

Julia met Ness, aka Hennessey Rich, while she was in DC this summer. Apparently Ness is also uber-involved in school and hoping to attend Harvard or Georgetown. I'm a little jealous of how quickly she and Julia became friends, which is petty and dumb, but you can't help how you feel, you know? Holden likes to say that high school friends aren't real friends, that they're just the people we're stuck with until we have the freedom to make our own choices. I don't want to believe that, but he tends to be right about most stuff.

Julia's family moved to Three Rocks from Bend the summer before seventh grade. Her dad is a writer and motivational speaker who can work from anywhere, and her mom got tired of the snow. Julia and I ended up as friends partly because I was the only other girl in Three Rocks in the same grade as her. Before Julia, most of my friends were girls from school who lived in Tillamook, but I had no way to see them during the summers because Mom and Gram were always too busy working to drive me back and forth. Julia and I met at Three Rocks Beach, where both of us always went on days when it wasn't raining—her to read and me to take pictures. We stayed friends when school started because we ended up in three classes together.

Frannie is kind of the same. I consider her a good friend, and she once told me I was the closest thing she's ever had to a sister, but she's more like Julia than me. She wants to do ROTC in college and then become an air force nurse. Afterward she's interested in getting a graduate degree in public health and working for an NGO like Doctors Without Borders. I think of it like Frannie wants to save the world, while Julia wants to conquer it. Me, I just want to carve out a little place in it where I can survive, and maybe, if I'm lucky, be happy someday.

After school, I head to my mom's coffee shop, officially called the Oregon Coast Café. The door groans audibly as I open it. It's hanging a little crooked because one set of hinges is messed up. Mom keeps saying she's going to call someone to come repair it. Maybe after the holidays. Honestly, there's a lot about the coffee shop that needs fixing up, but the place is cozy and warm and we serve delicious food and drinks at reasonable prices. Mom has done as well as she can to keep it going with limited resources.

Kendra, the day cashier and barista, is pacing back and forth behind the counter in her jacket and hat, her purse slung over her shoulder. She heads for the door as I stroll back into the back. "I've got to run," she says. "My mom is waiting for me to pick her up from work."

"No worries," I tell her. "See you later."

I pop into the back office, where my mom is hunched over her computer squinting at the screen as usual. "Hi." I tug playfully on her pale blond wig. "I still think you should get a pink one."

Mom glances up at me. "Oh yeah? You think I'm hip enough to pull off colored hair?"

"Well, I did, until you used the word 'hip' unironically," I say. "But I could tutor you if you want."

Mom laughs. "As fun as that sounds, I think I'll stick to being a clueless old lady. It's just easier."

"Points for knowing your limitations," I say with a wink. "Kendra left already. I'd better go make sure Matt's not messing everything up." With a grin and a little wave, I duck out of the office, tie on my Oregon Coast Café apron, and head up to the front counter. Matt Sesti is the guy working in the kitchen making the soup and sandwich orders. He's twenty-one but got held back a year, so he graduated from Tillamook High the same year as Luke. He's been hitting on me off and on ever since Luke left for basic training. Today he gives me a long look as I slide behind the cash register. I pretend not to notice.

Mom strolls up to the front about twenty minutes after I get there. She glances around the dining area, her expression neutral despite the fact we have only two customers right now. "Call me if you need anything," she tells me. "Otherwise I'll see you when you get home."

"Whatever, old lady," I joke. "We both know you'll be tucked in bed by eight p.m. like a proper senior citizen."

Mom gasps in fake outrage, even though it's true. She goes to bed early almost every night so she can be up at five a.m. to come back here. That's what made it so easy for me to meet up with Holden at the Sea Cliff. As long as I left after eight and got back before five, my mom had no idea I wasn't at home, studying or sleeping like I should have been.

"I need a lot of beauty sleep," she tells me. "So my hair will grow back thick and lustrous."

"I hope it grows back pink so you have to learn how to be cool," I joke. Her oncologist warned her that sometimes after chemotherapy hair grows back a different color or texture, but I'm pretty sure he just meant she might go from blond to light brown or something.

Mom heads out, and over the next hour I serve the after-school usuals: Thea and Janine, who clean the rent-a-cottages up on Cape Azure; Holden's friend Zak, who gets coffee on his way to work; a trio of freshman girls who show up almost every evening to divvy up their math and science homework and then share answers; and the geometry teacher who drives forty-five miles from Lincoln City twice a week to run a small group tutoring session.

Then the tiny Christmas bells Mom has hanging over the door jingle as a new customer comes in—it's Lourdes, my mom's best friend, who owns the Shop-a-Lot across the street. ("More like shop a little," Julia likes to joke. The inside is about the same size as my mom's bedroom, but it's the closest thing Three Rocks has to a grocery store.)

"Hey, Lourdes. The usual?" Smiling, I prepare to ring in her favorite drink—a cinnamon vanilla latte.

"Actually, I'm feeling like a sandwich today." She tosses her long black braid back over her shoulder. "What do you recommend?"

"Hmm." Whenever I eat here, I normally just slap some turkey and provolone on bread. I pluck one of our to-go menus from the stand by the register and scan the choices. "The Courtney Love and the Raymond Carver are both popular," I say. "The Ahmad Rashad is also good. And the River Phoenix." All our sandwiches are named after famous Oregonians.

Lourdes squints at the paper. "Why is this sandwich called the Courtney Love?"

"Order it and find out," I say with a grin.

"It didn't kill Kurt Cobain or anything, did it?"

"Ha. No," I say. "Our food has never killed anyone, thank you very much." I clear my throat. "Come on, Lourdes. Chunks of tender pot roast on a single piece of Texas toast, smothered in cheese and gravy? Clearly, it's a hot mess."

"Ah, I get it. Well, it sounds delicious. I'll give it a try. Plus a medium cinnamon vanilla latte."

I ring up her order and swipe her credit card through the machine. Matt starts working on her sandwich while I make her drink. I grind the beans for her espresso, and while it's brewing I add flavor shots of cinnamon and vanilla to her paper cup.

"Seems like your mom's doing pretty well," Lourdes says.

"So far so good." I knock gently on the wooden countertop as I start steaming some milk.

"How's Luke?" she asks. "Have you talked to him lately?"

"Yeah, a couple nights ago. He's good too," I say. "He'll hopefully be back for a visit in January."

My hand shakes a little as I pour the espresso and hot milk into her cup. I might be a temporary town hero because of pulling Sam out of the fire, but Luke is one of the golden boys of Three Rocks. The whole O'Riley clan is sort of famous for running the best restaurant in town, but Luke also happens to be the guy who led our school to the state hockey championships three years straight. And then two summers ago he was working as a lifeguard when the mayor's daughter tipped her sailboat over. She got caught up in the ropes and would have drowned if Luke hadn't commandeered a kid's kayak and paddled out to rescue her. He's been semi-famous ever since.

I'm not sure what other people would say if they found out I'm not with Luke anymore—that I'm hooking up with Holden Hassler instead. Actually, that's a lie. I do know what they'd say. It wouldn't be as bad as what some people still whisper about my mother, but it wouldn't be good. My cheeks flush a little as I imagine the gossip. That's another thing about small towns. Not only does everyone know everything, but they all have a strong opinion about everything, too. And they all feel perfectly justified in sharing it.

After the shop closes, I wipe down all the tables and then count the money in the register and put it into the safe.

"I made more brownies and sugar cookies, and I've got trays of croissants ready to go in the oven tomorrow," Matt tells me as we're grabbing our jackets and signing out on our time cards in the back. He does a lot of the prep work for our baked goods.

"Cool," I say. "My mom will really appreciate that. Thanks."

"What are you up to tonight?" Matt slides into his coat. It's black and wool, like Holden's, except Matt's smells like marijuana instead of charred hotel. He keeps talking without giving me a chance to reply. "My friend is having a house party. You should come check it out. You must get bored in this crap-ass little town with almost no one else your age."

"Sounds fun, but I can't," I say. "My boyfriend is supposed to call me from Afghanistan, so I'd better get home." This is a blatant lie, but Matt doesn't know that.

He retrieves a knitted hat from his pocket and pulls it over his spiky blond hair. "Maybe another time, then? I mean, it's not like O'Riley owns you, right?"

I grit my teeth. "Look, I don't mind working with you, but you should probably stop hitting on me, okay?"

sh, I was just being friendly." Matt pushes through
r out into the cold and I'm right behind him. As I
o lock the front door, he turns to me and says, "You
know, some girls would be flattered."

I jam the keys into my back pocket. "And some girls would
tell their mom to fire you for sexual harassment."

Matt lives his hands up in mock self-defense. "Whoa.
Calm down, Woods. No reason to go nuclear." He turns away
and starts down the sidewalk.

"Wait," I say. "I didn't mean that. I'm just stressed. I won't
say anything to my mom if you promise to knock it off. And I
was flattered, the first couple of times, okay?"

"Message received." Matt pulls a pack of cigarettes from
his coat pocket. "I'm going to guess you don't want a ride
home."

"No thanks. I'm good."

Matt crosses the street to the small paved lot behind the
Three Rocks Community Center where he usually parks his
car. I head in the opposite direction. Pulling my jacket tight
around my body, I tilt my chin down toward my chest to keep
the wind from directly hitting my face. All the businesses
on Main Street are dark. I pass the ice-cream shop (closed
for the season), the descriptively named Tacos & Burgers (our main source of competition at lunchtime), and the
post office (staffed by one person on Monday, Wednesday,

and Friday, for all your three-day-a-week postal needs). On the other side of the street is the community center (which also doubles as a nondenominational church every Sunday), the surf and scuba shop (open on weekends), the Shop-a-Lot, and the Three Rocks Motel, the last two being some of the only businesses in town that are open every day. Luke's family's restaurant, Fintastic, is open every night for dinner and for lunch on weekends, but it's located on the way out of town, on the highway that leads toward Tillamook in one direction and Cape Azure in the other.

When I reach the end of Main Street, I turn toward Cape Azure. On the left side of Highway W, a gravel road leads into the Three Rocks Memorial Park, a small cemetery that takes up the lower eastern section of Puffin Hill. There are only about sixty people buried there. My grandparents are two of them. My neighborhood is on the other side of the highway, in a recessed area about a half mile from the beach.

Mom's house—which we have only because my grandparents owned it before us and paid off most of the mortgage—is smashed in alongside twenty other small houses and Three Rocks Manor, our town's only apartment complex. Unlike the houses on Puffin Hill that are partially sheltered by tree cover, our neighborhood might as well be on the plains of Kansas. The wind blowing in from the ocean cuts right through the fabric of my coat as I hurry across the damp lawn. When I open the storm door, I'm surprised to see a white envelope wedged in next to the doorknob. Whoever left this must have done it in the last couple of hours, and without Mom seeing them. I'm even more surprised when I flip over the envelope and see my first name neatly printed on the outside in small red capital letters. It's probably a Christmas card.

I slip the envelope into the back pocket of my jeans and insert my key into the lock, clucking my tongue in disgust when I realize my mom left the door unlocked again. She's kind of lax about security because Three Rocks is so small and almost nothing bad ever happens, but I hate the thought of her sleeping in her bedroom, completely vulnerable to some deranged lunatic who might break in.

I step inside the house, closing the door behind me. Betsy is sprawled out on the living room floor. She rises to her feet and wags her tail when she sees me.

"Shh," I tell her. I toss my jacket on the back of the futon couch and then tiptoe into the kitchen, where I give Betsy fresh water and refill her bowl of kibble. "You need to go out?" I whisper.

Even at the low volume, Betsy gets excited at the word "out." I open the back door off the kitchen and let her into our small, square backyard, which is nothing but a patch of dead grass and an old dilapidated shed where Mom still keeps her gardening stuff, even though the thing looks like it's two good gusts from blowing all the way to the beach. While I wait for Betsy to finish her business, I pull the envelope out of my jeans pocket and open it.

Instead of a card, there's a folded piece of paper tucked inside. It's a printed note. I flop down at the kitchen table and start to read:

"It was instinct for me to try to save that guy. It wasn't a hard decision. Maybe I'm just good under pressure." That's what you told the police. That's what you told the newspaper. Let's test that theory.
A. Write a full confession about what really happened at the Sea Cliff Inn that night. Post it to your Facebook page by eight p.m. tomorrow. It might ruin your life, but . . .
B. If you don't post a confession, I will ruin the life of someone you care about.
Choose wisely.

SIX

THERE'S A SUDDEN SCRATCHING SOUND, and I jump so hard I nearly drop the paper on the floor. But it's just Betsy. When she's ready to come in, she's ready to come in. She lifts up onto her hind legs and drags her toenails down the outside of the door again.

"Okay, okay," I mutter.

I let Betsy inside and then go back to the letter. My hands shake as I read it a second time. Fuck. Who could have left this for me? And why? There's no way I'm posting a confession online. My Facebook friends include my mom, Luke, about thirty of my classmates, most of the people who work at the café, and some of Luke's family. I imagine all of them reading my scandalous summary of that evening's activities. *Well, Mrs. O'Riley. First I evaded a marriage proposal from your son, then I slammed some vodka, then I hooked up with another guy, then I burned down a hotel. Pretty standard night.*

How long would it be before everyone in town heard about the post? Five minutes? How long would it take someone to call the cops? An hour? It kills me that I can absolutely envision the look on my mom's face if Holden's mom showed up at the door with an arrest warrant for me.

I consider the specific wording of the letter. It's very vague. It doesn't mention Holden *or* the fire. If someone was really watching me that night, I would have seen them, wouldn't I? And if they weren't there, the only way they could possibly know what happened is if Holden told someone.

I know he wouldn't do that.

I replay what I remember from that night in my head: I left work, went home to take a quick shower and make sure my mom was asleep. Then I headed up the hill, paused to take Luke's phone call, and finally crept inside the back of the Sea Cliff Inn as usual. The only person I even saw after leaving work besides Holden was Mrs. Roche.

I grab my phone and text Holden. You around?

He doesn't answer right away, and I spend the next few minutes pacing back and forth in the living room rereading the letter, losing my mind a little when I think about the consequences of obeying—or disobeying—the sender's instructions. Trespassing, minor possession, destruction of property. And those are just the criminal charges, before Holden and I are held liable for hundreds of thousands of dollars in damages. "That's a big nope," I mutter. But then: *ruin the life of someone you care about.* What does that even mean?

I blot some sweat from my upper lip, even though it's freezing inside the house. I suddenly feel a bit dizzy. As I reach out for the edge of the futon to steady myself, I realize I'm hyperventilating. "Calm down, Embry." I try to channel my mother. What was it she used to say about how she survived mammograms and ultrasounds and biopsies and chemo and surgery without completely losing her mind? *I focus on the things I can control and try not to obsess about the ones I can't.* It sounds very motivational poster, I know, but there's no denying that it seemed to work for her.

But what do you do when there's nothing you can control?

There's always something, my mom's voice says.

As usual, she's right. Shoving the note into my back pocket, I slide back into my coat and step outside, closing and locking the front door quietly behind me. The house on the left of ours is owned by Mr. Mancini, a man in his sixties who still works full-time at the cheese factory in Tillamook. I know he leaves for work even earlier than my mom does, so

I'm not going to disturb him.

I head to the house on the other side of me instead—the Lerners. They've got about seven million watts worth of Christmas lights going in the front yard, but there's no car in the driveway and no one answers the door. I try the house next to them. Cori Ernest, a single mom who works at the Three Rocks Motel, comes to the door, her two-year-old daughter, Corinne, propped up on her hip. "What's up, Embry?" she asks.

"Weird question," I say. "But someone left a note in between our doors and didn't sign it. Have you seen anyone around my mom's house?"

Cori shakes her head. She gestures at Corinne. "This one has been throwing up for most of the day, so I haven't been outside much." She pauses. "What did the note say?"

"Nothing too important," I mumble. "I'm just trying to figure out who sent it so I can, um, reply."

Corinne squirms in her mom's arms. "I'm thirsty," she whines, tugging at Cori's hair.

"Sorry I can't be more help," Cori says, adjusting her hold on her daughter and peeling Corinne's hand loose from her hair.

"That's okay," I say. "Thanks anyway."

Cori gives me a quick wave before shutting the door. I hear the dead bolt slide into place.

I'm debating whether there's any point to ask anyone else when a couple of grade school boys on bikes turn the corner onto my street. The Jameson brothers. They live a couple blocks away, in Three Rocks Manor.

I flag them down as they pass by. "Hey. Have you guys been riding around for a while?"

"What's it to you?" the older one asks. I should know his name, but I don't.

I point at my house. "I was just wondering if you saw anyone around that house in the past half an hour or so."

The older brother shakes his head. "Nope. Sorry."

"What about the kid in the hoodie, Cam?" the younger brother says.

Now I remember. Cameron and Cayden, those are their names.

"That kid was farther up the street, wasn't he?" Cameron says.

"What kid?" I ask. At this point any leads would be helpful.

"I don't know. We only saw him from the back. Jeans. Hoodie. Walking fast. Turned toward the beach."

"Did you see him in my yard or on the porch or anything?"

Cayden shakes his head. "I thought he was on the sidewalk in front of your house, but maybe I'm wrong. He might have just been looking at your neighbor's Christmas lights."

"How old was he?" I ask.

"I don't know. Like middle school or high school probably," Cameron says. "Skinny. Not that tall."

"What color was the hoodie?"

"Gray, I think," Cayden says. "Or maybe black?"

"All right. Thanks a lot," I tell the boys.

"Did he do something bad?" Cayden asks.

"I'm not sure," I say. "Trying to figure that out."

My phone buzzes in my pocket. I pull it out and the boys ride off. A soft rain starts to fall as I head back to my house, my eyes focused on the new message from Holden.

Holden: At work. What's up?

Me: Have you received any weird letters lately?

Holden: ?

Me: About the other night?

Holden: No clue what you're talking about. Want me to swing by later?

Me: I don't want to wake up my mom. Can we maybe meet on the beach?

Holden: Sure. I'll be heading home in about 30 min. Meet at the pot hole?

I make a face. The Pot Hole is this natural cave at the far end of Three Rocks Beach. It's carved into the side of Cape Azure, and during low tide it's a passage from our beach to Azure Beach, but during high tide it floods. And anywhere in between, it serves as a place where high school and college kids go to get high.

Me: Okay. Text me 15 min before you get there.

Holden: Will do.

Stepping back into the house, I close the door quietly behind me and read the note again. The person used my exact words from the *Tillamook Headlight Herald*, the only paper of any decent size around here. But that means they could live anywhere in Tillamook County, which takes in a ton of small towns. Not to mention they could have just accessed the info from the paper's website, so there's no guarantee whoever sent this note is a subscriber.

I duck into my bedroom and close the door behind me. My chest goes tight as I think again about what would happen if I told everyone the truth. I take in a deep breath, hold the air inside my lungs until they start to burn. Then I let it out slowly, just a bit at a time through pursed lips. I close my eyes, count to ten, count to twenty, count to thirty. I keep counting until my chest stops hurting, somewhere around 145.

I read the note a sentence at a time, trying to figure out what the sender's motive might be. Do they want me to confess about Holden or about the fire? Why would anyone demand I do either of those things unless they were personally invested? The only people who would care about Holden and me are Luke and Julia, but Luke is on the other side of the world, and if Julia knew I was hooking up with Holden, I'm fairly certain she'd confront me face-to-face. As far as the fire goes, the only people who ought to care about that are the relatives of the guy who owned the Sea Cliff Inn, and most of them live out of state. I saw one of his sons around at the end of the summer, but not lately. And if his family somehow had proof I was the one who started the fire, they could just give it to the police without threatening anyone.

"Why threaten to ruin the life of someone I care about?" I murmur. That's also a pretty short list. My brain cues up a grisly montage of exactly what that might mean, everything from sabotaging Julia's shot at going to Harvard to burning down my mom's café. *You're being paranoid*, I tell myself.

But am I?

I lift the letter up to the light, looking for any clues to who might have left it. But there are no special markings or anything—it's just a piece of printer paper used by basically anyone with a copier or computer printer. The envelope looks like the type that would be used with Christmas cards, but there's no brand stamped on it. The red letters on the front are round and straight and all the same size, as if someone purposely tried to mask their style of printing.

Sighing, I slip the letter back into the envelope and set it on my desk. I've done all I can do for now. Pulling my homework out of my backpack, I try to focus on my latest list of vocabulary words for Spanish III, but they blur together in front of my eyes. I push Spanish to the side and grab the novel my English class is reading—*A Separate Peace*—but it's even harder to focus on that. The whole book is about how a boy betrays his close friend out of jealousy, and it hits entirely too close to home when I think about Holden and Julia. I wouldn't say I'm actively jealous of Julia, but I can recognize the differences between us. She has money and connections. She's super-ambitious. She'll end up rich and powerful someday. Me, well, I win when it comes to making a latte. So yeah, there's no denying I like the fact that Holden picked me over her.

Like I said, it's possible I'm not a very good person.

I drop the novel on the floor next to my bed. Could Julia have sent me the note? No, she wouldn't be able to keep it a secret if she knew about Holden and me, and besides, it's not her style. When she has a problem with someone, she tells them. She almost got suspended last year because she didn't agree with the grade she got on her research paper and went after our Advanced Comp teacher in the parking lot before school.

My phone buzzes. Holden. Be there in 15.

I grab the note from the desk and slip it and my phone into the pocket of my jeans. Maybe Holden will have a fresh perspective. Maybe he'll see something I don't see. Sliding back into my jacket, I leave the house and shut the door quietly behind me, locking it as usual.

Ten minutes later, I cross Main Street in front of the community center and cut through the small parking lot for our beach access. A paved ramp leads down to the sand. It's another quarter mile to the far side of the beach and I quicken my stride, moving closer to the water's edge where the sand is firm enough to easily walk on.

The surf rumbles in my ears. The ocean dances in my peripheral vision, a dark and deadly ballet. About fifty yards from shore, waves crash against the three rocks the town is named for—Arch Rock, Ridge Rock, and Fin Rock. There's actually a fourth rock a little closer to the beach called Seal Rock, because sometimes when the sun is out you can see seals basking on it. That rock is low and flat and blends into Fin Rock when you're looking from a distance, though, so I guess it didn't count to whoever named the town.

Beyond the rocks, the blackness of the ocean stretches out into forever, disturbed only by the red light of a winking buoy, hundreds of yards from shore.

I approach the cliff at the far side of the beach, a high wall that actually makes up part of Cape Azure, a hand-shaped piece of land with several fingers that protrude out into the ocean. A lighthouse, still in use, stands at the top of the cliff. Most of that area is part of Cape Azure State Park, but I haven't been there since Julia's dad took us hiking in middle school.

Turning my attention back to the beach, I scramble over a field of loose pebbles as I make my way toward the opening in the cliff. Some beaches have seashells. Three Rocks Beach has, well, rocks. The entrance to the cave starts about ten feet up from the water level, but kids have pushed the biggest rocks into a pile to form a sort of natural stairway. I scale the boulders and pause in the opening to the dark hole. I shine the flashlight on my phone around the inside. It's dry and deserted. It's also creepy as fuck.

I decide to hang out in the opening of the Pot Hole while I wait for Holden. Swiping at my phone, I access the internet and check out a movie review site that I read frequently. I scroll down to see the new on-demand and DVD releases. Every week, Mom and I do a Sunday night sundae party with ice cream and movies. Well, first we watch the latest episode of *911 Fire Rescue*, which I have nicknamed Sexy Firefighting Models. But she always lets me pick a movie to watch after that.

After the movie stuff, I skim some of the science and tech news on a national website, being careful to avoid the international links. Those always seem to be full of natural disasters and bombings and stuff. Even though I'm sure

Luke and I aren't getting back together, it's still terrifying to think of him in the scary situations that the big national papers write about.

A few minutes later, a lone figure dressed all in black approaches the Pot Hole at a steady jog. Holden is up away from the waterline and wearing combat boots that sink down in the sand with each stride. He transitions from sand to the rocks without slowing down, expertly picking his way across the sea of boulders. When he reaches the opening to the cave and pulls off his black knitted cap, he doesn't even look winded.

"What's up?" He bends down to brush his lips against mine. "Your texts seemed a little . . . frantic."

I glance furtively around. "Not here. Someone might see us." I step through the opening and slide down a short incline, into the belly of the cave, wincing at the musty odor. Holden follows me. Hitting the flashlight on my phone again, I double-check to make sure we're totally alone. Then I turn back to him. I pull the wrinkled note out of my back pocket. "I think someone saw us that night. They left me this—at my house. It says I have to post a confession of why I was at the Sea Cliff on my Facebook page."

"What? Let me see it," Holden says.

I hand him the note. Holden uses the flashlight on his own phone to read the note. He scrunches up his forehead as he finishes reading. "Ruin the life of someone you care about. What does that even mean?"

"I don't know," I say. "I mean, why not ruin *my* life if I'm the one you're pissed at?"

"Maybe this asshole saw us but doesn't have any actual proof. So he can't hurt you, but he might have stuff on other people. Any idea who left it?"

"The Jameson brothers said they saw a kid in a hoodie near my house, but they don't know who it was and they didn't see him on the porch or anything."

"Hmm. That doesn't exactly narrow it down. Everyone in town probably owns a hoodie." Holden rubs at the bridge of his nose. "It's probably some troll who doesn't like all the attention you got in the newspaper and stuff. I would just throw this away and pretend you never got it."

"You think?" I tuck my hands into my pockets. "But what if they really hurt someone?"

"Are you going to risk getting arrested and/or sued over that remote possibility?" Holden asks. "Besides, *ruin some-one's life* sounds a little dramatic, doesn't it? It's not like any of your friends are hard-core criminals or in the witness protection program. What's the guy gonna do? Out someone for using drugs or having an eating disorder or something? Those are *good* things to have out in the open."

"So you don't think I should do *anything*? I mean, whoever

wrote this might be crazy."

"What *can* you do? I can show it to my mom if you want, but you know what she's gonna think."

"That we started the fire." Again I see that look on my mom's face, a mixture of resignation and despair. I won't do that to her.

"Yep," Holden says. "Plus, it's not like the cops could do much with this note. Assuming whoever it is was smart enough not to leave fingerprints, this is just regular paper and a generic envelope. And this printing looks like someone tried to be as nondescript as possible. Look how round and even it is. Not exactly a major clue."

"You would tell me if you got one too, right?" I say, my voice wavering.

"Of course. The fact that I *didn't* get one is what makes me think it's just some asshole jealous of the attention you got." Holden slips the note into the envelope and hands it back to me. Then he runs one thumb down the side of my face. "I know you're used to flying under the radar, but heroes have haters, that's just how it is."

"I am not a hero," I mumble. "I risked my life because I didn't want to be a murderer. And now some whack job is threatening to target totally innocent people in my honor."

Holden looks down at me for a second, his expression deadly serious. "No one is totally innocent," he says finally.

"Yeah, but you know what I mean."

"I still think it's some troll." Gently, Holden removes my hands from my pockets and wraps his own hands around them. His fingers eclipse mine completely. "Look, Embry. I know you're a little freaked out, and I am too, but I say we call this asshole's bluff. He can try to ruin my life if he wants. Not like there's much to ruin." Holden continues before I can reply. "If we don't tell anyone about that night, chances are no one will be able to prove we were in the hotel. I looked it up online, and apparently fire investigations almost always end up inconclusive. There's never enough evidence left after the flames burn out to know for sure what started the fire. A couple of weeks from now the whole drama will be forgotten."

"Will it?" I want to believe Holden, but I have a bad feeling about this note, a bad feeling that the trouble from the Sea Cliff fire is just getting started.

SEVEN

December 15

I'M NOT SCHEDULED TO WORK on Saturday, but I volunteer to go in and help out because my other option would be pacing around the house going crazy until after eight p.m. to see if someone I care about gets their life ruined.

Part of me wants to call Julia and Frannie and tell them to be careful, but you can't really give advice like that without being more specific. I'm pretty sure the standard follow-up question to "Be careful because a crazy person is blackmailing me and threatened to hurt my friends" is "What did you do?" I try to reassure myself by thinking about how someone would have to work really hard to ruin either of their lives.

They're both smart, sensible, hardworking, well liked. I still feel like shit, though. At least I can look out for my mom since we're both going to be working all day.

Business is steady in the early morning as some of the beach walkers come in for coffee and a hash brown breakfast sandwich called the Beverly Cleary. I float between the front and the back, helping out both the cashier and the cook. After ten, things slow down and I throw myself into deep cleaning the customer seating area, scrubbing away the dust that has accumulated on light fixtures and windowsills. I work around the strands of tiny white lights we've strung up as Christmas decorations. Next, I gently Windex the glass fronts of each of the framed photos hanging in the café—mostly B-list actors and professional athletes who've stopped by for a sandwich or a latte in the past. Then I turn to the big mural on the back wall. It's a painting of Three Rocks Beach—a faded yellow sun shines down on the rocks, sand, and clear blue water. My great-grandmother had it painted when she first opened the shop, because she wanted people to be able to enjoy the beauty of the coastline even when it's cold and rainy. But after fifty years it's looking a little dingy.

With a damp cloth, I wipe the whole thing from top to bottom, brushing a few loose chips of paint to the floor. As my hand passes over the swirls of color, it occurs to me that maybe Holden would be willing to touch this up. It's not exactly his style, but I bet he'd be able to mimic the brush-strokes of the original artist.

"Embry." My mom's voice startles me.

I spin around. "Yeah?" I clutch the damp cloth tight in my right fist. "What's up?"

"Are you sure you want to be doing all this today?" Mom's eyes flick to the front window. A couple of girls my age walk by in puffy winter jackets. I don't recognize them—they must be tourists. We get college kids from Portland and families from other parts of the coast coming through on the weekends. "It's not even that cold out today," Mom continues. "I thought maybe you'd rather hang out with Julia or Frannie?"

"Nah. Julia is busy working on her college applications, and Frannie is probably volunteering at the food bank or helping out at the restaurant today."

"Still, I could hire a professional cleaner to come in and do this detail stuff. You don't have to do it."

I start to reply, but then get distracted. A man wearing a brown bomber jacket and a baseball cap is standing in the doorway of the market across the street. There's something familiar about him, but I'm not sure what it is. He's got sunglasses on, so I can't tell if he's staring at us or looking past the edge of the building, out toward the ocean.

Mom turns around to see what has caught my attention. The man pulls out a pack of cigarettes and slides one between his lips, turning his face toward the building to shelter himself from the wind. Cigarette lit, he pulls a phone out of his pocket and starts walking down the street toward the beach access parking lot.

"I don't mind cleaning." I turn back to the mural. "Holden Hassler might be willing to come brighten this up a little. He was in one of my art classes and he's an amazing painter."

Mom turns toward the mural. "It is looking a bit faded, isn't it? You know, your grandmother had an idea for that wall before she died."

"Oh?"

Mom makes a swiping motion with her arm. "She wanted to tear down the whole thing, put in a big picture window that looks out onto the ocean."

"That would be amazing," I say. "But probably expensive."

"True." Mom wilts slightly, and I feel bad for bringing reality into her fantasy. "Let me think about the touch-up. If you see Holden, ask him how much he would charge."

"Okay," I say, even though I know he'd do it for free.

Mom glances around the coffee shop. I follow her gaze, from the Christmas lights strung around the front window to the painted tables and chairs to the walls that now seem just a bit brighter. "It looks fantastic in here."

"Thanks." I smile. "Is there anything I can help you with in the back?"

Mom grins. "Wanna scrub the employee toilet?"

I shudder. "Noooo. But I guess I could."

My mom snickers. "I was kidding. I make the staff who show up late do that. You can help me with the holiday orders if you want. We don't have as many as last year, but I've got some people who want to pick up their cookies early next week."

Mom's sugar cookies are a favorite of the kids in Three Rocks. She sells them in different shapes depending on the time of year—flowers in the spring, leaves in the fall, and stars and snowflakes in the winter. Several of the people who live here order dozens to bring to work and family holiday parties.

"I'm on it," I tell her, heading back into the kitchen area of the shop. Mom and I sometimes make the cookies at home, too, so I know the recipe by heart. I quickly assemble all the ingredients on one of the big prep tables and start mixing the batter in our industrial mixer. Once the batter is ready, I get into a rhythm: roll out the dough, cut out the cookies, put the pans in the oven, roll out more dough, pans out of the oven, loosen cookies with spatula, and put them on a tray for cooling. Start again from the beginning. The repetitive motions soothe me and the work keeps me from thinking about the note and the slowly approaching deadline of eight p.m.

Two hours later I've managed to roll out, cut out, and

bake over six dozen holiday cookies. After that, I neaten the storeroom and make up a batch of chicken noodle soup for Monday's soup of the day, pausing occasionally to help out Adele, today's cashier and barista, when it gets busy out front.

Mom gathers her things to leave around five, as usual, but balks when I offer to stay until close. "That's too much time here, Embry."

"You work twelve-hour shifts all the time," I protest.

"Because I own the place," Mom says. "And I don't want you to end up like me, even if you decide you want to own the place one day, too." She tugs me toward the back hallway, where both of our coats hang on hooks outside the manager's office. "I do appreciate all your help, though. Even if I'm not sure what motivated it."

"Can't I just want to help my mom?" I ask. A twinge of guilt pricks at my insides as I think about the best way to pass three more hours.

"Hmph." Mom shrugs into her coat. "First time for everything, I guess."

"Hey!" I protest. "That's not—"

Mom laughs. "I'm kidding. What's got you so wound up today?"

I slide into my own coat and we turn toward the front. "Nothing. Just some stuff going on at school."

"Anything I need to know about?" She adjusts her wig

slightly as she slides on a fuzzy cream-colored hat and pulls it down over her ears.

"I've got it under control," I tell her. At least I hope I do.

We wave to Adele as we pass by the front counter. The bells above the door jingle as we step out into the cold. Fog has rolled in off the water. It twists and swirls around us, painting the entire street a hazy gray. I pause in the doorway of the post office to pull out my phone and snap a couple of pictures.

Mom and I continue walking along Main Street. We pass the row of shops and then turn away from the ocean, walking on the shoulder of Highway W as we round the base of Puffin Hill. Someone has strung tiny white lights along the top of the fence that runs the length of the cemetery. Headstones cast dark shadows across the grass. I can just barely make out the feathery leaves of poinsettia plants that some people have left by their loved ones' graves. The skin on the back of my neck prickles. When I was little, living so close to the cemetery never bothered me, but now that some of my relatives are buried there I can't pass it without getting a weird feeling in my gut.

As we approach the road leading into our neighborhood, the mix of fog and our neighbors' Christmas lights creates an interesting swirly red-and-green effect. I take a couple more pictures.

"Let me see what your photos look like," Mom says.

I scroll back through my image gallery and show her the best one from today, taken right outside the post office. It's a picture where the red-and-black cobblestones of the street and the houses at the top of Puffin Hill are in focus, but the area in between them is blunted a ghostly gray.

"Pretty," Mom says. "Especially considering what a piece of crap this phone is. Have you thought about studying photography at college?"

"Why? So I can work at the coffee shop forever? Not that there's anything wrong with that," I add quickly.

My mom smiles. "I definitely do not expect you to work at the coffee shop forever, unless you want to. I don't know how people make money taking pictures, but it might be worth looking into, if it's something you really enjoy."

A gust of wind rattles the windows on one of the hill houses above us. Mom grips onto her fuzzy hat with her free hand to keep it from blowing away. She's still looking at the picture on my phone.

"I'm actually taking a photography class next semester," I say. "Hopefully we'll talk about stuff like that."

"You've definitely got a good eye." Without asking, Mom flips back through the previous few pictures—a couple of the street, a couple of the beach, and one of Holden. Luckily it's just him on his motorcycle, nowhere near the Sea Cliff Inn.

She shakes her head. "I can't believe his mother lets him ride that thing. She must worry every time he goes somewhere that he might not come back."

"Well, she is a cop," I say. "It'd be kind of hypocritical of her to forbid him from doing anything dangerous."

"Good point," Mom says. "Do I even want to know if you've ever ridden on the back of that thing?"

I blink innocently as we turn onto the cracked asphalt road that cuts through the middle of our neighborhood. When my mom was in the hospital and I couldn't be with her because she was getting chemo, Holden would pick me up and take me for rides up and down the Oregon Coast to distract me.

"Don't you just love what the Lerners have done to their yard?" I say, changing the subject and pointing at a giant inflatable snow globe with two polar bears dancing inside it. Fake snow rains down on their heads. "I swear every year they add more and more Christmas decorations. Soon they'll be charging people just to drive down our street."

"That is not an answer." Mom clears her throat. "Just promise me that you'll never take unnecessary chances, okay?" She wraps an arm around my back. "You're all I got, kiddo. I don't want to lose you."

I pause in front of our house and turn to my mom. "I don't want to lose you either."

Mom pulls me into a full hug right next to the mailbox.

"I'm not going anywhere, Embry. My doctors say I'm doing great."

"I don't know what I would do without you," I murmur into the zipper of Mom's winter jacket.

"Oh, probably fall apart completely," Mom teases. "But if you're lucky, Betsy would take care of you."

As if she somehow heard her name, Betsy pops her golden head up in the living room window, which means she's standing on the futon couch.

"Get down." My mom claps her hands.

Betsy prances back and forth on the futon. She barks twice. She's loud enough to hear through the glass. Her tail thumps against the windowpanes.

"This is why we can't have nice things," Mom says with a grin.

"She's completely hopeless," I agree. A smile forms on my face as my dumb dog disappears from view. She's probably scratching on the front door.

Mom fishes her keys out of her purse, and sure enough Betsy explodes out into the cold as soon as Mom opens the door. I have to grab her by the collar before she makes it across the yard and into the street. I drag the dog back into the house and shut the door behind us.

"Are you hungry?" Mom asks. "I was thinking about driving into Tillamook and picking up a pizza."

"Sure," I say. "I'm always hungry for pizza." Heading into the kitchen, I do a quick check of our refrigerator. It's mostly empty except for a half gallon of milk and some cheese and lunch meat that Mom brought home from the coffee shop because it was getting close to the expiration date. "But I could make us sandwiches if you don't want to drive all that way."

"You know what? I have a better idea. We got so much accomplished today that I think we should celebrate. Let's go to Fintastic. I know how much you love their sautéed scallops, and with Luke gone you probably haven't had them in forever."

"I do love those," I admit. "But Fintastic is so expensive. We could probably buy some scallops from the market and make—"

"Embry!" Mom scolds. "You shouldn't be worrying more about money than I am. How long has it been since we went out to eat? We can afford to have a nice meal every once in a while."

"You're right," I mumble. *As long as no one finds out I burned down the Sea Cliff Inn.*

"What do you say?" Mom continues. "Dinner at Fintastic, and then afterward we can even get a Christmas tree if you want. I heard the lot has marked them down to half price."

"Really?" Mom and I both love Christmas, and every year we have fun decorating the coffee shop and our house with knickknacks and lights, but we haven't gotten a tree since my grandmother died.

"Sure. Your dad sent a little extra money this month to buy some holiday things, and now that they're marked down—"

I scowl. I hate it when she calls him my dad. "Dad" implies involvement. I prefer the term "father" or perhaps "genetic donor." When I was little, it was different—back then I really wanted him to be part of my life. All the other kids at school had a dad they saw at least occasionally if not every day. I felt cheated, like I was missing out. But when I turned fourteen, my grandmother told me the whole ugly story of his affair with my mom—how his wife told all of Three Rocks that Mom was a stalker who got him drunk and seduced him, how he begged and pleaded and even tried to bribe her into getting an abortion, how my mom agreed to take less child support in exchange for him promising he would never try to get custody.

I looked my father up online a couple of times after I heard that story. I think I was hoping to find some evidence it was false, or at least exaggerated. But all I found was a sandy-haired executive type with a Pilates instructor for a wife and two sons in college on the East Coast. After seeing all that, I decided I wanted nothing to do with a man who didn't even want me to exist. I'd say that I hate him, but I know the money he sends my mom every month is what's keeping us afloat, so I guess maybe I just dislike him a lot.

"I don't want to use his money," I say. "I mean, obviously we should use his money for things that we need. But I have some cash saved up we can use for the tree."

"What difference does—"

"It makes a difference," I say. "In fact, hold on a second." Ducking into my room, I return with a wad of bills. I hold them out toward my mom. "I was thinking we could use this toward fixing the furnace. I know you've been looking into that."

Mom's eyes flick to the thermostat on the wall. We have it turned all the way up, but it's barely sixty in here. "I was thinking you might want to use it to buy yourself something special," she says. "Or maybe some presents for your friends?"

I shake my head. "I never buy stuff for anyone besides you and Luke. I'd feel better if the money went toward something we both need."

"What about Julia?"

"Julia and I always make each other things or exchange little gifts," I say. "This year I'm surprising her with the official Julia Worthington sandwich, remember?"

After much begging and cajoling, my mom agreed to let me create a new sandwich for the coffee shop menu and name it after Julia. It might seem like a silly gift, but Julia will love seeing her name up on our painted board, and I'm going to make sure she loves the sandwich too.

"As long as it doesn't have glitter on it," Mom says.

I grin. Julia is known for her sparkly makeup, especially in the summer when she's showing a lot of skin. "No glitter. Just hummus and vegetables and low-fat Greek dressing."

"Sounds good," Mom says. "So how about this? We'll put half of this money toward the furnace. The other half you can hang on to or put in the bank just in case something comes up. If nothing else you can put it toward your college textbooks next year."

"Fair enough. Just let me change and I'll be ready to go." I hand Mom five of the fifty-dollar bills and tuck the rest of the cash into my purse. I'm still not going to use it if we get a tree. My father has taken a lot of happiness from Mom and me. He doesn't get to mess up Christmas.

"Great," Mom says. "I'm going to call for a reservation just in case it's busy and then take a quick shower. Can we plan to leave at six-thirty?"

"Sure." That'll leave one and a half hours until the deadline. My brain replays that montage of potential life-ruining things. I tell myself I'm being silly. No one can wreck Julia's chances at college just because they want to. And no one would risk vandalizing the coffee shop or really hurting someone I care about just to teach me a lesson. It's probably a dumb prank, like Holden said.

I wish I could be with him when that clock counts down, but I think he's working at the gas station tonight. Maybe I'll catch a glimpse of him when Mom and I get to the Christmas tree lot—it's right across the street from the station.

My phone buzzes with a text. Swiping at the display, I smile when I see who it's from. It's like he heard me thinking about him.

Holden: Just checking to see if you're freaking yourself out worrying about that note.

Me: I decided to help Mom out at the café today, but now that I'm home I might be mildly freaking out.

Holden: Anything I can do?

Me: I just feel like I should be doing something. Like warning everyone I care about to be on guard.

Holden: You're with your mom and I'm looking out for me. Luke is in Afghanistan so who does that leave that you're worried about? Just Julia?

Me: Julia, Frannie, some of the coffee shop peeps.

Holden: Well, you can warn anyone you want, but without more to go on there's not a lot any of us can do.

I know he's right, but it still feels wrong to ignore threats against the people I care about. My chest feels heavy, like it's full of rocks. I hate this—this helpless out-of-control feeling.

Me: What if something bad happens?

Holden: It won't.

Me: But what if it does?

Holden: Then we'll deal with it together, ok?

I gnaw on my bottom lip. Holden's words aren't enough to reassure me, but right now they're the best I'm going to get.

EIGHT

ABOUT AN HOUR LATER, Mom and I pull into the gravel parking lot for Fintastic. The building is plain on the outside—just white concrete with a black shingled roof—which helps keep it what the townspeople like to refer to as a "hidden treasure." It's not the kind of place you would impulsively stop at if you were driving by. Still, each year a few more travel writers find out about it and it gets more and more crowded. Tonight is no exception and the parking lot is almost full.

A blast of warm air hits us as we open the door. The inside of the restaurant is the opposite of the outside. It's full of cozy booths and coastal decor, perfect for romantic dates or family outings. A tall Christmas tree stands behind the hostess stand, its thick, feathery branches decorated with green, red, and gold ornaments and adorned with hundreds of white lights.

Mom and I are greeted by the hostess, who turns out to be Frannie. She's wearing black pants and a knitted Christmas sweater with rows of reindeer and snowmen.

"Hi, guys," she chirps. "I saw your reservation in the book and I've got you all set up." She leads us to a table back in the far corner of the restaurant. She sets two leather-bound menus on the table. "Your server Katrina will be right with you."

"Wait, what?" I ask. "Katrina Jensen?"

"Yeah." Frannie glances over her shoulder at the front door, as if she's hoping for some new customers she can use as an escape.

"Is that a problem?" Mom asks. "Who's Katrina? Is she new in town?"

"She lives in Tillamook." I envision my nice dinner with my mom being ruined by Katrina's surly attitude and snide remarks. I turn to Frannie, who is now inching her way back from our table. "Can we have someone different?"

Frannie gives me a pleading look. "Sorry. I know she's not your favorite person, but I had to skip her in the rotation because the last guests wanted to sit by the fireplace, and if I skip her again she'll rat me out to my mom."

I know from Luke that Frannie's mom is really hard on her, that she feels like nothing she does is ever good enough for her parents. I definitely don't want to set her up for another lecture. "Ugh, fine." I roll my eyes. "Why do you hate me?" I mouth at Frannie as Katrina comes strolling up behind her.

"Welp. Here's your server. I'd better get back to the door." Frannie turns and scurries back to her post, her braids flapping.

Katrina is close to unrecognizable in the Fintastic server uniform—black pants, a blue T-shirt with a big fish logo across the chest, and a gray baseball cap with the word "Fintastic" embroidered on the front. Her blue hair is pulled back in a tight ponytail. Her robotic smile starts to contort into a snarl when she recognizes me, but she quickly pulls it together when she realizes I'm with my mom.

"Hello, ladies. Embry, our town hero, so nice to see you. Can I start you two off with something to drink?" she asks sweetly.

"Just water, please," Mom says.

"Water for me too."

"Two waters. Got it." Katrina's fake smile disappears, and I bet she's already decided Mom and I are going to be shitty tippers. Which actually isn't true.

"I take it you two aren't friends," Mom says, as Katrina heads toward the kitchen. "What's wrong with her?"

"How long do we have before this place closes?" I joke. "It's not a big thing. She's just . . . not my favorite person, like Frannie said."

"Well, speaking of you being a hero, I was wondering if you were planning to go see the boy you saved at the hospital. What was his name? Sam something?"

"Oh, right. Sam. Uh, I don't know. I haven't really thought about it." I haven't thought about it because there's no way I want to go see him. He'll probably act all grateful, and I'll end up feeling even worse about things than I already do. "I'm not even sure if he's still in the hospital or what."

"According to the newspaper, he is, but he's expected to make a full recovery. Did you know him at all? The article I read said he dropped out of Tillamook High during his junior year after his grandfather died."

"I didn't even know he went to Tillamook High, but I think maybe he's a couple years older than me," I say. "I might have just missed him."

"Well, it would be a nice gesture if you stopped by to visit," my mom says.

"Yeah, okay. I'll think about it."

Across the restaurant, Frannie seats an older couple I recognize—Julia's parents. I wonder what Julia is doing tonight. She retook her SAT last month and said she felt pretty good about it, but now she's obsessing about the essays she has to write. She and her friend Ness signed up for some "How to Write the Perfect Application Essay" online course that I know she's been logging on to a lot.

Luke's mom strolls out of the kitchen carrying a tray of food. She stops by the bar, where his brother Jonah adds a bottle of red wine to her tray. Jonah leans in close to say something to her and she pats him on the arm.

Mom follows my gaze. "So I haven't heard you mention Luke much lately. I take it he's not coming home for Christmas?"

"He can't," I say. "He said maybe after the first of the year."

"Are things still all right between the two of you?"

I pause for a minute, then say, "We kind of agreed to take a break while he was overseas. I didn't want to tell you because it was right when you were getting sick and I know how much you like him."

"I do like him." Mom smiles. "But what matters is whether *you* like him."

"He's a great guy," I say, convincingly. "But being in the army has put him on fast-forward. He wants me to move to Texas this summer. He even mentioned the idea of getting married the next time he's in town."

Mom whistles under her breath. "Gosh, you guys are so young to be talking about stuff like that."

"I know, right?" My shoulders slump forward as I think

about the last time Luke and I were alone together, after my junior prom. We got a hotel room for the night, and I was expecting it just to be about drinking and hooking up, enjoying our limited time together. He looked so hot in his dress uniform that I spent the whole dance daydreaming about how fun it would be to take it off him.

But Luke spent half the night on the hotel room balcony, staring out at the ocean. He kept talking about a friend of his whose wife had left him after a long deployment. "I'm just not sure what'll happen if I end up overseas for six months . . . or longer," he said. "We've never been apart for more than three months, and even that was really hard for me."

That was the night I first suggested that we take a break—less pressure, I told him. He needed to focus on staying safe, not worry about his lonely girlfriend back home who couldn't possibly understand what he was going through. He needed to be free to do whatever he had to do to survive the situation. I wanted to be a source of support, not stress.

He got angry at the idea, so I dropped it and led him back inside, to the bed, where he finally let me distract him. In the morning he acted like everything was fine.

But by the end of the school year, he had come around to my way of thinking. "Just a break, not a breakup," he told me on the phone. "So that way instead of being sad that we're apart, we can just be happy when we're able to talk to each other. And then when I return to base we can start making plans for after you graduate."

At that time I really thought we'd get back together. I mean, this was Luke, the guy who spent six hours helping me look for Betsy when she escaped from the backyard. The guy who took me sailing and kayaking and planned a romantic picnic for the day he first told me he loved me. Luke, the guy who was satisfied with second base for six months and then waited another four months for me to feel ready to sleep with him. Surely, the teensy little crush I had on Holden at the time wouldn't compare to all that.

How could I have been so wrong?

My mom clears her throat. "Well, just don't let him pressure you into anything. You'll always have a place to stay with me, and a job if you want it."

"Thanks." I blink away the images that flash through my mind—me at my mom's funeral after the cancer comes back, snow falling on Puffin Hill as I place a leafy red poinsettia next to her grave. "I've been thinking about breaking it off with him completely the next time he comes home. I wish I wanted the same things, but I just . . . don't." This is more than I've told anyone except for Holden. *Holden.* His name is on my lips. My mom knows we're friends. I could tell her the whole truth. It's the perfect opportunity, and it's not like she would judge me.

But I don't. Because the words won't come out. Instead I push my hair back from my face and change the subject. "Why don't *you* ever date anyone, Mom? You haven't since Jackson, right?"

Jackson Keller was a nurse who worked in the Tillamook General emergency room. Mom met him at the coffee shop. He used to come in a lot during the summer and order fruit smoothies to take to the beach. Eventually he decided to go back to school for an advanced degree and moved to Portland for classes. He and Mom saw each other on weekends, but it gradually fizzled out. Mom never told me what happened—I was about eleven at the time—but I saw her eyes red-rimmed enough to assume he'd been the one who ended it.

Mom toys with a strand of her wig. "Honestly, hon? I'm a lot happier when I'm not in a relationship." She shrugs. "There were a couple other men when you were little. Back then I really wanted you to have a father figure in your life. But as you're finding out, relationships can be extremely stressful. You have to make compromises. Everything you do suddenly has the power to seriously affect another person. I just decided it wasn't worth it, that I'd rather focus my attention on you and the shop. And then when I got sick, I had to find the time to focus on myself too." She grins. "Not a lot of time left over to deal with romantic bullshit."

"I just hate the idea of you feeling all alone because of me," I say.

"Silly girl." Mom pats me on the hand. "You're the reason I'll never feel all alone."

When Katrina brings our food (which I'm hoping she didn't spit in), the scallops are just as amazing as I remembered. There are five of them, sautéed to a golden brown and arranged in a circle on a bed of linguine. A scampi sauce made with butter and herbs is drizzled over the top and the edge of the plate is garnished with fresh parsley and lemon wedges. I pull out my phone and snap a picture of the dish.

The time is 7:18. Less than an hour until the deadline.

"Are you going to Snapgram that or whatever?" Mom asks.

I smile. "Nah. It's just almost too pretty to eat."

"You must not be as hungry as I am, then." Mom cuts off a big bite of her herb-encrusted salmon with Florentine sauce and pops it into her mouth. "Mmm. Melts like butter." She dabs at her mouth with her napkin.

I cut into the first of the scallops. It's cooked perfectly. Crisp on the outside, soft on the inside without being rubbery. I swirl a few strands of linguine around my fork, the long narrow pasta making me think of the hoses unspooling as the firefighters hurried into the Sea Cliff Inn. Was someone else really there that night, watching Holden and me?

The fork flies out of my trembling fingers and rolls halfway across the table. "Sorry." I snatch the fork back and give it a quick wipe with my napkin, hiding my still-shaking hands in my lap.

Mom blots at her lips again. "Are you sure you're all right? You've seemed kind of jumpy all day."

"Sorry. I just have a lot on my mind."

"Well, if you ever want to share . . ." My mom trails off meaningfully.

I nod. "I know. Thanks. It's no big deal." I hope it's not, anyway. I check my phone again as I tuck it into my purse—7:21. Is someone else watching the clock just like I am, waiting to see if I post on my Facebook page? Or is Holden right and they're just sitting somewhere laughing at the thought of me worrying about all this?

Turns out Mom and I are both starving and we eat mostly in quiet, save for the occasional murmuring of how delicious everything is. I try not to gulp down my food. I glance around the restaurant, chewing slowly, savoring each bite. The hardwood floor gleams like it's freshly polished, and the fisherman decor hanging from the walls—stuffed fish, anchors, historical pictures, nets and ropes, etc.—has all been strung with tiny white fairy lights for Christmas. The big glass windows have been decorated with fake snow, except for the ones along the back that look out on the ocean.

My eyes land on a seahorse-shaped wall clock hanging above the bar. Twenty-seven minutes to go.

I cut into my fourth scallop and swirl it around in the scampi sauce. When Mom gets up and excuses herself to go to the restroom, I grab my phone and call Holden. I know if he's at work he probably won't answer, but I just want to hear his voice.

His voice-mail message plays. "This is Holden Hassler. Please leave a message." No frills. All business. I hang up the phone and send him a text:

Me: I'm at Fintastic with my mom, going a little crazy wait-ing for 8pm. Everything okay with you?

When he doesn't reply, I log on to the internet and check out some of the local news stories. One of the articles is about the Coast Guard rescuing two college boys from a cave south of Yachats, the town where my father lives.

I try to imagine what my father would say if he found out what I did. Is he the kind of guy who would support me and say I shouldn't be held responsible for an accident? Or would he judge me and lecture me about sneaking around with boys and underage drinking? I wonder if he'll end up hav-ing to pay part of the damages to the Sea Cliff if I get caught. He could probably just write a check for the whole thing. I search "signing away paternity rights," but I can't find anything about whether that protects a parent when it comes to financial judgments against their child.

"Fuck," I mutter under my breath. What would even happen to my mom if we ended up having to sell the Oregon Coast Café? She could probably find a job at a coffee shop or restaurant in Tillamook. Maybe she could be a manager or do their books or something. But what if the Oregon Coast Café isn't even worth what we'd owe for my part in the Sea Cliff fire? The shop space is rented, not owned, and Mom is always grumbling about how she's barely breaking even.

If someone finds out the truth, Mom and I could end up losing our house.

I swallow hard. The scallops start tumbling around in my stomach like shoes in a clothes dryer. How did this happen? How did *any* of this happen?

My mom slides back into the booth. "They even decorated the bathrooms for Christmas."

"No kidding?" I tap the X on my browser to shut the window so she doesn't see what I was looking at. The time display on my phone is practically pulsing now.

Twenty-two minutes to go.

"Are you going to finish?" Mom points at my one remaining scallop and a bit of linguine.

My stomach is still twisting and turning. I force a smile.

"I'm full, actually. You want?"

"Sure." Mom cuts the scallop in half and pops each bite into her mouth with a forkful of linguine. "Mmm." She signals for the check. She hands her credit card to Katrina and waits for her to come back with the charge slip to sign.

Frannie returns to our table while we're waiting. "Was everything okay?" she asks brightly.

I'm pretty sure by "everything" she means Katrina. "I guess," I say grudgingly. "Food was amazing as always."

"That's what I like to hear. You guys hang on a second before you go. I have something for you, from my mom and dad."

I nod. It's probably a Christmas card or a small gift. A lot of the business owners in town exchange little presents with each other. As Frannie heads for the kitchen, I check my phone again. Seventeen minutes to go.

A few minutes later, Frannie returns with a white plastic bag with a couple of Styrofoam containers in it.

"What is it?" I peer into the top container and see a couple of uncooked salmon fillets.

"Just some extra fish and some of our deer sausage. Mom mentioned I should hook up any of our friends who come in. The sausage comes in three different flavors—teriyaki, cheddar, and chipotle. I made the chipotle. My parents won't let me go hunting until I'm eighteen, but my dad let me help fabricate the deer he shot earlier this month."

"Gross," I say. "Not the sausage, which is amazing. Just the dead deer part, and whatever is involved with *fabricating*."

"It's when you—"

"Stop right there," I tell her. "Before you ruin sausage for me forever."

My mom shifts awkwardly in her chair. "Thank you, Fran. But your mom doesn't have to feed us."

She waves her hand. "Pssht. You know how it is. There's no way to order exactly enough food for the restaurant, especially when it comes to perishable stuff. And my dad and brothers killed three deer this season, which is enough meat and sausage to last us like a year."

"Well, if you're going to twist my arm." Mom flashes Frannie a smile as she ties the top of the plastic bag into a loose knot. "Is your mom available so I can thank her?"

"She actually left early tonight," Frannie says. "I think the stress of the holiday season is getting to her this year."

"Is she still in charge of the nativity play?" I ask. Every year on Christmas Eve we have a Three Rockin' Christmas Eve Party at the community center next to the Shop-a-Lot. The party kicks off with some remarks from the mayor, who used to be the Tillamook fire chief. Then there's a traditional nativity play, which is full of the local kids and usually a lot of fun, and later cookies and punch provided by local volunteers. Mrs. O'Riley has directed the play for as long as I can remember. One year Luke, Frannie, and I were cast as the three wisepeople. Luke kept calling his present Frankenstein instead of frankincense, and his mom got really cranky about it. The audience thought it was hilarious.

"Yes, and she is overachieving as usual. She's actually trying to recruit a Baby Jesus from Tillamook since there are no infants in Three Rocks right now. I keep telling her to just use a doll."

My mom chuckles. "I think Jesus would be impressed by her commitment to authenticity."

"Moms." I roll my eyes at Frannie and she giggles.

"Moms indeed," my mom says wryly. "Can't live with 'em. Can't eat delicious food without 'em." She turns back to Frannie. "Well, tell her I said thank you. Embry and I will enjoy the salmon over the next couple of days and eat this yummy deer sausage all the way into next year."

"Seriously. That sausage is responsible for all this." Frannie pats the front of her fuzzy holiday sweater, which I'm pretty sure is about 95 percent yarn and 5 percent girl. She's almost as skinny as I am.

"Whatever." I roll my eyes at her again.

Frannie disappears with a wave as Katrina returns with

my mom's charge slip. "Thanks, you guys. Have a great night," Katrina says. She's halfway back to the kitchen before my mom can say, "You too."

Mom nudges me in the ribs as we head for the exit. "I forgot to tell you. The mayor dropped by the coffee shop yesterday while you were at school and asked if we were planning on attending the Christmas Eve party. Seems you might be the recipient of a Rocky Award this year for what you did the night of the Sea Cliff fire."

"Ugh." I make a face. The mayor likes to hand out cheesy awards to residents who have gone above and beyond in exemplifying the mission of our town, which is like "honesty, bravery, camaraderie" or some bullshit. "Did you tell him I had other plans?"

Mom snickers. "No I did not. I told him we'd both be there like we are every year."

"Great." It figures the one time someone wants to honor me it's for one of the worst things I've ever done, but right now I have more important things to worry about.

My phone buzzes just as we're getting ready to head out into the cold. Eight more minutes.

I tap at my messages icon and see a text from Holden. A huge knot of tension in my back starts to dissipate just from looking at his name. "Thanks for dinner," I tell my mom.

"Thanks for your help at the shop. I can't remember the last time . . ." Mom trails off as something across the parking lot attracts her attention.

I follow her gaze. There's a man near our car. It looks like the guy who was checking us out at the coffee shop earlier today. The guy in the baseball cap and the brown bomber jacket.

NINE

I HURRY TOWARD OUR CAR with my mom right behind me. The guy ducks between the rows of vehicles and gets into a black BMW. He backs quickly out of his spot and heads for the exit, his tires spitting gravel as he transfers from the parking lot to the paved road.

"Do you know that guy?" I ask my mom.

"Not sure. I didn't get a good look at him." She pulls her keys out of her purse. "I was just wondering why he was by our car."

"You would tell me if you had a stalker or something, right? I thought I saw that same guy looking at us earlier today from in front of the Shop-a-Lot." My voice sounds frantic. I struggle to dial it down a notch.

"If you did, it's probably a coincidence," Mom says. "It's a small town. If he's a tourist or passing through, this is one of the only places to get a good dinner."

I check my phone. It can't be related to the threatening message I got. I still have seven minutes before the deadline. Unless that guy came lurking around just to scare me.

As Mom pulls out of the lot, I remember the text from Holden. I swipe at my screen.

Holden: Sorry. At work. Anything bad happen?

Me: No, not really. But the official deadline isn't for a few more minutes.

Holden: Want me to come pick you up after I get off? We could go for a ride on the bike. Take your mind off things.

Me: Brrr! Too coooooold!

Zipping along the coast on the back of Holden's motorcycle during the summer was great. I'm not sure how much of an escape it would feel like in thirty-degree weather.

Holden: Wuss ;)

Me: Mom and I are actually heading your way to get a Christmas tree.

Holden: Cool. Glad you're not alone.

Me: Me too.

Mom glances over at me. "You kids work those phones something fierce," she says. "I'm always amazed at how fast you guys text."

I laugh under my breath. "We're all going to have carpal tunnel when we're your age." The lock screen lights up. It's 7:55. Five more minutes. I glance up at the road. We're only a couple of blocks from the Christmas tree lot. I do my best to watch both my phone and the road until Mom turns into the lot and cuts off the engine. I don't know what I'm expecting— it's not like whoever threatened me has been stalking me for the past twenty-four hours and is going to jump out in front of the car as the time runs out on my deadline.

I feel better, though, now that we're off the roads.

The lot has been pretty picked over, but there are still about a dozen trees left to choose from. Mom gives the smaller ones that will fit in our living room a thorough examination, going from tree to tree and feeling the branches, checking to see if the needles are falling off already.

I peek at my phone every time I can get away with it, my heart thudding in my chest when the display hits 8:00 p.m. As Mom flags down the tree salesman to check the price on a tree that isn't marked, I spin a slow circle, scanning the entire area for anyone who might be looking at me.

Across the street, the lights flick off in the body shop attached to the gas station. Holden is in the parking lot, pumping gas on a couple different cars. He sees me and taps at his wrist as if to say, "Look what time it is."

I nod at him, but I'm not sure if he saw the motion, so I

give him a tentative wave. He waves back and then turns to the gas pump. He removes the hose from his customer's fuel tank and hangs it back on the pump. He reattaches the customer's gas cap and offers the man a receipt.

Mom returns with a man about her age wearing a red-and-black plaid jacket and brown work pants. He's got standard blue-and-orange gardening gloves on his hands.

"This one is twenty dollars, Emb. What do you think?"

"I think we should take it." I force a smile, for the benefit of both my mom and the tree salesman. I cast another glance all around me as I follow them up to the front of the lot, where the man puts netting around the tree.

Mom and I both go for our purses at the same time. She shakes her head at me. "I have cash. Not from your father, okay?"

I nod. I feel bad about being so picky. "I'm sorry if I was stupid about that."

"You weren't stupid. You were sensitive. You're allowed to be sensitive, though I do hope you'll consider talking to him someday."

"Maybe someday," I say. *But not anytime soon.*

Mom gives the tree salesman the twenty-dollar bill, and he offers to write her a receipt. She shakes her head. "That's all right. Thank you."

He carries the tree to our car and helps secure it to the roof with a couple pieces of strong twine. As mom pulls her keys out of her pocket and heads for the driver's side, the tree salesman presses a little card into her hand. "Give me a call if you ever need any plants or flowers for your yard. I run the nursery over in Tillamook and I can get you a good deal."

Mom blushes as she accepts the business card, and I suddenly realize this guy is flirting with her. Seeing Mom and this guy smiling at each other kind of makes me wish I could disappear. It also makes me wonder if everything she said at dinner was true.

Maybe love is just one more thing she sacrificed for me.

Back at home, Mom and I work on getting the tree into our tree stand. I close the blinds and pull the curtains across the front window. I can't quite shake the image of the guy in the brown bomber jacket lurking in the Fintastic parking lot. I hope my mom hasn't picked up some creepy guy from an online dating site or something. I think she'd tell me if she were seeing someone, but she probably thinks the same about me.

Holden calls in the middle of Mom holding the tree straight and me tightening the bolts of the stand, while Betsy wags her tail and paces back and forth, excited at the presence of anything new in the house.

"Go lie down," I tell her. With one hand on the trunk of the tree, I use my other hand to silence my phone.

Betsy barks once and then sits back on her haunches and smiles at me.

"Dumb dog," I say, but my lips twitch. I can't ever resist her doggie smile.

We finally get the tree bolted in securely. Mom steps back to see if it's straight. "Looking pretty good. Did you want to decorate it now or tomorrow?"

"Maybe tomorrow." This is later than my mom is usually awake, and I can see the dark circles under her eyes, her shoulders starting to droop. I gesture toward my bedroom. "I've actually got some homework I should work on."

Mom snickers. "First you want to work all day on Saturday, and then you want to do homework? If you're some alien pod person, you're doing a terrible job of impersonating a normal teenage girl."

"You calling me abnormal?"

"In the best possible way." Mom winks. "Tomorrow sounds good. We can decorate it during our Sunday sundae party."

"It's a date." I give her a quick hug. "I had fun today. Good night."

"Night." Mom yawns. "I'll see you tomorrow."

Betsy follows me as I head for my room. I kick off my boots and flop down onto my bed fully clothed. My mom isn't the only one who's exhausted. I don't know if I wore myself out working or if it's just the stress of worrying about what might happen after the deadline for posting a confession, but I'm about ready to fall asleep too.

Betsy clambers up onto my bed and lies down at the foot of it.

"Rough day for you too, huh?" I stroke her soft fur. Then I pull my phone out of my pocket, lie back on the bed, and call Holden. "Hey," I say. "Sorry. We were dealing with the tree."

"No worries. I was going to jog over and check out your tree, but you guys were gone before I finished with my customers." He pauses. "So nothing bad happened?"

"There was this weird guy by our car at Fintastic, but it was probably just a coincidence. I'm still keeping an eye out for trouble, though."

"Like I said, I bet it was just some troll," Holden says. "They're everywhere nowadays."

When nothing happens on Sunday, I start to believe him. And then when nothing happens on Monday or Tuesday, I completely believe him. But then everything changes at school on Wednesday.

TEN

December 19

THE FIRST THING I NOTICE is that Julia isn't at her locker before first hour. She usually drives herself to school instead of taking the bus with most of the Three Rocks kids because she swims laps in the mornings for exercise. Still, she's always at her locker by the time I finish eating breakfast in the cafeteria. I send her a text, asking if she's sick or staying home today and she doesn't respond. When my phone buzzes a few minutes later, I assume it's her, but it turns out to be Holden.

Holden: Did you check your email this morning?

Me: Yeah. Mostly spam. Why? Did you send me something?

Holden: No, but someone made a Gmail account under my name and sent something out to our entire class.

Shit. I don't generally log in to my school email account unless a teacher tells me to because it's full of boring stuff like announcements and cafeteria menus. I use my phone to pull up my inbox. Sure enough there's a message from HoldenHassler226@gmail.com—a message with a video attachment. The text of the video says: *Christmas came early for me . . .*

A sense of dread creeps over my body as I click the video. I recognize the background immediately—the lobby of the Sea Cliff Inn. The image focuses and I see Holden sitting on the sofa, me kneeling in front of him. It's pretty obvious what's going on. It's pretty obvious we're both enjoying it.

The camera is zoomed in, so all you can see of me is my back and blond hair. A lot of people probably won't even recognize me. But Holden is undeniably Holden. I blush furiously as I watch the video to its conclusion, desperate to know but terrified to find out how much more it shows. The clip cuts off before he lifts me back onto his lap, before I kick over the candle and start the fire.

I'll ruin the life of someone you care about. Maybe this video is supposed to hurt Holden. It'll be awkward for him, I'm sure, but it's not like most people are going to care if he was hooking up with some girl. Julia might care, but even though it might embarrass her, she and Holden are broken up, so it shouldn't be a big deal. Still, I bite my lip as I imagine her face flushing red as she watches this.

I shut my email account and text Holden back.

Me: Has Julia seen this?

Holden: Not sure. She's not responding to my texts.

Me: Mine either. What do we do?

Holden: I'm not sure there's anything we can do.

It's tempting to toss my purse right back into my backpack and walk out the front doors of Tillamook High. I'm not sure I can sit through all my classes wondering what Julia is thinking, wondering if my classmates know that's me in the video. Holden and I have been pretty careful about the way we appear in public, but everyone knows we started hanging out more after Julia went to DC for the summer.

But before I can decide whether to cut and run, Frannie rounds the corner. She's wearing black jeans and a hoodie that says "ARMY"—probably something Luke sent her. "Embry," she calls, as she crosses the hallway and heads toward me. "I'm glad I caught you."

Her eyes are a little red, like maybe she's been crying. I'm hoping she hasn't heard about the video. Her name wasn't on the email recipient list, probably because she's only a junior. Seeing me with another guy wouldn't ruin Luke's life or anything, but I know it'd upset him and that's not the way I want to end things between us.

"Hey, Fran," I say cautiously. I rummage through my purse until I find a ponytail holder. Casually, I twist my hair up into a bun.

"I'll walk with you to first hour." She shifts her books from her right arm to her left.

Frannie's class is right next door to mine. She's in an AP English class that focuses on advanced grammar and vocabulary to help kids excel on their college entrance exams. I'm in Multimedia and the Web, an elective designed to show students how to set up web pages and LinkedIn accounts. It's basically a blow-off class, since by the time kids can take it they usually know more about the internet than the teacher.

"Yeah, sure." I shut my locker and head down the hallway beside Frannie. As we walk, I glance furtively around, trying to see if people are looking at me more than usual. There's definitely some whispering and giggling going on, but no one seems to notice Frannie and me as we walk by.

"Have you heard from Luke lately?" she asks.

"I talked to him on the phone a few days ago, but nothing since then. He said something about maybe going on a mission."

"Did he say anything special when you talked to him?" Frannie asks. "Maybe about something he wanted?"

I throw her a sideways glance as we head down the stairs at

the end of the hallway, wondering if she knows Luke asked me about getting married. Most guys don't talk to their little sisters about stuff like that, but Luke is not most guys. He and Frannie are super-close, since the rest of their siblings are several years older than them. Plus, Luke is the only one in the O'Riley family who supports Frannie going into the medical field. Their parents want her to go to school for business so she can run one of their restaurants someday.

"Nothing out of the ordinary. Why?"

"I bought him some stuff for Christmas that I know he's been wanting, but I was hoping to get him something extra as a surprise."

"He didn't mention anything specific," I say. "Did he send you that sweatshirt?"

A smile flits across her features. "He did. In fact, he wore this exact sweatshirt when he was doing one of his physical fitness tests in Basic."

I make a face. "Ugh. I hope he washed it before he gave it to you."

Frannie doesn't laugh. She just fiddles with the end of one of the hoodie's strings. Her smile evaporates as we near our classes.

I pause outside the doorway to her room. "Are you okay? You seem sad."

She tugs at the end of her ponytail. "I'm okay. I just got into it with my mom about something. She can be kind of unreasonable."

"You said she was under a lot of stress, right? Maybe that's all it is."

"Yeah, maybe." Frannie shifts her weight from one foot to the other. "You know, Luke said once that if things got too bad, I could move in with you and him next year. Do my senior year in Killeen." Her eyes flick up to mine. "Of course, that was before you guys decided to take a break."

"Fran," I say softly. "No matter what Luke and I do, you can still live with him if you want."

"Yeah. I guess." Before I have time to respond, she adds, "See you around, Embry," and ducks into her classroom.

I start to follow her, but then stop. I hate that Frannie is having such a hard time with her mom right now, but she's not going to want to talk about it in front of her classmates, and I can't really afford to be late to class.

Sighing, I stroll into the school computer lab next door and head to my assigned workstation in the back corner. For the past week we've been working on creating a web page using a Blogger or WordPress template. Most of the kids in class are creating blogs. I'm actually working on a website for the coffee shop. Mom has a really basic page with our location, hours, and phone number, but I'm trying to create something a little fancier that will hopefully draw in more business. So far, I've added a menu page and a link to Google Maps. The assignment isn't due until after the holidays, but I'm hoping to have a functioning page by Christmas so I can give it to her as a present.

"Today we're going to focus on adding images to your website," our teacher, Ms. McClellan, says. "Please keep in mind they need to be rated G or PG so that I don't lose my job. You'll want to experiment with different sizes and alignments, as well as give them captions and consider linking them to other pages. And remember, if you're going to make your site public, these need to be images in the public domain, or images that you own."

"So no famous people?" a perky girl in the front row asks. I can see her computer from where I'm sitting. She's making a fan page for an all-girl K-pop band.

"Sometimes there are public domain images of celebrities on Wikipedia or IMDB," Ms. McClellan says. "But when in doubt, throw it out."

I upload a few pictures I took of the food at work. I place them on the menu page of the website, trying different sizes and placements until I hit on something that looks both clean and aesthetically pleasing. I save a spot for a photo of the Julia Worthington, the new sandwich Mom and I are going to unveil the day after Christmas. I open my purse and peek at the screen of my phone. Julia hasn't replied to the text I sent her.

Focus on the things you can control. I'm sure by now someone in school administration has gotten wind of the video and deleted the email from our server. I have no idea how many people have seen it or whether Julia knows it's me. I drum my fingernails on the tabletop for a few seconds before accepting that there's nothing I can do right now to improve the situation.

I glance around at what some of my classmates are doing. Two boys in front of me are both making fantasy football sites. Watching them upload pictures of NFL players makes me think of Luke. Even though hockey is his fave sport to play, he's obsessed with watching football. I wonder how much of it he gets to see being stationed so far from home.

The girl next to me is creating a web page full of holiday gift ideas. As I watch, she clicks her mouse and uploads a photograph of a gingerbread Christmas house. I shudder. Mom bought one of those houses once when I was a kid. It took forever to put together and the end product looked more like our dilapidated garden shed than a festive holiday cottage. The worst part was that the icing that held everything together turned hard like cement and the actual gingerbread went stale in a couple of days, meaning after all that work we didn't even end up eating it.

Ms. McClellan strolls up and down the rows, observing our progress and offering tips. She tells a couple of kids on the other side of the room to put their phones away and get to work. I wonder if they're looking at the video of Holden and me together. I have no idea how many students might have downloaded it or passed it on to their friends in other grades. My face burns with shame. I'm not embarrassed because I did it—and still want to do it, if we're being honest—I'm just embarrassed because I got caught. I hope whoever recorded us has had their revenge and will leave Holden and me alone now. Maybe this is a good thing—a chance for me to come clean, both to Julia and to Luke.

Julia shows up to third hour—Spanish III. She never responded to my text, so I figured maybe she saw the video, got upset about it, and decided to go home. But when she breezes into the classroom ten minutes after the bell rings with a pass from the office, she seems totally oblivious.

"Siento llegar tarde," she tells Señor Martinez. She tosses her blond hair back from her face. As she heads to her seat in front of me, the boy to my left—Lowell Price, the kid who Misty Whitehawk punched at the swim meet—clears his throat. I glance over at him and he coughs the word "slut" into his hand. I'm about to tell him to fuck right off when I realize he's directing it at Julia, not me. "Yeah right." I snort. Julia might be flirty, but calling her a slut is like calling her dumb or lazy. Nothing could be further from the truth.

A couple other kids glance over at Julia as she makes a production of settling into her seat and pulling out her textbook and laptop. I hear whispering from the back of the class.

"La Navidad llegó anticipada para mí," a boy in the back row says. *Christmas came early for me . . .* There's quiet laughter from the seats around him.

"Silencio, por favor!" Señor Martinez glares at us from beneath his severe brow. There are a few residual whispers and giggles, but then most people go back to working on their assignments.

I don't put it all together until after class, when Julia and I head back to our lockers.

"You would not believe the day I'm having," she hisses. "I'm guessing you saw the video."

My breath catches for a second before I say, "I mean, I didn't watch it all or anything."

"Everyone is just assuming the girl is me. Half the boys at this school have been making lewd blow job gestures at me all day," Julia says. "Why are guys such idiots?"

"No idea," I mumble, my brain still reeling. The lighting in the video was pretty bad and you couldn't see my face, but still, I guess I expected Julia to recognize me right away.

She slams her locker and turns to me. "Are you okay? You look pale."

I look up. "Yeah, I'm fine. Are *you* okay?"

Julia tosses her hair back over her shoulders. "Holden can get with whoever he wants—I don't care. Everyone knows we're just friends now. But I'm a little worried about what might happen to him. Even Principal Blake thought the girl was me. I spent first hour in the office with the police. They want to investigate Holden for some sort of child pornography sex crime."

"What?" I swallow hard. "If they don't know who the girl is, how do they know she's underage?"

"It doesn't matter, because he's only seventeen. Isn't that messed up? They're trying to accuse him of spreading child porn where *he's* the child. Apparently Oregon's pornography laws are really draconian and he can get charged as an adult. Hopefully he can prove that Gmail account doesn't belong to him and it'll all blow over."

I think about what it would mean if Holden got arrested for distributing pornography. If he was convicted, he'd have to register as a sex offender. Even if he wasn't convicted, that could still ruin his life. Not to mention make life pretty difficult for his mom. Holden said she's been taking online classes, hoping to be able to move up to detective someday.

I check my phone. No new messages from him. I wonder if

he's in the office or if he had to go to the police station over this.

"Have you talked to Holden since all this went down?" I ask.

Julia shakes her head. "I haven't seen him at all today."

A couple of varsity hockey players named Eric and Alex burst into laughter as we pass them. "Hey, Julia," Alex asks. "How about a ride home after school?" He thrusts his hips at her.

"You want something more filling for lunch?" Eric pokes his tongue into the side of his cheek.

Julia flips the boys off. "Pretty sure both of you together wouldn't even add up to today's chili dog."

"Only one way to find out." Alex waggles his eyebrows.

Julia rolls her eyes as we stroll past. "This is the bullshit I've been dealing with since I got here this morning."

"Why don't you tell them it's not you?"

Julia spins around. "Hey, mouth-breathers!" she yells down the hallway. "By the way, it's not even me."

"Can you repeat that?" Alex lifts a hand to his ear. "I couldn't understand you with Hassler's dick in your mouth."

Eric grins. "Methinks the lady doth protest too much."

Julia turns back to me. "That's why. Nothing better than brain-dead morons misquoting Shakespeare, right? Better to just ignore them."

"Okay, but you could probably get those guys in trouble if you want," I say. "That's straight-up sexual harassment."

Julia waves it off. "I don't care about those assholes. They're basically the poster children for 'peaked in high school.' I almost feel bad for them."

"You're right, they're probably not worth it. But let me know if you change your mind and need a witness." I turn around and glare at the boys, who have forgotten all about Julia and are now engaging in what looks like a slap fight with a couple other guys from the team.

Julia reaches out and gives me an impulsive hug. "You're such a good friend, Embry."

If she only knew.

Julia does a great job of ignoring the occasional bits of whispering and giggling as we go through the cafeteria line and carry our trays to our usual table. I take note of everyone around us who is acting like an asshole. A lot of them are people who made a point to suck up to Julia last year when she was the head of the junior prom committee. Now that we'll be graduating soon, people are showing their true colors.

"What's wrong?" Julia asks. "You look like you just ate a piece of bad fish."

"Just thinking about how stupid people can be." I take a big bite of my spaghetti, which is lukewarm at best. I wash it down with a swallow of milk.

"Oh yeah. It's an epidemic. Don't let it get to you." She pulls her water bottle out of her backpack and shakes it up so her diet drink mix isn't all settled on the bottom. Then she leans over the table and speaks in a low voice. "Is it wrong that I want to know who the girl is?"

I cough. "I thought you said you didn't care—"

"I don't care that he's moved on or whatever. I was just wondering if she's the girl he cheated on me with." She pauses. "Do *you* know? I know you two talk more than he and I do these days."

My spaghetti threatens to crawl its way back up my throat. "Uh, he doesn't really talk to me about stuff like that."

Julia drizzles fat-free Italian dressing on her salad. "I guess it doesn't matter. If he's happy, I'm happy."

Julia and I talked on the phone a couple of days after she and Holden broke up. Apparently he told her the girl he'd hooked up with was "just some girl at a party." She asked me then if I knew who it was and I told her I had no idea. I feel bad just thinking about it. I feel bad that I'm still lying about it. Unfortunately, feeling bad and doing something about it are two different things. Guilt is one of my superpowers. Confession, not so much. *Soon*, I promise myself. *I'll figure out a way to tell her soon.*

"Sorry. I didn't mean to get weird." Julia reaches out for my arm. "I'm just glad I have you to go through stuff with. I wish I had been here this summer when your mom was sick. You should have called me."

"I knew you were busy. I didn't want to burden you with my shit while you were studying and working." *And hanging out with Ness.*

"You still should have called me," Julia insists.

And it hits me like a kick to the chest that she's right. I swallow hard and try to compose an answer, but I've got nothing. Maybe if I *had* called Julia, I wouldn't have relied so heavily on Holden. Then we never would have hooked up and started sneaking around together. The Sea Cliff wouldn't have burned, a psycho wouldn't be tormenting me, random boys wouldn't be calling Julia a slut.

Maybe Holden is wrong. Maybe high school friends *are* real friends. Maybe I'm the only fake friend here.

ELEVEN

I DON'T SEE JULIA AGAIN until we meet up at our lockers after school. "Swim practice is canceled until January because Coach Smyth had to go out of town," she says. "Do you want to go Christmas shopping with me?"

"Here?" I ask. Tillamook doesn't even have a mall. Unless Julia wants to buy antiques, gourmet cheese, or produce from the grocery store, Christmas shopping will involve a longer trip.

Julia wrinkles up her nose. "What about Portland?"

"That's over an hour and a half each way," I remind her. "Plus Portland traffic. Unless you're planning on spending the night there, we won't have any time to shop."

"You're right. I guess I'm just lonely for civilization." She sighs. "Maybe Lincoln City? I can probably find presents for my parents at the outlet mall."

"Let me check with my mom."

I text her and ask her if I can go shopping with Julia, telling her I'll be home by nine p.m. She says it's fine and that she might work late, but she can get away from the shop for half an hour to walk home and let Betsy out. I feel a little guilty putting the responsibility of the dog on her, but I know she hates it when I treat her like an invalid, and she did just tell me this weekend that I should spend more time with my friends.

"Let's do it," I say.

Ignoring a few more whispers and curious looks from our classmates, Julia and I head to the back parking lot where she parks her Subaru. We hop in, and Julia pulls her water bottle out of her backpack and puts it into the center cup holder. A slice of lime floats on the surface of the cloudy liquid.

I scrunch up my face. "What is that sludge again?"

"This *sludge* is super acai berry fat-burning concentrate." Julia huffs. "And it tastes good, like raspberry tea."

"It looks like some old guy's bathwater."

She smirks. "Whatever, skinny bitch. Been bathing a lot of old men lately?"

"I've got to pay the bills somehow," I say.

Julia laughs as she starts the engine.

We make our way through the town and quickly turn onto US 101, otherwise known as the Oregon Coast Highway. Julia fiddles with the radio while I focus on the landscape flying past.

A recent hip-hop tune starts playing. "I love this song," she says. She bobs her head as she sings along under her breath. "Ness has seen these guys in concert twice. She says their live show is epic."

My mom and grandma took me to Burning Man once when I was five. Otherwise I've never been to a concert. "Cool," I say. I can't figure out why Julia seems so blasé about everything that happened today.

As we travel south, tiny beach towns with faded pastel buildings are interspersed with gaps of coastline and the occasional breathtaking ocean vista. I snap a couple of pictures with my phone. They turn out blurry and distorted from the window and the movement of the vehicle, but there's still something kind of magical about them.

"You take great photos," Julia says. "You should do something with them someday."

"Something like what?"

"I don't know. Enter them in contests? Or at least put them

up on stock photo websites for people to buy."

"Yeah, maybe." It's not a bad idea. I don't have a good enough camera to win contests, and most people just steal photos from online to decorate their blogs and web pages, but it's always possible some ad agencies or small companies would pay to use my coastal pictures for official business.

It's funny, both my mom and Julia telling me I should try to make money from my pictures. I've never really thought much about trying to turn my photography hobby into a career. I'm like Holden in that way. He says he doesn't want to make his art his job, because then he'll lose the joy, but I think a lot of losing the joy is when you try to sell your art and no one buys it. Even if you have confidence in your work, it's probably hard to hold on to it after you're forced to realize no one else loves what you do as much as you do.

It's only a little after four, but already the sun is starting to drop low, coloring the sky a mix of pink and orange. The road inclines for a short distance, and I manage to snap a great picture contrasting the blue of the water with the soft pastels of the sky. It reminds me of one of the Monet paintings I learned about in Art Appreciation class.

It's not just the ocean that's beautiful here, though. The coastline is a mix of soft sand and dark jagged rocks, of cliffs and flat areas dotted with driftwood. Even the towns have a quiet beauty about them. Holiday banners hang from ornate lampposts that look like they belong in another time. Quaint shops selling antique furniture or fancy chocolate are intermingled with gas stations and convenience stores.

I watch a family of four make their way down a narrow sidewalk, stopping in front of a seafood restaurant to consult a menu. The mom carries a toddler dressed in a fur-lined white jacket in her arms while the dad keeps a firm grip on an older girl—maybe six or seven.

I think about that life a lot—what it would have been like to grow up with two parents and siblings. It feels like a fairy tale to me.

My phone buzzes in my purse. I dig it out and tap at the screen. It's a text from Holden. I want to read it, to know for sure that he's okay, but it feels weird to do that around Julia.

The phone buzzes a second time, and then a third.

Julia accelerates through a sharp curve. We're in between towns now, a wide-open road in front of us. She hits a giant pothole at about sixty miles per hour and my shoulder bangs into the side of the door.

"Whoops. Sorry." She glances over at me. "You going to answer those?"

Crap, now it'll look weird if I don't. I flick my phone on silent.

"Um, yeah," I say. "It's Holden, actually."

Holden: I was wrong. Maybe lives can be ruined.

Holden: My mom is freaking out. She's worried I'm going to get arrested. I'm being investigated by some hard-ass detective.

Holden: Are you with Julia? Neither one of you is answering my texts.

Me: Yeah. We're headed to Lincoln City.

Holden: Call me later?

Me: Sure.

"Is he in trouble?" Julia asks.

"Maybe," I say. "His mom is freaking out about stuff. He says he texted you too."

She nods. "I got a message in sixth hour but haven't had time to reply yet. He heard I got called down to the office and wants to know what I told the principal, and the police."

I start to slide my phone back in my purse.

"You can call him, if you need to," Julia says. "We're still friends, you know."

It takes me a second to realize she's talking about her and Holden, not her and me.

"Tell him I'll call him later tonight," she adds.

"Oh, okay." I swipe at the *H* in my contacts menu.

Holden's phone rings twice. Then he says, "Hey."

"Hey." I clear my throat. "Are you going to be okay? Surely they can figure out it wasn't you who emailed that video around, right?"

"Hopefully," he says. "The cops should be able to track the IP address. But if it was sent from public Wi-Fi, I'm not sure if that'll rule me out or not. Either way, until they've investigated thoroughly, I've been asked to stay home from school. Good thing I don't care about my class ranking."

"They suspended you?" I ask.

"Seriously?" Julia says. "That is bullshit."

"Unofficially suspended," Holden says. "The school wants me to take the next couple days off, and then it'll be winter break, so . . ."

I relay the info to Julia. "Still bullshit," she says. "They have to know he wouldn't send out something like that."

"You'll be okay," I tell Holden. "You could probably skip all your finals and still stay in the top five."

"I guess. At least I'm not trying to get into a fancy college. I'm glad whoever this asshole is, they went after me instead of Julia."

"Speaking of Julia, she's driving right now but says she'll call you later."

"Thanks for getting me called down to the principal's office, you dirty perv," she yells from the driver's seat.

Holden laughs. I can't help but smile. For a second, as

messed up as things are between the three of us, I feel a flash of hope that somehow everything might turn out all right. But then I remember the secrets I'm keeping, the lies I've told, the horrible things I've done. And that momentary sense of lightness sinks like an anchor.

TWELVE

WHEN WE GET TO LINCOLN CITY, Julia snags the first spot we find in the outlet mall parking lot, and we make a plan to work our way from one side to the other.

"Want to try on some dresses?" She cocks her head toward a store called Red Carpet—a new addition to the mall since the last time I was here.

I smile. "Let's do it." It might be just the thing I need to get my mind off what happened at school today.

A few minutes later, Julia and I are inside the store flipping through racks of glamorous party dresses. "What categories are we going to do?" she asks me.

Sometimes when we go shopping for clothes, we pick categories ahead of time and then find outfits that work for them.

I think for a moment. "Best-dressed list, worst-dressed list, matchy-matchy."

"Works for me. What about this one for best dressed?" Julia holds up a black velvet gown with an asymmetrical hemline and spaghetti straps made of rhinestones.

I tilt my head to the side. The dress is gorgeous, but the black makes Julia look even paler than she is and washes out her blond hair. "Does it come in other colors?"

Julia finds the same dress in royal blue and holds it up. She does a twirl in the middle of the store, the toe of her ankle boot getting caught in the thick carpet, causing her to stumble.

I laugh. "Perfect. Now me."

Julia and I dive back into the racks, looking for my best-dressed gown. Unsurprisingly, she's the one who finds it. It's green and flowy. The bodice is strapless and made of overlapping satin and lace. Julia assures me this will make "the girls" look bigger.

We change to a different rack full of dresses with lots of tulle and feathers. Julia's face is a mask of concentration as she pores through the possible offerings for our worst-dressed contender. She holds up a gold dress with a skirt made of overlapping peacock feathers.

I shake my head. "Not tacky enough."

She finds the same dress in red and then grabs a green

cardigan from a rack across the department and layers it on top.

I laugh. "There we go. Très festive."

For myself I pick out a dress that's a mess of pale pink tulle with a white satin bodice. "Imagine this, with black thigh-high boots."

"And a hat!" Julia snatches a black fedora off a nearby mannequin and tosses it to me.

"Sad ballerina is sad," I say.

"It's terrible to be sad at Christmas!" Julia exclaims.

We both giggle. It hits me that this is the most normal I've felt in days.

"And now for the matchy-matchy gowns." I cross the store to a rack of Grecian-inspired draped gowns in ivory and pale gold. "Goddess-style?" I hold one of the pale gold gowns up to my frame.

"Goddess-style," Julia agrees. She finds a gold one in her size and we head to the fitting rooms, our arms laden with tulle and taffeta. As always, we share one of the larger rooms, helping each other with straps and zippers. We slip into our best-dressed gowns, and I can't help but gasp at my reflection in the mirror. The cut of the dress adds soft curves to my boyish frame, and the green color brings out the golden tones of my hair.

"Embry, you look amazing," Julia says. "You should totally buy that."

The price tag reads $159.00. "In my dreams," I say.

Julia twirls in front of the mirror in the royal-blue dress. "How much is this one?" she asks.

I find the tag, dangling from Julia's left armpit. "Two hundred and eighty-nine dollars," I tell her. "So basically *not even* in my dreams."

She laughs. "Yeah, I don't think my parents would go for that either. I got my New Year's Eve dress from Nordstrom and it was only a hundred and twenty, but that's partially because it was a discontinued style and I had to buy a six instead of an eight."

"Is that why you're only eating salads at school?"

"Yeah. It's a killer dress. I want to look good in it."

I arch an eyebrow. "Good for who?"

"For whom," she corrects. Then she grins and adds, "For me, of course." She points at the next dresses. "Worst-dressed time!"

We sip into the second dresses, trying not to laugh at how ridiculous we look. Then we put on the matching dresses, which really do flatter both of us.

"We are gorgeous," Julia declares.

"We are," I agree, grabbing my phone and snapping a

picture of the two of us in the mirror.

"Should we actually shop for other people now?" she asks.

I let out a huge sigh. "I guess . . . if we have to."

After we leave Red Carpet, Julia drags me from the Nike store to the North Face store to the Columbia store, presumably to look for fleece gloves for her mom and "anything cool" for her dad. But it seems like in every store Julia starts out shopping for others and then gradually reverts to shopping for herself. When I see her striding toward the Columbia fitting rooms with an armful of workout pants and several colorful fleece tops, I flop down in a nearby chair and pull my phone out of my purse. This might take a while.

I tap my passcode into the screen. At some point I missed another text from Holden.

Holden: Hey. My mom's going to be on patrol all night. Wanna come by?

Me: Why?

Holden: Er, do you want me to paint you a picture? ;)

Me: Don't you think with everything going on, that's probably a bad idea right now?

Holden: It was a bad idea the first time, but that didn't stop us, did it?

I don't respond right away. The first time Holden and I hooked up, it was sort of an accident. Well, it definitely wasn't planned. I'd developed an awkward crush on him after I got to know him in Art Appreciation class at the start of junior year, but I convinced myself it was just a physical thing. Back then Luke was still around and I was still delusional enough to think we were going to live happily ever after. I wasn't going to let the new kid in town mess that up. Hormones, whatever. I could handle it. Until Luke went away. Until Julia left for the summer. Until the night I couldn't.

My mom was spending a few days as an inpatient at Tillamook General to get one of her chemo treatments back in early July when Holden ran into me walking Betsy along the beach. He and Julia had been dating since April and the three of us had hung out together multiple times. After Julia left, Holden and I had continued hanging out, though he never showed any indication he was aware of my feelings for him. I remember coiling Betsy's leash around my palm that day while we made small talk for a few minutes. Nice day. Works sucks. Et cetera.

But then Holden reached out and touched my arm. "What's wrong?" he asked.

"My mom," I said. The tears came from nowhere. It was like he'd snapped one of my secret inner pieces into place.

He knew my mom had cancer, that she was going to have surgery in a couple of weeks, but I never brought up the way her illness made me feel around him or Julia. I never talked about worrying obsessively that she wouldn't get better or the way I sometimes cried in my sleep. It felt selfish for me to be such an emotional mess when my mom was keeping it together and she was the one who was actually sick. Holden didn't even ask for details. He just wrapped his arms around me and pulled me into a hug. That was the first time I'd ever been close enough to him to smell him, that mix of deodorant, laundry detergent, and paint.

When I managed to quit crying, I tried to explain. "She's okay. She's just staying a couple nights in Tillamook for some chemo. But every time she goes to the hospital I feel like maybe this is the time she won't come home."

Holden petted my hair. "That must be so scary. I wish I knew what to say to make it better."

"Honestly, just the fact that you're listening makes it a little better. I normally don't talk about this stuff with anyone, not even Julia."

"Why not?"

I turned away from him, looked out at the ocean. "I don't know. Maybe there's something wrong with me. The more serious something is, the harder it is for me to confide in anyone about it."

"People don't normally talk to me about serious stuff either. I mean, sometimes they do, but usually it's just shit that doesn't matter."

I nodded, thinking again of my inner pieces. I could almost feel them clicking together, filling up that gap. "It's hard to be real, to be honest. But there's something about you that makes it a little easier."

"Well, if you figure out what it is, let me know so I can avoid more of these awkward encounters." Holden laughed at the look on my face. "Kidding. I'm not a total ass, I swear."

He invited me to a Fourth of July party that was being thrown by a girl a year older than us, who lived in one of the biggest houses on Puffin Hill. Neither of us really wanted to go, but there's not a lot to do in Three Rocks and we knew the alcohol would be flowing, so we figured it would take my mind off things.

When we got there, the house was thick with smoke and the music was cranked so loud that the floor was vibrating. I made an immediate move toward the deck at the back out the house. The sun was setting over the ocean, and I pulled out my phone to take a couple of pictures.

Holden grabbed a beer from a cooler in the kitchen and met me outside. As he held the bottle out in my direction, I turned and snapped a photo of him. It was candid, no warning. His lips were pursed in a funny way and his hair stuck up like a rooster's feathers in the breeze. He made me show it to him and talked shit about what a bad picture it was, but I'll never forget the look on his face right after I took it. It was surprise, mixed with . . . pleasure.

He drank from his flask while I nursed the single beer. We looked out at the ocean as darkness filtered away the remaining daylight. Our bodies edged closer to each other as people came and went. I remember making vague chitchat with him, thinking about that look on his face, thinking about how close we were. At one point his arm brushed against mine. I waited for him to move it, but he didn't. The tiny physical connection felt enormous to me.

But there was no way I was going to hit on my best friend's guy. When Holden said he was going inside to look for a bathroom, I nodded and leaned back against the wall of the house, relieved for the opportunity to pull myself together.

I finished my beer and a guy named Thomas who I sat next to in American History offered me another. Beer Two turned into Beer Three, and as I finished that I glanced down at my phone and realized Holden had been gone for over half an hour. I sent him a text and he didn't answer.

I checked the bathroom on the main floor of the house but it was unoccupied, so I asked a few people lurking around if they'd seen him. When they all shrugged, I continued to look for him, first downstairs and then upstairs.

When I pushed open the door to what turned out to be the master bedroom, for a second I was too shocked to speak. Holden was there all right, sprawled out on the bed, his neck tilted at a funny angle. Katrina Jensen was kneeling between his legs, the folds of her silky sundress gathering around her hips. She tugged at the button on his jeans. "Just relax," I heard her say. Holden didn't respond. His eyes were closed. I wanted to close mine too, but all the blood had rushed to my head and I was afraid if I did that I might fall over. I settled for training them on the plush, cream-colored carpet.

As I backed away toward the hallway, my foot hit the edge of the door frame.

I heard Holden swear under his breath. Then he said, "Embry, wait."

I looked up. Holden was hurriedly rebuttoning his jeans.

"Sorry to interrupt." I imagined my cheeks as two bright red circles, like the face of a doll. "I was just . . . wondering where you went. I think I'm going to go ahead and take off."

"Embry." Each time Holden said my name it made my insides tremble. "Wait up. I'm coming with you." He slid off the bed.

"Fucking figures," Katrina said. "Rich Bitch went away but assigned you a chaperone, huh?"

"I'm not anyone's chaperone," I told Katrina. Without looking at either of them, I added, "I just wanted to let you know I was leaving. You can stay. I'll be fine walking home alone." I hurried from the room and back down the stairs, moving through the house as fast as I could without making a scene.

Holden's feet pounded the steps behind me. He caught up to me outside in the dark, before I even made it to the black pavement of the street. He tried to grab my arm but I shook him off.

"Please. Just talk to me," he said.

I turned and started walking down Puffin Drive, the three beers I drank feeling like both too much and not enough at the same time. Holden followed me without speaking. I kept waiting for him to say something, explain how I was wrong about what I saw.

Finally I spun around to face him. "Give me one reason why I shouldn't tell Julia."

He had to stop short so he wouldn't run into me. "Tell her if you want. I don't care. Hell, I'll tell her."

"Then why did you come after me?"

The wind blew his hair back from his face. "Because I could see that I hurt you."

"I'm not hurt. I'm just . . . surprised. I can't believe you would cheat on your girlfriend."

"Things with Julia and me are . . . complicated," Holden said. "I'm pretty sure she's hooking up with someone in DC."

"No she's not," I said. "She would have told me."

"The way you told her about how you were feeling earlier?" Holden arched an eyebrow.

"Screw you," I said. "Even if she *is* hooking up with some

dude in DC, that wouldn't make what you did okay."

"You're right," Holden said. "You're absolutely right. But come on, Embry. She's your best friend. Can't you tell she's not that into me?"

I sort of agreed with Holden here, just based on the way Julia acted when the two of them were together and on the things she said (or didn't say) when he wasn't around. Her initial interest came from finding out Holden was one of the smartest guys in our class and then deciding he looked like Jared Leto. (He does, sort of.) She asked him to junior prom on a whim and he agreed. I didn't think they were going to go out again, but I guess her parents said they didn't want her dating the Gas Station Boy, and after that she doubled down on her supposed attraction. But still.

"Does she know you're hooking up with other girls?"

"No." Holden coughed. "And I mean, nothing really happened in there."

I scoffed. "Whatever you say, but I don't think Julia would see it like that."

"I'm not telling Julia. I'm telling *you*."

"Why?"

"Your friendship means a lot to me."

Something about that admission made my chest get all hot and tight. "Why Katrina?" I spat out, imagining her down on the beach with Luke. Did she somehow know I liked

Holden? Did she do it on purpose? "I've never even heard you talk about her."

"She's in my gym class," Holden said. "I never really took her flirting seriously until tonight."

"And then tonight you were just all in for some reason?"

"Tonight I was half drunk and a hot girl accosted me as I was leaving the bathroom and pulled me into a bedroom and offered to blow me."

I winced. "TMI, Holden."

"What? It's not like you didn't see what was happening."

"Trying to forget," I muttered.

Holden pushed his hair back from his face. "Look. I was stupid. But that's sort of a hard thing for a guy to turn down, you know?"

"Oh, I hear you. Biological urges and all that," I said coolly. "Poor men just can't control themselves, right?" I tried not to focus on his cheekbones. They were high and sharp—I had noticed them the first day of Art Appreciation class. He looked like one of the statues we studied.

"Not an excuse, Embry. I was just trying to explain. No girl has ever—actually, forget it. Let's just leave it at I fucked up majorly." Holden crossed his arms. "But why are *you* so angry?"

"I'm not angry," I snapped.

"Could've fooled me."

"Whatever. I'm out of here." I turned away and accelerated into a jog, hoping Holden wouldn't follow me, that he'd go back to the party and leave me alone.

But instead he caught up in about three strides and insisted on running beside me. "I thought it'd be you, you know?"

"You thought *I'd* be the girl who you cheated on my best friend with?"

"I thought you'd be the first girl I was, you know, close to like that. Ever since we started talking in class. To be honest, I still kind of think that."

My jaw dropped slightly at the thought of Holden being a virgin. I knew Julia hadn't slept with him, but he seemed so worldly and self-assured. I guess I figured he had to have more experience than did. But then I got offended again. "Why would you think that?"

"Because I know how you feel about me," Holden said, as the two of us ran down the hill in the dark. "I've suspected for a while, but now I know."

I didn't answer him until we got to my house and he made a motion to follow me inside. "Go home, Holden," I said.

"Say it, Embry," he challenged. "Admit how you feel about me and I'll leave you alone."

My house keys shook in my hand. "I think you're an asshole."

"Entirely possible, but what about down on the beach? What was that bullshit about me being so easy to talk to?"

My lower lip trembled. "You *are* easy to talk to," I said hoarsely. For the second time that day, the tears came. "But you're right. You hurt me."

"I'm sorry." Holden brushed my tears away with his thumbs. "I'm an idiot."

I didn't respond. I just looked at him for a few seconds, paralyzed, voiceless.

"Tell me to leave again," he whispered.

But I didn't. And then he kissed me. Soft, then harder. And when I didn't resist, he pulled me inside and pressed my body up against the wall. And then I kissed him back.

It was openmouthed and hungry, almost violent. Our teeth knocked together before we found the best angle for our lips and tongues. Kissing him was like puncturing this balloon that had been growing inside me—pain and fear and loneliness expanding and crushing my vital organs. Holden was right, and I needed a break from pretending otherwise. I needed him—all of him. I dragged him to my bedroom, where we stripped off each other's clothes. I pushed him down on my bed. He tried to stop me because we didn't have protection, but by that point I was beyond rational thought.

The next day, reality came crashing down. The health

clinic in Tillamook was closed so Holden had to take me all the way here to Lincoln City on his motorcycle so I could get Plan B. He offered to go in with me, but I told him to wait outside while I ran into the pharmacy. I didn't blame him for my epic stupidity, but I didn't really want to talk to him about it either.

"For what it's worth," Holden told me on the ride back, as I was ignoring him and focusing intently on the coastline whipping by, "I'm not sure if I'll ever want kids, but if I did I'd want them with someone like you."

I tried to pretend that didn't mean anything, but it did.

Julia called me the next day to say that Holden had broken up with her.

I tried to pretend *that* didn't mean anything either, but it did.

Still, I avoided Holden for the next couple weeks, right up until the day of my mom's surgery. He texted me on the way to the hospital. I couldn't believe he remembered what day it was. But I ignored his text. I was 100 percent focused on my mom. Around one a.m., Holden texted me again. The nurses had let me spend the night in Mom's room on a cot, and I was lying next to her, watching her breathe. If Death wanted her, he was going to have to fight me for her.

Holden: Everything ok with your mom?

Me: Yeah. She's in a lot of pain, but they think the operation went well.

Holden: Glad to hear it. I figured you'd still be awake.

Me: I might never sleep again. I'm watching her breathe, making sure she's okay.

After a few seconds I texted again:

Me: Why are you awake?

Holden: Making sure you're both ok.

After that I couldn't avoid him anymore. I needed that solace, that safe place, that person I didn't have to hide from.

I still need him, but it's different now. Back then I felt like our relationship was one-sided—he was comforting me. Now I want to give something back, and admitting that terrifies me. Where's the line between mutual comforting and mutual expectations?

I shift in the dressing room chair. Julia is taking forever. Glancing down, I realize I missed a second text.

Holden: Nothing to say to that, huh?

Me: I was just thinking about that night. I still can't believe I was the first girl.

Holden: What can I say? Girls don't exactly line up to bang the salad-eating pansy gas station boy :P

Me: Those things do not define you.

Holden: Yes they do, at least partly, and I wouldn't have it any other way.

Julia pops out of a fitting room stall in flamboyant neon-green-and-pink exercise pants and a black fleece top with pink trim. "Oooh, are you messaging Luke?"

"What?" My face flushes as I slip my phone back into my purse. "No, just checking my email."

"Bullshit," Julia says gleefully. "You were about five seconds away from licking your phone. You guys were sexting, weren't you?"

"Um, no," I say. "And I don't even know how you could joke about that right now."

Julia shrugs. "No use crying over spilt BJ video, even if it's not mine."

"But doesn't it bother you that people think—"

"Nope," she says. "People are going to think whatever they want no matter what I do. No sense feeding into it by getting angry or defensive. And I'm sure Holden will be fine. He always lands on his feet."

She's probably right about Holden. There's got to be some way the police can figure out who actually owns that Gmail account, or at least trace where the video was sent from. But man, I wish I could be as calm and collected as Julia is in the face of a scandal.

She twirls around in a circle. "What do you think of this? Do these bright colors make me look fat?"

"You look amazing," I sat. "Fifty extra pounds wouldn't

make you look fat."

"Whatever. I wish I was as skinny as you."

"You *are* as skinny as me," I point out. "Plus, you have breasts. And muscles. Best of all worlds." I know I'm lucky to be naturally thin, but sometimes I wonder what it would be like to see my biceps or actually fill out my A-cup bra.

"I am *not* as skinny as you." Julia inhales, puffing her chest out a little. Julia is what she likes to call "a solid C." "But you're right. If losing more weight means giving up the girls"—she flexes one arm—"or the other girls, maybe we should stop at the cheeseburger place on the way home." Julia rests her hands on her waist. "I can cheat on my diet just this once. Shopping burns a lof of calories, right?"

"Absolutely," I agree. "Cheeseburgers for all the girls."

"Okay, let me just try on a couple more things and then I'll make my final decisions."

"Good Lord. You're *still* trying stuff on?" I joke.

"Almost done," Julia says in a singsong voice. "I might be retrying one or two of these." She disappears back into the fitting room.

The envelope icon pops up on my phone, indicating another text message. I'm expecting it to be Holden again, and I smile in anticipation. But instead, the name *Unknown* comes up on the screen.

THIRTEEN

I GLANCE UP TO MAKE SURE Julia is completely out of sight before swiping the screen. Two more messages buzz in while I'm waiting for her to close the fitting room door.

Unknown: I should have known you'd let your boyfriend get in trouble instead of taking responsibility for your choices. Clearly you've learned nothing. So . . .

Unknown: A. Steal Julia Worthington's purse before school tomorrow. Put the purse and its entire contents in the trash can by the bike rack in front of the school.

B. If you don't do this, I'll do more than ruin a life. I'll end one, and you'll have only yourself to blame.

Unknown: You have 12 hours. Choose wisely.

My hands start to shake. I read the messages a second

time. Is this psycho actually threatening to kill someone unless I steal Julia's purse? Those two things seem so unrelated that for a few seconds I just stare dumbly at the screen.

Julia pops out of the dressing room again, this time in a teal-blue-and-black outfit. "You like this one better?" she asks.

I turn my phone over to hide the screen. Looking up at her, I force a smile. "You're going to buy both no matter what I say, aren't you?"

She giggles. "Maybe."

"Then yes. This one is my favorite."

"Mine too, I think."

She vanishes into the fitting rooms again and I take a deep breath, hold it in for as long as I can, and then exhale it slowly. I flip my phone over and start to reply, unsure if it'll work because I've never tried responding to a text from an unknown number before.

Me: Who are you?

No answer, but my phone doesn't give me a failure message either. It looks like the text went through.

Me: How do you know Julia?

Me: Why do you want her purse?

Me: Why are you doing this?

I send a couple more texts pleading for more information, but Unknown doesn't reply. Sighing, I cram my phone back in my purse and close my eyes, rubbing my temples with my fingertips. The messages sound so angry. The only person I know with a legitimate right to be pissed at me is Julia. I stare down the hallway of the fitting rooms. Is it possible she found out about Holden and me? That she's been in there sending me threatening text messages while pretending to try on clothes?

She reappears with an armload of bright fabric while I'm still mulling over this possibility. Julia and I have been friends for years. I see her every day at school, and I've spent entire weeks at her house when her parents were traveling. She's never struck me as the type of person who would concoct an elaborate anonymous revenge scheme instead of just telling me she found out I was sleeping with her ex-boyfriend and she's mad about it.

Then again, maybe she's hiding a lot of inner pieces too.

"Ready to go?" She smiles brightly.

"Sure." I follow her to the front registers, trying to dissect the sound of her voice and the expressions flitting across her face. She seems the same as always. She can't be the one—why would she ask me to steal her own purse? That makes no sense.

I'm momentarily distracted by a rack of lavender fleece zip-up hoodies. Light purple is my mom's favorite color, and I suddenly remember I've got the money from my father in my purse. The hoodies are forty dollars even on sale, which normally I wouldn't consider, but they're marked down from $79.99 and it seems like a really good deal.

Julia stops talking and glances back over her shoulder. "Ooh, you should get one. That's such a pretty color."

The cashier calls her forward, and I don't even bother telling her I'm shopping for my mom. I find a medium hoodie and hold it up to my frame. It'll work, and now my mom will have something to open on Christmas, which is always fun. I get in line behind Julia and test the zipper to make sure it works while I'm waiting for my turn to pay.

A few minutes later we're both headed back outside. The sun has set completely and our breath makes white puffs in the dark. Both of Julia's wrists are laden with plastic bags.

I gesture at her haul as we head toward the Subaru. "Did you remember to pick up anything for your parents?"

She grins. "I got my mom some gloves like she wanted and a fleece pullover she can wear in the mornings when she does her walking. My dad always tells me he doesn't need anything and that I shouldn't waste my money on a present for him. I think I'm going to order him one of those Steak of the Month Club things off the internet. Or Wine of the Month."

I arch an eyebrow. "They'll let you order Wine of the Month for someone even though you're not old enough to drink?"

Julia winks at me. "I might have gotten hooked up with a fake ID while I was in DC."

"No way," I say. "Let me see."

Julia unlocks the doors to the Subaru and deposits all her bags into the back seat. Then we both slide into the front. She clicks the locks and then digs through the center console of her car, removing a small plastic card. She hands it over to me.

It's a Washington, DC, driver's license that has her picture but someone else's name and date of birth. "Ashtyn Crawford? That sounds very fancy of you."

"Doesn't it?" Julia grins. "Ness said it's best to have a fake name for when you go out, even if you don't have ID. Otherwise it's too easy for people to stalk you."

"Wow. I've never thought about using a fake name."

Having a stalker feels like something that happens only to rich and famous people. Then again, whoever is threatening me is sort of like a stalker. I wonder if they've been online, if they've searched through my social media to learn more about me. I have a Facebook page I hardly ever use and an Instagram account with like twenty followers where I post mostly pictures of the beach. Other than that I've been mentioned on the Tillamook High website a couple of times and in the newspaper for pulling Sam out of the fire, but that's about it.

"If you want, I can see about getting you a fake ID too when I'm in DC for New Year's. That way we can go out drinking this summer before I leave for college."

"I don't know," I say, the hot flames of the Sea Cliff fire rising up in my mind. "I've been thinking maybe I should quit drinking for a while."

Julia glances over at me. "Okay. But let me know if you change your mind."

I set Julia's fake ID back into the center console of the car. Last year she used to lecture me about drinking. It's almost like she went away for the summer and came home a different person.

By the time I get home, my mom is already in bed. I let Betsy out into the backyard and refill her food and water dishes. While she's sniffing around at the grass, I reread Unknown's messages and then call Holden.

"Hey," he says. "So are you coming over or what?"

"Sure, but I need to talk to you."

"Oh, the dreaded 'we need to talk' conversation. If you're blowing me off, you can just do it right now if you want."

I can't even tell if he's serious or joking around. "Actually, the creeper who emailed that video to the senior class is back with another twisted request."

"Seriously? Getting me accused of distributing child porn

wasn't enough? What do they want now?"

"I'll show you when I get there," I say. "What unit are you in?"

"Apartment twenty-six. Second building. Second floor."

Julia has been over to Holden's place before, but she never talked much about it, so I have no idea what to expect. I find a set of wooden stairs at the front of the second building and climb to the second floor. Apartment 26 is one of the corner units.

Exhaling deeply, I knock gently on the door. A few seconds later I hear the sound of a dead bolt disengaging. The door opens and Holden stands before me looking strangely casual in a pair of gray sweatpants and a black T-shirt with a ripped sleeve.

"Come on in," he says.

He closes the door behind me as I step into their living room. It looks so different from my own home. Whereas my mom likes knickknacks and handmade things, Holden's mom seems to prefer a more minimalist environment. My eyes skim over a navy-blue sofa and a set of gray Formica tables, their tops polished and empty except for one box of Kleenex and a TV remote. A small flat-screen television sits on a black-and-gray TV stand, a DVD player, and stack of DVD boxes on shelves behind glass. Only one thing stands out in this room—a large painting that hangs above the TV. I recognize that it's Holden's work right away. It's a picture of a beach, but one I've never seen before. The sand is made of small white rocks that seem to have almost a gravelly consistency. The water is a softer, brighter blue than anything we have along the Oregon Coast. There's one tree in the painting, growing out of the sandy soil. It's small, but still somehow majestic, with a bifurcated brown trunk topped with dark green leaves.

"Wow." I step up to the painting, fighting the urge to reach out and touch the canvas, to run a fingertip across the different textures that give it such a lifelike feel. The sand is sparkling in places, almost like real sand when the sun hits it.

"You like it?" Holden asks.

"Yeah, it's amazing. What's making it glisten?" I ask. "Some kind of special paint?"

"Regular paint, with actual sand mixed in," Holden says. "There's also bits of dried plant matter mixed into the green of the tree. I like experimenting with mixed media."

"It's seriously incredible," I say. "How many of these have you done?"

"Like fifteen or so. I made this one special for my mom. Most of my finished paintings are over at my grandparents' house. They're not all this big."

"Are they all this good?"

"No, but they're not bad," he says.

Something in the background of the canvas catches my eye. I lean in to get a closer view. "Is that the Parthenon off in the distance?"

"Yes. This is Greece. It's an olive tree."

"Why do you paint so many solitary trees?"

"I don't know. They require you to use multiple brush-strokes for the different textures. And I like the idea of one living thing off by itself, in a strange environment, yet thriving." Holden cocks his head as he looks at his own work. A smile plays at his lips.

"Is that how you see yourself? I always kind of wondered if the solo tree thing was you asserting your independence from the rest of the world."

"Nah." He laughs under his breath. "I think that might be projection on your part."

"What do you mean?"

"That maybe you see yourself in my paintings of trees. You're always talking about how you have trouble letting other people get close to you."

I never thought about it like that. Maybe I *do* see myself in Holden's paintings. "You should try to sell them online," I say.

Holden flops down onto the sofa. "No one would want to

pay the shipping for a big-ass painting."

"You never know." I sit next to him. From this vantage point I can see into the kitchen. Black laminated paper peels from one of the cupboard doors, revealing unpainted wood beneath.

"Yeah, maybe," he says, but I can tell he doesn't believe me.

"Speaking of making money off your awesome talent, my mom was wondering how much you would charge to touch up the mural on the back wall of the café."

"You know I'd do that for free," he says.

"You don't have to. I mean, she could pay you like a hundred bucks or something."

"That's not necessary. Just let me know when would be a good time to work on it." He yawns. "Enough about painting. What's going on with you? More messages, you said?"

I hand him my phone in response.

Holden clicks through the texts from Unknown. "This is fucked up."

"I know, right?"

"Who could have sent these?" he asks. "How many people know your cell phone number?"

"Not sure. Not too many people call me, but I think it might be on my Facebook page."

"Seriously?" Holden scrolls through the texts again. "Why would you put your phone number on your Facebook? They sell that info all over the place, don't they?"

I'm pretty sure I added it because I made my Facebook account when I was thirteen, right after Mom gave me my first phone, and it felt so cool to finally have my own number. I shrug. "I never answer if I don't know the number anyway, so who cares? Either way, almost every teacher asks for it at the beginning of the year. It wouldn't be that hard for someone at school to find out."

"So then it has to be someone from school, right? First they wanted you to embarrass yourself on Facebook. Then they emailed that video around to school accounts. And now they want you to steal Julia's purse? No random outsider would care about that stuff, especially Julia's purse."

"Well, it is a three-hundred-dollar purse," I mutter. "But no, I agree. This feels personal to me."

"So who has a personal reason to be pissed about you and me or the fire?" Holden crosses his legs at his ankles, the toes of one foot tapping against the floor.

I tick people off on my fingers. "Julia," I say. "Luke. Frannie, I guess, if she was pissed on his behalf. Oh, and maybe Katrina Jensen."

Holden arches an eyebrow. "Why Katrina?"

"I don't know. Maybe she somehow found out about the two of us." I pause. "Also, she and Luke apparently hooked up before he and I started dating."

"Whoa," Holden says. "I did not know that."

"Yeah, it happened before you moved here. I don't know the specifics, if it was a onetime thing or what." I make a face. "I don't really like thinking about it."

"Okay, so do you think any of those people would send you this kind of message?"

"No. Not really. Julia would just confront me to my face. Luke has more important things to worry about right now. Frannie would never threaten to hurt innocent people like this. And Katrina is a bitch sometimes, but I've always assumed her bark was a lot worse than her bite. I mean, whatever happened with her and Luke was a long time ago, and it's not like I stole you away from her or anything." *Like you did with Julia*, a little voice reminds me.

"So then what are you going to do?"

I lean forward and rest my head in my hands. "I think I have to go to the police, Holden. This is getting out of control. I can't let this whack job *kill* someone. We can wait and talk to your mom first. Maybe I could make a report about being blackmailed without mentioning what happened at the Sea Cliff."

"Maybe." Holden rakes his hands through his hair. "Or maybe someone is just trying to trick you into going to the cops because they know our role in the fire will be discovered if you do."

"How? The video isn't time-stamped and it doesn't show the fire starting. Even if someone recognizes the Sea Cliff lobby, you used to work there. There's no proof we're responsible for what happened."

"There might be wax residue from the candles," Holden says. "I bought those with cash in Tillamook a while back, but it's always possible they could trace them to me."

"You really think the Safeway has security footage from over a month ago? And of everyone who shops there?"

"Probably not," Holden admits. "But the video might screw us. Sometimes tech guys can pull metadata from recordings that shows the time they were taken."

"Shit," I say. "Maybe we should just tell the whole truth."

Holden turns away from me, his eyes skimming across the neat and angular surfaces of the apartment. I wonder if he's afraid of the same thing I am—that confessing to the Sea Cliff fire could lead to actually losing his home. His eyes meet mine again. "Or I could help you steal Julia's purse if you want. I can distract her while you grab it or whatever."

"What?" I stare at him. "You think I should actually do what this psycho wants me to do?"

"I don't know. It's not like it'll be any big thing to Julia. She can just buy another one, right? You and I stand to lose a lot more by getting blamed for the fire."

"I know. But steal from my friend? Ugh. That's so gross."

Not any grosser than hooking up with her boyfriend while she's out of town. I frown. Some people have an inner voice that supports them and helps guide them in their actions. Mine just likes to point out my hypocrisy and moral failings.

"Well, you could also tell her the truth. Then maybe you could just ask her for the purse and offer to pay her back."

It's a good idea, and one I wouldn't have come up with on my own, but then I remember the message said I had to steal the contents of her purse too. "She might give me her purse, but she's not going to give me everything inside it too, like her wallet and her ID and stuff." I pause. "You know, Julia has a fake ID now. She got it this summer while she was hanging around that Ness girl. Do you think that's what this is about?"

Holden shrugs. "I don't really see how Julia's ID would connect to the fire or you and me."

I bury my face in my hands. "You're right. Fuck. I feel like someone is just torturing me."

"Well, I support whatever you think you should do."

I peek through my fingers. "Run away from all of this and never come back?"

Holden chuckles. "That I do not support."

"You can come too if you want." I rest my head against his shoulder.

"Well, in that case." Holden hops up from the sofa. He

pulls a set of keys from his pocket. "Let's go."

"Your bike? But it's freezing outside."

"I'll block all the wind with my massive body," he says.

I snicker. "Yeah, right."

"And I'll loan you my warmest hoodie, if you promise not to make fun of my body again."

"Better, but I'm not sure a motorcycle ride will fix things."

"It won't fix the future, but it'll fix the present. And best of all, it'll clear your mind."

FOURTEEN

AS USUAL, HOLDEN IS RIGHT. It's impossible for me to think about anything while I'm zooming through the dark on the back of his bike. Anything other than surviving the harrowing turns and blistering cold.

Holden made good on his promise to loan me a hoodie, so my middle parts are warm, but the wind cuts right through the fabric of my jeans and after ten minutes on the bike, I'm pretty sure my face has literally crystallized.

"How you doing?" he yells back, as he leans into yet another hairpin curve.

I do my best to mimic the way he angles his body. "I'm alive . . . so far."

Holden laughs. We hit the outskirts of a small town and

leave the shelter of the trees. We're headed the same way I went with Julia to get to the outlet mall. It's funny how the same scenic vistas I snapped pictures of out the window of her car look totally different at night.

Holden slows the bike as we ascend a large hill. I gasp as we hit the top of it. The view over the dark ocean is otherworldly, the waves silvery in the moonlight, robotic in their endless ebbing and flowing.

I position my cold lips next to his ear. "This is so beautiful."

"Isn't it?" He slows his speed temporarily so it's easier to talk to me. "The coast is something else. It's like we live on a movie set."

Before I can reply, we come to a steep downhill grade. Holden guns the engine and accelerates sharply. I tighten my grip around his waist as the bike picks up speed again. The wind whips my hair back from my face like a blond flag. My eyes water, blurring the highway's dotted yellow line into a single stripe. My lips start to go numb. We hit a dip in the road and my stomach lodges into my throat.

Then suddenly we're back on flat pavement, trees on either side, racing into the dark unknown. I bet this is what skydiving feels like. Just plummeting through sharp, cold air at high speed. Fast, free, almost flying.

A reflective sign for a beach overlook comes up on the right. Holden signals and then turns into the parking area.

He pulls the bike into a parking spot and cuts the engine. There's no one here but us. He angles his head toward the overlook platform. "Wanna hop off for a few? Stretch your legs before we head back?"

"Sure." I rest my hands on his shoulders and lift myself off the motorcycle.

Holden slides off after me. He unhooks the chinstrap of his helmet and lifts it off his head, shaking out his hair. "Feeling any better?"

"A little." I remove my own helmet and hand it to him. "Holy shit. That hill was intense."

"Holy shit is right." He loops the helmets over the motorcycle's handlebar and then rubs at his waist. "You were grabbing onto me so hard you probably left marks through my clothes."

I scoff. "Well, that's what you get for trying to kill me."

"And yet you're smiling." As we head down the path to the overlook platform he adds, "I'm glad you still have your survival instinct."

"We've all got something." I lift my fingertips to the exposed skin on my face. It's colder than the night sea. Cupping my hands, I blow into them, let my breath warm my nose and cheeks. "I apparently still have a face, which is good."

Holden vaults up onto the wooden platform and I step up

after him. "That is good," he says, pulling me in close. He lifts his gloved hands to my cheeks. "After all, this is one of my favorite faces."

I scrunch my lips into a pretend pout. "One of?"

He grins. "Well, you know. I'm a sucker for the classics. Helen of Troy, the Mona Lisa, that—"

"Hey. The Mona Lisa isn't even hot." I give him a little shove away from me, toward the edge of the platform.

"Disagree," Holden says. "She's beautiful in her own way. That mischievous smile, those dark, soulful eyes, the way she—"

"Fine, whatever." I cross my arms. "But I insist on being ranked above her."

"Okay, okay," Holden says. "Yours can be my second-favorite face . . . right after that guy from *The Scream*." He pulls me in close again.

"You're such an ass," I say, as our lips touch.

Holden laughs. "My girl Mona Lisa would never be so rude." He kisses me again before I can reply, and after a few seconds I quit trying to think of a response and just drink in the sensation of his closeness.

We break apart a few minutes later and wander to the edge of the platform, both of us bending down and leaning out forearms on the railing. The moon is almost full, its light shining down on the ocean like a beacon.

"The only thing that would make this more perfect is if we saw a whale," I say.

"And if that whale came up out of the water and offered us hot chocolate," Holden adds.

I smile. "I like the way you think."

"I haven't seen a whale since I was kid," Holden says. "My family used to drive over to Depoe Bay from Portland."

"We used to go too—me, my mom, and my grandma. We couldn't afford the boat trips, but we looked from platforms like this one. I've never seen anything but a couple of spouts."

"Really? No heads or tails or flippers?"

"Nope. No pretty whale tales for this girl. Talk about childhood oppression."

Holden rests his head on my shoulder. "I meant what I said before, about your survival instinct."

"What? Am I supposed to just give up when life gets hard?"

"No, but your life has always been hard, growing up with one parent, and then your mom got sick, and now you're being harassed by some psycho. And not only are you keeping it together, you don't seem bitter toward people who have it way easier." He pauses. "Sometimes I get angry at the people who seem oblivious to how lucky they are."

"Well, it's debatable whether I'm keeping it together. And as for the other stuff, I guess I'm just a realist. Life isn't fair.

It's not right that some people have so much and others have so little."

"It isn't," Holden agrees.

"But knowing that doesn't change anything." I shrug. "It used to bother me how Julia and I would talk about wanting to go to Greece or Australia, and then her parents actually took her on trips to those places and all I got were postcards. But I know I can see those places too someday—it just won't be as easy." I watch the waves roll in below us. "I also know a lot of people have it worse than me too. My mom likes to say that happiness isn't a zero-sum game. Julia getting to travel the world and go away to a fancy college and all that isn't what's keeping *me* from doing any of those things. So there's no reason to be bitter toward her. That's one of the reasons I feel bad about you and me. I feel sort of like I took you away from her. Like I don't deserve happiness if it came from hurting another person. Life shouldn't work like that."

"You didn't take me away, because I was never hers," Holden says. "No one belongs to anyone. And trust me, I was just a novelty—the brainiac gas station boy who is smart enough to be worthy but also safe because I don't try to one-up her with grades or school activities."

"Maybe, but I still lied," I say. "She's going to DC for New Year's Eve, to visit her friend Ness. When she gets back from that trip, I'm going to tell her everything. And after that,

Luke will be in town and I can tell him everything too. It'll feel good to get it all out."

"It will," Holden agrees. "It'll be scary, but you'll be glad afterward."

"I hope so."

Without warning, rain starts to fall and Holden and I hurry back to the bike. As we head for home, I press my body tight against his for warmth and angle my face to the left so I can look out at the ocean. The wind takes my hair and the night air freezes my face again. As we fly across the slick roads and the ocean water blurs to a mix of black and silver, it occurs to me that Holden and I haven't slept together in almost a week, and yet somehow I've never felt closer to him.

Back in Three Rocks, the rain has faded to a soft drizzle. Holden cuts the engine to the motorcycle across the street from my house. He kicks down the kickstand and I swing my leg over the bike to dismount, using his shoulders for balance.

He slides off after me. "So do you know what you're going to do yet?"

"About the text messages?" I shake my head. "My mind does feel clearer, though. Or at least it did until you asked me that."

"Glad I could help." Holden laughs under his breath. "And

then mess things up afterward."

I lean in to give him a kiss on the cheek. "What are guys for?"

"Seriously. I'm always here if you need me." He wraps his arms around my lower back and gives me a gentle squeeze. "And text me if you need me to help with whatever you decide to do."

"Okay." Reluctantly, I untangle myself from him and head across the street. He fires up his bike and pulls away as I make my way up the driveway. I pause on the porch, watch his motorcycle fade into the night, swirls of mist swallowing him up in a way that makes it seem like he was never there at all.

I turn to let myself inside, but then something moves in my peripheral vision. I freeze, expecting a cat or a raccoon to emerge from the fog, but instead I see the silhouette of a man. He's walking along the far side of the street, looking down at his phone. *It's nothing. It's just someone out for a late walk*, I tell myself.

But as the man approaches I see he's wearing a baseball cap. I can't tell what color his jacket is. Is it the man in the brown bomber jacket who Mom and I saw in the parking lot of Fintastic? I can't be sure.

I'm tempted to call out to him, but what do I say? What if he's just a tourist or someone visiting one of my neighbors for the holidays? Before I can say anything, the man realizes I'm watching him and quickens his stride, cutting across someone's lawn in a shortcut back to Highway W. He turns toward town.

Trying to stay quiet, I hurry across our front lawn and follow him. When I get to Highway W, the man is turning right onto Main Street. I cross the highway and jog past the cemetery, trying not to notice the wavering shadows, the half-frozen flowers adorning the graves.

By the time I hit Main Street, the man has vanished. I peer into the lobby of the Three Rocks Motel, but there's no one there except for an older man sitting behind the front desk. Nothing else is open this late—I don't know where the man in the hat could have gone.

Shivering in the damp air, I walk to the end of the street and take the stairs to the beach, just in case he's down on the sand. But there's no one out here except for a couple of college kids walking hand in hand out by the water.

As I turn back toward my house, a car pulls out of the lot from behind the community center. It's a black BMW, like the car the man jumped into at Fintastic. I fumble my phone out of my pocket and snap a picture of his license plate. 896TRE. I'm not sure what I'm going to do with it, but maybe Holden knows how to access his mom's DMV database. It's worth asking at least.

I head home and slip back inside the house without waking my mom. I shrug out of my jacket and lay it on the back of the futon couch so it can dry out. There's a pile of mail there that I didn't notice earlier. My eyes are drawn to red printing on one of the envelopes. My heart accelerates in my chest as I fish the letter out from the bottom of the stack, praying it's not another message from Unknown. But it's actually a business length envelope with a plastic window in it. Stamped on the front, above the window, are the words "FINAL NOTICE."

I sigh. Mom has never been one to tell me about money stuff, but since she got sick she's gotten even more secretive. I understand—I mean, it's not like I can do much about the bills we're behind on—but still, I'd rather hear it from her that the electricity is going to get turned off than just come home to a dark house one night. Maybe instead of fixing the furnace she'll use the money I gave her from my father to pay whatever this is.

Flipping through the other envelopes, I find two more that look like bills—one from Tillamook General and one from a group of radiologists, probably whoever reads the scans Mom has done. I want to open all these and see just how bad things are, but my mom would not be okay with that, and I wouldn't be okay with her opening my mail either.

As I set the envelopes back on the edge of the futon in a

neat pile, my stomach drops low in my gut. There's no way I can make things harder on her by being arrested or sued over the Sea Cliff fire.

Which means I'm going to have to do what Unknown wants.

I'm going to have to steal Julia's purse.

FIFTEEN

I TOSS AND TURN, unable to get much sleep. For a fleeting moment I imagine calling Julia, waking her up in the middle of the night to confess everything. *Hi. I slept with your boyfriend, lied about it, kept sleeping with him after you broke up, started a fire, almost killed someone, lied about that too, and now some whack job is threatening me and people I care about. Oh, for some reason he wants your purse and everything in it. Can you hook a sister up?*

Yeah, no. That would not go over well. I have to steal it. I am going to steal from my best friend. I keep saying it over and over in my head, like eventually it'll sound less horrible and gross. What's a little petty theft to go with my trespassing and destruction of property?

My mind plots and replots exactly how I'm going to get away with it. I'm sure Julia will be swimming laps tomorrow morning since swim practice is canceled for the rest of the year. That means her purse will be locked in her gym locker, which luckily is the same gym locker I shared with her freshman and sophomore year when we were both on the swim team. I'll take Mom's car to school so I can arrive earlier than usual. Julia usually swims for about thirty to forty-five minutes. That's plenty of time to slip into the girls' locker room, grab her purse, and deposit it into the trash can in front of school. Assuming she hasn't changed the lock, I can probably pull this off. Still, the step up from liar to thief makes me hate myself. And Unknown—I hate Unknown for putting me in this position.

If only there were someplace where I could hide and watch and see who comes to get the purse. The student parking area is behind the school, so I can't sit in my car. Also, if I'm late for first hour, the school will call my mom and I'll have to explain myself to her.

Then I remember Holden isn't allowed in class for the rest of the week.

Grabbing my phone, I dash off a quick text message:

Me: You awake?

He calls me instead of texting back. "I'm always awake," he says. "Until fifth hour anyway. Civics and American Lit make for some great napping."

"You're not going to class tomorrow, though, right?"

"Nope."

"If I grab the purse and toss it, can you watch the front of the school to see who picks it up?"

"As long as I get out of the house without my mom catching me. She gets home from her overnight shift around six-thirty and goes right to sleep, so I should be able to watch in the morning at least."

"Thanks," I say. "If I have to become someone I hate to protect the people I care about, at least maybe we can figure out who's blackmailing me."

"Then what?" Holden says.

It's a good question. I've been so focused on protecting Holden and me, and keeping Unknown from hurting anyone else, that I haven't really thought about what would happen if we met face-to-face.

"Then we put a stop to this," I say. "One way or another."

"Sounds like a plan," Holden says. "If I don't recognize the person, maybe I'll recognize the car."

"Hey, speaking of cars. I've been seeing this guy around town—first outside the coffee shop, then Fintastic. I think I saw him again tonight outside my house. I'm worried my mom might have a stalker. Do you know any way to look up a license plate?"

Holden clears his throat. "Legally?"

"Ideally. Or I thought maybe you could access a database or something through your mom?"

"My mom's search capabilities are through the sheriff's department, via a laptop she checks out of the police station to plug into her cruiser. I'd not only have to be able to hack her account, I'd also have to break into her police vehicle during one of her shifts to use it."

"Okay, never mind. Mom swears she doesn't know who this guy is—it might all be a coincidence, not worth getting in trouble for."

"Give me the plate just in case. There's a guy who works at the gas station who might be able to run a search for me."

I read Holden the letters and numbers.

"This guy hasn't threatened you or anything, has he?" Holden asks. "Do you think he could be related to everything else that's been going on?"

"I don't see how," I say. "But I guess we shouldn't rule out the possibility. There's a lot of stuff that's not making much sense right now."

December 20

The next day, I drive to school and pull my mom's car into the student parking lot just as the sun is starting to rise. Sure enough, Julia's Subaru is parked in one of the corner spots. My stomach feels like it's full of bees. I blink back tears just thinking of what I'm about to do.

But then I think of that stack of bills on the arm of the sofa, that stamped letter with its ominous warning. *Just get it over with.*

It's a frigid morning, but my hands are sweating and I nearly drop my mom's keys as I remove them from the ignition. Swearing under my breath, I grab my backpack from the passenger seat and head into the school.

The hallways are mostly empty at this hour. I stop off at my locker to stash my backpack in there, but then realize I'm going to need something to hide Julia's purse with. Slinging the backpack over my shoulder, I head off toward the girls' locker room on the other side of the school. I breathe in deeply. *You can do this.*

My footsteps echo on the tile floor. I pass a couple of girls sitting on the ground, textbooks splayed out on their laps. One of them looks up at me—it's one of the freshman girls who come into the coffee shop a lot. I give her a tight smile as I round the corner and head for the athletic wing.

As I approach the door to the locker room, it occurs to me I should probably have some reason for being there before school, just in case I run into someone I know. I decide I can tell people I was looking for Julia. Of course that excuse isn't going to work if I run into Julia, but if that happens this whole plan is going to crash and burn, so I'd better get my ass in gear before she finishes her laps.

I duck into the locker room. The main area in front of the mirrors, where students blow-dry their hair and put on makeup, is empty. As I walk down the rows of lockers, I pass a couple of girls who are changing, but they both have their backs to me. To the left of me, the bathroom and shower area is also empty, but the steady patter of water on tile means at least one person is taking a shower.

Praying Julia hasn't changed her routine in the last year and a half, I turn down the last aisle and look for her telltale sky-blue lock. It's there, on locker 86. She picked this locker as a freshman because her birthday is August 6 and she said she'd never forget where her stuff was.

I glance furtively around and then take a seat on the bench in front of the locker. Dropping my own backpack to the floor, I unzip it so I'll be able to quickly tuck Julia's purse inside. I breathe in deeply and then exhale. I steady my shaking fingers against the lock and start to turn. 12-36-24. This was always one of the easiest combinations to remember. But when I pull down after the 24, nothing happens.

Shit. Sweat begins to bead up on my forehead. Maybe I forgot the extra turn in the middle of the combination. I start to dial the lock again. Behind me, the running shower goes silent. I hear the plastic curtain being pushed to the side, imagine a girl reaching out for her towel. Whoever that is will be finished soon, and if her stuff is in this row, I'm going to be busted.

With shaking hands, I pull down on Julia's lock again. Success. With my breath whistling in my throat, I grab Julia's purse and quickly tuck it into my backpack. Hurriedly I pull the zipper closed. I start to shut Julia's locker and then decide it'd be best to leave it open, make it look like maybe she forgot to shut the lock or that someone went around pulling on them and got lucky with hers. I leave the door hanging half open and set the lock on the ground. Hopping up from the bench, I peek around the corner and am relieved to see that the common area is still empty. I head for the door to the locker room at high speed. A couple more girls are in the rows changing now, but it's no one I really know. I keep my chin tucked, my hair forward obscuring my face as I hurry by.

I'm almost to the door when a voice from behind me asks, "Embry?"

SIXTEEN

I SPIN AROUND SLOWLY. Frannie is standing in front of the mirror, a towel wrapped around her body. Wet hair dangles down over her pale, freckled shoulders.

"I thought that was you," she says. "I didn't know you worked out before class."

"I don't," I say quickly. "I mean, not usually, anyway. I came to school early to work on a project in the computer lab and just ducked in here to go to the bathroom." There's at least one bathroom closer to our school computer lab than this one, but hopefully she won't think about it too hard.

"Oh. Cool." Frannie tucks a strand of hair behind her left ear. "Well, good luck on your project. I should probably stop dripping all over the floor and get dressed." She angles her head toward the rows of lockers.

"See you later," I say. I watch her retreating form and breathe a sigh of relief when she turns down the middle row of lockers. Hopefully she'll be out of the locker room before Julia notices her purse is missing.

I slip into the hallway and head for the front of the school. There's still about forty minutes before class starts, but the first buses will be arriving in the next ten minutes so kids have time to eat breakfast. When I reach the front lobby, a couple of guys I don't know—freshmen or sophomores, maybe—are sitting on one of the benches in front of the building, in plain view of the trash can. Throwing away a fancy purple purse without them noticing is probably going to be tough.

I tap one foot repeatedly as I try to figure out what to do. I sneak a peek at my phone. I'm running out of time. I start walking toward the trash can. Maybe if I get close I'll be able to figure out a way to dump the purse without anyone noticing.

I pull out my phone as I stroll past the guys, pretending that I'm making a call. I walk to the edge of the school property, continuing my fake phone call. I glance around for Holden, but I don't see him anywhere. If he's here already, he's doing a good job of staying out of sight.

I turn back to the school, the phone still up to my ear. One of the guys on the bench points toward the street. They both hop up and head toward a black pickup truck that's turning into the lot. I walk back toward the school at a fast clip, inching down the zipper on my backpack as I approach the trash can. I rest my backpack on the top of the can like I'm looking for something in it. Glancing around one more time, I grab Julia's purse in one hand. Wrapping the leather strap around the middle, I slip the whole thing into the can, forcing it down beneath some greasy fast-food paper bags.

Then I head for the glass doors leading into the school, my heart pounding two or three times for every step I take. I force myself to slow down, to stroll, to look like any other kid dreading a long day of classes. I duck back into the building just as the first buses pull into the parking lot.

Made it, I think. But now it's Unknown's turn, and God only knows what they're going to do next.

I stop off at the nearest girls' room, where I lock myself in a stall and lean up against the metal, my heart galloping in my chest. I think back through every move I made this morning, trying to decide if I might get found out.

It's possible Julia might suspect me just because I know her locker combination, but she's more likely to be suspicious of someone who changes clothes next to her that she doesn't like. If she somehow hears from Frannie that I was in the locker room, that's probably game over for me, but I'm not really expecting that to happen. Julia and Frannie don't talk that much outside of swim practice and official meets. Plus, it's not like my using the locker room bathroom should be grounds for a big discussion.

Probably everything will be fine.

Well, no, everything is really screwed up, but at least maybe this purse thing will be fine.

My stomach rumbles, reminding me that I haven't eaten anything in over twelve hours. I wash my hands and then head into the cafeteria, where I pick up my breakfast tray. I grab a seat at our usual table, even though Julia never joins me for breakfast. In between nibbling on my sausage biscuit and slightly crispy scrambled eggs, I swipe at my phone and send Holden a message:

Me: Are you here?

Holden: Yep.

Me: Did you see me?

Holden: Yeah. Nice fake conversation on your phone.

Me: How did you know it was fake?

Holden: Because I'm smart ;)

Me: Do you think anyone else saw me?

Holden: No. I mean, there are probably security cameras that cover the front of the school, but someone throwing something away isn't exactly going to be a red flag.

Me: Have you seen anyone scoping out the trash can yet?

Holden: No one besides you.

I catch movement out of the corner of my eye. It's Julia. She's headed toward the table and she looks furious.

Me: Keep me posted.

Julia pulls out the chair across from me with a vicious yank. "You are not going to believe what happened!" Her eyes are flashing and her nostrils are flared in anger.

"Hair dryer broken?" I ask, my eyes focused on the dark blond bun on the top of her head. A trickle of water is running down her left temple.

She kicks at the chair next to her. "No, I'm just too pissed to dry it today. Apparently I left my gym locker unlocked and someone broke in and stole my purse."

"Your new purse?" I ask, my voice rising in pitch. *No, Embry. Some other purse.* I probably should have worked out what I was going to say during this conversation ahead of time.

"Yes." Julia flops down in the chair. "Can you believe it?"

"Ugh. That sucks so bad. Did they take anything else?"

She shakes her head. "No, but it's not like these clothes are worth all that much."

Her jeans are Diesel brand, with artfully ripped knees and spatters of bleach. They're probably worth at least a hundred and fifty dollars.

"God, that would have been an even worse nightmare," she continues. "Imagine having to go to class in your swimsuit!"

"I'm sure someone would have lent you some clothes," I say. "I think the nurse has a box of stuff in case students throw up or bleed on their clothes."

Julia shudders. "I'd rather wear my swimsuit." She swears under her breath. "I'm totally screwed for lunch now—my school ID and all my cash were in my purse."

I want to ask her how much cash she had, because I'm curious if maybe that was the motivation—someone knew Julia had hundreds of dollars floating around in her purse—but there's no way to ask that without sounding kind of sketchy. Instead I say, "I can buy you lunch."

"Seriously?" Her frown starts to thaw. "You're the best."

My stomach twists. I am not the best. I'm the worst. The worst friend, possibly the worst person. For a fleeting instant I want to spew the whole truth right there at the lunch table. My mouth gapes like a fish as I try to spit out the words. But all that comes out is, "It's no problem." I clear my throat. "Did you report the theft to the principal?"

"Not yet," Julia says. "I guess I'd better, huh? I don't think she's going to do a full locker search or anything, and it's not like there are cameras in the locker room, so chances are it's gone for good. But I guess I should at least tell her it's missing, just in case anyone finds it and turns it in."

"Hopefully it'll turn up," I say lamely. I suppose it's possible it might turn up, since I don't know why Unknown wanted me to steal it.

"Yeah, maybe," Julia says. "They can keep the purse if they want. I just don't want to go through the hassle or replacing all the stuff that was inside it." She sighs. "I'm going to drop by the office right now so I can fill out a report and get a temporary ID before first hour. I'll see you later."

"Sure," I say. And then, "Hey. Do you need to borrow anything else?"

Julia spins around. "Like what?"

"I don't know." I try to imagine what kind of stuff Julia had in her purse. "Pens or gum or anything?"

"Nah." Julia starts to turn around again but then stops. "I don't suppose you have any eyeliner or lip gloss on you, do you?"

"I have eyeliner, but it's nothing fancy." Julia buys most of her makeup online from Sephora. My makeup comes from the drugstore in Tillamook.

"I can roll with whatever," Julia says. "I feel like a ghost without makeup."

I find a Maybelline eyeliner pencil in the zippered pocket of my purse and hand it across the table to Julia.

"Thanks!" She blows me a kiss. "See you in Spanish."

I struggle not to flinch. Every time Julia says something nice to me, another knot forms in my gut. It's almost like she knows exactly which words will hurt me the most.

I head to first period, where we get the entire hour to work on our websites again. I flip through the tabs at the top of the page, but I can't really concentrate. My stomach is still churning, my blood coursing with adrenaline. I sneak a peek at my phone, but Holden hasn't texted me. Pressing my fingertips to my temples, I try to channel my mom's quiet strength.

There's nothing I can do right now except try not to lose my mind while I wait for Holden to report in. I take slow, steady breaths and try to concentrate on my project.

I flip through the different sections of the web page again. My mom is really going to be surprised by this. Ever since I was little, she's told me that homemade Christmas gifts are the best, but this is the first year I'm making her something that is actually helpful and functional.

I sneak peeks at my phone throughout class, but there's no text from Holden. When I haven't heard from him by lunch, I duck into the bathroom on the way to the cafeteria and tap out a message.

Me: Well?

Holden: A few people have thrown away trash, but no one has taken anything out of the can.

Me: You're sure?

Holden: Yes, unless they're some sort of magician.

Me: Can you keep watching?

Holden: I can at least until my mom wakes up and calls me and starts screaming.

Me: Okay, thanks.

I slip my phone back into my purse, and it hits me that maybe Unknown was after Julia's phone for some reason. She didn't mention whether it was stolen this morning.

Flushing the toilet, I exit the stall and wash my hands. Then I head for the cafeteria.

Julia is waiting for me right inside the main entrance. She turns toward the hot-food line and I get in line behind her.

"Any word on your purse?" I ask.

"No. The principal was really upset. She said there hadn't been a locker break-in all year. She wanted me to call the police and have an officer come take an official statement, but that seemed a bit extreme. I ended up just emailing them a description of my purse and wallet."

"Did they get your phone too?" I reach under the plastic guard and help myself to a hamburger with fries.

"Thankfully no." Julia grabs a Styrofoam plate of rice and

grilled chicken. She wrinkles up her nose at it. "I bring my phone into the pool area when I swim laps so I can use it as a stopwatch and also check messages."

I select a green apple from the fruit section of the line and then take a tiny chocolate brownie from the dessert section. Julia grabs a bowl of cut-up cantaloupe and a container of green Jell-O for dessert. As we head for the cashier, she eyes my brownie enviously.

"What, exactly, are you planning on wearing for New Year's Eve again that is the reason you are torturing yourself with creepy diet drinks and school Jell-O?"

Julia sighs. "It's this extremely formfitting dress with a big slit up the front. And like I said, I bought one size too small. I still need to lose another inch off my hips or I'm not going to be able to sit down without the risk of a big slit up the back too."

"I sincerely hope this is the party of the century." I pull a five-dollar bill out of my purse and give it to Julia. "And that you meet the guy of your dreams and he appreciates all your suffering."

"Let's not get crazy," she says, as she hands me back my change. "I'm not looking to meet anyone. I just love the dress. I want to feel beautiful in it. Powerful. That means actually being able to move."

"I get it. Well, I expect to see some pictures." I hold my badge out for the cashier to scan and then Julia and I both head for our usual table.

"Of course," Julia says. "Even better, you should come over sometime and see the real dress. You could try it on for me so I can how it's really supposed to look."

"Whatever." I roll my eyes at her.

We cross the cafeteria and take our usual seats. Bending down, Julia pulls her phone and her water bottle out of her backpack. She shakes up her bottle as I take a big bite into my hamburger. Flicking through a few screens on her phone, she checks Twitter and Instagram. Julia has over two hundred followers on both, many of whom she got during her internship this summer.

I check my own phone to see if I have any new messages. Nope. I wonder if Holden is still outside somewhere, keeping an eye on the trash can in front of the school.

While Julia flips through her social media feeds, my eyes rove across the nearest tables. Several girls are wearing red and green in anticipation of the holidays. I can't believe it's almost the end of the year. It seems like just yesterday it was summer, my mom was sick, and Holden and I were both fighting our attraction to each other.

I scan the far corners of the room, looking for anything that seems off. If Unknown is in this cafeteria, I feel like

I should sense it. I mean, how can someone be the type of person who threatens to hurt innocent people and not give off some sort of creepy vibe?

But then I think about how much of myself I manage to keep under wraps, and I realize Unknown could be almost anyone. Across the cafeteria, Lowell Price sits at a table by himself, shoveling French fries into his mouth three at a time. I remember him calling Julia a slut in class yesterday, but as far as I know, he'd have no motive to blackmail me into stealing her purse or confessing my role in the Sea Cliff fire.

Katrina Jensen sits at the next table with a few of her Tillamook friends. Her lunch tray has already been picked clean and she's reading a thick paperback novel. She seems to despise both Julia and me, but that doesn't mean she's a deranged stalker.

It hits me that I should respond to Unknown's latest text right now. Maybe I can trick him or her into starting a conversation with me and narrow down my pool of suspects.

Grabbing my phone I text Unknown:

I did what you want. Are we done now?

Lowell continues eating his French fries at the exact same pace. Katrina slips her book into her purse and then hops up from her table to dump her tray. She waves good-bye to her friends and heads for the girls' bathroom in the main hallway, giving me a long look as she passes.

I could get up and follow her, see if she checks her messages in the bathroom, but it's not like that's going to prove anything, and she's not just going to show me her phone.

Julia looks up from her own phone. "Why are you staring at Katrina Jensen?"

"I don't know," I lie. "Something about her is a little off."

"Yeah," Julia says. "I overheard someone in the locker room saying that in sixth hour yesterday Katrina was bragging about buying a pistol."

"Seriously?" I ask, somewhat shocked. Hunting rifles aren't a rarity in Three Rocks or Tillamook, but handguns are. "She's not even old enough to buy a gun, is she?"

"Supposedly she bought it off some college kid."

"That's messed up." I shake my head. "I know she likes to be outrageous, but I can't believe she would want to risk getting caught with a weapon."

Julia's face grows serious. "I heard her stepdad used to get drunk and beat on her mom. Supposedly, her mom kicked him out, but still. Girls can't be too careful anymore. Ness actually takes Krav Maga classes. She wants to get a concealed-carry permit once she's old enough."

I shudder. "I'd be afraid I would shoot off my own foot."

"I don't know. I think it'd be cool to learn how to handle a gun." Julia spears a bite of chicken and chews slowly. She takes a swig of her acai berry diet whatever and starts composing a tweet. She stops halfway through, lifts a hand to her lips.

"What is it?" I ask.

She picks through the rice with her fork, her brow furrowing. She starts to bend down toward her backpack and then stops. "Shit, my purse," she says. She stands up so suddenly that she tips over her chair.

"What is it?" I ask. "What's wrong?"

"Must have . . . eaten . . . a nut." Julia's voice is thick and wheezy now. "Need. Nurse." She turns toward the exit to the cafeteria but makes it only about five steps before she collapses to the ground.

SEVENTEEN

"JULIA!" I SCREAM. Immediately, a crowd starts to gather around her. I leap out of my chair and drop to my knees beside her. "Get back," I tell the curious onlookers. I grab Julia's hand. Her skin is clammy and cold. "You're going to be okay," I say. I do a quick calculation. Even if I could go to the front of school and get Julia's purse from the trash can, the nurse's office is closer and I know the nurse has backup EpiPens for situations just like this. Lifting my head, I say, "Someone needs to go get the nurse."

But no one is listening to me. They're all just crowding in for a look at Julia Worthington flailing around on the ground.

My gaze lands on Frannie and her friends Mona and

Patrice, standing at the periphery of the crowd, their eyes wide and their faces pale. Frannie and I make eye contact, and it seems to snap her back to reality. "I'll get the nurse," she volunteers. She scurries off down the main hallway, her strawberry-blond braids bouncing against her shoulder blades. Mona kneels beside me, the edges of her head scarf dragging on the ground. "My mom's a nurse," she says. "Is she choking? If so we should roll her on her side."

"It's her allergies," I say. "Her food must have touched peanuts or something." But inside, a darker suspicion is taking root. Was this why I was supposed to steal Julia's purse? So she wouldn't have her EpiPen?

Julia wheezes as she curls onto her side. Her face has gone red and is starting to swell up. She tries to say something but it comes out like a wet gurgle. I push a lock of sweaty hair back from her eyes. "Hang on, Julia," I say. My heart pounds hard against my breastbone. I've known she was allergic since the summer we met, but I've never seen her have a full-blown reaction. When she had to stick herself at the swimming conference, she did it before there was any noticeable change in her voice or appearance. Some of the noises she's making don't even sound human.

Her face starts to turn from red to purple. Her lips look positively blue. My own throat goes tight just from looking at her. I glance down the main hallway. Shit. There's no sign of

Frannie and the nurse. I raise my head to the crowd. "Does anyone else have an EpiPen?" I ask.

"I do," Patrice says timidly. She pulls a plastic cartridge from her purse with shaking fingers. "But I'm allergic to bees. I'm not sure if it's the same."

"It is," Mona says.

"Do you know how to inject someone else?" I ask.

"In theory." Patrice chews at her lower lip. She pulls the cap off the EpiPen and holds it against Julia's leg, her hands still trembling. "Are you sure I should?"

Julia's eyes are rolling back in her head now. Her extremities are twitching like she's having a seizure. Behind us, I hear the snapping of cell phones as people take pictures. I look toward the entrance to the cafeteria once more. Still no nurse. What is taking her so long?

"Give it to me." I grab the pen from Patrice's hand and jam it in Julia's thigh, right through her jeans and depress the plunger.

There's no immediate change to her condition. *Come on, come on, come on.* I've never given anyone an EpiPen before, but I took a first-aid class last summer where they went through the basic procedure. It's pretty idiot-proof as long as you manage to penetrate the fabric of the victim's clothes.

Five seconds pass. Then another five.

"Are you sure you did it right?" Patrice asks.

"Clear the way, please. Clear the way." Mrs. Heller, our school nurse, pushes through the throng of onlookers, her shiny gray bob bouncing with each step of her sensible nurses' shoes. She's got an EpiPen clutched in her hand. Frannie hovers behind her. "And put your phones away," the nurse adds. "This is a personal medical emergency, not something you should be sharing with strangers."

"I just injected her with someone else's EpiPen," I say. "Maybe I should've waited, but I was afraid she was going to die."

Mrs. Heller squats down beside me. She reaches out to feel for Julia's pulse. The swelling in her throat seems to have diminished slightly. Her color is looking more pink and less purple now. The nurse attaches a small electronic clip to one of Julia's index fingers and nods to herself as a number pops up on the display. "Let me see what you used."

I hand her the empty EpiPen cartridge and she squints at the fine print. She compares Patrice's pen to the pen in her hand. "Should be fine," she says. "EpiPens only come in two sizes—child and adult. I am going to need you to give the office a statement, though, for legal purposes."

"Why isn't she waking up?" a kid yells from behind me.

His voice sounds familiar. I glance back over my shoulder. It's Holden's friend Zak, who works at the gas station with him.

Mrs. Heller ignores his question. "Please, all of you, back up or I'll start assigning detention. Give her some space to breathe." The crowd has grown to about forty people now.

Julia's eyes flick open. She makes a gasping noise as she reaches for my shoulder and tries to pull herself up to a seated position.

Mrs. Heller grabs her shoulders gently and restrains her to the floor. "Don't try to sit up yet, Ms. Worthington. You had an allergic reaction and we administered epinephrine. It's best if you stay lying down until the paramedics get here."

"My p-purse," Julia chokes out.

I squeeze her hand. "I stuck you with someone else's EpiPen. The nurse said it's the same as yours."

"Paramedics?" Frannie asks. "Isn't she going to be okay?" Frannie looks back and forth from the nurse to me.

"She should be, but we always send anyone who has a serious allergic reaction to the ER for them to make sure the patient is stabilized," Mrs. Heller explains.

Julia tries to say something else, but when she opens her mouth, no words come out. My phone buzzes in my purse. It might be Holden, telling me who grabbed Julia's bag from the trash. I'm dying to look at it, but I'm not going to do so while Julia is lying on the floor.

"Don't try to talk," I tell her. "Just relax. You're going to be fine."

She nods weakly. Her eyelids flutter shut.

A few minutes later, two navy-clad paramedics enter the cafeteria and load Julia onto a stretcher. The entire cafeteria rises to its feet and starts to clap.

Mrs. Heller nods at Mona and me. "Good job, ladies. Way to stay calm under pressure."

I nod back, but now that the crisis is over, the reality of what just happened is crashing down on me. My eyes water and a lump starts to form in my throat. I can't believe Julia could have died.

My phone buzzes with a text. There are two messages from Holden:

Holden: Still haven't seen anyone take anything out of the trash can.

Holden: You ok? An ambulance just pulled up. What's going on?

With shaking fingers I respond to the second one and let him know what happened to Julia. Then I reread the first one. It seems to confirm my worst suspicions. Unknown didn't want me to steal Julia's purse so they could have it or anything inside it. They wanted me to steal her purse so they could try to kill her.

EIGHTEEN

I SPEND THE NEXT three hours sick to my stomach. Julia almost died because of me. I'm not even sure if she'll connect the fact that someone snatched her purse with the allergy attack, but I do. Unknown had me steal her purse with her EpiPen and then somehow laced her food with peanuts or peanut oil. I think back to right before she collapsed. I paid for her lunch, she gave me back the change, and then we sat down. I try to remember all the things she touched on her tray, but I can't. I know she had the chicken and rice, and the green Jell-O. I don't remember what else.

I get another text from Holden right as school is ending. He watched the trash can all day and no one showed up. I meet him in the parking lot of the community college across the street. Most of Tillamook Bay Community College is down on Third Street, but the Industrial Technology Department is right across from the high school.

His motorcycle is parked along the edge of the lot. I pull my car in next to him and he hops into the passenger seat.

"I can't believe no one has come to retrieve the purse yet," Holden says. "You think they're waiting until tonight when it's dark?"

"I think they only wanted me to steal it so Julia wouldn't have her EpiPen," I say grimly.

"That's seriously fucked up. Should *we* go get the purse?" he asks.

I shake my head. "No. At least not until I talk to Julia. Unknown might be hoping one of us does that. Then they can try to set us up for attempted murder."

"I still can't believe she had an allergy attack." Holden shudders. "What a messed-up thing to do to someone."

"Yeah." A lump rises in my throat as I think of the wheezing and choking sounds Julia made. Tears leak out of my eyes. "I can't believe I almost got her killed. I'm going to tell her everything the next time I see her. I don't expect her to forgive me, for the purse or for you, but I don't want to keep stuff from her anymore." I turn toward the side window as

I hurriedly wipe at my eyes. I don't want Holden to console me right now—I don't deserve it. I need to make things right with Julia on my own.

"I'm glad. I think that's a good idea." He pats me on the leg. "She's not necessarily going to hate you, you know?"

I shrug. "If she does, I'll understand. I should have told her the truth so much earlier. What's wrong with me, Holden? How come I know the right thing to do but can't ever manage to do it?"

"Because doing the right thing is hard," he replies. "But you're doing it now, and I respect that. Eventually Julia will too."

I sigh. "I feel like the worst person in the whole world."

"Stop," Holden says. "You did a bad thing. Maybe several bad things," he adds before I can correct him. "But we all do bad shit sometimes. It's what you do now that matters. If you don't like the person you are, take responsibility for your past mistakes and do better."

It reminds me of my mom's advice about controlling what I can and not obsessing about other stuff. The only thing to do now is confess, apologize, and let Julia decide if she's going to forgive me.

I sigh again and smile wanly. "Maybe I can't talk to Julia the same way I can talk to you, but I still care about her so much. I can't even imagine my life without her in it."

There's a long beat of silence. Then Holden says, "Don't take this the wrong way, but did you ever think that the reason you can confide in me but not people like Julia and Luke is because you're more afraid they're going to leave you?"

"What do you mean?"

"Come on, Embry. Your dad left before you were even born. You can pretend that didn't affect you, but you're only kidding yourself. That sort of thing screws a person up. Of course you have issues with people leaving. Luke left for the army. Julia started talking about going away to college. I know you think there's some deep and special reason you can talk to me, but maybe it's just because you know I'm going to be sticking around town for a while."

I start to object, but then I purse my lips tightly and force myself to think about Holden's words. It's not even just my dad and Luke and Julia. Before my grandmother died, I confided deeply in her too. It's entirely possible I've gotten so sick of being left that I've started pushing away all the people I think might leave me.

My phone buzzes again—a text from Julia:

Julia: Hey. I just got home from the hospital. Thanks for saving my life ;)

Me: You doing okay?

Julia: So well my parents would probably make me go to school tomorrow if it wasn't the last day before winter break.

"It's Julia," I tell Holden. "She's okay."

"Thanks to your quick thinking," he says.

"Yeah," I reply. But we both know my actions are what put Julia in danger in the first place. Unknown targeted her because she's my friend, and I made it even easier. I turn my attention back to my phone.

Me: Can I come by and see you?

Julia: Yes. And can you bring some chocolate? Almost dying has recalibrated my priorities.

I smile.

Me: I'm on it.

I use some of the money from my father to splurge on a box of fancy chocolates to bring to Julia. Fred Meyer, the biggest store in town, has a selection for Christmas and they're even gift-wrapped. I look them up online to find one that's peanut-allergy safe and then triple-check with the cashier before buying it. I know I can't bribe Julia into forgiving me, but if our friendship is going to end today, I don't want her last thoughts of me to be that I tried to kill her with poisoned candy.

Thunder rumbles above my head as I pull out of the parking

lot and take Highway 101 across Tillamook to get back to the smaller highway that leads to Three Rocks. I drive the speed limit, past the library and the hospital and the farms at the edge of town.

The road narrows as I head into the hills. I decelerate to navigate the sharp S and C curves. Pockets of fog hang in the higher-altitude air, forcing me to slow down even more. A hard rain begins to fall, individual droplets smacking into the windshield like tiny pebbles. I flip on the windshield wipers, frowning as a couple of pickup trucks blow past me in a no-passing zone. I breathe a sigh of relief a few minutes later when I descend the final stretch of road into Three Rocks. Mom's fifteen-year-old Mazda isn't much, but it's all we've got and I'd hate to get in an accident.

I drive past the turnoff to my neighborhood and take a sharp left onto Puffin Drive. Halfway up Puffin Hill, I veer left onto Terresea Way, the street Julia lives on. I've been over to her house tons of times, because when we used to have sleepovers and stuff, I always suggested her place. "You've got more movies and better snacks," I always told her. Truthfully, I'm a little embarrassed of where Mom and I live. I love our house, but it's small and cramped and we've been known to let dishes pile up in the sink and trash pile up in the trash can. Hanging out at my place probably feels like slumming it at a cheap motel for Julia.

She opens the front door in pink sweatpants and a Victoria's Secret T-shirt, her hair twisted up in a messy bun. Other than her face looking a little red, there's no evidence of her earlier attack. Still, I tear up a little just looking at her. "I'm so glad you're okay," I choke out.

"Me too," she says. "Come on in out of the rain, silly."

I step into her warm foyer. "Wow. It feels so good in here."

"Yeah? I think it's kind of hot. But you know old people and their bad circulation." She rolls her eyes and grins. Julia's parents are in their fifties, almost old enough to be my grandparents.

"Better hot than my house. Our furnace is messed up, so it's freezing right now."

"I have a space heater you can borrow if you need to," Julia says. "My mom bought it for me because I sometimes study in the basement, but as you can tell I don't really need it."

"I think we'll be okay, but thanks." A sharp pain spikes through my chest as I imagine the look on Julia's face after I tell her about Holden and me. But I have to do it. I won't lose my nerve. I can't.

I follow Julia deeper into the house. Her living room has matching leather sofas and a vaulted ceiling. Like Holden's apartment, there is no clutter, no knickknacks. A huge artificial Christmas tree stands in one corner of the room. It looks professionally designed, with clear glass ornaments and garland made of metallic golden ribbon. Even the television remote has its own special holder, a small black marble case that matches the coffee tables.

There's a knitted blanket balled up on the floor on the far side of the sofa. Julia reaches down, snatches the blanket from the floor, and folds it loosely. "I was just watching some TV," she says.

"Where are your parents?" I was expecting them to be hovering over her.

"They're both in the study. My dad is writing and my mom is reading, probably. Wanna go upstairs?"

"Sure." I follow Julia up to her bedroom on the third floor.

She closes the door behind us. I wander over to the far side of her room. There's a huge glass window looking out toward the ocean. Her house is one of the lower ones on the hill, so the view is partially obstructed by trees, but you can still see the dark blue water, the waves rolling in. I watch the white froth hit the beach and soak into the sand. Then the tide pulls the water back to the ocean. In and out. In and out.

"You love the ocean more than anyone I know."

"Hmm?" I hear Julia, but I'm still sort of hypnotized by the relentless push and pull of the waves.

"I just think it's cool how you've lived here your whole life but you're still in love with the ocean. I feel like most people eventually start to take it for granted."

I turn back to face her. "I am," I admit. "I love it exactly the same as I did when I was little."

Julia gestures at the wrapped box in my hand. "Is that for me?"

"Oh, right." I almost forgot I was holding the chocolate. "It is, actually."

I hand Julia the wrapped box and then perch awkwardly on the edge of her bed. She crosses the room to her white wooden dresser. She opens the top drawer and pulls out a flat wrapped package. "Do you want your present too?"

"Well, that's not really a present," I say. "I mean, I have something else for you for Christmas."

"Two presents?" Her eyes light up. "I'm not sure I've been nice enough this year for that." She presses the flat package into my hand. "Open yours," she says eagerly.

"You first," I say.

She shakes her head. "You first."

"Okay." I turn the thin package over in my hand and start to loosen the tape on one end, doing my best not to rip the paper.

"Embry. You don't have to save the wrapping," Julia says. "Trust me, we have plenty."

"Sorry. Force of habit." Quickly, I undo the tape to find a Shutterfly photo book. The title is *Embry and Julia's Three*

Rocks Adventures. There's a picture of the ocean on the cover, our town's famous three rocks in the background.

"Julia," I say. "This is so . . . thoughtful." Shit. I wasn't expecting a personalized gift. Just when I thought things couldn't possibly get any harder. I start to set the book down on the comforter. "Look, I need to—"

"You need to look at that book." Julia sits next to me on the bed. "I bet you don't even remember some of those pictures."

"Okay, okay," I say, trying to keep my voice light but dying a little inside. My brain starts a blinking red countdown, like the timer on a bomb. *Three minutes until total annihilation.*

I flip to the first page. It's a collage of pictures from junior prom. Luke had just finished his specialized training and had flown home from Texas to go with me, and Julia was with Holden.

Seeing all four of us together sends a rush of emotions through me. I thought we were happy that night. I thought we had what we wanted. Julia was happy with Holden. I was happy with Luke. But it was all a lie.

She points at a picture of the four of us as we enter the dance. "I love that picture because they both look so pissed."

It's true. Julia and I are giving the camera our best dazzling smiles, but both Luke and Holden look like they'd rather be fist-fighting than posing in the same picture.

"Remember how mad they got at dinner?"

I snicker. "Yes. I thought Mrs. O'Riley was going to kick us out of the restaurant."

"Have you talked to Luke lately?" Julia asks. "When is he coming home again?"

"He said hopefully in January."

"Do you think you two will get back together?"

"Probably not." Another current of sadness moves through me. Not at the thought of losing Luke, because he deserves to be with someone who can love him completely and give him the things he needs. Just at the thought of hurting him, even temporarily, when I tell him the truth. He doesn't deserve to get his heart broken, but he also doesn't deserve to be lied to.

Sometimes no matter what you do, someone is going to get hurt.

Two minutes until total annihilation. I trace my finger around the biggest picture on the page. Julia's mom had taken it before the boys picked us up at her house. We're both wearing our dresses with paper crowns from Burger King that we got earlier in the day.

It's funny, I think a lot about the differences between Julia and me, but no one looking at this picture would see them. We almost look like sisters.

The next page is pictures from school. I'm not even sure who took some of these. There's one of Julia and me sitting in the hallway before first hour and another of me hugging Julia after one of our sophomore swim meets. Frannie and some of the other girls on the team are visible in the background.

As I flip farther back in the book, Julia and I get younger. There's a picture of us hiking with her dad at Cape Azure State Park, and then one of us at the zoo in Portland. The last few pages are the two of us at the beach: Julia and I skipping rocks and making sand angels, bending down over a jellyfish that washed ashore, perching like flamingos on a driftwood log, frolicking out in the shallow water with Betsy.

Each picture brings back memories. I forgot how deeply enchanted we were by the beach when we were in middle school. As Julia got older, she started traveling with her parents. She saw new places and developed new interests. Slowly, the allure of the ocean faded for her. Still, these pictures tear me up inside, because this book is nothing if not a physical manifestation of real friends, and I screwed that all up for a guy. Not even for a guy—I screwed it up because I cared more about hiding parts of myself than just being honest with my friend. *One minute until total annihilation.*

As I shut the book, I hop up from the bed and go to the window again. I bite back the tears that are threatening to spill out. I don't want Julia to see me crying. "Thank you for the amazing present," I say, struggling to hold my voice steady. "Both of my gifts are nothing compared to this."

"Doubtful." Julia tears into the wrapping paper and squeals at the chocolate. "Wow, when I said bring chocolate, I wasn't expecting this."

I blot at my eyes and then turn to face her, the closest thing I can manage to a smile plastered on my face. "I wanted to get you something good, especially after everything that happened today. And I looked up that company on the website to make sure the chocolates were peanut safe, that there was no danger of cross-contamination."

"Very thorough." Julia slits the plastic wrap of the box of chocolates with her fingernail.

"What do you think happened?" I ask. "You're only allergic to peanuts, right? Do you think somehow one got into the rice or something?"

Julia selects a circular chocolate from the center of the box. "Peanuts and tree nuts. I don't know. I'm pretty sure the school isn't allowed to have any nut products to prevent accidents like today from happening. The ER doctor said maybe one of the cafeteria ladies was eating a granola bar and somehow she contaminated my tray by accident. Or my mom said there have been issues with contaminated gelatin in the past. I guess some of the factories make pistachio pudding too."

"So you don't think someone tried to hurt you on purpose?" I pace back and forth across the plush carpet.

"God, no. Why would I think that?" Julia holds out the box of chocolates to me.

I shake my head. Pretty sure if I tried to swallow anything right now, it would crawl right back up my throat. "Because your purse was stolen, with your EpiPen in it."

"Oh, right. No, I hadn't even thought about that." She furrows her brow. "Why are *you* thinking about that?"

Once more, tears well in my eyes, but I bite them back. I don't get to be sad right now. Right now I just get to be honest . . . finally. *Three . . . two . . . one . . .* "Because I'm the one who stole your purse," I blurt out.

NINETEEN

"YOU WHAT?" Julia's cocks her head to the side like she's confused, like she honestly thinks she heard me wrong.

My legs go a bit weak and I lean back against the wall of her room. I wipe my sweaty palms on my jeans and then jam my hands into my pockets. I train my eyes on my shoes. "I went to school early, sneaked into the locker room while you were swimming, and took your purse." My words get faster. "I'm sorry. I might be able to get it back for you, but if not I'll give you the money to get a new one. It'll take a couple of months, but—you know what, that's not even the worst part. I've also been sleeping with Holden. I'm the girl in the video." I take in a deep breath and keep going before Julia can interrupt. "I'm the girl he hooked up with this summer. While you were away, Holden and I started hanging out. I talked to him about everything that was going on with my mom. I never thought anything would happen. But then one night things got weird between us and we hooked up. And I'm sorry I didn't tell you."

Everything is sort of bleeding together now. I'm not even sure if she can understand what I'm saying, but I have to get it all out this time, every bit of it, before she gives me a reason or an opportunity to hold something back. "I lied to you repeatedly when you asked me if I knew who she was. I don't expect you to forgive me for any of this." My shoulders slump inward as I finish. It takes intense effort just to look at Julia. I'm so afraid of what I might see.

Her lips are pursed, but there's no obvious anger in her expression. "Back up," she says. "Why the hell would you steal my purse?"

"I didn't want to do it. I've been being . . . blackmailed, I guess. I got this text message that said I had to steal it or else they were going to . . . get me in trouble. I'm the reason that video of Holden and me got sent out too." Quickly I give Julia a rundown on the messages I've received from Unknown.

"But what does this guy have on you?" she asks. "I'm assuming it's more than just hooking up with Holden."

I hesitate. I want to tell her everything, but there's still that natural urge to hide parts of me, the deepest, darkest inner pieces. *Can you trust her?*

"Whatever, don't tell me if you don't want to." She hops up from the bed, considers her reflection in her dresser mirror. "But then why are you even telling me any of this right now?"

"A lot of reasons," I say. "Mostly because I can finally see that Holden was right. Not telling you about me and him was stupid and selfish. I didn't want to tell you over the phone, and then when you came back from DC you were stressed about your SAT scores and I didn't want to tell you then and maybe distract you from studying. And then it got to be near the holidays and I . . . I kept telling myself I was protecting you, but really, I've been protecting *me*. I knew telling the truth would mean losing you as a friend. I've been so terrified I was going to lose my mom. I couldn't think about losing my best friend too." I swallow hard. "I know how selfish that makes me."

"So now you're *okay* with losing your best friend?" Julia's voice is level, but tears are pooling in her eyes. "What, just because your mom is doing better?"

"No," I rasp. "I'm not okay with it. But look at what happened. Keeping secrets almost got you killed. I'd rather that you hate me than we stay friends and you end up getting hurt."

"Do you love him?" Julia asks.

I pause, caught off guard by Julia's abrupt change of subject. Just the thought of loving Holden makes my heart accelerate, and not in a good way—in a "Charging . . . CLEAR!" kind of way. "I don't know, but either way that's no excuse."

"Why didn't you just tell me you had a thing for him when I told you I was going to ask him to prom?"

It's a good question, and not an easy one for me to answer. "I guess because it didn't feel right for me to be with Luke and have feelings for some other guy. Like how could I tell you not to date him when I had a boyfriend and you didn't?"

"You could've told me how you felt and then let me make my own decision," Julia says quietly. "I never would have asked him out if I knew you had a crush on him."

She's right. I should have told her. But I didn't want her to think I was greedy or slutty or a bad friend. And yet, here we are—me confessing that I've been a bad friend for the past several months.

It's Julia's turn to pace. "The truth is, I knew Holden was hooking up with someone else," she says, her voice level. "I just didn't know who. Until I saw the video. I've sat behind you in so many classes. I've braided your freaking hair, Embry. Did you really think I wouldn't recognize you?"

"Then why didn't you say something?" I clench my jaw.

"I guess I've been waiting to see how long it would take

you to tell me the truth, trying to decide if there's anything about our friendship worth saving. That's what hurts—how long it took you to come clean. My relationship with Holden was never serious. But you thought you were betraying me and you kept it up for *months*."

"I'm sorry," I whisper.

"And now you're telling me you're in some kind of trouble, being threatened by some stranger, but rather than confide in me, you break into my locker, steal my things, and end up almost getting me killed. I could have helped you! I would have given you the purse."

I drop my chin. "You're right. I should have come to you and told you everything. I just, I don't know. How was I supposed to ask you for your money and makeup and driver's license and stuff?"

"Those are just things. They're replaceable." Julia's voice cracks.

"You're right," I say again. "But asking you for that stuff would have meant telling you the truth. And I'm *ashamed* of the truth. Every time I say it, I have to face the reality of it all over again."

"Then why did you do it?"

"I don't know." I throw up my hands in frustration. "I guess because I do stupid things."

"And you kept all this a secret from me because you

thought I would judge you," Julia says, her voice flat.

"More stupid things," I say miserably. "Holden says I push people away once I realize they're going to leave me. I did it with Luke when he joined the army, and with you when you went away last summer."

"Just because someone is in a different place doesn't mean they're gone from your life."

"I know," I say hoarsely.

"I mean, Jesus." Julia's voice takes on a sharp edge. "Give people a little more credit. I understand why you kept being with Holden a secret, even though it was the wrong thing to do. But you didn't even confide in me about your mom. I would have been there for you this summer—phone calls, Skype, midnight texts, whatever."

I slide down the wall and end up sitting on her floor, my knees pulled in, my arms wrapped around them. I am both grateful for and shamed by her words, by the fact she's being honest, by the fact she hasn't thrown me out of her house. I want to explain the way I am to her, but it's hard, because I don't even really understand it myself. "It wasn't really a conscious choice. Just every time I tried to say something my throat closed up. Like 'Hey, how's DC? By the way, my mom has cancer and I'm scared she's going to die and leave me all alone.'"

"But you could talk to Holden?"

I sigh. "Yeah. I don't exactly understand why he's different, but he is."

Julia flops down onto her bed again. "I get it. I've also confided in him about stuff. I think it's partly because he sees things and calls people on them, and it's easier to acknowledge something is true after someone else puts it out there. Maybe I should have made more of an effort to reach out to you. My mom told me about your mom's diagnosis. You just never brought it up, so I figured you didn't want to talk about it."

"I don't know if I did or not. It's been hard for me to be . . . openly scared about my mom's condition because she's been so strong throughout most of it. If she can keep her shit together, then I feel like I should too." I shrug helplessly. "But none of this is your fault. I have been a really shitty friend, so shitty I almost got you killed, and all of that is on me."

"You also saved me," Julia reminds me. "Don't forget that part."

Just like I saved Sam, I think. *Right after putting his life in danger.*

"But back to Holden. He was never my boyfriend, not really. I asked him to the dance because he's cute and smart and I didn't want to go by myself. I only started dating him because it irritated my parents." She laughs under her breath. "But it also kept them off my back."

"Off your back about what?"

Julia lifts her chin. "About whether I'm gay."

"Wait. What?"

"Holden figured it out somehow and called me on it, but I didn't know for sure until Ness." Her face brightens momentarily, like a flower blooming in a storm. "I just knew I didn't feel the way about boys that you and my other friends seem to feel."

"Why wouldn't you tell me that?" I ask, hurt bleeding into my voice. "Did you think I wouldn't support you?"

"No, it's just like you said. Some things are hard to bring up out of nowhere. I kept thinking maybe Holden would mention it or you'd pick up on something and ask me, but you always just assumed I was straight, and I never knew how to correct you."

She's right. Even just the other day when I was teasing her about her New Year's Eve dress, I assumed she was trying to look good for some guy. "I'm sorry. I didn't mean to assume things . . ."

"It's fine," Julia says. "I mean, I also assumed I was straight for a while, so I'm not blaming you or anything. Just saying I know what it's like to need to talk but freeze up when it comes to starting the conversation."

"So you and Ness are . . . together?"

"Not officially. But who knows what might happen if we end up at the same school next year."

"But no one knows about you two?"

"Just Ness, and Holden, and now you. It's not some huge secret, but you know how my parents are. They don't mind gay people but they don't want one in their family. Last semester I was reading an LGBT website on my iPad and I left the page open and my mom found it and started acting really weird, suggesting maybe I should look into getting a remote internship instead of going to DC for the summer. I played it off, like I'd been doing some research for a class, but my parents still seemed to be second-guessing letting me go away. So I figured, why not ask a boy to prom to get them off my back."

"I hate that your parents would . . ." I trail off, unsure of how to finish that thought.

"Me too, and I'm hoping they'll come around, but like you said, there's only so much stress a person can handle at one time. So I figured I could wait and tell them in a year or two. Dating Holden helped assuage their fears, even though they didn't think he was good enough for me. He agreed to play along for a while."

"No wonder he kept saying you were never that into him, that I should just be honest with you."

She shakes her head. "I can't believe he didn't tell you the truth. He's a better guy than I even imagined."

"Probably too good for me," I say. "Just like Luke . . . Just like you."

Julia softens slightly. "Look. I don't hate you or anything. But I'm not sure I'll ever be able to trust you again. You really hurt me." She looks away, toward the window.

I can see her lower lip trembling. "I understand." I scramble to my feet and turn toward the door. "Thanks for hearing me out."

"Hang on." Julia turns back to me. "I don't want anything bad to happen to you either. What did the police have to say about your blackmailer? Can they trace the text messages?"

"Um . . . I actually haven't gone to the police."

"Embry!" Julia's eyes widen. "If this guy really tried to kill me, who knows what he might do next?"

"The problem with that is . . . Holden and I are kind of responsible for the Sea Cliff fire. We used to hang out there sometimes. With candles." I look down at my hands. "It was an accident."

Julia sighs deeply. "I thought I recognized the background of that video. Well, if it was an accident then the cops aren't going to charge you with arson or anything, right?"

"No, assuming they believe us, probably just trespassing

and some sort of reckless-negligence kind of thing. The bigger problem is when we get sued for hundreds of thousands of dollars."

"Shit," Julia says. "I didn't think about that. Did you tell your mom?"

I shake my head. "She's doing okay physically, but she's behind on some bills from when we had to close the coffee shop all summer because of her treatments and I . . . I just can't." I blink hard. "She's the reason I stole your purse. I didn't know what to do, and then I saw some mail she'd left out and it was stamped with stuff like 'Final Notice.'"

Julia nods likes she understands, but there's no way she could really get it. Her family has probably never gotten a "final notice" for anything in their lives. She doesn't know what it's like to worry about losing her home.

"Do you have any idea who's sending you the messages?" she asks.

"Not really. I've considered a few suspects, but no one that I can honestly believe would try to kill you."

"What about the guy you pulled out of the fire? Do you know if he's okay?"

"Sam? The newspaper said he was supposed to make a full recovery, but I haven't checked up on him or anything."

"I was just thinking that if he died, maybe someone close to him found out the truth and is after you for that."

"Don't you think I would have heard something if he had died?"

"Maybe not if the cause of the fire is still under active investigation. Look, I'll let the police know about my allergy attack and how it might be connected to my purse getting stolen. But you have to tell someone about being blackmailed—Holden's mom at least. Otherwise what if the next time this psycho wants you to do worse than steal?"

"I'm kind of hoping there won't be a next time." Even as I say this, I know it's unlikely. If Unknown really wanted to kill Julia, they're not going to be satisfied with a close call.

TWENTY

JULIA LOOKS EXHAUSTED from her time in the ER and I've said everything I need to say, so I tell her I'm going to go home so she can rest.

The two of us head back downstairs. Julia's mom is striding around the kitchen in a black pantsuit and three-inch pumps. She's tall and thin, with light blond hair that requires biweekly touch-ups according to Julia. You'd never suspect she was in her fifties, though. Right now she's putting fresh herbs and vegetables into one of those fancy Vitamix blenders. "Embry, hi," she says. "Julia mentioned you were coming by. Do you want to stay for dinner? I'm making tomato basil soup."

I force a smile. "Thank you, Mrs. Worthington, but I

actually need to be getting home."

"Okay, maybe next time. Tell your mother Merry Christmas for me."

"Will do," I say.

There's an awkward moment when Julia and I reach the front door. I want to hug her, but I don't want her to push me away. And worse, I don't want to make her uncomfortable. I settle for another forced smile. "Thanks for listening." I shift my weight from one foot to the other.

She nods. "You're welcome. Thanks for, you know, telling me everything."

I wait a few seconds for her to say more. I'm hoping she'll tell me she's going to call me after she thinks about everything or that we should get together after the holidays to talk again. I'm hoping she'll tell me she wants to still be friends.

But she doesn't say any of that. So I say, "I guess I'll see you around."

"Yeah," she says. Her voice wavers, and I realize I'm not the only one who's about to cry. But Julia turns back to the house before the tears start to fall.

By the time I get home, I have multiple messages from Holden.

Holden: I just got off the phone with Julia.

Holden: You ok?

I want desperately to respond, or to call him, but even Holden feels wrong right now, so I ignore his texts. I head into my room and flop down onto my bed. The urge to cry has left me but the sadness hasn't. It's a dull, heavy ache, like a bag of bricks sitting on my chest. After lying there for a few minutes, struggling to breathe, I decide there's one other thing I can do that'll maybe ease the weight a little.

I'm going to tell Luke the truth too.

I try calling him, but when his voice-mail message pops on I hang up without saying anything. Flipping to my email account, I start to compose a letter.

Dear Luke,

I'm sorry to put this in an email, but it can't wait anymore. It shouldn't have waited this long, but I'm a coward who didn't want to lose you, even though I've known for a while now that I can't be the girl you want. You are amazing and when we first started dating, all I wanted was to be amazing back to you. I convinced myself that I could make you happy.

As much as being apart from you has sucked, it's also helped me realize some things about myself. Mostly, I'm not sure what I want. I'm not sure if I want to get married, especially before college. I'm not sure if I want kids. I'm not sure what I want to study or where I want to live. I admire you for having so much of your life figured out, but I'm not there yet.

When I suggested that we take a break, I really did do it because I wanted you to be free. I wanted you to be able to deal with the stress of being a soldier without any danger of feeling guilty if you needed someone else. But it turns out, I'm the one who needed someone else. I've been seeing someone here. I've been with him for months. I should have told you, but I thought I was hiding the truth for your benefit. But lying only benefits the liar. I know that now.

Again, I apologize for sending this to you in an email. I tried to call you, but you didn't answer, and I figured a letter would be better than a voice mail. Call me when you get this, though, if you want to talk about things. I don't want to lose you from my life completely, but I'll understand if you don't want to be around me anymore.

I'm so sorry, Luke. I hope someday you can forgive me. I know you'll find someone who wants the same things you want, a girl who will be able to make you happy without pretending to be someone she's not.

As I'm thinking of how to end the message, there's a knock at the front door. I slip my phone into my pocket and pad down the hallway into the living room.

When I peek through the peephole, I see Holden standing in the rain, shocks of brown hair peeking out from under the hem of his black knitted cap. I open the door.

"Are you okay?" he asks. "You didn't respond to my texts."

I nod, letting him in. "Sorry. Long day. What'd Julia have to say?"

"Thank you, mostly, for keeping her secret."

I smile slightly. "She told me you were a good guy."

"She's not wrong." He cracks his knuckles. "Look, this is just my opinion, but I think she'll forgive you someday. The tougher question is whether you'll forgive yourself."

I nod. "Trying. I'm actually writing Luke an email right now."

"Ah," Holden says. "That's cool. I don't want to interrupt. I wanted to give you this and I didn't want to just leave it in the door because I didn't want to freak you out." He thrusts a green envelope at me.

My fingertips close around the envelope. "What is it?"

"It's a Christmas card, duh." He grins. "Okay. I'm going to take off. Good luck with the Luke thing." He slips back outside. I watch him jog toward his motorcycle, which is parked at the end of our driveway.

He gives me a little wave as he pulls away. Betsy pads into the living room to see who is at the door. "We got a Christmas card," I tell her. I shut the door and take a seat on the futon. For once she curls up obediently at my feet.

With shaking fingers, I open the envelope. The card inside is handmade and hand-painted. It's a single Christmas tree left in a lot, illuminated by fluorescent streetlights. There are no people around, but two deer stand off to the side, as if they've come to investigate. The inside of the card simply says *Merry Christmas* in Holden's neat handwriting.

There's a folded piece of paper tucked inside the card, an advertisement for a small art gallery in Cannon Beach, a city about an hour north of here. Apparently they're running a photography exhibition through the end of December. Holden has written two words at the bottom of the flyer: *Wanna go?*

I glance up at the clock. He lives only a couple blocks away. He should be home by now. Grabbing my phone, I dial his number. "This card is beautiful," I tell him. "You should sell these online too."

"No way. That's a one-of-a-kind. I made it just for you."

"Well, in that case, you should sell other, less special designs."

"You are bound and determined to make me into some sort of Etsy mogul, aren't you? Not all beautiful things need to be mass-produced and sold."

"Sorry. Maybe I'm projecting my own fears about not knowing what to do with my life onto you."

"Yeah. Maybe you are. Stop doing that." He laughs lightly. "So what do you think? Wanna get out of town for a day? I have to work at the gas station on Saturday morning, but we could go Sunday morning."

"You mean . . . like a date?" I hold my breath while I wait for him to answer.

"We don't have to call it that," Holden says. "I just wanted to take you somewhere fun. I figure your mind could use a break from everything that's been happening here."

"I'd love to check out this gallery with you," I say. "But I don't want to hide from what's going on. Julia yelled at me for not going to the cops—she said letting Unknown run wild might be putting other people in danger, and she's right. I want to figure out who's blackmailing me, make sure they don't hurt anyone else."

"Fair enough. What do you suggest?"

"I don't know, but I think we should get together and strategize," I say. "Can I come by?"

"Sure," Holden says. "My mom is working. I'll leave the door unlocked."

"Okay, give me about ten minutes. I need to finish up this email."

"Take all the time you need," Holden says. "And Embry, it probably sounds lame, but I'm proud of you . . . for telling the truth."

"Thanks, I guess." It feels like more credit than I deserve.

I disconnect the call and switch back to my email. I reread the message to Luke and envision the way he's going to feel when he gets it. I can see his smile fading, his jaw clenching as he realizes after the first few lines that I'm breaking up with him. Then what? Sadness or anger? Probably both. My index finger hovers over the trash can icon for a few seconds. *Focus on the things you can control*, my mom's voice whispers. *There's always something.*

Being honest with Luke is never going to be easy, just like it wasn't easy to tell Julia the truth. But telling her was the right thing to do, and so is this. I type "I'm sorry" again at the end of the message and sign my name. Exhaling hard, I press send.

TWENTY-ONE

TEN MINUTES LATER I'm sitting on the sofa in Holden's living room, one leg twitching repeatedly as I try to figure out if there's a way we can unmask Unknown without going to the police. I think about what Julia said about Sam, how if he had died it would give anyone who cared about him motivation to hurt me.

I glance over at Holden. "Do you think the guy I pulled out of the fire could have died?"

"I don't know. I guess anything is possible."

"I mean, if Sam died in the fire, it was my fault for starting it. Morally and legally. I would be guilty of manslaughter."

"*We* would be guilty, not you. It's as much my fault, and even Betsy's. I brought the candles and alcohol, which probably helped the fire spread. Her big silly tail spilled the vodka." He taps one foot. "And I don't like to point fingers at the less fortunate, but anyone squatting in there was breaking and entering, so he wasn't a completely innocent victim."

"Great. Except none of that makes me feel any better, Holden."

"No? I guess misery doesn't always love company."

"No it doesn't. I always thought that was the dumbest saying ever. If I'm suffering, seeing that other people are suffering too just makes me feel worse." I pick at a loose thread on the edge of the sofa cushion.

Holden laughs lightly. "I like that about you."

I scoff. "That I'm not a huge bitch who enjoys seeing other people in pain?"

"Yeah. And that you don't cut other people down to build yourself up."

"Well, I'm sure not going to try to pin the blame for the fire on a homeless guy," I say. "Dead or alive."

"Well, let's try to figure that out first," Holden says. "Maybe he's totally fine and you're considering this angle for nothing."

"Okay." I open a browser window on my phone and do a search for "Sea Cliff fire." I avoided most of the news write-ups in the days after it happened because each time I saw my name or "a local teen" mentioned as a hero who saved a man from the burning building, it was like swallowing a rock.

I find the article my mom read that mentions how the man pulled out of the fire was Sam Lark, a twenty-one-year-old former Tillamook resident who dropped out of Tillamook High his junior year.

I pass the phone over to Holden. "The article lists him in stable condition and says he's expected to make a full recovery. But there's no updated information on whether Sam has left the hospital or where he is now."

Holden scans the article and then gives the phone back to me. "So call the hospital."

I glance at the time. "Now? It's pretty late."

"It's not like they aren't open twenty-four hours. Just say you need to leave a message for Sam Lark."

I search for the number for Tillamook General Hospital. When the operator answers, I clear my throat. "Hi," I say. "Uh, I know it's late, but I was trying to leave a message for a patient—Sam Lark. Can you transfer me to someone who can help me with that?"

"One moment." There's a long pause and then the operator returns. "Did you say Lark? L-a-r-k?"

"Yeah."

"I'm sorry. It looks like Mr. Lark checked out earlier today."

"Checked out? So he got better already?" I ask. "He's okay?"

"Checked out means the patient has left the hospital," the operator says. "I don't have access to whether they've recovered or left against medical advice."

"Thanks," I tell her. I hang up the phone and summarize the info for Holden.

"So he's fine," Holden says. "He can't be involved."

"Unless . . ." I think back to that night, to Sam rambling about Beau and Elvis as we made our way down the stairs. "Do you think it's possible someone *else* was trapped in the Sea Cliff that night and the newspapers didn't report it? Would they keep something like that a secret?"

Holden shrugs. "I'm not sure."

"Can you ask your mom if the firefighters found anyone else in the hotel?" I swallow hard. "Or any bodies?"

"I can try." Holden pulls out his phone and rattles off a text to his mom. The response comes almost instantaneously. He frowns. "She says as far as she knows they're still waiting for a fire investigation team to come from McMinnville and she's not allowed to discuss the details of an ongoing investigation. She also says you should stop worrying about this and go home and get some sleep."

"What did you ask her?"

"I just told her I was with you and that you were wondering what happened to Sam and if there was anyone else in the Sea Cliff that night."

"So does the fact that she won't answer mean there probably was someone?"

"No, it's just my mom being a stickler for procedure. She might not even know herself. She's not personally involved in the case." Holden shakes his hair back from his face. "Either way, you did everything you could. I mean, I guess it's possible there was someone else in the building that night."

"Do you want to go look?" I blurt out.

"Look at the Sea Cliff? It's not like if there was someone else they'd still be there."

"No, but we can look for evidence that more than one person was living there."

"Okay," Holden says slowly. "But wouldn't finding out there was more than one person in the building that night just make things worse?"

"I would feel worse," I admit. "But it'd be a legitimate motivation for whoever is harassing me. If Sam knows that we started the fire, and a friend of his was left inside and died that night, chances are Sam is the one who's after me." I call up Unknown's text messages. "I mean, read these. Don't they sound angry to you? This isn't just some sicko who's playing a game."

Holden frowns as he swipes through the texts. "You're right. There's rage here. But I still say these messages sound personal." He slides the phone back to me. "Sam doesn't know you or Julia."

"I know. But since he went to Tillamook High, he might know *of* me, or know other people who know me. Maybe he's working with a partner."

Holden rubs at the bridge of his nose. "I guess it's possible. Let's go see what we can find."

The Sea Cliff Inn actually looks a little better than I imagined. I think I was expecting there to be nothing left but a charred husk, the smoking remains of a concrete foundation, and the basic skeleton of a house. But the roof and third floor of the building aren't even discolored, and the lower levels still look structurally solid. Superficially, anyway. Sexy Firefighting Models has taught me that when it comes to the structural integrity of a building, looks can be deceiving.

The entire area is cordoned off with yellow police tape and there's a sign on the lawn that says the building is part of an active investigation and trespassers will be prosecuted. Holden and I duck under the yellow ribbon and creep up to the porch. At this point I've lost track of how many crimes I've committed.

The front door to the hotel is just a gaping hole—the firefighters having rammed it in to bring in their hoses and gear. Holden and I stand on either side of the blackness, listening for the sounds of footsteps or breathing.

"You hear anything?" I whisper.

He shakes his head and then gestures at the doorway. I follow him inside. We both activate the flashlights on our phones.

The lobby, where Holden and I used to meet, is nearly completely destroyed. The walls are black and burned through in some places, exposing wood and concrete beneath. The sofa is completely charred, only parts of the metal framework remaining. The carpet has turned to ash beneath our feet. The air looks clear but the whole room reeks of smoke. My eyes start to burn.

"Cover your mouth and nose," Holden says. "The smoke damage means there's probably a lot of particles in the air, even though we can't see them."

I pull my shirt up over my nose and mouth and head for the staircase. The banister is blackened with soot, but the steps look mostly damage-free. Still, I rest my weight heavily on the first step to test it before ascending farther. It feels sturdy under my boot. Gripping the banister, I take a second step.

"Slow and steady," Holden cautions, his voice muffled through his shirt.

Once I make it to the top, Holden climbs the stairs one

at a time. We ascend to the third floor and enter the room where I found Sam. I'm amazed at how different it looks. The smoke has cleared, leaving behind a bed, desk, and chest of drawers. The wall is scorched here and everything again is covered with soot, but the fire didn't get a chance to completely destroy this room.

I walk over to the chest of drawers and open each one. They're all empty. Holden checks the desk and under the bed. "There's nothing here," he says.

"Let's check the other rooms." I turn back to the hallway.

Holden and I go from room to room. In the last room on this floor, we find the charred remains of a pink backpack and a single fleece glove with a hole in the thumb.

"Looks like someone else was here at some point," I say.

"True. But who knows how long ago it was. Let's check the second floor." Holden turns toward the door and I go to follow him, when all of a sudden there's a cracking sound. At first I think it's a gunshot. I instinctively drop to the floor. But then there's a rumble, and I feel the boards beneath me start to give way.

A hole opens up in the floor near the doorway and Holden disappears down into the darkness.

TWENTY-TWO

"HOLDEN!" I SHOUT, completely forgetting that we're not supposed to be here. "Oh my God, are you okay?" He doesn't answer right away, and I immediately cycle through the worst possibilities—he's dead, he's bleeding out, he's been impaled on a coatrack, he's buried alive.

"I'm okay," he calls up to me. "But my leg is trapped under something heavy. Can you shine your light down here?"

I pull my cell phone out of my pocket and angle the light at Holden. He's half covered by a pile of debris. "Hold on. I'm coming down there."

"Be careful!"

I backtrack to the stairs. My heart races as I carefully descend to the second floor. Blood pounds in my ears. Why did we come here? Is it like those unsolved mysteries shows where the criminals always return to the scene of the crime? I swear under my breath. When will this nightmare end?

There's a sharp clattering sound as I reach the landing. I find Holden in the room directly below where we were, trying to lift boards off his body. I kneel down and help uncover him, keeping a wary eye on the hole in the ceiling above us. There's one board lying across his leg that we can't move because it's connected to a heavy metal beam that was used to support the ceiling. I grunt as I try to put all my weight into moving the beam.

"Shit," I say. "This weighs more than I do."

"Let me rest a second and I can try to help you." Holden's breathing is short and choppy, his face moist with sweat despite the cold.

"Are you hurt?" I ask. He shakes his head, but his jeans are ripped and I can see by the light of my phone that he's bleeding in at least one spot on his thigh. "What about your leg?"

He moves the torn denim to the side so he can see his skin and then makes a face. "It's not that bad."

"Let me see." I angle the light from my phone at the hole in his jeans. The gash is ragged and bleeding steadily. "Not that bad? Put pressure on it. I'm going to call someone."

"No, Embry. Are you nuts? We're not supposed to be here. Trespassing. Tampering with evidence. How many crimes do you want to go down for?"

"But you're going to need stitches," I protest.

"You guys need help?" a low voice asks.

I whirl around, expecting a cop or a firefighter, but Sam Lark stands in the doorway. He's wearing the same black hoodie and camo pants he was wearing the night of the fire, but it looks like the hospital must have washed them for him, because they're not crusted in mud anymore. A tan-and-white Chihuahua is nestled in the crook of his arm.

"Holy shit. You scared me." It's hard to see in the dark, but I do my best to analyze Sam's expression, his posture. Can we trust him? I'm not sure. "What are you doing here?"

"I was looking for my dog." He steps forward. "Whatcha got going on here? Did the ceiling collapse on him?"

"I fell through the floor." Holden groans softly.

If Sam was Unknown, he could just walk away and leave Holden trapped. Instead he's leaning in like he wants to help.

"There's one board I can't move," I tell him. "It's too heavy."

Sam sets the dog down on the ground. "Stay," he orders. The dog is dusty and shivering. It sneezes twice and then shakes its head violently.

Sam turns to me. "Let's see if I can help."

I shine my flashlight the length of the board. Sam rubs at his chin. "All right. You lift at the end. I'll lift in the middle."

"What do I do?" Holden asks.

Sam scoops up the Chihuahua and presses him into Holden's arms. "Hold my dog."

We get in position, and on the count of three Sam and I both lift with all our strength. Holden pulls his leg out from underneath the board and Sam and I drop it back to the ground. The dog yips at the noise.

Holden clambers to his feet. "Thank you," he tells Sam.

"Yep," Sam says. "You gonna be okay?"

"I'm fine." Holden hands the dog back to Sam. "But your buddy seems like maybe he has a cold."

"Beau." Sam strokes the Chihuahua's bony skull, and the dog makes a wet hacking sound. "I had to come back for him, but he's not doing so hot."

"So Beau is your *dog*," I say. "I remember you mentioned him that night. I was afraid it was another person."

"Nope." Sam shakes his head. "Since my gramps died a few years back, all I got is Beau." He steps closer to me, and his face lights up with recognition. "Hey, it's you. I kept hoping you might come by the hospital so I could thank you."

"Sorry," I say. "I've been working and going to school. Plus, it wasn't that big of a deal, you know? Probably anyone would have done it."

"You hear that, Beau?" Sam says. "Brave and humble."

I swallow hard. The way he's looking at the dog is the way

I look at my mom. *All I got is Beau.* "What are you going to do now?" I ask. "Where will you sleep?"

"I think Beau and I are going to head toward California," Sam says. "I got a cousin in Oakland that I never met, but he says I can crash with him for a month or so, longer if I can find a job."

I dig in my purse and pull out the rest of the money from my father—a little over two hundred dollars. I hold it out toward Sam. "Here. Before you go, take a bus back to Tillamook tomorrow and take Beau to the Animal Emergency Hospital. They'll make sure he doesn't need any medicine."

Sam looks worried. "You think he's really sick?"

I start to tell him the dog is fine, that everything will be okay, but I can't bring myself to lie to him after he just helped us, even though a lie is probably what he wants to hear. "I'm not sure," I admit. "He might need some antibiotics for that cough."

Sam takes the money from my hand tentatively, like he's worried there are literal strings attached. "What if his bill is more than this? Will they take him away from me? I can't lose Beau."

"I understand," I say. "Just tell them that's all you've got. They won't take him away." I pray that I'm right about this. Homeless people deserve to have pets. Homeless people deserve to feel love.

"I have some money," Holden says. "I can give you a ride into Tillamook tomorrow. And if the bill is more than expected, I can cover the rest."

Sam looks back and forth between the two of us. "Why are you guys being so nice to me?"

"You just helped us," I say. "And I have a dog too. Also, I know what it's like to be almost alone in the world."

Sam's dark eyes soften at this admission. "You seem too . . . normal to know what that feels like."

A tear leaks out of my eye. "There's nothing abnormal about loneliness."

Holden adjusts the pressure he's holding on his wound. "I'll pick you up at ten. And if you want to crash here tonight, I recommend the gardening shed out back. It's not all that comfortable, but it's warm and dry and won't collapse on you."

I wish I could bring Sam back to my house—feed him and let him take a shower—but my mom would never allow it. I know he's not the one sending the messages, though. He's just one more unlucky person struggling to survive.

Holden shows Sam where the shed is, and then the two of us head around to the front of the Sea Cliff. I once again suggest he should go to the ER, but he refuses. "I don't need stitches. I just need some of that liquid Band-Aid stuff."

"I think we have some of that at my house," I say.

"I'm not sure if I feel safe driving the motorcycle back down the hill."

I nod. I don't want him trying to maneuver it on the slick road while he's bleeding. He could get light-headed and pass out. "We can walk."

"All right. Just give me a second." Holden shucks out of his heavy flannel. He pulls off the Henley he's wearing underneath and slips the flannel back over his bare chest. I remember the first time I saw him shirtless, the night we hooked up after the party. He'd always seemed to be wearing at least two layers, even in the summer, so I had no idea what to expect. But I was pleasantly surprised.

Holden ties the Henley around his leg. "You're staring," he points out.

"Sorry. I was just thinking about the way you remind me of some of the statues we studied in Art Appreciation."

"You know those statues have smaller than average junk, right?"

I laugh out loud. "Of course your mind would go there. I wasn't making a comment on your genitals, dumbass. I was trying to say you look nice with your shirt off."

"Oh, well in that case, thank you."

I roll my eyes. My gaze lands on the bay window that looks in on the lobby of the hotel. "Hang on a sec." I jog over to the window. Maybe whoever recorded Holden and me left behind a clue.

I peer in through the glass, trying to remember the exact angle that the video emailed around school was shot from. Whoever made it was standing on the right side of the bay window, looking in through one of the smaller panes of glass. I kneel down and examine the shrubbery growing alongside the building.

"What are you doing?" Holden asks.

"Looking for anything. A hair, a thread, something Unknown left behind." The dirt at the base of the bushes is hard and packed, but I feel around in it anyway, just in case there's something down there that I can't see. Right when I'm about to give up, my hand lands in a shallow impression. "I think I found a footprint." I pull out my phone and turn the light on again.

Holden kneels next to me. He holds back the shrubbery so I can get a clear view.

"It's only a partial," he says. "It looks like the heel of a boot."

I snap a few pictures with my phone. There's not anything truly identifying about the boot print, but maybe the images will look different in the light. "We can put these on a computer and blow them up really huge."

"Cool." Holden tightens the Henley around his thigh. He

crosses his arms over his chest and I realize he's freezing.

"Sorry. We'd better get going before you bleed to death."

Holden and I start heading down Puffin Drive. Every couple of minutes, I peek at his leg out of the corner of my eye, relieved to see the blood hasn't seeped through the fabric of his Henley. "Aren't you worried that might get infected?"

"I'll rinse it good. And I had a tetanus shot last year, so don't worry about that either," he says. "By the way, what you just did for that guy—giving him all that money—is one of the kindest things I've ever seen anyone do. You didn't even pull out ten bucks for yourself. So I don't want to hear any more bullshit about you not being a good person."

I flash him a half smile. "It's like you said. If I don't like the person I am, I should change. This is me trying to do better."

"Yeah, no," Holden says. "I'm betting you did that without even thinking about it, so quit trying to sell yourself short. Also, that stuff about knowing how it feels to be almost completely alone?"

"Yeah?"

"I know I'm not much, but you'll always have me. No matter what." Leaning in close, Holden slings his arm around my shoulder, and the horror of everything that's happened fades ever so slightly.

TWENTY-THREE

BETSY IS WAITING at the door to greet Holden and me. I intercept her before she can jump on him and mess up his leg worse. "Shh," I tell her. "Don't wake up Mom or we're all going to get in trouble."

Holden pets Betsy while I duck into the bathroom and find the liquid Band-Aid in the medicine cabinet. I bring it to him and then start to follow him out the front door.

"What are you doing?" he whispers.

I shut the door behind us. "I'm coming with you so I can be sure you don't pass out from blood loss or anything."

He smirks. "Aww, that's kind of sweet. Almost like something a girlfriend would do."

I slug him hard in the arm. "Would a girlfriend do that?"

"Mine probably would," he says, a smile still playing at his lips. "But I probably would have deserved it."

We walk the two blocks to Holden's apartment building and he bounds up the stairs, his injury not seeming to affect his mobility very much. We slip into the darkened apartment. I close the door behind us while Holden heads for the bathroom.

I flail around until I locate a light switch that works. My eyes flick to the painting of the olive tree as I cross the living room and find the bathroom halfway down the hallway. The door is mostly closed, but I can see Holden moving around in there.

"You need some help?" I open the door far enough to peer in.

"Maybe," he says. "Let me rinse the wound first." He starts to undo his pants.

Holden steps into the bathtub in his boxers and directs the showerhead at his leg. Water flies everywhere, and he swears under his breath as he tries to hold open his wound and adjust the stream at the same time.

I laugh. "Here. Let me help."

"Ooh. Our first shower together," he teases.

"Super-romantic." I angle the spray right onto his wound. He winces as the water hits his skin. The dried blood washes away, exposing a cut that is deep and jagged.

"Oh, Holden," I say. "Are you *sure* you don't want to go to the ER? That looks so nasty."

"I've cut myself before working on cars. It'll be fine, as long as I make sure it's really clean. Can you see if there's any Neosporin or anything in the medicine cabinet?"

I find him a tube of off-brand triple antibiotic and watch as he squeezes the goo into the cut. "Can you help me hold the edges of the cut apart?" he asks.

I make a face, but I bend down and put my thumbs on either side of the jagged wound. Holden squeezes more antibiotic gel into it and then has me press the edges tight together as he paints over the whole thing with liquid Band-Aid.

"Does it hurt?" I ask. "I saw some ibuprofen in the medicine cabinet."

"It's throbbing a little bit."

"I'll be right back." I leave Holden sitting on the edge of the tub and go to the kitchen for a glass of water.

While I'm gone, he gets dressed again. When I return, he swallows two pills and washes them down with the water. "Let's take another look at that footprint now that we've got some light," he says.

We head into the living room. I enlarge the images on my phone while Holden peers over my shoulder. Only a little bit of the boot tread is identifiable, but it looks like a circle of diamonds forming a sunburst shape in the center of the heel. I Google "boot prints" and "boot tracks" and end up with a lot of forensic databases, none of which are free, unfortunately.

"I think my mom has one of those programs on her tablet," Holden says. "She doesn't use it as a patrol officer, but she's studying to become a detective, and I'm almost positive I've seen her looking at shoe treads."

"Can you access it?"

He arches his eyebrows at me. "Let's find out."

I follow Holden into his mom's room, where he locates her tablet on the top of her dresser. This room is as sparse and streamlined as the living room—metal bed frame, black bedspread, black dresser and chest of drawers. Absolutely no clutter.

"Needs a painting," I say, my eyes skimming across the blank white walls.

"I tried." Holden laughs under his breath. "She said it would be wasted because all she does in here is sleep. Is it wrong that I was relieved?"

I snicker. "That sounds like something my mom would say."

We take the tablet back out into the living room and flop down next to each other on the sofa. Holden logs on to the computer, and the latest version of Windows loads on the screen. He searches through a couple of work-related folders. "Here we go." He clicks on an icon of a shoe print.

A program called TreadAware loads, and then a password log-on box pops up.

"Cross your fingers." Holden types a string of letters and numbers into the box and taps enter. The start screen for TreadAware pops up.

"Oh my God. You're amazing," I say. "How did you know her password?"

"Well, I know her general log-in because she lets me use this for homework. I was hoping it was the same password for this."

"Oh, your mom is one of those people, huh?" I tease.

"Old people." Holden scoffs. "So bad with technology. But at least her password isn't PASSWORD or like one-two-three-four-five or something."

I point at the menu bar. "How does it work?"

"Not sure." Holden scans through a few different menus until he finds one that says "upload photo." "Worth a try," he says.

I hand him my phone, and he uploads the best photo of the boot heel onto the website. Then he clicks "search database."

"I don't know how long this is gonna take." Holden sets the tablet on the coffee table. He turns to me and blinks innocently. "What shall we do while we wait?"

I blush. "What did you have in mind?"

Instead of answering, Holden brushes my hair back from my face. He runs one fingertip down my jawbone. A shiver races through me. My body trembles.

"There's that convulsing thing again." He laughs under his breath.

"Good convulsing," I remind him.

He leans in and touches his lips to mine. "Glad to hear it."

I wrap my arms around his neck and extend the kiss. My hands get lost in his soft hair.

He exhales hard. "I've missed this," he says. "I've missed you."

"I haven't gone anywhere," I murmur.

"Yeah, but you know what I mean." Wrapping his arms around my middle, Holden tries to pull me onto his lap.

"Holden, come on." I squirm out of his grasp. "What about your leg?"

"It's fine."

I clear my throat. "Yeah. Well. You should probably refrain from . . . strenuous activity for at least a few hours so you don't rip open the cut."

He grins. "I could just lie there. You could be extra gentle."

I scoff. "It does sound pretty tempting when you describe it like that."

His smile widens. "Really?"

"No." I punch him in the arm again.

He collapses back on his cushion and contorts his face into a fake pout. It reminds me of the way Betsy looks when her bowl is empty and I make her wait for food. "Are you bored with me, Embry Woods?"

"What? No. I just—"

"I was your little plaything, but now I'm all used up, huh?" Holden sighs dramatically, holding one hand to his forehead.

I laugh. "Are you high? Did you take something besides ibuprofen when I wasn't looking?"

Holden snickers. "Nope. Who knew ibuprofen was such good shit."

"I guess." I poke him in the ribs. "You big weirdo."

"Seriously, though," he says. "If what happened at the Sea Cliff freaked you out to the point where you want to be just friends, I can handle it. You can tell me the truth."

"I thought we *were* just friends," I remind him.

"Yeah, but I mean the kind of friends who don't get naked together on a regular basis."

I've considered more than once whether being Holden's friend with benefits is a bad idea, but I don't regret anything that's happened between us, aside from that first night we were together. Even the fire—I don't regret meeting him at the Sea Cliff or sleeping with him. I just wish I hadn't knocked over the candle. I know I use physical intimacy to avoid emotional intimacy—it's easier for me and the chance of rejection is less—but I'm okay with that for the time being. Still, I know Holden's feelings have developed beyond friendship, and if I'm being honest, mine have too. At some point I'm going to have to decide exactly what I want from him . . . and what I'm willing to give.

"It's not that," I say. "It's just a combination of trying to focus on Unknown and . . ."

"And what?"

"And I don't know. Figuring out my feelings."

He clears his throat. "And, uh, what are your feelings?"

I narrow my eyes at him. "I'll tell you when I figure them out."

"Fair enough." He grins. "You're still gonna go to the gallery with me on Sunday, though, right? I have a surprise for you."

"You know I hate surprises."

"You'll like this one," Holden says, his eyes bright with mischief.

Before I can reply, the tablet beeps and a list of possible matches comes back. We both turn our attention to the screen.

"Only four different brands," Holden says. "Not bad."

I barely hear him. I'm too busy staring at the second name on the list: Rendon Hiking Boots. The same type Katrina Jensen was wearing in the cafeteria at school.

TWENTY-FOUR

I POINT AT THE SCREEN. "Katrina has these boots."

"They're a pretty popular brand," Holden says. "Don't a lot of people at school have those?"

"Yeah, but a lot of people at school don't have the means and motive to blackmail me."

"Let's see if we can find a picture of exactly what a Rendon sole looks like." Holden skims through the TreadAware menus until he finds a master database of pictures and prints. He pulls up a picture of the bottom of a Rendon boot. This one is a different style from the ones I saw Katrina wearing, but it's clear that the heel design matches the heel in my picture.

I tap one foot repeatedly against the carpet. My body is

filled with nervous energy at the thought of finally putting an end to this madness. "It's her, Holden. It has to be."

He sets the tablet back on the coffee table. "Maybe, but we can't accuse someone without proof."

"What if I go talk to her? Tell her I know what she's doing. I might be able to get through to her."

"Assuming she's Unknown, is that what you want? To get through to her?" Holden asks dubiously. "After what she did to Julia?"

"I want to understand why she's doing this, and I don't want anyone else to get hurt. That's what matters to me. I know she's having some issues at home. She might need help."

He shakes his hair back from his face. "What if she's dangerous, Embry?"

"I'll be able to figure that out by her response," I say. "If she seems dangerous, I promise I'll go straight to the police."

"Okay, but I'm going with you." Holden's voice is firm.

"That's not necessary. I can talk to her at school tomorrow."

He crosses his arms. "I can still go. They told me not to go to class. They didn't say I couldn't go into the building."

"You have to take Sam and Beau to the vet, remember? I'll be perfectly safe, I promise."

"Julia probably thought she was perfectly safe too," Holden

mutters, but he's not going to back out of helping Sam, and he's definitely not going to tell me what I can and can't do. That's not his style.

December 21

Unfortunately, Katrina doesn't show up to school on Friday. I text Holden after class to tell him I'm going to look for her at Fintastic.

Holden: Wait for me to get off work. I'll be home by 9:30.

Me: That's too late. If she's not closing she might have left by then.

Holden: Do you even know she's working?

Me: No, but I figure it's worth a try. I won't go anywhere alone with her I promise.

Holden: I still don't like it. How are you going to get home after you talk to her? She could follow you.

I start to tell him I can hold my own in a street confrontation with Katrina Jensen, and then I remember Julia talking about how she might have bought a gun. But Katrina wouldn't shoot me—that's crazy. *No crazier than her poisoning Julia.*

Me: I'll drive my mom's car.

Holden: Good. Come see me at the gas station afterward. It's supposed to rain. You can give me a ride home ;)

Me: Ha, I knew this wasn't about my safety ;)

Holden: You know it is though, right? I care about you, Embry. I don't want anything to happen to you.

I care about you too, I think. But I don't type it. I can't type it. My mom cared about my dad, and look how that turned out. And Holden's parents—he said they used to be so happy, and now they barely speak. I like the way things are with Holden. I don't want to mess that up unless I have to.

Me: You're sweet.

Holden: You too, even though you like to pretend you're not.

Me: Whatever. Did the trip to the vet go okay?

Holden: Yeah. They're keeping Beau overnight to give him IV antibiotics, so I dropped Sam off at the Tillamook shelter and he's got a bed lined up for tonight.

Me: Good. I'll text you before I head to the gas station.

Holden: Ok. Be careful.

Me: I will.

The Fintastic parking lot is nearly full as usual when I pull my mom's car into it at about 8:30 p.m. I hop out and click the locks, even though I'm not planning on staying long. I do a quick survey of the parking lot, just to make sure the guy in the leather bomber jacket isn't lurking around. Nope, it's just one elderly couple and me out in the cold right now. The gravel crunches beneath my boots as I head for the front door.

I pause outside the entrance to peer through one of the front windows. Frannie is standing at a server station that has urns of coffee and iced tea. She's rolling silverware for tomorrow, her hands moving methodically as she stares off into space. I watch for a few seconds as she lays out a maroon cloth napkin, stacks a knife, fork, and spoon in the center, folds in the corners of the napkin, and then rolls the bundle into a tight cylinder.

Behind her I catch a glimpse of Katrina as she glides past with a tray of food. Good. I don't know exactly what I'm going to say to her or how she'll respond, but this madness needs to end.

I hold the door for the elderly couple who have made it across the slick parking lot, the man leaning heavily on a cane. The warm air of Fintastic wraps around me as I duck into the restaurant behind them. Frannie looks up from where she's standing, as if robotically linked to the opening and closing of the front door. A quizzical look appears on her face. She knows there's no way I'm dropping by to eat by myself.

The man and woman in front of me both head to the restrooms. Frannie makes her way over to the door. "Embry. What's up?"

"Hey, Fran," I say. "I just need to talk to Katrina about something."

Frannie makes a face. "Good luck. She's been in a foul mood all night. Also, I wouldn't say anything about her eye."

"Her eye? What do you mean?"

Frannie starts to reply, but then the front door opens again and a middle-aged couple who live up on Puffin Hill enter. She gives me an apologetic look and then dashes off to seat them.

Katrina is working the back section again, where my mom and I sat the other night. She has only one table of customers right now—a family of four in a booth—so she's busy gathering all her salt and pepper shakers onto a tray to refill them. She turns around as I approach.

Immediately I figure out what Frannie was talking about. Katrina is wearing a thick coat of makeup, but it's obvious that she has a black eye. It looks like someone punched her. I remember what Julia said about her stepdad being violent toward her mom.

"Sorry if you want to sit up here," Katrina says. "I'm not supposed to get any more tables tonight."

"I'm not eating. I came to ask you about something."

"Oh yeah?" Katrina gives me a curious look. "Make it quick. I still have half my sidework to do."

I glance behind me at the family of four. "I, um, is there some place we could talk alone?" As I say the words, I realize I'm doing exactly what I promised Holden I wouldn't do.

"No," Katrina says flatly. "Look, Embry, whatever it is, just spit it out. I'm not here for your melodramatic bullshit."

I'm still trying to figure out exactly how to phrase things. "What happened to your eye?" I ask, stalling for time.

"You have got to be kidding me." Katrina moves to the next table and adds the salt and pepper shakers to her tray. "I fell. I bumped into a wall. Take your pick."

"I heard that your stepdad—"

"Just stop," Katrina says. "We both know you don't give a shit about me, and my mom fell even harder than I did, if you know what I mean. I need to get my work done so I can get home to her."

"I do give a shit," I say, as Katrina adds another pair of salt shakers to her tray. "I hope you at least called the cops. But I came here to ask you about the video, the one of Holden and me that got sent around school."

Katrina laughs under her breath. "That was *you*? I thought it was Rich Bitch, but why am I not surprised? You should try finding your own guy sometimes instead of stealing everyone else's."

"Look. I don't know what happened with you and Luke, but whatever it was, it ended months before the two of us started dating."

"You're right," Katrina says. "Funny, though, how Luke

and I were together for an entire summer, and then he ended it because he said I was too young for him. And then there he is with you a few months later, and we're the same age."

"So is that why you've been threatening me? Because you think I took Luke away from you?"

"Threatening you?" Katrina's face twists into a scowl. "What are you talking about?"

"I know you're the one who filmed Holden and me," I say firmly. "And the one who's been sending me the messages. Julia could have died that day, you know."

"Okay, no, I did not film Holden and you—like I said, I didn't even know that was you. And unless sarcasm kills, I haven't done anything to your precious bestie either." Katrina looks past me, to the family of four. "Please leave before your bullshit talk gets me fired. I need this job." She sets her tray of salt and pepper shakers on the nearest table and strides past me.

"Can I get you guys anything else?" she says sweetly to her customers, like everything is fine and I didn't just accuse her of attempted murder.

The mom orders a triple-layer peanut butter fudge brownie to share with the kids, and Katrina sashays off toward the service station to put in the order. She taps quickly at the computer screen and then tosses a glance over her shoulder.

Her face hardens into a glare when she sees I haven't moved. "Go away," she mouths at me before heading into the kitchen.

I'm filled with conflicting emotions as I watch her disappear. She honestly did seem surprised to learn I was the girl in the video with Holden. And if she's the one who poisoned Julia and asked me to steal her purse, she played that off like a pro. But then I think of the way she checked in with her table, the kindness in her voice, most likely manufactured to encourage maximum tipping. Maybe she's just good at being fake.

Katrina returns in a few minutes with a single plate and four spoons. She sets the brownie in the middle of the table and leaves a small leather book with the bill in it next to the dessert. Then she stalks back over to where I'm standing.

"Please go, Embry," she says. "I don't know who's been spreading lies about me, but that's all they are—lies."

"I found a boot print at the Sea Cliff Inn where the person stood to record Holden and me," I admit. "It was a Rendon hiking boot. I know you have a pair."

"So what?" Katrina says. "That's your big evidence? Half the kids at school own Rendon boots. Even your precious bestie probably has a pair."

"I have reason to believe Julia's allergy attack at school wasn't an accident," I say. "And Julia didn't poison herself."

"You sure about that?" Katrina asks. "She got an awful lot of attention, didn't she?"

"Yeah, but other stuff has happened," I say. "And I know things about Julia that you don't. She wouldn't have spread that video of Holden and me around, especially not considering most people thought the girl was her." *Then again, if she didn't want people to know she was gay, spreading that video would have been a great way to hide the truth.* I tell my inner voice to shush. Julia is my friend. She is not Unknown. Katrina is just messing with my head.

"Maybe she plans on telling everyone it's you at some point. Or maybe she just wanted to scare you." Katrina grabs the last of her salt and pepper shakers. "People like her aren't friends with people like us unless there's a reason."

"You're wrong," I say. "Julia has been my friend for years."

"She uses you. You're just some sidekick she drags around so she can feel better about herself in comparison."

"Wrong again," I say, my voice wavering slightly. "If anything, I've been using her."

"Whatever you say." Katrina balances her tray of salt and pepper shakers on her arm and slides past me. "We're done here. Don't bother waiting around for me, because I'll be in the kitchen for about thirty minutes, and if you're still here I'll go out the back way."

Katrina disappears and I turn toward the front door. I don't know whether to believe her. I guess it was dumb to think she'd confess to multiple crimes in the middle of Fintastic, but I hoped I'd be able to tell in my gut if she was Unknown.

Frannie looks up from the hostess stand as I pass. "What was that about?"

"Nothing important." I glance around the restaurant. "Did your family all take the night off without you?"

She laughs lightly. "Something like that. I don't mind, though. Sometimes it's nice to be away from them, you know?"

"Yeah, I guess you don't get much of that when you live and work with the same people."

"You sure don't." She smiles. "I hope you have a good Christmas, Embry."

"You too." I reach out and give her an impulsive hug. I'm not sure if she and I will be as close after she finds out I broke up with her brother, but I hope she doesn't take it too hard.

I send Holden a quick text and then head to the gas station to pick him up. I pull into a parking spot behind the pumps and replay the conversation with Katrina in my head as I wait for him to finish up.

When he slides into the passenger seat, I give him a quick

recap of everything that happened. Then I pull out of the lot and head for his apartment.

"Katrina's right," he says. "A lot of people at school probably do have a pair of Rendon boots."

"Yeah, but she's not right about Julia," I say. "She likes attention, but not that much."

Holden nods. "I agree. Julia might have been really angry at you for lying, but she wouldn't try to get me in trouble after I did her a favor."

I sigh as I pull my mom's car into a parking spot outside Holden's building. "It's frustrating. Julia and Luke are the two people with real motivation to be angry at me, but there's no way either one of them could be Unknown."

"How did that go with Luke anyway?" Holden asks. "Did you finish your letter?"

"I did. I sent it last night, but I haven't gotten a response yet."

"You think he'll call you when he gets it?"

"I hope so." I get nauseated every time I imagine Luke reading that email. "How's your leg doing?" I ask, eager to change the subject.

"I'll live." Holden yawns. "It looks ugly, but the liquid Band-Aid held through the night and it hurts less today."

"I'm glad something is doing better," I mumble. "I feel like

I've made no progress figuring out who Unknown is at all."

"Maybe your brain just needs to take the weekend off," Holden says. "When you get too immersed in stuff, it's hard to see the whole picture."

"Maybe," I say. But inside I'm not so sure I have time to take the weekend off. Unknown is still out there, and who knows what they're planning next.

TWENTY-FIVE

December 23

SUNDAY MORNING ROLLS AROUND and I haven't received any new messages from Unknown. I also still haven't gotten a reply from Luke. He's either too upset to talk to me or still out on his mission. I'm hoping it's the latter.

My mom is on the sofa, watching that TV show where Gordon Ramsay visits failing restaurants and helps them turn things around. I wonder if she's trying to pick up some tips for the Oregon Coast Café. Through our front window, I see Holden pull his mom's car onto the driveway.

"Where are you off to?" Mom asks, as I head for the front door.

"Holden and I are going to check out a photography exhibit at an art gallery in Cannon Beach," I say.

"Like a date?" Mom cocks her head to the side, a smile playing at her lips.

My stomach flops around at the thought. "Nah, just friends."

She grabs her purse from and pulls a twenty-dollar bill out of it. "Just in case you need to pay for something. I know I owe you for last week's shifts at the café."

I start to tell her I can use the money my father sent, but then I remember I gave the rest of it to Sam. "Okay, thanks. And I'll be home in time for our usual."

Mom reaches out to ruffle my hair. "Honey, you don't have to spend every Sunday night with me. Hang out with your friend. Live a little. Have fun."

"Sunday night sundae parties are fun," I inform her. "And anyway, Holden has to work later, so don't think you can weasel out of *our* date."

"All right. I'll pick out a movie while you're gone."

"Please don't."

Mom laughs. "Just for that, I'm going to let Betsy pick out the movie."

The dog is in the kitchen crunching down a bowl of kibble. When she hears her name, she stops eating long enough to woof in agreement.

Rolling my eyes, I open the door. Holden is standing on the porch in jeans and a black rain jacket, his normally unruly hair tucked behind his ears. A set of car keys dangles from one hand.

Mom hops up from where she's sitting. "Hi, Holden," she says, nodding when she sees the car. "No motorcycle?"

Holden looks up at the sky. "Well, the forecast is a little dicey. We're going to be driving for over an hour each way. I don't mind the bike in the rain, but I'm not trying to give Embry pneumonia or anything."

"Smart boy," Mom says. "Have a good time and drive safe. Call me if you need me, Emb. I've got two cookie orders I need to bake for a couple last-minute customers, but I think I'll just go in early tomorrow and knock them out."

"Good idea. Remember, your doctors said it was important for you to take at least one day off a week." I lean in to give my mom a quick hug. Then I follow Holden out the door and into a brisk, overcast day. "Your mom didn't need her car?" I ask.

"Not until tonight." Holden opens the passenger door for me and then jogs around to the driver's side. He turns the key in the ignition and the engine purrs to life.

I click my seat belt and recline the seat slightly as he backs down the driveway.

Holden drives to the end of my street and turns onto Highway W. We follow the winding highway past Fintastic and out of town, this time turning north toward Washington State rather than south toward the outlet mall.

We hit a clearing and then pass a logging field littered with stumps and dead branches. A painted sign reads: PLANTED 2017. I can just barely see tiny saplings poking out of the ground. I fumble for my camera, but by the time I get my phone out of my purse the field is long gone.

"Is it weird that I find deforestation beautiful?" Holden asks.

"Kind of." I slide my phone back into my purse. "But there is something majestic about a big swath of open land cut out of the middle of the woods, especially when it's been replanted."

"Right," Holden says. "It's reforestation, not deforestation. New baby trees sprouting from the remains of their elders."

"I like that," I say. "Hope for the future."

Cannon Beach is a small town that has only a handful of streets running through it. Holden and I find the Dragon Fire Gallery on Hemlock Street, across from the Cannon Beach Cooking School. He pulls into a parking spot and we both hop out of the car. He takes my hand as we walk toward the front of the building, a gesture that's both comforting and confusing. Holden is not my boyfriend, so why is he acting like it so much lately?

That troubling question is quickly washed away as I step into the warm, cozy gallery. I take a deep breath and inhale the scent of cinnamon and cardamom. This is my happy place, surrounded by beautiful artwork. The walls are painted vibrant colors and the hardwood floor under my boots is gleaming. Glass display cases hold small sculptures and handmade jewelry. A recording of what sounds like monks singing and chanting plays quietly in the background.

"Welcome!" Holden and I are greeted by a bubbly woman in a flowered dress. Her jet-black hair hangs to the middle of her back. "I'm Anaba," she says. "Here's a pamphlet that explains the art for sale and our current installation. Let me know if you have questions about any of the works."

"Thank you," I tell her. I fold open the glossy brochure. Most of the artwork in the gallery is by artists from the Pacific Northwest, several of whom are Native American. A circular cutout in one wall leads into a second room where the photography exhibition is being held. Photos hang on all four walls, as well as on triangular display columns interspersed throughout the room.

I knew the exhibition was called *Sea and Sky*, but I didn't realize the details of the photographer's work. She's created a collection of photographs of beaches and rocky coastlines at different times of the day. Each location has photos showing sunrise, afternoon, sunset, and the middle of the night. The first few displays are locations close to home—I even find a set for Three Rocks—but as Holden and I move deeper into the room, I find photographs of coastlines from different states and even different countries.

I stand in front of a photo of New Zealand fjords for a long time. "Can you imagine?" I ask Holden. "Can you imagine what it would be like to travel to the other side of the world?"

"Sure," he says. "And someday you won't have to imagine. You'll be able to go anywhere you want, take the same kind of photographs. And if you need an assistant . . . this guy." He pats himself on the chest.

I smile at him. "You are such a good friend."

"Friend . . . right," Holden says, his voice light. "Does that mean you're done figuring out your feelings?"

"Well, you know. Given the circumstances, I never really considered that the two of us could be more than friends."

"And now that the circumstances have changed?"

"I still have to talk to Luke," I remind Holden. "I'm hoping he'll call me soon."

"And after you guys talk?"

"I don't know," I say honestly. "Part of me thinks that if we were in a relationship I might push you away, the way I did with Luke. Maybe it's better to stay friends than to risk losing yet another person I care about."

"Maybe we're already more than friends and you just don't want to admit it because it scares you." Holden arches an eyebrow.

I poke him in the ribs. "One of the things I've always liked best about you is the way you never pressure me."

"Ouch," he says. "All right. I'll back off so you can enjoy the exhibit. But think about it later, okay?"

Holden lapses into silence, but he continues to follow me from display to display. It should bother me, but it doesn't. I like having him close. I wonder what it'd be like to be his girlfriend. Would it stay like this—easy and relaxed? Or would it change things? Just because our parents' relationships didn't work out doesn't mean we'd be doomed to fail, does it?

I try to imagine my future without Holden, and I can't. I'm not talking about marrying him or anything—I just mean next semester, a year from now. No matter what I envision, Holden is there. We're studying together and going for rides on his motorcycle, finding places to hook up when our moms aren't around. We're talking and laughing and being ourselves, no hidden pieces required. Maybe that *is* love. It occurs to me I don't actually know any people in love, not since my grandparents died. There's Julia's parents, I guess, but their relationship has always felt more like a business to me.

Holy shit. Am I in love with Holden? I knew my feelings were intensifying, but I guess I thought at some point I'd be able to make a choice, to love him or not love him. I didn't expect things to sneak up on me.

"You okay?" he asks. "You're looking a little flushed."

"Fine," I say quickly, moving to the next display. "It's just a little warm in here."

When we reach the final display in the room, it's a set of four photographs taken in India, a stone temple located on a beach. In the foreground of the sunrise and afternoon photographs, fishermen cast nets from long-tail boats while women and children dig for clams in the sand.

"What does this one make you feel?" he asks.

"Like it's happening in another world, at an earlier time," I say. "I should feel sad. The people, even the kids, are working hard. But everyone seems so happy."

"I love the midnight picture." Holden points to the lower-left corner. "Look, there are a couple of seabirds who have come out now that the humans are gone."

Sure enough, if I squint I can make out the tiny silhouettes in the dark photo. I might have missed them completely if Holden hadn't pointed them out.

We head back into the main room of the gallery, where

Anaba is explaining some jewelry in a display case to an older couple. I wait until she's finished and ask her if I'm allowed to take photographs.

"Absolutely," she says. "We just ask that you refrain from using your flash and that anything you post online you be sure to give credit to the artist."

I nod. I don't want to post of any of this. I just want a few snaps to keep for myself so I never forget this day.

After we leave the gallery, Holden and I grab some lunch at a place called the Perfect Pancake. They serve all kinds of breakfast foods, including thirty-five types of pancakes, as well as sandwiches for lunch. It makes me think of the big brunches my grandma used to make for Mom and me when I was little.

The waitress seats us in a booth next to a window that looks out on the parking lot. I order red velvet pancakes that come with cream cheese frosting, and Holden gets vegan pecan pancakes with real maple syrup. We eat mostly in silence. I keep thinking about the gallery exhibit, about how Holden saw things in some of the photos that I missed completely. Maybe there are clues to the identity of Unknown that I've missed somehow. I call up the messages on my phone and read through all the texts.

"Everything okay?" Holden soaks up some syrup on his

plate with the last bite of pancake.

"Yeah, I was just rereading the messages from Unknown. I can't help but feel like I'm missing something—some basic piece of information that would make all the other clues fall into place."

"It's not usually that easy," he says.

"I know. I just keep thinking that if Unknown had actually wanted Julia's purse, we would have caught him or her fishing it out of the trash. Then this would all be over."

"True." Holden pops the last bite of pancake into his mouth. He chews thoughtfully. "Maybe the next message will give us a better chance to set a trap."

"I hope so." As much as I hate the thought of more messages, I like the thought of setting a trap.

A black BMW pulls into the restarant parking lot. My heart skips a beat until I see the driver is a woman. It's not the same car I've been seeing around Three Rocks.

"Hey, did you have any luck with that license plate?" I ask Holden.

"Shit. I forgot all about that. I've got it written down on a piece of paper in my room. I'll call my friend when we get back, I promise."

"Cool. I don't see how some middle-aged dude in a BMW could be related to all this, but if I can figure out who he is, at least maybe I can rule him out." I glance at the time as I slip my phone back into my purse. It's a little after one p.m. "Time to head back?"

He grins mischievously. "Not quite yet. I've got one more stop planned."

"You didn't have to do all this." My heart thrums in my chest. I get that weird trembly feeling like I get when Holden touches me, only this time it's just from the look on his face. He looks so . . . happy.

"I told you I had a surprise. Think of it as your Christmas present."

I bite at my lower lip. "But I didn't get *you* anything."

He shrugs. "This is kind of my present too. I haven't gone anywhere besides Portland in a while because of school and work. It was good to get away."

"It was," I say. "Thank you."

The waitress drops off the bill, and I grab it before Holden can get his wallet out of his pants. "Let me pay. Since you drove and everything."

His smile dampens slightly. "No, I got it. I didn't ask you out so that you could pay."

"This isn't 1950," I inform him. "Besides, think of it as your Christmas present."

"Fine. You can pay half if you really want to."

"Thank you." I pull the money my mom gave me out of my purse.

Holden takes the twenty-dollar bill from my outstretched hand and gives me a ten in return. We head up to the register to pay, and then he jogs back to the table to leave a few singles for a tip.

I buckle back into the car and watch the scenery fly by, curious as to where Holden and I are going next. I roll down the car window so I can take some pictures of the town. The air outside is damp, but so far the clouds overhead haven't done more than rumble threateningly.

I'm surprised when Holden pulls into an opening for Ecola State Park. I've never been here, but most of the state parks on the coast are mainly for hiking and picnicking. We just ate, so . . . "Are we going hiking?" I ask. "I'm not sure how good I'll do in these shoes."

"Very limited hiking," Holden says. "You'll do fine." We drive past a set of restrooms and a couple of picnic shelters and park down in the far parking lot alongside several other cars.

"Limited hiking is popular today, huh?"

Holden smiles, but he doesn't say anything. We both hop out of the car and I follow him down a short trail to a small fenced-in square platform. A family of four is standing at the railing. The sun is hidden behind thick clouds, but it's still fairly bright outside, and the dad has one hand up, shielding his eyes from the glare. A girl about six years old is resting her chin on the top of the wooden fence while her older sister, maybe ten or twelve, is taking a picture with her phone.

Holden steps to the opposite side of the platform and scans the horizon. I follow him, squinting out at the water. Below us, a pair of surfers in full-length wetsuits are paddling out into the ocean.

"Are we watching surfers?" Occasionally there are surfers on Three Rocks Beach, though not usually in the winter because the water is so cold.

Holden pulls a pair of binoculars from the pocket of his rain jacket and suddenly I realize why we're here.

"Whales?" I ask loudly.

"Shh." Holden smirks. "You're gonna scare them away."

The six-year-old girl crosses the platform. She points out at the ocean, to what is approximately the eleven o'clock position. "My mommy said she saw a spout over there."

"The top of the whale's head surfaced, actually," the woman corrects. "Come over here, Serena. Don't bother the nice couple."

My stomach gets a weird feeling at Holden and me being called a couple. Do I like it? Do I not like it? How do I not know? Oblivious to the warring feelings inside me, Holden hands me the binoculars. "Give it a try. Let me know if you see anything."

I peer out into the water, scanning systematically, top to bottom, left to right. I'm not used to using binoculars and I end up having to close my right eye to see clearly. For almost a whole minute, Holden and I are totally silent. I hear slight mutterings from the family of four, but I can't make out any words. I'm too focused on the ocean, on examining every wave, every splash of water. I find seagulls bobbing on the surface and once the dark swirl of what I think is a sea lion moving around a formation of rocks. But no whales. I'm just about to hand the binoculars back to Holden when I see a puff of mist.

"There!" I point. "Ten o'clock." I watch the spot, waiting for the whale to show itself, to let its broad back break the surface of the water. But when it happens, it's not the rounded crest of the whale's back, it's the tail fin, all fin-shaped and perfect, like childhood me used to dream about.

Next to me, Holden's breath is hot in my ear. "I saw it," he says. "Wow. I think that's the second-most beautiful thing I've seen all day."

I snort. "Oh yeah?"

"Right behind the pecan pancakes I had for lunch."

"Ass," I whisper.

"What? First you had to be hotter than the Mona Lisa and now you want to be prettier than pancakes too? You've got a real problem with vanity, Embry Woods."

I bite back a smile. "You're right. I'm being unreasonable. Those pancakes were exceptionally sexy."

He pulls me into a hug. "Luckily for you, I like vain, unreasonable girls."

I press my head against his chest. "Seriously, Holden. This has been the most amazing day. Thank you."

Holden leans down and kisses me on the cheek. "You're welcome."

Warmth radiates through my body. For a few seconds, I think again about us being more than friends. The idea scares the hell out of me, but part of the reason I never thought about it is because I couldn't imagine betraying Julia like that, at least not until after she left for college. And yeah, I know it's stupid to be okay with betraying her privately and not publicly, but I wasn't okay with betraying her privately either. I just did it, and then I was too much of a coward to find a way back from that until it was literally a matter of life and death.

But now that I know Julia doesn't have romantic feelings for Holden, it feels less impossible that he and I could actually be together, once I talk to Luke, of course.

Holden drops me off at home around four p.m. He heads to the gas station, and Mom and I drive into Tillamook, where we get a large pizza from Upper Crust and a container of ice cream from the Tillamook Dairy.

We take our treats back to the house and prepare for our Sunday night sundae party. Mom splays the pizza out on the coffee table after giving Betsy a stern warning. I fetch a couple of doggie treats from the kitchen cabinet so the dog doesn't feel too left out. All three of us curl up in the living room and my mom starts the latest episode of Sexy Firefighting Models. This week, the fire lieutenants Zander and Gray (I'm still trying to figure out if those are their first names or last names) get into a fistfight at work over Alicia Ramos, one of the firehouse's paramedics. This complicates matters when both firefighters then have to work together to rescue a car that's slid half off a bridge and is in danger of plummeting into a freezing river. Ramos stands off to the side next to a gurney as Zander and Gray stabilize the car with ropes and pulleys, her long black hair cascading over her shoulders in a style I'm pretty sure most paramedics would find inconvenient for work.

"Who are you rooting for?" I ask Mom. "Team Zander or Team Gray?"

Mom clucks her tongue. "I'm rooting for Alicia. You know she wants to go to medical school, right? She doesn't have time for either of those guys."

"Good for her," I say. Even fictional people have more concrete goals for the future than I do.

After the TV shows ends, Mom puts in *Ladder 49*, which I'm pretty sure was not Betsy's movie of choice. Halfway though, my phone buzzes with a text.

I smile to myself as I reach for it. I don't know what I'm hoping for exactly. Maybe a sweet text from Holden telling me he's still thinking about me, or a coolly polite message from Julia saying she thinks we should talk. What I get is another message from Unknown, and this time they want me to steal a gun.

TWENTY-SIX

I STARE AT THE WORDS, unblinking.

Unknown: It's time for your next choice. Shouldn't be a tough one since you're so good under pressure.

Unknown: A. Steal the handgun from Katrina Jensen's glove compartment and leave it in the Pot Hole. Her car is in the Fintastic parking lot.

B. If you don't do this, I'll kill someone you love. And this time I promise you won't be around to save the day.

Unknown: You have 2 hours. Choose wisely.

I read the message again. Why does Unknown seem to create tasks for me that involve people I'm with or have been with recently? I was shopping with Julia when I got the message to steal her purse. And now, two days after confronting Katrina at Fintastic, I'm being told to steal her gun?

"Hon. You okay?" my mom asks. "You're white as a sheet."

"Huh?" I look up from the screen. "No, I'm fine. I just . . . need a little air. I think I'm going to take Betsy for a quick walk."

Mom frowns. "It's awfully dark outside. Be careful."

"I am. I mean, I will." I suck in a sharp breath of air. My lungs feel swollen, or maybe shriveled—whatever lungs do that makes it hard to breathe. Why the hell would Unknown want me to steal a gun? Is Julia right? Are they going to ask me to shoot someone? And who are they going to go after if I say no?

Mom pulls off the purple head wrap she wears around the house. "My hair is finally starting to grow back," she says proudly, running one hand over her scalp.

"That's . . ." My mind completely blanks out on the word I want. "Super," I finish. Mom gives me another strange look. I have to get out of here before I lose it.

I tuck my phone into my pocket and grab my jacket from where it's sitting on the back of the sofa. "Betsy," I call. "Want to go out?"

As far as getting a dog's attention, "Want to go out?" is second only to "Want a treat?" Betsy's collar jingles as she stands up from her bed and hurries across the living room. She skids to a stop in front of me and sits back on her haunches.

"Good girl." I grab the leash from a hook on the wall and attach it to her collar. "We'll be back," I tell my mom. Before she can even reply, I head out into the cold, letting the door slam shut behind me.

My heart beats three times for every step I take, and thanks to Betsy I'm practically running. I have to go to the cops now—there's no question. Stealing Julia's purse was one thing. I'm not breaking into any cars. I wouldn't even know how to. *But Holden would*, a little voice whispers. I don't care. I'm not messing around with any guns. Enough people have gotten hurt. There's no reason to believe Unknown won't try to kill someone even if I follow their instructions.

I pull out my phone and start to send Holden a message, but then I stop. Every time I told him I wanted to go to the police he tried to talk me out of it. He was right at first—neither of us knew whether the initial message was just a dumb prank. But I should have confessed everything instead of stealing Julia's purse. I need to figure everything out in my head before I bring Holden back into this. That way he won't be able to talk me out of it.

I try to figure out exactly what I'm going to say to the police as Betsy and I walk along the main street of town, past the post office, Tacos & Burgers, the ice-cream shop, and the Oregon Coast Café. The coffee shop looks so sad with the lights off, the tiny chalkboard that reads CLOSED hung on the door.

We keep walking. I watch dead leaves turn end over end as they tumble across the cobblestones. Ocean waves crash in the distance. A tang of salt hangs in the air.

We pause at the far end of the street. Betsy tugs hard on the leash. She wants to go down to the beach. She *thinks* she wants to go in the water, but that's only because she doesn't remember how freezing it is.

"All right, all right," I grumble as she tries to yank my arm out of its socket. We take the paved path from the parking lot down onto the sand. Betsy starts to run and I do my best to keep up with her. We make it all the way down to the cliff wall and then turn around and run back toward the parking lot. Betsy paws at something in the sand and suddenly starts to dig. Sand flies everywhere. "Hey, stop it!" I tell her.

She proudly unearths her treasure—a dead crab—and picks it up in her mouth.

"No, gross." I wrench the crab from her teeth and she turns her head out toward the water hopefully, like she thinks we're going to play a game of catch.

"Not today, friend." I fling the crab into the water but keep a tight hold on Betsy's leash. I tug her over to a big driftwood log set back from the water's edge. "Let's chill for a few minutes."

I plunk down on the log. Betsy lies down by my feet, her warm chin right on my boots. I lean over, rest my forearms on my thighs, rub my temples with my fingertips. "I just want this to be over," I mumble. But that's not true. I want to know who Unknown is—I want to understand why they're doing this to me. I just can't believe someone I know would ask me to steal a gun or threaten to kill someone.

But if it's not someone I know, then who could it be? The only other person who comes to mind is the mysterious guy in the baseball cap and brown leather jacket who's been lurking around town. But I don't even know who he is. Like my mom said, that could all have been a coincidence. Maybe that wasn't even him walking through my neighborhood that night. What motive would a total stranger have to hurt me?

The tears come from out of nowhere—quiet at first and then big racking sobs. So many tears for so many reasons, because of Luke and Holden and Julia and the fire. Because of Unknown and the things I've done. Because I am completely terrified at the thought of turning myself in, and crushed at the thought of having to implicate Holden too.

But I'm going to do it. I have to do it. No more excuses.

Pulling out my phone, I send Holden a quick text:

Me: Meet me tonight? Usual place?

Holden: I have to run a quick errand after work. 10 pm ok?

Me: Yeah.

Holden: You ok?

Me: No. I got another message. It's messed up.

Holden: Oh. Sorry. I'll be there at 10.

Me: See you then.

I start to slip my phone into my pocket, when I hear a noise behind me. Footsteps. Soft and slow, like someone is trying to sneak up on me. I glance down at Betsy. She's resting her chin on her paws, oblivious. Holding up my phone like I'm snapping a picture of the moon, I flip to reverse camera so I can see behind me. Sure enough, there's a man on the path down from the parking area. My blood chills as I realize he's got a pair of binoculars and they're trained on Betsy and me.

My heart stops when I focus in on what he's wearing—a baseball cap and a brown jacket.

TWENTY-SEVEN

I'M NOT SURE WHAT TO DO. Part of me wants to turn around and chase him, catch up with him and demand to know why he's been following me. The rest of me wants to pretend like I don't see him, sit quietly, hopefully lure him closer. If I can get a picture of him, I might be able to plug it into a Google image search and figure out who he is. Maybe he's some sort of insurance investigator for the Sea Cliff or something.

Betsy ends up making this decision for me. As the man inches closer to me on the path, she lifts up her head. I zoom in my camera, but I still can't make out any of his features. Betsy hops to all fours and starts barking. She vaults over the log and starts running in the direction of the path.

The man turns and flees. Betsy and I run after him.

"Wait!" I shout. "Who are you?"

The man turns the corner onto Main Street and disappears into an alley on the other side of the market. The next building is the Three Rocks Motel. He's probably staying there, but there's no way they're going to give me the names of their guests.

I start to turn away when I notice who's behind the check-in desk. It's my neighbor Cori Ernest. She's probably not going to help me, but it's worth a try.

I secure Betsy's leash to the metal pole of a no-parking sign and duck inside the lobby of the motel. Cori is sipping from a paper cup with a lid on it.

I stride up to her. "Hey, I need your help."

She looks up at me, one eyebrow arched in curiosity. "What's going on?"

"I'm looking for a man," I say. "Brown leather jacket, baseball cap. Is he staying here?"

"Hon, even if I knew what sort of coats the guests were wearing, which I don't, I wouldn't be able to give out that information."

"Please," I say. "I'm in trouble. I think that man has been following my mom and me. I just want to know his name. Can you do that much? I promise I won't tell anyone that you told me."

Cori's lips tighten into a hard line. "If someone has been

following you then you need to tell the police about it. Have them come down here and I'll give them all the information they want."

I start to protest, but then I realize she's not going to budge. It was probably stupid of me to even ask. The clock behind the check-in counter reads 9:40. I should bring Betsy home before I go meet Holden because it's not safe for her to walk across the slippery rocks by the Pot Hole.

"Okay. Sorry to bother you. Thanks anyway."

I leave the motel and let Betsy pull me into a jog down Main Street. We reduce our speed when we get to Highway W. I coil her leash around my palm a few times so she can't run out into the street if something scares her. The Christmas lights strung along the edge of the cemetery bathe the whole area in a ghostly hue. I try not to think about my mom ending up there if her cancer comes back. She believes that she beat it. I should have the same faith.

I slip back into the house with Betsy, closing the door softly behind me. I free the dog from her leash and pour her an extra bowl of food. Then I return to the beach. Halfway there, it starts raining again. I pick my way carefully along the rocks and pebbles, hurrying toward the Pot Hole, a few minutes behind schedule.

Out closer to the waves, I see two people walking along the sand. They're heading toward town. I squint, trying to see who it is, but thick clouds are blotting out most of the moonlight and I can't make out anything beyond their shadows.

As I approach the Pot Hole, I see Holden's silhouette in the opening to the cave. He gestures with one hand, almost like he's talking to someone. As I grow closer, I hear snippets of his voice—Holden *is* talking to someone—but I don't see a second figure. The other person must be just inside the opening to the Pot Hole. The wind steals away most of their words and I can't make out any responses. I hang back for a couple of minutes, waiting to see who he's talking to, but no one ever emerges from the cave.

Holden's eyes scan the beach and I freeze, thinking maybe he won't be able to pick out my form amid the driftwood and boulders, but I can almost feel it when he zeroes in on me. He waves and I clamber up the slippery rocks, all the while expecting to see someone besides him at the top. But no one else is here.

The wind whips Holden's hair back from his face. He hugs his arms across his chest. "Shit, it's cold. And my boots apparently leak."

I glance down. His boots are soaked. Behind him, water sloshes back and forth in the cave. It's not high enough for me to see it, but I can hear it. "Tide's coming in quick, huh?"

"Yep. Drier out here, believe it or not." He pulls the collar of his thick flannel shirt up to cover the back of his neck.

Lightning slashes across the sky, illuminating the swirling, choppy waters of the Pacific. White froth paints the tops of gray-green waves. Out in the distance, a buoy dances maniacally, its red caution light carving a scarlet streak into the darkness.

Most people describe the ocean with words like "beautiful" and "mesmerizing," but when you live in a coastal town, you're more likely to use words like "powerful" and "deadly."

Raindrops hammer against my cheeks like tiny nails. I lean back against the wall of the cliff and wrap my scarf around my mouth and nose. "Who were you talking to?" I ask, my voice slightly muffled by fabric. "I thought I saw you talking to someone a few minutes ago."

Holden cocks his head to the side. "You mean on the phone? My mom called to say that the cops had traced the location of where the email was sent from. Apparently someone sent it from a public computer in the community college lab. Detective Reyes is trying to find out if there's security camera footage from that day she can review."

"Do they think they'll have it?" My heart pounds in double time at the thought of finally knowing who's been blackmailing me.

"I don't know, but just that info should hopefully be enough to clear me. I stopped by my grandparents' house that day on the way to school. Their neighbor was over borrowing a tool from my granddad. They can tell the cops I couldn't have been at the community college at the time when the email was sent."

"That's awesome," I say. And then, "So you were on the phone? I thought someone else was here with you."

Holden shakes his head. "You're the only person I meet here, Embry."

I peer past him into the crevasse again. The water level rises each time another wave rolls in. If there was anyone in there, they've already escaped out the other side, onto Azure Beach. I guess I could have been mistaken about what I saw.

I mean, why would Holden lie to me? He wouldn't, unless he's involved somehow. But that's crazy. Holden has been my number one supporter throughout this whole mess. And he's just as guilty as I am. I've got to stop seeing threats everywhere I look. That's part of what got me into this mess in the first place—not trusting anyone, being too afraid to tell the truth.

"I think of this as our spot now," he continues. "You know, since we torched our other one."

I wince at the wording. "Our spot is a natural cave that's flooded half the day and always smells like weed." I hold up one arm to block a sudden barrage of cold rain from hitting my eyes. "How romantic."

"I can't help it that all the teenage pot smokers of Three

Rocks enjoy chasing each hit with some fresh ocean air."
He chuckles. "Speaking of which, you'll never guess who I
caught crawling out of here when I arrived."

"Who?"

"The littlest O'Riley."

"Frannie? No way. She does not smoke weed." But even as I
say this, I think back to her bloodshot eyes at school. I know
she's been fighting with her mom, but maybe that was only
part of it.

"I mean, she didn't stick around to talk, but she was with
Matt Sesti, that guy who works with you. Everyone knows
he's the guy you go to if you want weed but don't know anyone
old enough to buy it for you. If they weren't smoking, then I
don't want to know what they were doing in here together."

I frown. "Matt is like twenty-one. There's no way he'd be
messing around with a sixteen-year-old." I try to remember the shadows I saw walking along the beach. It could have
been Frannie and Matt. It could have been a lot of people.

"You're only seventeen. Didn't you tell me he hits on you
sometimes?"

"Yeah, but at least I'm *almost* eighteen," I say.

"Well, this particular hideout is really only good for a
couple of things. But who could blame the girl for smoking a little weed growing up in her family? It's probably a

high-stress environment." Holden coughs. "Anyway, you said you got another message?"

"Yeah. I wanted to show you in person." I hand him my phone, still thinking about Frannie, wondering what kind of issues she could be having with her mom that would cause her to turn to drugs.

"Jesus Christ," Holden says. "Why do they want you to steal someone's gun?"

"I don't know, but I'm going to the cops," I say. "Tonight. If you want, we can show this to your mom first, get her advice on what to do, whether we need lawyers or whatever."

"What about *your* mom?"

"She's already asleep, but I'll tell her everything tomorrow."

"You sure you wanna do this? We could both end up going to jail . . ."

"I know. I—I just can't take the chance. This person tried to kill Julia. If I don't go to the police and something happens to someone else, I will always wonder if I could have prevented it."

"But you did what they wanted with Julia. Maybe they knew she'd be okay and were just trying to scare you."

"Yeah, well. Mission accomplished."

Holden taps the screen of my phone. "You know, there's

still some time. I've filled Katrina's car up at the station before. I might be able to break into it. Then we could try to trap Unknown. Hide out by the Pot Hole and see who comes to get the gun."

A chill creeps up my spine. Once again, Holden is trying to talk me out of doing the right thing. He's probably just looking out for both of us, but what if he's not? What if there's a darker reason he doesn't want me to go to the cops? *Stop being paranoid, Embry.* I take in a deep breath and let it out.

"No. Absolutely not. Neither one of us is getting caught breaking into a car or stealing a gun. I'm done letting Unknown blackmail me," I say. "Besides, if we go to the police and explain how the email with the video and what happened to Julia are connected, maybe they'll figure out who Unknown is before they can try to hurt anyone else."

"I understand how you feel. I just wish there was some way to report this guy without confessing to a major crime . . ." Holden swipes through the messages again, his face contorting into a scowl. "Forget it. If it'll make you feel better, then I think you should make a police report."

I nod. Tears pool in my eyes as I consider the gravity of my decision. "I'm scared, Holden," I whisper. But then I think of my mom's words again. This is something I can control. I just have to be brave.

Holden pulls me in close and wraps his arms around me.

I can feel his heart beating in my ear. The slow and steady thumping calms me. "Me too," he says. "My mom is going to be so pissed at me. I have no idea how we're going to be able to pay for the damages. But whatever, we'll figure it out. We'll all figure it out . . . somehow. The important thing is that this guy doesn't get to hurt anyone else."

The rain has tapered off and the wind has died down, making it feel a little warmer than it was on the way here. Mist hangs in the air, giving the beach a ghostly shrouded look. I press my face against Holden's chest, drinking in the scent of laundry detergent, the dampness of his flannel shirt cool against my cheek. I start to let my eyes fall shut, but suddenly there's a flicker of movement. A shadow crosses my field of vision—a shadow from inside the Pot Hole.

Someone is watching us.

TWENTY-EIGHT

I BREAK AWAY FROM Holden's embrace and lunge for the opening in the cliff.

"Embry!" he shouts.

Fueled by adrenaline and the overwhelming need to confront Unknown, I practically fly through the hole and slide down the incline into the cave. Immediately I'm waist-deep in water.

"Embry? What are you doing? Are you—" The rest of Holden's words are stolen by the wind, but I'm sure they included something like "crazy" or "insane."

I am not those things, but I will be if I don't figure out who's tormenting me, and why. As my eyes begin to adjust to the darkness, there's movement in my peripheral vision.

I jerk my head just in time to see what I think is a wavering shadow ducking through the exit onto Azure Beach. I slosh through the water after him—or was it a her?

"Wait!" I shout. "I just want to talk to you."

"Embry!" I hear Holden drop down into the water behind me. "Come back. We're going to drown."

I register the fear in Holden's voice, but I don't understand it. He's being paranoid. The water isn't even up to my chest. I push forward. Just a couple more yards and I'll emerge out the other side of the cave, hopefully in time to catch a glimpse of whoever was spying on us.

There's a crashing sound as a particularly fierce wave hits the rocks. Then there's a rushing, a roaring, and I realize my mistake. The cave is filling with water—quickly. In a few seconds it'll be over my head.

"Shit," I mumble as I flail toward the opening onto Azure Beach. I lose my footing on a slippery rock and my head goes under. The shock of the icy water on my face steals away my breath. My eyes burn and I have to squeeze them closed and swim for what I think is the exit. I wonder where Holden is. Did he get out in time?

The current pushes my body toward the opening and spits me back out into the night. I fight for the surface and my head emerges from the waves. I forgot that Azure Beach is completely covered at high tide. I'm only about ten yards out from the shore, but right now the shore is just a slippery wall of rock.

Stars shine down between breaks in the thick gray storm clouds, providing only the faintest bit of light. Doing my best to tread water against the push and pull of the ocean, I suck in a huge breath of air and look around for Holden. I don't see him anywhere.

The current pulls me farther out to sea. My heavy winter clothes are starting to drag me toward the bottom. A wave crashes down on me. The icy water is everywhere now—my entire body is going numb.

"Holden!" I scream in exasperation, but it comes out like the bleat of a dying sheep. *Come on, Embry. You can't die here. I can't. My mom needs me. Focus on the things you can control . . . There's always something.* I grit my teeth as I kick off my heavy rain boots and shuck my way out of my jacket.

"Embry! Over here." Holden's voice sounds far away, like an echo of a video of a radio. Wisps of fog twist and twine around me like blindfolds. I can't swim toward him because I have no idea where he is.

"Holden," I croak. I fight to stay afloat, but I can't even tell if my arms and legs are moving. The fog that's swirling around me grows thicker. I imagine it penetrating my eyes and ears, clouding up my brain. Am I farther away from the shore now?

The waves toss me one way and then the other. Everything is twisting. Everything is slowing down. I'm not quite sure where the land is anymore. I'm not quite sure what my name is anymore.

"Embry!" Holden yells.

That's right. Embry. Like Ember, only different. Mom said she got the name from a Jehovah's Witness who came to our door once with his daughter. Her name was Embrie. Mom liked the sound, but liked the *y* better than the *ie*.

"Seal Rock," someone says.

Not someone—Holden. I struggle to remember what Seal Rock is. Another wave crashes over my head. Somehow, the water feels less cold. My eyelids are getting heavy. My whole body is like a big giant anchor, weighting, weighting me down. I need to let go of it and then I can float up into the clouds. I close my eyes. My body starts to sink. My mind flutters its wings and prepares for flight. But then my head collides with something jagged and hard.

My eyes flick open. "Seal Rock," I whisper.

Seal Rock is a long, angled rock at low tide. At high tide it's just a small shelf of limestone sticking up above the water. I grab onto the side of it, my fingers still numb and barely working.

Holden appears out of the fog, his hair a cascade of blackness against his pale skin. He's still got his boots and his heavy flannel, which hangs open, exposing the soaked Henley underneath. "Hang on." He reaches toward me. "Give me your hand."

It takes me a few seconds to peel my frozen fingers from the jagged stone. Holden tugs me—mostly deadweight, unable to help—from the frigid ocean and up onto the rock, where the even more frigid air rips through my wet clothes and freezes my skin.

Instinctively I curl into the fetal position.

"No, you gotta get up, Embry." Holden points across the jagged outcropping. "If we get to the other side of the rock, we can make it back to Azure Beach. But we gotta go now before the tide comes in the rest of the way."

"There's no beach," I say. "It's just a wall of rock."

"Yeah, but there's a trail. It starts at the far side of the cliff. We just have to climb up onto it."

"Is that all?" I choke out. The fog is growing thicker. Shapes form before my eyes. Triangles. Hearts. Tongues of fire. Burning hotels. An oval that reminds me of dog tags. Luke's dog tags. I curl tighter into a ball. "Maybe I deserve this," I whisper.

"Yeah, no. Fuck that," Holden says. "We're getting out of here." He grabs me under my armpits and lifts me to my feet. "Other side of the rock. Now."

It looks like an impossible journey, but my teeth are

chattering too hard to reply, so I let him half drag, half carry me to where there's a narrow finger of slippery rock formations leading halfway back to the shoreline.

"You want me to walk a balance beam right now?" I ask, my legs buckling at the thought. "I'll fall."

"You don't need to stand. You can crawl. Or get back in the water if you want. Just don't let go until you're ready to swim to the cliff."

Nodding, I lower myself to my knees. Slowly, I crawl my way back toward the shore. Waves crash around me. Raindrops batter my skin. The fog continues to taunt me with images. There's a book, like the book Julia made me. There's a tombstone, only I'm not sure who it's for.

At the edge of Seal Rock, Holden and I still have to swim about ten yards back to land, and then somehow lift ourselves about eight feet onto the bottom of the muddy trail that cuts back and forth up the side of Cape Azure.

"We're going to die," I tell Holden.

"No we're not. You were on the swim team. This is nothing. You can do it."

I plunge back into the icy water. Visions of my mother dance in my head as I flail toward the cliff. Just like I knew how her face would look if I got arrested, I also know how it would look if I drowned. Stroke. *I'm the reason my mom is alone.* Stroke. *I'm the reason my mom is poor.* Stroke. *If she didn't have me, she wouldn't have to work so hard. She could sleep better, eat better.* Stroke. *Maybe I'm the reason she got cancer.*

All those thoughts hitting me like bolts of lightning are enough to make me stop swimming, start sinking to the bottom. It's like all the pieces I've been hiding from myself are suddenly snapping into place. But then: *I can make it up to her. I can make things better for her, somehow, someday. But only if I live.* New pieces. New hope.

My fingers touch the slippery side of Cape Azure. I find a lip in the rock, wrap my hand around it, and look up at the trail. Holden appears beside me. "Now what?" I ask.

Holden hooks his foot into a crack in the cliff. He threads his fingers together and lifts them waist high. "Now I give you a boost."

I look at his hands, look above my head at the start of the trail. It's possible. "Then who gives you a boost?"

"Put your fucking foot in my hands before we both drown," Holden says.

I do it. He lifts me. I grip onto a tree that's growing out from the path and somehow crawl my way into a puddle of mud. Holden appears beside me a few seconds later.

I curl into a ball again. "S-s-sorry," I say, my teeth chattering. "I f-fucked up."

Holden laughs. "Yeah, you kinda did."

"I swear I saw somebody watching us from inside the Pot Hole."

"Were they wearing a wet suit and flippers?"

"It was just a sh-shadow, and then movement."

"Could it have been a seal?"

Seals don't generally come onto Three Rocks Beach, but I guess anything is possible. "I don't know. Maybe I'm going crazy."

"It's okay. Sanity is overrated." Holden brushes my wet hair back from my face. "Let's just get up this cliff so we can cut across the hill and get you home."

"Fuck," I say. Since I quit the swim team, my stamina has definitely dropped off. This is the kind of trail I would have struggled to complete when I was in top form. I can make it only a few steps before I have to stop and rest.

But then a blast of wind rattles through the trees and I realize my ears and nose are both totally numb. I blow into my hands to warm my nose, but there's nothing I can do for my ears.

"Fuh-freezing." I tug on my earlobes with my fingers, rub my hands back and forth across the tender skin.

"Me too. But you got this," Holden says. "Just keep moving. Just focus on how good it's going to feel to get into a nice warm bath."

"Oh God. Heaven." I plod up the trail in my waterlogged socks, trying not to focus on the fact that my feet are also starting to go numb.

Slowly, Holden and I ascend the cliff. I feel a momentary burst of relief when the top comes into view, but then I remember how much farther we still have to walk. All the way across to the Sea Cliff and then down Penguin Hill. Wait, not Penguin. What is the name? Shit. Why can't I remember it?

I stumble without warning, windmilling my arms to keep from falling on my face. My head is feeling cloudy again. I sink to my knees in the middle of the trail. "I just need to rest for a few minutes," I say. "I just need—"

I can't even finish the sentence. The dirt beneath the fabric of my wet jeans is dry, and compared to the water it feels so incredibly warm. I lower myself to the ground completely and sprawl out on the soil. I just need to sleep. I hear Holden saying something, but I can't make out the words. Whatever he's trying to tell me is going to have to wait. Just a little rest. Just a few minutes. Just a few . . .

TWENTY-NINE

December 24

I WAKE UP WARM BENEATH an electric blanket. Holden is sitting on the edge of the bed, a thin book closed around one of his hands. "Jesus Christ." He breathes a sigh of relief. "I was just about to call 911."

I rub my temples with my fingertips. "What happened?"

"You passed out at the top of the trail."

"I vaguely remember dropping to my knees in the dirt." I push up on my elbows and look around. "I'm at your apartment? How did I get here?"

"I carried you, mostly."

My eyes widen. Holden's not weak, but I'm five foot eight

and weigh about 120, and my waterlogged clothes probably added at least ten pounds.

"I see you," he says. "Trying to figure out how my scrawny ass got you here. You don't have to be a Captain America super-soldier to carry a girl. I do landscaping in the summer, remember. It builds up your strength."

Sitting up, I cover my chest with one hand as I glance around the small room. The floor is a mess of books. Some of them have ripped or missing covers. I bet Holden got them from the Goodwill in Tillamook. There's a desk here with more books and a handful of sketches scattered across the top of it—some of them are trees, some oceans, some just free-form designs. One corner of the floor is covered with a plastic drop cloth. An empty easel sits on it.

My eyes flick back to Holden, and to the book he's holding. "Were you reading?"

"I was reading to you actually."

"Reading what?"

"*The Metamorphosis.*"

"What's it about?"

"A traveling salesman who randomly wakes up one day as a cockroach. His family is grossed out by him, so they lock him in his room and eventually he dies."

"Uplifting." I swallow back a yawn. "Super-disappointed that didn't make it into my dreams."

He shrugs. "There's something about it I find soothing."

"Speaking of soothing, this blanket is pure heaven." I lie back down and pull the cover up to my chin. "Why am I wearing your boxer shorts?"

"I had to get you out of your wet clothes to start warming you, but I didn't want you to wake up and feel all exposed or whatever."

"Thanks." I peek under the covers again. "They're surprisingly comfortable. What time is it?"

"A little past four a.m.," Holden says.

"Holy shit!" My heart thrums in my chest. "I've been asleep for four hours?"

"More than three, anyway. It took a while to get home."

"I need to get to the police station." My brain is still foggy, and it takes me a few seconds to calculate how much time has passed since I got my latest message. Too long. Unknown could have already gone after someone else. Sliding out from beneath the covers, I haul myself to my feet. My knees start to buckle, and Holden has to grab me around the middle to keep me from face-planting on his bedroom floor.

"Whoa," he says. "Slow down. You're recovering from hypothermia, Embry. You might need to go to the hospital."

"That's not happening." Mom has health insurance for the two of us, but it has a high deductible and doesn't cover everything. I think of that stack of bills on the back of the couch. "I just need my clothes and I'll get out of your way."

"Oh. Um. We generally wash and dry stuff at my grandparents' house. There are washers and dryers in the basement of the building, but I didn't want to leave you alone long enough to go down there. I can run them down now or if you're in a hurry I can loan you some stuff of mine."

I nod. "If I could borrow stuff from you, that'd be great."

Holden rummages in his closet and comes back with a pair of sweatpants and a long-sleeved Henley. "I'd say you could borrow my coat, but the smell would probably kill you."

"It's only a couple blocks," I say. "This'll work."

Holden pulls a ball of white fabric out of his pocket. "And these."

"Dry socks. Oh my God," I say. "Thank you. My feet are still cold. I don't suppose you have a pair of shoes I could wear."

"What size are you?"

"Eight, but I don't care if they're too big. I just need them for the walk home."

"I think that's about what my mom wears. Hang on." Holden disappears and returns in a couple of minutes holding a pink-and-black pair of tennis shoes. "She's an eight and a half, and she won't care if you borrow these. You get dressed and I'll put your wet clothes in a plastic bag."

Holden shuts the door behind him and I quickly change,

trying not to notice how much the Henley smells like him. The pants are too long, and I have to roll the waistband a couple of times until the cuffs don't drag on the floor. The socks are longer and thicker than any socks I've ever worn, but they feel amazing on my feet and legs.

I take a moment to consider my reflection in the mirror on his dresser. My face is bright pink. I'm not sure if it's from being out in the cold or under the warm blanket or what. My hair is a tangled mess. I spend about thirty seconds trying to finger comb it before I give up. I squeeze the excess water from it and then just let it hang.

I duck out of the bedroom, half expecting Holden to be lurking right outside in the hallway, but he's in the living room.

"Before I forget." He hands me a Ziploc bag with my phone, the battery, and about fifteen small silica gel packets, the kind you get in vitamins and bottles of ibuprofen.

"My phone! How did you get it?"

"I was looking at it when you dived into the Pot Hole. I don't know if it'll ever work again, but give it a few hours and then put the battery back in and try to turn it on."

I shake the baggie. "Silica gel?"

"Yep, companies use it to soak up moisture. When it comes to phones, it's like rice, but better. And without the mess. I always save the packets because I use them to keep some of my tools from rusting during the rainy season."

"Thanks. I guess if it doesn't work I'm going to be without a phone for a while."

"Do you want me to give you a ride to the police station?"

"Would you?"

"Of course. They're going to need to get a statement from me anyway after you tell them the truth. Maybe they'll be willing to radio my mom and have her come in so she can take it."

I nod. It's just as depressing to think about Holden being blamed for the fire as it is to think about Mom and me. But seeing Julia so close to death the other day clarified things. I'm prepared to do whatever it takes to make sure no one else gets hurt. I just hope it's not too late.

A few minutes later, I hop onto the back of Holden's motor-cycle and we head to Tillamook. The ride reminds me of the ride to Lincoln City to get Plan B—two people who screwed up big-time and just want things to go back to the way they were.

Holden pulls the bike into a parking spot behind the police station. I dismount and unclip the chinstrap of my helmet. Above my head, clouds swirl. A few flakes of snow twist and flutter in the fluorescent parking lot lights.

"I can't remember the last time it snowed," Holden says.

He loops both helmets over one of the handlebars.

Normally snow is a magical thing to me, but right now I'm just exhausted—physically and mentally. I yawn. "I can't remember the last time I was awake this early."

"You ready to do this?" Holden studies me with his dark blue eyes.

"Nope," I say. "But I'm ready for this all to be over."

"Fair enough." He takes my hands in his and squeezes them gently. Bending close, he brushes his lips against mine. "Whatever happens, we're in this together."

"Together," I agree.

We stroll hand in hand across the parking lot and into the warm police station. Holden and I stride up to the window, where he asks the desk sergeant if his mom is around.

"Officer Hassler is out on patrol right now," the desk sergeant says. "She should be back to the station around six, unless she gets delayed on a call."

It's only an hour from now, but that feels like a lifetime. "This can't wait," I say. "We need to make a report."

The sergeant looks back and forth from Holden to me. "A report about what?"

I take in a deep breath. "Someone has been blackmailing me. I think they may have tried to kill one of my friends."

The sergeant's eyes widen slightly. He tells me to have a seat and that a uniformed officer named McKenna will be out to take my statement in a few minutes. I know just the guy he's talking about because Officer McKenna once stopped Julia for going fifty-five in a thirty-five when I was in the car with her, and she managed to flirt her way out of a ticket.

I take a seat in a hard plastic chair just inside the front door to the station. Holden paces back and forth with his hands jammed into his pockets. Officer McKenna strolls out into the lobby about ten minutes later, a laptop computer under his arm. He's put on a few pounds and grown a mustache since he stopped Julia last year, so now he looks a little like the overweight guy from *Mall Cop*. I fight the urge to flinch when he gives me a firm but sweaty handshake.

"Ms. Woods, is it?" he asks. "Follow me, please."

"Embry is fine," I say. "And Holden is coming too. He's also involved."

McKenna nods. "Hi, Holden. Come on back."

We follow Officer McKenna past a big open area with several desks to a narrow hallway at the back of the station. He unlocks a door that leads into a small room with a table and four chairs. I haven't even decided where to sit when another cop ducks his head in the door.

"Sorry to interrupt," he says. "But are you Embry Woods?"

"Yeah."

"Your mom is Claire Woods?"

"Yeah. Why?" My voice shakes. Next to me, Holden rests a hand on my lower back.

The officer glances at Holden. "I don't want to alarm you, but I need you to come with me."

"Too late," I say. "Just tell me what's going on. Holden can hear too."

"What is it, Hutchens?" McKenna says. "I was just getting ready to take a statement from her."

"Claire Woods is at Tillamook General. She's been shot."

THIRTY

MY HEAD GOES CLOUDY. Officer Hutchens reaches out and grabs me as I start to wobble. "Steady," he says. "Take a breath." He keeps talking, but I can't understand what he's saying. His words are soft and soothing, but they get scrambled up in my brain.

"She's alive?" I ask. *Please please please.*

"Yes," he says. "According to the dispatcher, the woman who owns the Shop-a-Lot was out for an early morning run and found your mom bleeding on the side of the road. She was responsive when the paramedics arrived. That's all I know. I can take you guys to the hospital in my car."

I nod rapidly. "Thank you."

"I'll meet you over there," Holden says, grabbing my hand.

"I'm here no matter what, okay?"

"Yeah." I squeeze his fingers. A tear falls, grazing the curve of my cheek on its way down to the floor. Wiping the remnants away, I follow Officer Hutchens out to his police cruiser. Outside, it's begun to snow, but I don't feel it. I don't feel the cold air. All I feel is the thudding of my heartbeat, my chest tightening like a drum as I once again imagine what life would be like without my mom.

Hutchens unlocks the passenger-side door for me. Under any other circumstances, I'd find the inside of a police car interesting, but right now everything is a blur. I fumble for the seat belt and struggle to click the buckle into place with my shaking hands.

Hutchens blasts the heat as he pulls away from the curb. When we reach the edge of the parking lot, he hits the siren and turns onto the street that leads to Tillamook General. He races around the corners almost as fast as Julia does in her car. I have a million questions, but Hutchens wouldn't be able to hear me over the siren, and my voice is stuck deep down in my throat anyway. I can hardly breathe. I just keep imagining my mom bleeding on the side of the road. I glance at the clock on the dash. It reads 5:38. Why was she even outside this early? Vaguely I remember her saying something about going to work early to finish up the holiday cookie orders.

I turn toward the side window and blink away tears. My

hands curl into fists, my fingernails digging crescent-moon impressions into the flesh of my palms. As snowflakes batter the glass, my fear morphs into something like rage.

Unknown has crossed a line.

When we arrive at the emergency room, a nurse tells us that my mother is still being evaluated and that it'll be a while before I can see her. I turn to Hutchens. "Do you know what happened? Do they have any idea who shot her?"

"My partner took a report from Ms. Morales, the owner of the Shop-a-Lot, but I haven't talked to her yet. I'll be the one interviewing your mother once she's able to answer some questions."

If she's able to answer some questions, he means.

The emergency room doors slide open and Holden steps into the waiting area, his dark hair flecked with snow. He hurries over to me. "Any news?"

"Not yet."

The three of us sit side by side in the ER waiting room. My phone is burning a hole in my purse. I want to grab it and send a million scathing texts to Unknown. The nerve of someone hurting my mom after all she's been through. What kind of monster does that? But then I remember my phone is in a Ziploc full of silica gel. There's no way it's dry already.

So instead I bottle up my rage and fear as I watch the small flat-screen TV mounted up on the wall. It's a cable news station reporting on international headlines. All the top stories are tragedies—a nuclear spill in Japan, an earthquake in Italy, a car bombing in Syria. I don't want to know about any of that. How does the world even keep going with so much pain and tragedy everywhere?

I glance over at Holden. He's staring intently at the TV. We might be similar in a lot of ways, but we're different too. Holden never hides from the truth. He takes in the violence without saying anything, his jaw tightening as the news anchor tallies up the casualties.

Hutchens taps one of his scuffed black shoes against the hospital's tiled floor. He flips through a nature magazine and then a brochure titled "You and Your Blood Sugar." Hopping up from his seat, he says, "I'm going to go see if we can get an update."

"I'll go with you," I say, trying to unsee the image of a beautiful Gothic church crumbling to pieces in the Italian quake.

We're quickly rebuffed by the registration clerk, who tells us that as soon as my mom's initial evaluation is done, a nurse or doctor will be out to retrieve me. "Try not to worry," she says. "If she weren't in stable condition, someone would have come to get you already."

"Super-reassuring." I sigh.

"Hang in there." Hutchens turns back toward our seats, slowing to check out a pair of brightly colored fish swimming in a glass aquarium.

"You don't have to stay with us," I tell him. "I appreciate the ride here, but Holden can take me home. You can go do whatever else you need to, if you want."

"Well, I've got to wait and take a statement from your mom, but I haven't eaten much this shift, so maybe I'll run down and see if the cafeteria is open."

"Take your time," I say.

"You want me to bring you anything?"

I shake my head violently. I don't remember the last time I ate, but I'm completely full—full of fear and anger and shame and regret. There's no room for anything else right now.

After Hutchens disappears, I walk a lap around the waiting area. There are five other people besides Holden and me. Three of them look like patients—an older woman with an oxygen canister, a man with a red nose clutching a box of Kleenex, and a girl a few years older than me who is sprawled out on her side across several chairs. She's wrapped in a plain white blanket that probably belongs to the hospital. I remember watching the nurses pile those blankets on top of my mom after her surgery.

I flip through the sparse selection of magazines, but there is absolutely nothing here that would interest anyone under the age of thirty. I end up plunking down in front of the fish tank, watching the bubbles from the filter push through the gravel on the bottom of the tank and float up through a small ceramic castle.

Holden comes to sit next to me. "This is a beautiful setup," he says. "And I think these are saltwater fish."

"They are." I'm not sure how I know. I just do.

"Embry Woods?" a sharp voice asks.

I hop up from my chair. "Yeah. That's me."

A woman wearing dark green scrubs with a name badge hooked to the breast pocket is standing in the doorway that leads from the waiting room to the ER. She gestures to me. Come on back, hon," she says, tucking a pen into the back of her silvery-gray bun. "I'm Margaret, your mom's nurse."

"I'll wait for you out here," Holden says. "Give you some time with your mom."

"Thanks." I shoot him a grateful look.

Margaret presses a plate on the wall and the wooden doors leading back into the emergency department open.

I follow her through them. "Is my mom going to be okay? You guys got all her records about her cancer treatments, right?"

"We do. It's all in the computer," Margaret says.

"So she's awake? How's she doing? The police couldn't even tell me where she got shot."

"She was shot one time, and the bullet passed cleanly through the leg. Honestly, it was more of a graze than an actual hit. A lot of blood, but no damage to muscles or other structures."

"So that's good, right?"

"Yes. It means she won't need surgery. She might not even need to spend the night, but I believe the doctors are planning to keep her for observation and watch for bleeding issues, due to some of the medications she's on." Margaret pushes open a door marked TRAUMA. There are three beds inside. Two of them are empty. Mom is in the one closest to the wall.

My lower lip starts trembling when I see that she's sitting up. Aside from looking a little tired, she looks fine—she's actually reading the same blood pressure pamphlet as Hutchens was reading out in the waiting room. Her right leg is wrapped in gauze from the knee to the middle of the shin.

"Brought you a visitor, Ms. Woods," Margaret says. "I'll be at the nurses' station doing some charting. Just give me a buzz on the call light if you need me."

"Embry!" Mom's face melts into a smile. She drops the pamphlet onto the bed. "Oh, don't cry, kiddo. I'm okay."

I try to swallow back a sob, but it's too late. Tears are streaming from my eyes. I hurry to her bedside. She scoots to one edge of the mattress so I can crawl in next to her. "I was so worried," I choke out.

"I'm sorry, honey. My battery died and they wouldn't let me borrow a phone until after they finished messing around with my leg. I tried to call you, but it went straight to voice mail. Is your battery dead too?"

"My phone got wet," I say. "Long story, but I think it'll be okay. What about you? Did you see who shot you?"

Mom shakes her head. "I don't even know what direction the bullet came from. It was so weird. I felt the pain in my leg before I even heard the gun go off. I didn't connect the two at first. The noise came from down on the beach and the wind muted it a little. I thought maybe a boat had run aground or something. Then when I realized I was bleeding, I couldn't call anyone because my phone was dead, so I was trying to walk home when I collapsed. And then Lourdes found me."

I wrap my arms around my mom's neck and rest my forehead on her shoulder. The tears are still streaming from my eyes. "God, I was so scared. I thought I was going to lose you." I lift my head and swipe at my face with one hand, but it's hopeless. The tears just keep coming.

"I'm fine, Emb," Mom says. "Really. The doctors say I might even be out of here in time to see you get honored at the holiday party tonight. You know, you'll be the first in our family to receive a Rocky Award."

"Ugh, Mom. Do I really have to go to that? Rewarding me for being dumb enough to go in a burning building would set a terrible example for kids."

Mom clucks her tongue. "You are so bad at taking a compliment. You totally get that from me, in case you were wondering. Your father always seemed to love having praise heaped on him."

Her words remind me of a different fear that's been niggling at the corners of my mind lately, ever since I got the Christmas card with money in it. "Speaking of my father," I say slowly. "Be honest. Why have you been pushing me to talk to him after all these years?"

"Because he's your dad and he seems to be showing a real interest in getting to know you."

"Now? When I'm almost eighteen?"

"Well, he did sign away his rights. He probably feels like now he can approach you without worrying about how I'll respond."

"What a hero." I scoff. "What if I don't believe you? What if I think you're worried about your cancer coming back? You're trying to get me to talk to him so that I won't be all alone in case something happens to you, aren't you?"

My mom's expression softens. She reaches out for my hand. "Well, I'd be lying if I said that hadn't crossed my mind, sure."

"Then you should have told me that." I huff. "Stop keeping things from me because you're trying to protect me. Trust me, all it does is make things worse."

"You're right," Mom says. "So far all my scans are clean, but my oncologist was realistic about the chances of the cancer having spread, or the chances of developing a different cancer someday. I feel good—hopeful even—but my number one concern is to make sure that no matter what happens, you'll be taken care of."

I sniff. "That's funny."

"What's funny about it?"

"My number one concern is that *you'll* be taken care of."

"It's not your job to take care of me," Mom says sternly.

"Agree to disagree," I reply.

Mom wraps me in a hug. "I didn't mean to keep stuff from you. I just didn't want you to worry. And in fairness to your dad, he has contacted me repeatedly, asking if I thought you'd be willing to see him. And he asked my permission before sending you the card and money."

"Okay. I'll think about talking to him. And I need to come clean with you too. I've also been keeping secrets, and I'm afraid—" My voice cracks. "I'm afraid one of them might be the reason you got shot."

"What? Oh, Embry, this wasn't your fault. It was probably just a stray bullet from stupid kids trying to shoot seagulls or something."

I shake my head. Suddenly, I'm crying again. The weight of everything comes crashing down on me. "I'm sorry I didn't tell you, but I've been being blackmailed. The messages threatened to hurt someone I love, so I was planning to go to the police last night, but then things got kind of messed up and I didn't make it there until this morning. And that's when I found out you were here."

"Blackmailed?" Mom asks. "Honey, what are you talking about?"

Before I can answer, there's a knock on the door and Officer Hutchens enters. "Mrs. Woods?" he asks.

"Ms. Woods," my mom corrects.

I look back and forth between my mom and the police officer, both frustrated and relieved by the interruption. I wipe hurriedly at my eyes.

Hutchens slides a chair up near the bed and takes a seat so he's eye level with my mom. He clears his throat. "I'm Officer Alan Hutchens from the Tillamook County Sheriff's Department. I've been assigned to your case. We've got a team combing the beach for any evidence of the gun or shooter, but we'd like to get a statement from you on anything you might have seen."

"Sure," Mom says. "I don't know how helpful I'm going to be, though. I didn't see much."

Hutchens nods. "We'll be talking to everyone who lives or works in that area to inquire about whether they saw anything."

"I'll let you guys talk." I swallow back a yawn. "I'm going to go track down a cup of coffee."

"Okay," Mom says. "We'll probably only need a few minutes."

I return to the waiting room right as Holden comes back from the cafeteria, a coffee in each hand.

"Thought you might need a little pick-me-up." He holds out a paper cup, a couple of sugars and creamers balanced on the lid.

"Thanks. It's like you read my mind."

"Well, I know you haven't had much sleep." Holden yawns. He's had even less sleep than I have.

I sink down in the same chair as before and add the sugar and creamer, swishing the cup back and forth a couple of times to mix everything up. I take a tentative sip, waiting to see how the coffee will mix with the emotions swirling inside me. My stomach is doing that shoes-in-a-clothes-dryer thing again, and the last thing I want to do is vomit in the middle of the ER waiting room.

"So how's your mom?" Holden sips his own coffee.

"She's doing okay. The bullet passed straight through her leg, so she didn't need surgery. The nurse said it was more of a graze."

"Well, that's a relief. Did she see anything?"

"No. It was still dark and she thinks the shot came from down on the beach and you know how pitch-black that gets. Officer Hutchens is getting her statement right now."

Holden's phone buzzes in his pocket. He digs it out and glances at the display. He taps at the screen. "Hello?" He pauses. "I see. Awesome. Do you know when?" He hops up and paces back and forth across the tiled floor. "Well, I'm glad this will be over soon. Thanks for keeping me posted." He hangs up the phone and turns to me. "That was Detective Alina Reyes from the Tillamook County Sheriff's Department."

"And?"

"Apparently the computer lab has a camera at the front of the room that ought to give us a clear view of whoever sent the email. They're working on getting security footage from Tillamook Bay right now. Once they get it they're going to have me come in and watch it, see if I recognize anyone." He bends down and takes my hands in his. "Embry, this is almost over. Once they have that video footage we should be able to identify Unknown."

THIRTY-ONE

"HOLDEN, THAT'S AMAZING. WE'RE SO close! How long until the cops have the security footage?" I ask.

"Sometime today, she said. Or the day after Christmas at the latest."

"I hope it's today." I slump back in my chair and exhale a sigh of relief. "I just need for this to be over. I want this psycho locked up where they can't hurt anyone else."

"Does that mean you want to wait until the police get the footage to talk to them?" Holden asks, sitting next to me again.

"We might as well." I lower my voice. "But I still want to tell the truth. Unknown has done some terrible things, but they didn't cause the fire. I need to take responsibility."

Holden nods. "*We* need to take responsibility."

When Officer Hutchens finishes talking to my mom, I hop up from my seat and stride toward the ER doors. As long as her nurse stays out of the room, I'm planning to take up right where we left off in our conversation. Maybe there are clauses in the law that protect a person's business from being seized in a lawsuit. Maybe we can file for bankruptcy and not lose our house. I don't know enough about legal stuff to know what's possible, but what I do know is that I should have told my mom the truth from the start.

But when I get back to the trauma area, my mom is curled on her side, her eyelids drooping. She yawns. "I think they gave me some really good drugs," she murmurs.

Figures. It's like the whole world is conspiring against me doing the right thing. "Do you want me to let you rest?" I ask. "I guess we can talk later."

"Would you mind? I forgot what we were talking about, but I feel like it was important." She furrows her brow.

I sigh inwardly. I don't know if it's fatigue or the pain meds she's getting, but she's in no condition to have a serious conversation. "It was no big deal," I say. "I'll let you get some sleep."

"You should go home and get some sleep too," Mom says.

"I don't want to leave you," I say. "Maybe I can nap out in the waiting area."

"Someone needs to be there to take care of Betsy," she says. "I'll be fine here. You can come get me later or tomorrow." She frowns. "I'm going to need you to call a few people who ordered Christmas cookies and let them know I'm not going to be able to fill their orders. There are some last-minute orders that I didn't get finished."

As much as I don't want to leave my mom's side, I also don't want to alienate any of the café's customers. We can't afford to lose them. "I can finish the orders," I say. "I think you've got Matt and Kendra working and it probably won't be busy except for people picking up cookies, so I can go in and knock them out in a few hours."

"You're a lifesaver." Mom yawns again.

I nod woodenly, even though it's not true. "I'd better go let Betsy out like you said." At least I can be a carpet saver.

"I'll call you once I know when they're going to release me." Mom reclines back on her pillow. "Sorry, my eyelids feel like anvils all of a sudden."

"It's okay. Get some rest." I head for the door to the trauma bay. I pause at the threshold and turn back for a second. "I love you, Mom," I say.

But she's already asleep.

Holden takes me home on the motorcycle and follows me inside the house. I'm still worn out from my near drowning and brush with hypothermia, and I don't even know how he's functioning since he hasn't had any sleep at all.

I let Betsy out, and the two of us stand in the kitchen and watch her through the back window. After we let her back in, Holden says, "Come on, you. Let's get some rest." He tugs me toward my bedroom.

I shake my head. "I have to go to the café. I told Mom I would knock out some last-minute cookie orders."

"Fine. But it's not even open yet. You have time to sleep for a couple hours. I'll wake you at ten."

"Okay." My face feels tight from my swim in the ocean, and my hair is twisted into a wet bun. I should take a shower and try to untangle it, but I'm just too tired.

I follow Holden back to my room and crawl into my bed. He slides under the covers next to me. I rest my head on his chest and wrap one arm across his slender waist. He caresses my back gently, his fingers slipping beneath my shirt to my bare skin beneath.

Even though I'm exhausted, a wave of pleasure rises up from his touch. It seems wrong to feel good right now, but at the same time, I could really use a break from reality. Maybe I can't fix things, but I can escape them, at least for a little while. I press myself tighter against Holden, will his fingers to keep exploring my flesh.

With one hand, he tilts my chin upward so we're looking at each other. His eyes are like the ocean during a storm. I reach up to trace the bones of his face with my fingertips. He brushes his lips against mine. Softness. Heat. The hellish morning starts to fade away as Holden's mouth finds mine again.

I arch against his body and turn my head to expose more of my neck. I want this—I want him—so much. But then my eyes land on my nightstand, on the Shutterfly book Julia made for me. My body goes tense. How can I do this when so many people have been hurt? How can I even think about doing this? It's not right.

"What is it?" Holden murmurs into my ear. "What's wrong?"

"Do you ever wonder if we're bad for each other?" I blurt out.

"Why? Because our sex literally burned down a building? It was an accident, Embry. When are you going to stop blaming yourself?"

"It wasn't just an accident. We were trespassing. We were drinking illegally. We could both go to jail."

"We could. But none of that affects how we feel about each other. Nothing has changed, except now we can actually be together. Now I can finally tell you that I lo—"

"Stop." I slide out from beneath him, my whole body shaking. "How can you say nothing has changed? We almost killed someone. You were being investigated for child pornography. A deranged stalker is threatening the people I love. You could have been seriously hurt when we went back to the Sea Cliff. My mom is in the hospital." I sit up in bed. "And none of those things would have happened if we'd just stayed away from each other."

Holden rakes his hands through his hair. "Avoiding risks and locking yourself away from people isn't the answer. Haven't you figured that out yet?"

I wince. Maybe he's right. Maybe I'm not pushing him away because he's bad for me. Maybe I'm pushing him away because I'm scared of what might happen if he stays. He almost said something that would've changed everything. I still haven't figured out if what I'm feeling for Holden is love, but hearing him say it isn't going to help me. It's just going to add more pressure.

"I don't know if I can handle any additional risks right this second," I say.

"Okay," Holden says slowly. "So then do you want me to go home?"

"No," I say, "but I can't let myself get lost in you while Unknown is still out there."

"Fair enough."

"I'm worried that if Unknown finds out my mom is okay, they'll go after someone else."

"Well, your mom is protected right now, and Julia is

probably with her parents. And I can handle it if this asshole comes after me. But I guess Luke's back in town now, right? Have you told him about any of this?"

"What?" My body folds in on itself. Hearing Luke's name from Holden's lips cuts like a knife. I still haven't gotten a response to my breakup email. "As far as I know, he's still in Afghanistan. Why would you say he's back in town?"

"I'm pretty sure I saw his car when I was working at the gas station yesterday."

"And you didn't mention it until *now*?" Luke drives a red Mitsubishi convertible with oversized tires and the vanity plate ORILEY4. I don't know jack about cars and even I would recognize it, so if Holden says he spotted it then he probably did.

Holden shrugs. "I was worried about us getting arrested. And then it slipped my mind when we almost drowned and then found out your mom had been shot."

"Shit, Holden!" I almost screech. "If he's here, I need to warn him. He might be Unknown's next target." I dig the Ziploc bag with the silica gel packets out of my purse. I slide the battery back in and the screen lights up. I send Luke a quick text.

Me: Hey, if you're back in Three Rocks, please call me. It's important. You might be in danger.

I watch the screen for about thirty seconds and then set

my phone on my nightstand. "If Luke's really back here, why wouldn't he have already called me?"

"Well, you did break up with him in an email, right?"

"Yeah, but it was a good letter. Honest. Apologetic. If he had read it, I know he would have called me. I'm almost positive . . ."

"Maybe you don't know Luke as well as you think you do," Holden says.

I bite my lip. "What are you trying to say—that he could be Unknown? As in Luke shot my mom? Hurt Julia? No. No way."

But then I think back to the times I saw Luke get angry at a car for cutting him off, or depressed when one of his sports teams lost. If he somehow found out I was hooking up with Holden before I wrote him that email, could it have made him snap to a degree where he would go after innocent people just to hurt me? It doesn't seem possible, but I know that sometimes combat changes people. Also, Holden said he saw Frannie buying weed, and that never seemed possible to me either.

I decide to text Frannie too.

Me: Odd question, but Luke didn't figure out a way to come home after all, did he? A friend thought they saw his car in town. Is he still overseas?

I wait a few minutes, but she doesn't reply either. "I should go by the O'Riley house, just to see if Luke's really back in town. Make sure he's okay."

"They're probably all still asleep," Holden says. "Like you should be. Luke's a big boy. He can take care of himself. Let's rest for a couple of hours. Maybe by the time we wake up he'll have texted you back. Maybe the cops will also have the security footage."

"I guess you're right," I say. "But there's no way Luke is Unknown. He would never hurt me like that. Never."

I'm not sure who I'm trying to convince—Holden or myself.

THIRTY-TWO

TRUE TO HIS WORD, Holden wakes me up right at ten. The first thing I do is check my phone. There's still no reply from Luke or Frannie. I call my mom to check on her, but she doesn't answer. I call the nurses' station, and the nurse assigned to her tells me that she's napping right now but she's doing fine.

I head into the coffee shop, passing the area where my mom was shot on the way. The police didn't want to block traffic on Main Street, but they've strung caution tape along the shoulder of the road and several yards out into the grass. I wonder if they found any evidence, if they have any idea who the shooter might have been. Hopefully when they get that camera footage from the community college everything will fall into place.

Matt and Kendra are working at the café. They've both heard about my mom going to the ER and ply me with questions about what happened. I tell them she's okay, but that the police don't have much information yet. Then I get to work on furiously baking, frosting, and boxing up the rest of the cookie orders.

Around noon, Matt asks me if I'll cover the back for a few minutes so he can go out for a smoke.

"Sure," I say. I still feel a little bad about snapping on him the last time he asked me out. He grabs his coat and heads out the back door, to the delivery area where he and a couple others on the staff sometimes smoke. As the door starts to fall shut, I notice there's a girl out there waiting for him. *Good*, I think. And then she turns and I catch a glimpse of her face. It's Julia.

My heart accelerates in my chest. What is Julia doing with Matt?

Kendra calls back an order for two Raymond Carvers, and I quickly lay out sourdough bread and top it with sliced roast beef, Swiss cheese, and spicy brown mustard. I put the sandwiches on the panini press to toast. Then I scurry to the back of the coffee shop and press my ear to the door. But it's a metal door and I can't hear anything through it. Cutting into the storeroom, I stand on a small step stool and peek out of a smudgy window close to the ceiling. The glass is thinner and I can hear snatches of conversation. It sounds like they're arguing. "You said you'd have it by tonight," she says.

"I said maybe. You didn't pay for expedited shipping."

Julia opens her purse and pulls out a small wad of bills. "Here."

Matt pockets the money. "I'll try, but this ain't Amazon." He drops his cigarette butt to the asphalt and grinds it out under his boot. He turns back toward the door to the coffee shop.

I hop down from the step stool and hurry back to the kitchen area, plating up the Raymond Carver sandwiches and garnishing them with pickle spears. I hand them through a pass-through window to Kendra, who looks at me a little strangely.

"Are you burning cookies?" she asks.

"Shit." I completely forgot I had two pans of cookies in the oven before Matt went on his break. I pull open the oven doors, and the smell of burned cookies fills the kitchen.

"Gross." Matt rounds the corner into the prep area, reeking of cigarette smoke. "Can't you do two things at one time without fucking one of them up?"

Ignoring his insult, I throw the burned cookies in the trash and pull the bag out of the can. "Hey, did I see Julia Worthington out there with you?" I ask.

"Maybe. You jealous?"

"Hardly." I scoff. "It looked like you guys were arguing. What was that about?"

"Relax, Woods, I'm not harassing your little friends. We were talking business."

"What kind of business?" I tie a loose knot in the top of the trash bag.

He clears his throat. "I don't ask you about *your* business, now do I?"

"Stay away from Julia," I say. "And don't *conduct business* out of my mom's coffee shop. This is the only thing she has. If someone gets caught with drugs here, she could get in trouble."

"I'm not dealing drugs here."

"I've heard otherwise," I say, my voice laced with scorn.

"Well, you've heard wrong," Matt says. "If you must know, I sold your friend some diet pills, but not anything illegal. You can buy them over the internet. She was just worried that her parents might snoop through her mail if she ordered them herself."

I swear under my breath. Julia and her obsession with looking perfect in her New Year's Eve dress. I hope she's not taking some kind of toxic herbs from some shady website. How can someone so smart be so dumb about certain things? I guess we've all got problems.

"What about Frannie O'Riley?" I ask. "Someone told me they saw the two of you together."

Matt smirks. "If she's buying anything from me, I assure you it's not here at the café."

"She's a good kid," I say. "You shouldn't be selling her anything."

Matt shrugs. "I'm in no position to judge." He turns his attention to Kendra as she calls back an order for two more sandwiches. I head to the back with the trash bag.

I hate the thought of Frannie using drugs, but I know enough about human nature to know that telling someone not to do something will just make most people want to do it more. Still, I'm going to ask her about it the next time I see her. If she gets caught with drugs, it could end up on her permanent record, which could mess up her whole future.

I don't want her to feel the way I do right now, like I made a mistake I'm going to pay for the rest of my life.

Thinking about Frannie makes me wonder about Luke again. Holden had to be mistaken about seeing his car. There's no way Luke would come home and not tell me. I dump the burned cookies in the Dumpster and then check my phone. Sure enough, Frannie has replied.

Frannie: He's not here. I drove his car a couple of times with my dad. I just got my permit.

That makes sense. I send Holden a quick text saying that

he probably saw Frannie driving Luke's car and then start remaking the cookies I just burned.

By one-thirty, I've got all the cookies frosted and just need to box them up.

I tell Matt I'm going on break and make myself a Sally Struthers—three types of locally produced Tillamook cheese on fresh-baked Texas toast. He watches me fix the sandwich but doesn't say anything. When the cheese is melted and the outside of the bread is golden brown, I slide it onto a plate and get myself a cup of water to go with it. I take a seat at an empty table out front.

After I finish eating, I box up the last few orders and call the customers to let them know their cookies are ready for pickup. I start cleaning up the back while Kendra handles a few more walk-in customers and rings out the people who arrive for their cookies. At three-thirty, I give my mom a call and let her know that all the orders are out except for one.

"You're the best, Emb," she says. "Literally." And then, after a moment, "The doctors said the bleeding stopped and I can take oral antibiotics, so I can go home whenever you're able to come pick me up. Have you thought about what you're going to wear tonight?"

"Oh, Mom. Forget the dumb holiday party. I would much rather just have a quiet Christmas Eve with you."

"But I assured the mayor you'd be there. It would be rude to stand him up."

"He's just an old retired guy who plays mayor for free. He won't care."

"We're going," Mom says. "We can sneak out before the nativity play, if you want, but we can't skip you being honored."

"The play is the best part," I mumble, thinking about how Frannie said her mom was trying to recruit an infant from Tillamook to play Baby Jesus. "Fine. I'll pick you up at like five-fifteen. I think I'm going to let Matt and Kendra go home. It's totally dead in here right now. I'll hang out until this last cookie order is picked up."

"Good idea," Mom says. "I'm sure they both have places they'd rather be on Christmas Eve. No need for them to stay until close if you're sure you don't need either one of them."

I hang up the phone and give Matt and Kendra the good news.

"Are you sure you don't mind staying by yourself?" Kendra nibbles at the end of one of her manicured nails. "My mom doesn't get off at the dairy until six, so I can stay if you need."

"It's fine," I say. "Go home and start celebrating early."

Matt and Kendra quickly finish their closing duties and grab their stuff from the back.

"Remember what I said," I mutter as Matt heads for the

door, his car keys dangling from his hand.

"Mellow out, Woods. It's Christmas," he says. "Try to have a little fun, okay? You're like seventeen going on seventy."

"Whatever. Drive safe." The last thing I want is for anyone else I know to end up in the Tillamook ER.

"Happy holidays!" Kendra gives me a hug and then ducks out into the street, the bells above her head jingling as the door swings shut.

I finish cleaning up the kitchen, running my dirty dishes through the dish machine and wiping down the counters. The door jingles again and I figure it's probably my last cookie customer. I head out front to find an older couple standing at the counter. I've seen them around before—I think they moved into a house on Julia's street earlier this year.

"We're here to pick up our holiday cookies," the woman says. "The name is Kriss."

I put their box of cookies into a paper bag with handles. The man orders a hot chocolate to go. I mix steamed milk and melted dark chocolate in a cup and top the drink with a generous amount of whipped cream. He leaves me a five-dollar tip.

As the man and his wife head back out into the cold, my phone buzzes in the pocket of my apron. I pull it out. There's a text.

Unknown: You should have done what I asked you to do.

Now someone is dead and it's your fault.

You wish, I think, saying a silent thank-you prayer just in case God is listening. I start to shove my phone back into my purse, but then I stop. Maybe if I can get Unknown talking they'll slip up and say something I can use to identify them.

Me: I hate to break it to you, but Julia is fine and so is my mom. You're not very good at killing people.

Unknown: I'm not talking about Julia or your mom.

Before I can reply, my phone buzzes again. Another message. This one includes an image—a picture of military dog tags with blood smeared on them.

My hand shakes so badly that the phone slips from my grasp and clatters to the floor. This can't be what I think it is. I scoop up the phone and enlarge the picture until I can read the name on the small metal plates: Lucas O'Riley.

"No," I whisper. "Not possible." *It's fake it's fake it has to be fake.* Unknown can't possibly have gotten to Luke. Frannie just told me he's still in Afghanistan. He's thousands of miles away. Whoever this is, they're just messing with me.

I flip over to my address book and call Luke. He doesn't answer. I hang up and try Frannie. She doesn't answer either. I try her a second time. *Come on, goddamnit.* Someone needs to pick up.

On the third try, Frannie answers.

"Embry?" Her voice is wavering, uncertain, like for some

reason she thinks someone else might be calling her from my phone.

"Yeah, it's me. Sorry for all the calls, but I need you to tell me that Luke's okay."

"I. Wait. What? The army people just showed up. How could you possibly have heard already?" Her voice breaks into pieces, and I realize she wasn't uncertain when she said my name—she was distraught.

"Heard what, Fran? He's fine, right?" I say hoarsely. "I mean, maybe you haven't talked to him, but that's because he's been on a mission or something. It doesn't mean anything is wrong, does it? You would know if something . . . had happened."

"Embry," Frannie says, "I don't want to lie to you, but my mom said not to tell anyone, not on Christmas Eve. She said to wait until after the holidays, until we had all the information—"

"Information about what?" I am almost yelling now.

"It's like the most horrible thing ever and if I don't tell you I'm afraid you're going to find out some other way and—" Frannie gasps for breath. "But I don't want you to feel the way I feel right now because I don't even know what I'm going to do and—"

"Slow down, Fran," I say. "Just tell me. What happened?"

"He's gone," she whispers. "Luke is dead."

THIRTY-THREE

I RAISE A HAND to my chest. "When? How?"

Frannie sucks in a sharp breath. "I don't know the details yet. There's someone from the army talking to my parents right now, but they kicked me out of the room and . . ." Her words disintegrate into sobbing.

Tears well in my eyes. It has to be a mistake. Surely Unknown couldn't get to Luke stationed halfway across the world. Unless of course he really *did* come home to surprise everyone like Holden thought.

"Are you absolutely sure about what you heard? There's no way you misunderstood?" My brain can't process the idea that Lucas O'Riley, town hero, army medic, boy who offered to marry me just so my mom and I could have an easier life, is dead.

"Embry, they brought my parents a folded flag."

I swallow back a mouthful of bile as I sink into a chair to keep from collapsing. The clock on the wall ticks like thunder. The inside of the café goes a little blurry.

"Embry? You there?"

"Sorry. I'm here. I'm just in shock. Look, can I come over? I'm at work, but I can close up early. No one is here anyway."

"I don't know." Frannie sniffles. "My family is going to need time to deal with the news. I'm not sure coming by tonight is a good idea."

"Oh, okay." My legs are trembling now too. My whole body is basically shaking. I squeeze my eyes shut and open them. Still here. I bite down hard on my lower lip. Nope, not a dream.

"I'll call you once I have more information. In the meantime, please keep this between us. My parents aren't going to inform the town until after Christmas. They don't want to put a damper on anyone's holidays."

"Yeah, sure." I taste salt. I must have bit my lip so hard I drew blood. "Call me anytime, day or night. For anything," I tack on.

She sniffles again. "Thanks, Embry."

"I love you, okay? I'll be thinking of you."

"Yeah. Same." Frannie hangs up and I stare at the screen of my phone for a few minutes. I always knew when Luke went into the military there was a chance he could die, but I never really thought it would happen, especially not now. I flip the OPEN sign to CLOSED on the coffee shop door and return to my seat.

My stomach is roiling and my chest aches. I bend over, rest my head on the table, and let the tears come. They're silent at first—tears of shock—but as the minutes pass they go from shock to grief to a hot and ugly anger. Unknown did this, somehow, for some fucked-up reason that I still don't understand.

My heart feels like it's being squeezed by a boa constrictor. I want to lash out, hurt something. I grab my phone and rattle off a text:

Me: How could you? Julia, my mom, and now Luke? Why would you go after them? They are some of the best people I know.

Unknown: And yet, you lied to all of them, didn't you?

I don't respond right away. I might not technically have lied, but I definitely hid the truth.

Unknown: I told you someone had to die.

Me: But why?

Unknown: So you would realize actions have consequences.

Me: But why Luke? How did you even get to him?

I'm praying the answer won't be sufficient. Frannie has been acting weird lately. If she's really buying drugs from Matt, then maybe she's wrong about this. Maybe it's all a horrible misunderstanding.

Unknown: I can get to everyone.

"Son of a bitch." I pound my fist on the tabletop. A dull pain arcs through my arms. I pound the wood again and again. I imagine sitting here until my hands are bloodied and the table is a pile of shrapnel.

Unknown: Stop acting like a child. This isn't over.

Gaping at the screen, I leap up from my chair and rip open the door to the coffee shop. The street is empty except for an older couple ducking out of the motel next to the market. They give me a strange look before hurrying down the sidewalk. I can only imagine what I look like right now.

Returning to my phone, I type: You can see me?

Unknown: Maybe. Or maybe I just know you.

Me: Well know this. It IS over. I refuse to play anymore. You win, for now. But the cops will find you eventually.

Unknown: This isn't a game. Games are fun. You think this has been fun for me? This is payback. Your choices hurt people. And we're not done.

Me: Fuck you. We're finished.

Unknown: We're finished when I say we're finished. You think I can't get to your mom or your friends before the police get to me? Willing to bet their lives on that?

Me: Why? Just stop. Luke is dead. Why isn't that enough for you?

Unknown: Because you haven't suffered enough.

I beg to fucking differ. Tears are raining down both of my cheeks, and I don't even bother to wipe them away. I lost my best friend, almost lost my mom. Now Luke is gone because some psycho has a vendetta against me and nothing will ever feel okay again.

Me: I've suffered plenty. I'm going to tell the police everything. I'm going to help them track you down. You're going to pay for what you did.

There's a long pause. I hope it's because Unknown is starting to realize their time is running out, that I'm serious about the cops closing in on them.

Unknown: You're really going to tell the truth?

Me: Yep. I can't wait. In fact, maybe I won't wait. Maybe I'll tell the whole town tonight at the Christmas Eve party.

Unknown: You don't have the guts.

Me: You don't know me as well as you think you do.

Unknown: Maybe I don't. I dare you. Go to the party and

stand in front of the town and tell them what you did that night.

Unknown: If you tell them everything, then I'll turn myself in.

Me: Why would you do that?

Unknown: Because I need for this to be over too.

Me: Why should I believe you?

Unknown: Because I haven't lied to you yet, have I?

Me: You tricked me into putting my best friend in danger. I did what you wanted and you tried to kill her anyway.

Unknown: Frustrating, isn't it? The feeling that no matter what you do, someone is going to get hurt.

I don't reply right away. It has been frustrating. Unknown has given me impossible choices, or at least that's what I thought, anyway. But the truth is, there's been one right choice the whole time—the choice to confess everything about what happened at the Sea Cliff, to take responsibility, to tell the truth. I didn't want to do that because it would hurt my mom and Holden and Julia and sure, it would hurt me too. But that doesn't mean it wasn't the right choice.

Unknown: See you tonight.

Me: Are you going to be there, at the party?

Unknown: I wouldn't miss it.

Me: And you'll turn yourself in after I do?

Unknown: I'll turn myself in, IF you do.

Me: Good. I want to look you in the eye as the police drag you away.

Brushing the tears from my cheeks, I grab my jacket from the back hallway and lock the front door of the shop as I leave.

I have a Christmas Eve party to get ready for.

THIRTY-FOUR

WHEN I GET HOME, I let Betsy outside to do her business and then refill her food and water. Ducking into my room, I try to figure out what I should wear. I settle on a pair of black dress pants and a dark gray sweater. Seems appropriate for my funeral.

My eyes well with tears as I realize Luke will be having a real funeral soon. It's wrong to think of the shame and humiliation I'm going to face as death when Luke is actually dead because I didn't come forward sooner. Yes, I'm going to confess to a crime and put my family hundreds of thousands of dollars in debt. I might even go to jail, but I won't be gone forever, like he is. I flip through some pictures of him in the gallery on my phone. "I fucked up so bad," I say. "You deserved better than me."

As I set down my phone, I see what time it is. Shit. I forgot I had to pick up my mom from the hospital. I can't imagine driving when I feel like this. I grab my phone again and call Holden.

"I have a favor to ask you," I blurt out when he comes on the line. "Is there any way you can pick up my mom at the hospital? I told her I would get her at five-fifteen, but I'm not in any condition to drive. Actually, maybe wait and get her a bit later. If you can stall her so you don't get back to town until a little after six, she won't have to see what I'm going to do at the Christmas Eve party."

"I can get her," Holden says. "If you're sure she won't mind riding with me. But what do you mean you're not in any condition to drive? And what does the party have to do with anything?"

I want to respect Frannie's wishes not to share the news about Luke, but this is too much to keep inside me. "Luke is dead," I say, my voice hollow.

"What? What do you—"

"He's dead, Holden. Unknown wins. And now the only way for me to end this is to tell the whole truth tonight, in front of everyone. I have to. I can't let anyone else die. I'm sorry if this messes things up for you with the fire and—"

"Fuck the fire," Holden says. "Fuck the money. I don't care about that. They can't take from us what we don't have. But what do you mean Luke is dead? Are you *sure*?"

"Unknown texted me a picture of Luke's dog tags. I could read his name on the metal."

"So maybe it's Photoshopped. Or maybe Luke is Unknown."

"No, that's not possible," I say. "Unknown killed him."

"Be reasonable, Embry. I thought you said he didn't come home. How could a text stalker from Three Rocks, Oregon, get to Luke in Afghanistan?"

"I don't know," I say. "His own sister verified it, though. Frannie doesn't know the details yet, but she said the army brought her parents a folded flag. Maybe he did come back here and no one knew about it, or maybe, somehow, Unknown just got to him. I don't know. I mean, fuck, Holden. What about the past week has been *reasonable*?" I swallow back a sob. "I just wanted you to know I was going to tell everyone the truth. So that way you could be prepared."

"Are you sure you don't want to just go back to the cops and tell *them* the whole story?"

"No. I'm done taking the easy way out. Plus, Unknown says that if I confess in front of the whole town, they'll confess too." My voice goes hoarse. "I need for this to be over, Holden."

"And you trust Unknown?"

"Not really," I say grimly. "But I have to do this either way."

"Okay," Holden says. "Tell your mom I'll pick her up at five-thirty. I can take the motorcycle to Tillamook and borrow my mom's car from the station parking lot. I'll show up ten minutes late and do my best to stall your mom so we don't get back here until at least six. And I'll be around later if you need to talk."

I hang up with him and call my mom's cell. She answers on the third ring. "Hi, Mom," I say in an artificially bright voice. "Slight change of plans. There were a couple last-minute customers, so I'm running a little behind and I'm sending Holden to come pick you up."

"Not on the motorcycle, I hope," Mom says.

"No, he's going to come in his mom's car. He should be there by five-thirty."

"That's cutting it a little close for the Christmas party. Are you still trying to get out of going?" Mom asks teasingly.

If you only knew.

"Oh no, I'll be there," I say. "I'll save you a seat."

As I hang up the phone with my mom, my eyes fall on the Shutterfly photo book again. I want to reach out to Julia, to remind her she's gorgeous and that she shouldn't be taking internet diet pills. But I don't feel like I have the right to contact her. I should give her space, let her come to me if she wants to be friends again. Grabbing the book, I skim through the pages, my eyes taking in the two of us in our prom dresses and at the swim meet. I pause on the picture of Julia and me at Cape Azure State Park with her father. Something about this photo bothers me, but I'm not sure what. I scan it left to right, top to bottom, looking for anything I might have missed when I first glanced at it.

I swallow back a gasp as I reach the bottom of the photo. Julia is wearing a pair of pink-and-gray boots, the hot-pink laces double-knotted and wrapped around her shins. I've seen them online.

They're Rendon hiking boots.

THIRTY-FIVE

I TELL MYSELF it doesn't mean anything. It's like Katrina said, lots of people wear Rendon boots. Still, a prickling sensation at the nape of my neck reminds me that Julia has the most motivation to be Unknown. I call her on the phone, unsure of what I'm going to say. I just want to hear her voice. If she just talks to me, I'll know there's no way she's Unknown. I'll be able to feel it.

I get her voice mail. Unfortunately there is no reassurance in her perky greeting. I hang up without leaving a message. I think about texting Holden, but he's probably already on the way to pick up my mom.

"I guess if it's her, I'll find out soon enough," I mutter. But it can't be. It just can't. In the same way my brain won't envision a future without Holden, it also can't comprehend a present where Julia would have killed Luke just to punish me.

Grabbing my keys, I head out the door.

The holiday party takes place in the gymnasium of the Three Rocks Community Center, which has been transformed into a winter wonderland, at least for today. The walls are covered with silvery snowflake cutouts and the doorways are all trimmed with ropes of red-and-green garland.

There's an elevated stage at one end of the room, with a giant screen behind it. Mrs. O'Riley uses the screen to make digital backgrounds for the nativity play instead of painted sets. My heart revs up as I imagine myself standing up on that stage, telling everyone the truth. People say you're supposed to envision success in order to cut down on your anxiety, but all I can envision is shocked silence. And then scorn—lots and lots of scorn and shaming, with the whole town filming away on their iPhones. I should feel terrified, but all I feel is numb. Maybe it won't be as bad as I think. Maybe it'll be cathartic.

The room is already about half full, even though I arrived fifteen minutes early. I take a seat in the very back on the aisle. A handful of people wander up to me before the festivities start, asking about Luke or congratulating me for my heroism the night of the fire. Each time someone mentions Luke, my insides twist a little more.

Most of my classmates aren't here, since Tillamook has its own holiday festivities, but there are about fifteen kids I know from school in the audience, including Holden's friend Zak and Katrina Jensen. I don't see Julia or her parents anywhere. I wonder if she's going to stroll out of the darkness at the back of the room to hear my confession before offering one of her own. I still don't believe that Unknown could be Julia. I would know if she hated me enough to try to kill my mom, to kill Luke. There's no way she could keep that kind of emotion a secret. There's no way she would do that to me.

I keep an eye on the doorway, grateful for each minute that passes without my mom and Holden arriving. I know they're going to hear about this, but I'd rather neither of them personally witness what's about to happen.

At six p.m. sharp, a spotlight appears front and center on the stage. The mayor makes his way up the side aisle and steps into the circle of light. He taps the microphone twice. "Happy holidays! Welcome, people of Three Rocks and neighboring towns," he starts.

I shift in my seat. Aside from Katrina, who probably came from work, and possibly one Baby Jesus from Tillamook, I seriously doubt any out-of-towners have shown up. I know the names of 70 percent of the people in this room. I bet all of them know Luke's name. Lucas O'Riley, hockey player, lifeguard, soldier, Three Rocks hero. When I tell them I was at the Sea Cliff with another guy, most of the women will probably hate me just for that, for having someone so decent and good and not being satisfied with him.

"It's my great pleasure to see so many of my constituents gathered together to celebrate the holidays," the mayor continues. "I know the kids here in Three Rocks really enjoy putting on the nativity play each year, and I was watching last night's rehearsal. Let me tell you that you've got a heck of a show coming tonight."

You have no idea, I think.

The mayor glances out over the crowd. "But before we start the play, as is the local custom, I've got a few special people I'd like to honor with our official Three Rocks Rocky Awards."

The crowd claps politely. Phones light up in the audience, ostensibly to take pictures but more likely to check Facebook or email. If only everyone would tune out for my little presentation. I tap one foot nervously. The mayor starts by calling up an elderly Three Rocks woman who rescued a baby who was left in a hot car in Tillamook back in August. The woman broke a window with her cane and then called 911. I dig my nails into my palms as the woman shuffles up to the stage to receive her award. The crowd claps again.

Next the mayor recognizes our local Girl Scout troop for having a fall fund-raiser to support starving kids in Yemen. The scout leader and two of the scouts make their way to the stage to accept the award. One of the Girl Scouts asks for the microphone. She reads some statistics about the war in Yemen and how it's affecting millions of people, including hundreds of thousands of children. She ends by asking for a donation for another fund-raiser. People in the front rows start reaching for their purses.

The mayor clears his throat. "And then our final Rocky Award winner of the night, Embry Woods, who helped a man escape the fire at the Sea Cliff Inn. Embry, come on up!"

I stand and head for the front of the room, my heart pounding so hard that I'm afraid I might pass out before I get to the stage. Actually, that might be preferable to what's about to happen. *Just get it over with.* Right. All I have to do is stand up and look out at over half the town, tell them I'm a liar and a criminal who slept with the guy my friend was dating while my own boyfriend was off risking his life for our freedom, and now that guy is dead because of me. Then everything will get better. Or something.

My stomach feels like it's full of wriggling worms. All I can do is give the mayor a tight-lipped smile as he hands me the trophy. I'm pretty sure if I open my mouth I'm going to vomit right here all over the stage. It's about a million degrees under this spotlight, and my entire body is suddenly wet with sweat. Then the door to the community center opens and a cool breeze blows through. People in the audience cross their arms and tuck their hands into their pockets, but to me it feels heavenly. I crane my neck to see who's arriving late. Is it Unknown? Is it my mother? I can barely make out the silhouettes of two people walking up the aisle.

For a brief instant I consider fleeing—pushing past the newcomers and running for that open door, running all the way to some other town where I can start over. But I can't do that to my mom. I can't do it to anyone else Unknown might punish for my cowardice. Taking a deep breath, I turn to face the mayor. Here goes nothing. "Can I say something?" I ask.

"Of course." The mayor gestures out at the crowd.

I take the microphone from his outstretched hand and look out at the audience. It's like a firing squad made up of moms and small children. *Fuck, this is going to be a nightmare.* Just when I think things can't possibly get any worse, I realize it was my mom who just arrived. She's standing in the side aisle, and she's not alone. She's with a man I've seen before—a man in a brown bomber jacket. He's not wearing the baseball cap tonight, and I recognize him immediately.

It's my father.

THIRTY-SIX

I LOOK AWAY FROM my parents and my gaze falls on Lourdes, my mom's best friend. Nope, not looking at her either. I try again. Katrina Jensen eyes me curiously, her thin lips folded into a smirk. Strike three. I train my eyes on a spot on the floor a few feet in front of me. "Here's the thing," I start. "I'm not a hero like these people." I gesture at the woman with the cane and the Girl Scouts. "They did really great things. Brave things. I didn't. The reason I went into the Sea Cliff that night wasn't to save a life. It was to keep from ending one." I take a deep breath. "I'm the one who started the fire."

The crowd murmurs. I scan the shocked and disapproving faces, searching for Unknown. *Come on, where are you? You promised you'd be here.* The spotlight on me seems to increase in intensity. I glance up at the AV booth, wondering if whoever is running the lights and sound is some kind of sadist. The mayor's face reddens. He reaches for the microphone, but I'm not done. I set the Rocky Award down on the podium. "I don't deserve an award. I deserve to go to jail. I sneaked into the Sea Cliff to meet a guy. We had candles. We were drinking. I didn't start the fire on purpose. I knocked one of the candles over when we were messing around. I know what I did was a crime, and I know hiding it was an even worse crime. I'm sorry," I finish miserably. I chance a look at my mom. Her face is a mix of sadness and sympathy. "I'm going to turn myself in to the police."

I hand the microphone back to the mayor. He's still flushed. "Well," he says. "Thank you for your honesty, Ms. Woods."

Just when I think things can't get any worse, the video of Holden and me from that night starts to play on the giant screen behind the stage. The two of us are on the sofa. We're kissing. I'm sliding my jeans down to my ankles. Parents cover their kids' eyes. My face burns as the mayor lifts a hand to his mouth. I spin around and look up at the AV booth again. There's a shadow at the glass, watching me. Unknown.

The mayor hollers for someone to turn off the recording. On the screen, Holden and I are going at it now. My foot hits the table and the candle falls to the floor, igniting the carpet. There's a collective gasp from the crowd. I can't believe Unknown felt the need to play this video. This wasn't part of our deal. I look up at the AV booth one more time. The silhouette is gone.

"Shit." I push through the crowd, heading for the lobby of the community center. Unknown didn't get me here so we could both confess. *You haven't suffered enough.* They just wanted to humiliate me.

The staircase leading to the second floor is empty. I race to the door. A figure in a gray hoodie is running across the street toward the beach access parking lot. The figure runs full speed down the paved ramp.

I do my best to follow, but by the time I've made it down to the sand, the figure is nowhere to be seen. There are at least two sets of private beach access stairs they could have gotten to, leading to two different levels of Puffin Hill. I pick the closest one and hurry toward it, but that's when I hear my mom screaming my name.

I look back and forth between the beach access parking lot that my mom is hobbling across and the set of stairs leading up to Puffin Hill. Wherever Unknown went, I lost them . . . for now. Better to turn back and make sure my mom is okay.

We meet at the bottom of the stairs leading up to the beach parking lot.

"I'm sorry, Mom," I start. "I know I screwed up big-time."

"Are you okay?" she asks.

"No. I need to find out who played that video. It's the person who's been blackmailing me."

"Mrs. O'Riley would know, wouldn't she?" Mom says. "Isn't she the one who hires the support staff?"

"Yeah, but I seriously doubt she's here tonight. The O'Rileys are . . . dealing with some family stuff," I say. I want to tell my mom about Luke, but I already broke Frannie's confidence once by telling Holden.

"Well, then you should let the police handle it," Mom says. "Blackmail is a crime."

"Yeah, I know." I'm pissed at myself for letting Unknown get away, but at least going to the police means a better chance of catching them. "Are *you* okay?" I ask her. "How's your leg?"

"It hurts, but the hospital gave me some pain medication, so I'll survive."

Movement up on the street catches my eye. There are a couple of silhouettes outside the Three Rocks Community Center. "That was my father, right? In the brown jacket? Or did I hallucinate him? It's entirely possible the last few days have driven me insane."

"No, he's still inside," Mom says. "He didn't think you'd want to see him right now."

"I'm not sure I want to see anyone ever again," I say.

"I know what that's like." Mom wraps an arm around me, gives me a half hug.

"Is that why you're not yelling at me?"

"I'd like to hear the whole story before I do any yelling. Though I will say I don't understand why you didn't tell me the truth about the fire."

"I was going to tell you, I swear," I say. "I mean, at first I wasn't because I was afraid the cost to repair the Sea Cliff would bankrupt us. But then all this shit happened and I realized I should have just told the truth anyway, but that was this morning at the hospital and then we got interrupted and later you looked so tired. . . ."

My mom sighs. "Oh, Embry. You should have come to me much earlier."

"I know," I tell her. "I messed up royally. I just don't want my mistakes to hurt you." Tears leak out of my eyes. "I feel like I'm going to ruin your life even worse now than I did when I was born."

"Embry!" My mom's voice is full of concern. It just makes me feel worse, because I'm the one who should be feeling concerned right now. "You did *not* ruin my life!"

"It's okay. Gram told me the whole story of what happened." I make a halfhearted attempt to wipe away the tears. "I know everyone started treating you badly because of me."

"Everyone started treating me badly because of things I

did," my mom says. "Your father and me. You were just an innocent bystander, sweetie. Please tell me you know that."

I turn away, look out at the ocean. "It's hard not to think about how much better your life could have been without me."

"No," my mom says emphatically. "You saved me, Embry."

I shake my head. "You don't have to say that. I know things have would been easier if . . ." I trail off.

Mom takes me by the shoulders and turns me so I'm facing her. "Easier, maybe. But not better. You were the thing that made all the pain worth it. Without you to think about, the sadness would've eaten me alive." Mom cradles my face in her hands. She wipes my tears away with her thumbs. "You saved me," she says again. "Even this summer—you gave me a reason to keep fighting, to never give up hope."

"Really?" I never thought of it like that, that my being born was actually a good thing.

"Really," Mom says. "You were my everything from the moment I found about you. I never regretted bringing you into this world for a single second."

I throw my arms around my mom's neck and embrace her tightly. "I love you," I say. "You're the best mom ever."

"I try," Mom says. "And whatever trouble you've gotten into, we'll figure it out together. We figured out how to survive without Grandma. We figured out how to beat cancer.

We can deal with this too, okay?"

I nod, but I'm not sure I believe her. I mean, I believe that we can figure it out, just not without losing something really important to her, like the coffee shop or the house. Not unless the Murray family will let me pay them back over the next hundred years or so.

I furrow my brow. "Where's Holden? I sent him to pick you up in Tillamook."

"I know. I got your message, but your father showed up in the meantime, and when Holden hadn't arrived by five-forty-five, I went ahead and took a ride with your dad. I left a message for Holden at the ER front desk."

"I'll text him in case he's still looking for you. If it's okay with you, I just need a little time to myself."

"Sure," Mom says. "See you back at home?"

"Will my father be there?"

"Not if you don't want him to. I shouldn't have invited him to the party without asking you. He was just so thrilled at the idea of watching you receive an award. I figured he could lurk in the back, watch you, and sneak out and you'd never know."

"Yeah, I guess I messed that up for him."

Mom ruffles my hair. "Definitely not the presentation he was expecting, but he's not in any position to judge."

"True."

Mom wraps me in a hug. "Be careful," she says. "We'll talk more when you get home."

"Okay." I watch her limp her way back up the stairs.

Mom disappears from view, and I turn to the ocean. I walk out toward the water and then make my way down to the end of the beach, to the Pot Hole. The tide is rising, the cave starting to fill with water. For a moment I imagine ducking inside the dark opening, letting the waves sweep in and take me out to sea, or perhaps trap me in the cave and drown me. I've really made a mess of things the past few months.

But I can't just give up. Not now, when I'm almost free. I told the truth to everyone and the police should be able to identify Unknown from the security footage from the computer lab. It's over, or at least it will be soon.

And then my phone buzzes with a text.

THIRTY-SEVEN

Unknown: Nice job with the mayor.

My fingers tremble as I compose a reply.

Me: Glad you enjoyed it. I was hoping you might join me onstage, but I should have known you'd go back on your promise.

Unknown: I'm not going back on it. I'm going to turn myself in. But first I have a surprise for you.

Me: Hard pass. I did what you wanted, so just leave me and the people I care about alone, okay?

Unknown: Don't you want to know who I am?

Me: If I say yes, are you going to tell me?

Unknown: No, but I was thinking we could meet up some–where, talk face to face. Don't you have questions?

Me: Again, pass. I'm trying to be less destructive to myself and everyone around me.

Unknown: Since when?

Me: Since my best friend and my mom both ended up in the ER.

Unknown: Don't you want to know how I got to your boyfriend?

Me: He wasn't my boyfriend. And no, not unless you show me how to make him magically come back to life.

Unknown: Well, not exactly. But you can still save the life of his little sister.

The next text is a picture of Frannie. She's sitting on a chair in a room. I know that room. It's the lobby of the Sea Cliff Inn. Peering closer, I see that her hands and ankles are tied. There's a piece of tape over her mouth. Her eyes are wide with fear.

Me: WTF is this? We had a deal. You promised no one else would get hurt.

Unknown: She won't get hurt . . . as long as you make the right choice.

Unknown: A. Come to the Sea Cliff Inn alone. If you do this, I will kill a murderer.

B. If you don't come, or if you bring the police, I will kill a girl named Frannie.

Unknown: You have fifteen minutes. Choose wisely.

Me: You'll kill a murderer? What does that mean? Are you going to commit suicide?

Unknown: I guess if you want to know, I'll see you soon.

Me: Screw that. I'm calling the police.

Unknown: It's your choice, but there's no way the police can make it to the Sea Cliff without me seeing them. If I see so much as a flashing light on Puffin Drive or a single officer creeping toward the door, I'll strangle Frannie O'Riley with her brother's dog tags.

Me: You are one twisted fuck.

Unknown: Thirteen minutes. Tick tock.

I shove the phone deep into my pocket. "Fuck!" I shout. "Fuck, fuck, fuck!" I kick at the nearest rock, sending pebbles spraying across the beach.

Unknown is right about the police. The top of Puffin Hill is accessible only by Puffin Drive, unless the cops are going to scale the side of the cliff, which they're not.

I head for the nearest set of stairs—it belongs to a trio of time-share condos located halfway up the hill. I pause on the way, bending down to run my fingers across the smooth stones littering the beach. I find one with a sharp edge that fits neatly in my hand. It's not much of a weapon, but it's better than nothing. Unknown has never threatened my life—just everyone else's—so hopefully I won't need it. All I can think about is rescuing Frannie and then turning myself in. Telling the truth hurt—it hurt with Julia, with Luke, and at the party tonight. But there's also a sense of relief. As terrified as I am to turn myself in to the police, I know it's the right thing to do. As my feet pound the wooden steps, it occurs to me there's one more person I need to be honest with tonight. I pause halfway up the stairs to dial Holden's number.

"Embry." His voice is breathless. "I'm so glad you called. Is your mom okay? The nurse said she checked out with a strange man."

"Yeah, it was my father. Long story. Look. I'm on my way to the Sea Cliff. Unknown has Frannie. I'm not sure what's going to happen, but I can't let them kill her. I just wanted to tell you that I love you."

"I, what?" Holden says, clearly taken aback.

"I love you, Holden. That's why I've been so weird lately. I was coming to terms with that, and what it meant. I'm not saying it's enough. I'm not saying we should be together. I'm saying I've spent my whole life hiding parts of myself. You were right about my abandonment issues, but I'm not just afraid of people leaving me physically. I'm afraid of them pulling away emotionally, that if I let people see who I am they'll decide that I don't deserve love. But you make me feel like I *do* deserve love, and I can't even lie anymore. I love you. I think maybe I have for a while. Now, finally, *everyone* knows the truth. And now I've got to go end this."

"I love you too," Holden says. "But are you at home right now? There are a couple things I need to show you. The first one is that license plate you asked me about. It's registered to—"

"Patrick Ryder?" I say.

"Yeah, how did you—"

"He's my father," I say. "Long story. Whatever the other thing is, it's going to have to wait. I only have nine minutes to get there."

"Did you call the police?"

"You know I can't do that. There's no way they can make it to the top of Puffin Hill without Unknown seeing them. If they see cops, cop cars, even flashing lights on the hill, Frannie might die."

"I'm still in Tillamook, but I can call my mom and tell her—"

"No, Holden. Unknown will see her coming."

"They can drive an unmarked car, you know. Be sneaky."

"Okay, but what if they're not? I can't chance it. Don't you get it? Luke is dead because of me. I can't take any more deaths on my conscience."

"Actually, what I wanted to show you has to do with Luke," Holden says. "I was looking—"

"I don't have time for this. I'm sorry. If anything happens

to me, look out for my mom, okay?"

"Wait. Does it make sense that—"

I can't try to make sense of anything right now. There's no time, and I'm barely holding it together as it is. I disconnect the phone and stuff it back into my pocket. I take the rest of the stairs two at a time, my heart pounding in my chest, my breath whistling in my throat.

When I finally make it to the top of the stairs, I turn left and run along the edge of the road as fast as I dare. The snow from this morning has melted, leaving the concrete wet and slippery. It's just slick enough to make my footing unsure. I check my phone when I'm about a block away from the Sea Cliff. Three minutes left. I debate stopping to text Unknown to say I'm almost there, but I decide to just press on. Unknown doesn't seem like the type of person who will give me a margin for error.

My feet land on the front porch of the Sea Cliff at exactly one minute before the deadline. Another text pops up on my screen:

Unknown: The present is for you.

There's a wrapped package just off to the side of the porch. It's tucked halfway behind the shrubbery. I might not have even noticed it without the text.

"Where are you?" I ask. "What is this?"

No answer. Reluctantly I reach down for the box, praying

that I won't open it to find someone's head inside. My hands fumble with the bow. I rip the rest of the paper and open the box. There, nestled on a bed of tissue paper, is a hand-gun. There's a note beside it. The handwriting looks vaguely familiar.

Last choice:
Kill yourself, and she lives.
Refuse, and she dies.
You have fifteen seconds to choose.

THIRTY-EIGHT

"WHAT THE HELL IS THIS?" I shout. "Where's Frannie?"

Reluctantly, I trade the rock I've been carrying for the gun. Holding it down by my side, I step into the darkened hotel. The chair she was sitting in is lying on its side in the middle of the lobby, the ropes that once bound her a snarl of coils on the burned carpet. Maybe she managed to escape.

"Frannie?" I call up the stairs. "Are you in here?"

There's no reply. I blink rapidly. The air burns my eyes. I pass from the lobby into the back—the kitchen and dining area. It's been more than fifteen seconds, but still no sign of anyone. And then something moves in the fog outside. My fingers tighten around the gun as I push through the back door out onto the grass.

Frannie is standing at the edge of the cliff, her back to me. Her clothes and hair are mussed, like maybe she just escaped.

"Fran, thank God." As I hurry toward her, she spins around. She also has a gun in her hand.

I skid to a stop. "What are you doing? It's me, Embry." I glance around, looking for Unknown. "Where's the person who brought you here?"

"No one brought me here. I brought *you* here," Frannie says. "So we could finish this."

"Finish what?" My eyes drop to the ground, to the gray Rendon hiking boots Frannie is wearing. My brain struggles to make sense of what is right before my eyes. Frannie must have followed Holden and me that night. She made the email address and sent the video only to the senior class because she probably figured it'd throw suspicion away from her. Somehow she poisoned Julia—maybe she spiked her water bottle in the locker room or something. And my mom—my lower lip trembles just thinking about it. Frannie tried to kill her.

But if Frannie is Unknown, does that mean she killed her own brother? Or was that just a lie so she could lure me here by myself and try to goad me into committing suicide?

I take in a deep breath and try to analyze her expression

and body language. Her chin is raised and her eyes are sharp with defiance, but her shoulders are also slumped forward, as if she's just as tired as I am. Is she capable of shooting me? I don't know.

Taking a step back, I say, "Look. I heard you've been buying stuff from Matt Sesti. I don't know what you're taking, but I can help you. Everything is going to be okay. Just please put the gun down."

Frannie laughs. The gun trembles in her hand. "You're such a liar, Embry. You're lying to me just like you lied to Luke. My brother is dead. Nothing is ever going to be okay again, don't you get it?"

"He's really dead?" I swallow hard. "But you didn't, I mean, I know you wouldn't hurt him . . . so what happened?"

Frannie's jaw tightens. "What happened is you lied to him and betrayed him."

"I don't understand," I say. My eyes skim the surrounding area, the shrubbery, the frozen grass, the edge of the cliff. There's nowhere for me to hide, no escape from her gun.

"Why did you do it? Why did you leave him for some other guy?" Her voice wavers. A tear trickles down one of her cheeks.

She looks so miserable that for a second I look past the fact she's pointing a gun at me, past the idea that this sixteen-year-old girl who once told me I was like a sister to her has apparently been stalking and terrorizing me. "I—shit. It's hard to explain."

Frannie cocks the gun. The expression on her face goes cold. "Try," she says.

"Luke is—was—amazing," I say. "Not just to me, but to everybody. When we first started dating, I let myself get swallowed up by his goodness, you know? He was everything I needed in my world—stability, kindness, loyalty, bravery."

"But then after he built you up you just moved on to another guy without even telling him? Out of sight, out of mind, I guess. Don't you ever think about the people you hurt?"

I sigh. "Without him here, it just became easier for me to face reality. That we weren't right for each other, that we wanted different things. I wouldn't have been able to make him happy."

"Bullshit," Frannie says. "He loved you. He was going to propose to you. That's why I . . ." She trails off.

"You what? Followed me? Recorded me? Threatened me? Tried to kill people I love?" I bite back the tears that want to fall. I have to stay focused. I can't give in to my emotions, not now, not if I want to survive this.

The gun shakes in her hand again. If I can figure out how to distract her, I might be able to tackle her before she can get a shot off. But she's so close to the edge of the cliff. If I do it wrong, we might both go over the edge.

"That's why I told him," she says finally. "And then he died. You took away the most important person in my life. And yeah, that's why I tried to kill your mom. I would kill every single person you love, if I could. Maybe then you would know how this feels." Her voice is hot with rage. Tears are streaming down over both cheeks now. "I never should have told him. But you put me in an impossible position."

"Told him what?" I ask. "About Holden and me?"

She nods. "I saw you and Holden together on the beach one night. I followed you guys to the Sea Cliff and saw you there. Luke was going to come home as a surprise for New Year's Eve. He wanted to propose. I didn't want him to get his heart broken, so I told him you were hooking up with another guy, but he didn't believe me." She clenches her teeth. "His own sister, and he thought I was confused, or maybe lying. So I followed you again and made him a video. I gave you the chance to post a confession yourself, so Luke could hear it from you, but you didn't want to do that. So I sent him the video myself." She kicks at the ground. "We got the call like two days later. He died in a raid. He was supposed to stay back, but he broke protocol, tried to rescue a guy who'd been shot. Insurgent bullets mowed him down before he even made it to the other soldier's side. His superiors said it was a *lapse in judgment*, that it could have happened to anyone. His team said that Luke had seemed distracted lately."

Suddenly more pieces slide into place. Frannie has known Luke was dead for a couple of days. She folded his death into her plan to hurt me when she failed to kill Julia or my mom.

"I don't understand. Why would your family keep Luke's death a secret?"

"Like I said, my mom didn't want it to ruin the holidays for the rest of the town. She said Luke would want us to be strong, to get through Christmas as a family and then tell everyone afterward so the town could mourn."

A flash of sympathy moves through me. As horrified as I am that Frannie tried to kill my mom and Julia, I can't help but think about what it'd be like to have to keep such a secret for *days*. To pretend I was fine while I was secretly devastated. The death of a loved one would be the deepest, darkest piece of all. I bet hiding something like that would break a lot of people.

"You made me complicit in my own brother's death," Frannie continues. "I wanted you to feel that pain, the pain of knowing that no matter what choice you made, it was going to end badly, the pain of knowing your actions killed someone." She brushes at her tears with her free hand. New ones pour forth to replace the ones wiped away.

"Frannie." I swallow hard. "Let's talk about this, all right?" I'm still trying to figure out how to get her to put the gun down without either of us getting shot. I understand where her pain is coming from. It's like I said before—guilt is my superpower.

Frannie wraps both hands around the gun. "Do you know what his last words to me were? They were a one-line email: 'I wish you hadn't shown me this.' Do you know how that feels? I'm always going to wonder if he did it on purpose."

The idea that some of Luke's last thoughts were about me and Holden together is like a kick in the stomach, but I shake off the pain. This isn't about me. "No, Luke wouldn't do that. He wouldn't kill himself," I say. "I know what it's like to feel responsible for all the bad things that happen. But this wasn't your fault. Luke didn't rush into enemy fire because he was sad. He probably broke protocol because he's a medic and he's trained to save people's lives. He saw a friend suffering and acted on instinct. You know him, Fran. He wouldn't think twice about risking his life if it meant saving someone else. Remember how he rescued the mayor's daughter? That's the guy he's always been."

She doesn't respond immediately, so I keep talking. "If he *was* distracted that day, it's my fault, not yours. I thought I was protecting him, but I was really protecting myself. You did the right thing. Telling the truth is always the right thing to do."

She shakes her head. "I thought it was. But my mom said I

shouldn't have meddled, that I'm part of why he's gone."

"Well, your mom is wrong," I say firmly. My own mom flashes in my head. I hear her words down on the beach. *We figured out how to beat cancer. We can deal with this too, okay?* My throat goes tight when I think about how lucky I am to have a mom who is so incredibly supportive, a mom who backs me up even when I don't deserve it.

"She's never wrong," Frannie chokes out.

"She is this time. Look, Frannie, you can still walk away from this. We can both walk away. Julia and my mom are fine. Luke isn't your fault. You didn't really hurt anyone. Think about the things you've always wanted for your future. Think about what Luke would want. He wouldn't want you to go to jail."

She shakes her head. "We have to be punished for the consequences of our actions, intended or not. That's what my parents always say. We have to take responsibility." She takes a step backward, toward the edge of the cliff. "But I'm not planning on going to jail. I'm tired, Embry. I want it all to go away. I want to be with my brother again." She slides her finger onto the trigger. "Last chance. Shoot yourself, or I'll do it for you."

"Wait. Hold on." Maybe I can pretend like I'm going to shoot myself and then lunge for her gun at the last minute. I'm not going to shoot at her—not even to wound. I don't even know how to use a gun. Chances are I would kill her or miss her completely. "I'm tired too," I say, slowly stepping sideways, repositioning my body so if I end up knocking Frannie to the ground we won't go over the side of the cliff. "My whole life has felt like one tragedy after the next. But I brought most of them upon myself, and you're right—I never thought about the other people I hurt." Slowly, I lift my gun to the side of my head, rest the barrel on my temple. It's one of the strangest feelings I've ever felt. To be so close to death and yet to want to live so badly. "But if I do this, no one will know the things you've done. You can live."

"I don't want to live," she says. "I want to be with Luke."

"But think about what Luke wants. He would want you to live, right?" I watch Frannie's body, the flicker of different expressions, the tiny unconscious movements. I can tell she's thinking about it.

As she opens her mouth to reply, I lunge, doing my best to duck low under her line of fire. My shoulder collides with her stomach. We both end up on the ground.

A gun goes off.

THIRTY-NINE

A PAIR OF COPS COME charging around the side of the hotel, their guns drawn. "Drop your weapon!" one of them shouts.

I step back from Frannie, my face frozen in horror. There's a puddle of red growing on her shirt. "Help her," I say weakly. "I didn't mean to . . ."

"I said drop your weapon!"

I realize I still have the gun in my hand. I bend down, put it on the ground. Before I know what's happening, a cop has his knee in my back. My wrists are being shoved into handcuffs.

I turn my head to the side and catch sight of a familiar pair of boots hurrying across the grass. "Holden?" I say. "What are you doing here?"

The police stop Holden before he can get near me. "Making sure you're okay," he calls to me.

I turn my head the other way. Officer Hutchens is bending down next to Frannie, applying pressure to her wound.

"It was an accident," I say. "I was trying to get her gun. I didn't mean to shoot her. I don't even know how to use a gun. Is she going to be okay?"

"I don't know," Hutchens says. "But an ambulance is on the way."

Frannie curls onto her side. Our eyes meet. I fight the urge to look away. "Just let me die," she says. "I can't fix things. I can't go on like this."

"Yes, you can," I say. "What happened to Luke isn't your fault. You just need help to see that."

"It feels like my fault." Her voice cracks.

"I know what that's like," I say.

Sirens cut through the night as additional police officers and an ambulance arrive at the Sea Cliff Inn. Officer Hutchens hands off care of Frannie to a paramedic. One of the new officers on the scene is Holden's mom. She rushes over to him. "What are you doing here? I told you to stay away."

"You know I never do what I'm told." Holden turns to me. "Uncuff her, Mom. Embry was just protecting herself."

Officer Hassler bends down to talk to me. "I can uncuff you, but you're coming back to the station so we can get a full statement." She removes the handcuffs and I scramble to my feet. She walks me around to the front of the Sea Cliff where her police car is parked.

Holden and I slide into the back together. I massage my wrists. *Second time in a police car today*, I think, my eyes peeking through the bars to the front seat.

"Stay put. Both of you," Office Hassler says.

Holden and I both watch as she walks a few feet across the frozen grass. She calls someone on her cell phone. I try to read her body language. How much trouble am I going to be in? More important, is Frannie going to die?

Officer Hassler tucks her phone into her pocket and turns back to the cruiser, her expression neutral.

"Uh-oh. She looks pissed," Holden murmurs.

She opens the door and slides into the driver's seat. "Okay. Seat belts, please. The sheriff said to go ahead and bring you down to the station."

I buckle my seat belt with trembling fingers. As we pull back onto Puffin Drive, I let out a sharp gasp. Tears trickle from my eyes.

"Are you okay?" Holden asks.

I nod. "Just glad to be getting out of here."

"Extremely same," he says. "Holy shit. You about gave me a fucking heart attack, you know that?"

His mom clears her throat. "Language, please."

"She almost got shot, Mom. I think the swear words are earned in this instance."

"Perhaps," his mom says. "Then again, there's no reason for you to be here, Holden. I could drop you off at home on the way to the station if you like."

"All right. All right. I'll shut up." He curls his fingers around my right hand. "I promised Embry I'd be there for her if she was ever in trouble."

"Well, from what I've heard, you're both going to be in a world of trouble with respect to the fire you started, but we'll deal with that mess after we finish dealing with this one."

The ambulance with Frannie passes us on the way down the hill, its lights flashing.

"What's going to happen to her?" I ask.

"Not sure," Holden's mom says. "Depends on the DA. Does one of those guns belong to you?"

"No, she left one for me next to the porch, wrapped like a present," I say. "I think her plan was for us to both commit suicide. She blames the two of us for Luke's death."

"Her brother died?" Officer Hassler asks.

"That's how I knew something was up," Holden says. "When you told me he was killed but Frannie didn't have specifics, I Googled it. A page from the Department of Defense came up with a listing that showed Lucas O'Riley died a few days ago in Afghanistan. I knew there was no way some local stalker could get to him on the other side of the world. At first I thought Frannie might just have been confused about the timing, like maybe her parents had been trying to keep it a secret from *her* until after the holidays. But then the pieces started to fall into place. Frannie knew your cell number. She knew Julia had an allergy. She knew your mom walked to work. I didn't know exactly why she was luring you back to the Sea Cliff, but it made sense she might hate you if she had seen the two of us together." He reaches up, cradles my face with one hand. "I called my mom the second I got off the phone with you."

Holden's mom clears her throat. "Do you know who the guns belong to?"

"One might belong to a girl named Katrina we go to school with," I say. "Or Frannie might have taken them from her family. I know they own a lot of guns."

Holden's mom nods. "You should probably call your mom to meet you at the station. She'll want to be present for your questioning."

Holden and I are separated when we get to the police station. The detective handling the sexting email case, Alina Reyes, is the one who interviews me. I show her all the messages I've received from Unknown while we wait for my mom to arrive. She shows up a few minutes later, her eyes wide, a fuzzy hat pulled low on her head. She didn't even take a minute to put on a wig when she heard I was at the police station.

Reyes explains to my mom that I haven't been charged with anything, but I'm being questioned about my role in the shooting at the Sea Cliff Inn. She asks me why I went there, and when I tell her about the threats she asks me when the first one arrived. She goes back over the stuff Holden's mom asked, about the guns. She asks me why I didn't come forward and file a report about being blackmailed, and I tell her how Holden and I started the fire.

Detective Reyes nods. "Frannie O'Riley had a burner cell phone on her. Any texts she sent on previous days were deleted, but the messages sent today were still there. I'm pretty sure when we get the security footage from the community college we're going to see her on it."

"So what does that mean for Embry?" my mom asks.

"Well, someone is going to need to take a detailed statement about the Sea Cliff fire, but I'm assuming you're going to want to talk to a lawyer first and you're not going to find one on Christmas Eve, so that can wait. I'm not sure where the fire department is in their investigation, but someone will be in contact."

Mom nods. I can see the light fade from her eyes as she calculates how much that is going to cost.

"You guys can appoint me a public defender, right? If I can't afford a lawyer?"

"That doesn't really come into effect unless you're charged," Reyes says. "But stop at the desk on your way out. I think they keep a list of free and low-cost legal resources."

Mom nods.

"I'm sorry," I whisper.

"I know you are," she says. "I'm just glad you're safe."

We run into Holden and his mom in the parking lot. He rushes over and wraps his arms around me, his hug lifting me a few inches into the air.

His mom hurries behind him. "Holden, I think you two need to spend a little time apart until we get all these legal matters squared away."

"Mom. Come on, that's bullshit." Holden places me back on the ground.

"I agree with Officer Hassler." My mom rests a hand on my lower back. "Let's go, Embry."

"Call me Nadia, please," Holden's mom says. "Claire, why don't you and Embry enjoy your holiday as best you can, and I'll give you a call in a couple of days after I've spoken to Holden's father and an attorney."

"Sounds good." Mom slips Officer Hassler one of her business cards.

Holden cradles my face in his hands. "Fuck Edvard Munch and *The Scream*. You're my very favorite face." He kisses me lightly on the lips. "I'll see you soon, I promise."

EPILOGUE

BUT HE DOESN'T SEE ME, at least not soon. Holden ends up going to Portland to hang out with his dad for Christmas, and I even end up spending a couple of days with *my* dad. Turns out he's divorced now and lives in Eugene, which is still about three hours away, but he also bought a cabin in Netarts, which is just a few miles down the coast. He's been staying at the Three Rocks Motel for the past week or so while waiting for all the paperwork to go through. That's why I've seen him lurking around town.

Mom shuts the coffee shop until after New Year's so she and Betsy can come with me to visit him. I even get to talk to my half brothers on the phone. They both live in Pennsylvania. One is a brand-new lawyer and the other is in grad school.

They didn't even know I existed until a few months ago.

Dad—we'll see if he can keep that title—has a long talk with me on the beach one night while my mom goes to the store for s'mores fixings. As we work on building a fire together, he apologizes about fifteen times in fifteen minutes for the things he did before and after I was born. It reminds me of how I must have sounded apologizing to Julia. So desperate to fix things yet so clueless when it came to how to go about it.

"I get it," I say, as the kindling finally ignites. "Enough with the apologies. I can't just forgive seventeen years of hurt all at once. But you can do better, all right? From today onward, do better. Not just for me. For my mom too."

"I'll do better," he says.

Our eyes meet across the fire. His are misty. So are mine. "Good," I say. "That's a good start."

Later, after my mom returns, the two of us exchange presents while my father watches with a smile. She is super-excited about the upgraded web page and pets the lavender fleece like it's Betsy or something.

"You shouldn't have, Embry," she scolds. "This is beautiful, but I don't need stuff this fancy."

"It was on a good sale," I assure her. "And it's the perfect color for you."

"It is," my dad agrees. "And it looks so warm."

Mom bought me mostly little things—clothes, candy, a pretty blue shade of eye makeup—but the last thing I open from her is tickets to a photography exhibit at the Portland Art Museum.

"I wanted to surprise you with something, and I figured since you went to that exhibit in Cannon Beach with Holden . . ." She trails off.

I look up the exhibit on my phone. "This sounds amazing," I tell her. "Are you going to go with me?"

"If you want me to. Embry's really big into photography," my mom explains to my dad. "She's going to be taking a class next semester."

"What kind of camera do you have?" my dad asks.

"Oh, I'm just going to use the camera on my phone. It's enough for now."

"Are you sure? We could go shopping for one if you like," he offers.

I shake my head violently. "You don't have to buy me expensive stuff." I know he means well, but I never wanted a dad for the things.

"Well, how about I loan you mine, then," he says. "I bought one that has detachable lenses on sale a couple years ago, but I never really learned to use the advanced features. You'll put it to much better use, and maybe by playing around with it you can figure out what kind of camera you want for yourself someday."

I nod. "Yeah, that would be okay."

"So is photography what you think you want to study at college?" my dad asks.

"I don't know," I say. "Maybe. I've also been thinking about marine biology, or marine mammal science."

"You do love the ocean," Mom says.

"I think it's good to start college without a definite plan," my dad says. "Explore all your options with an open mind."

Mom snorts. "Like you've ever not had a plan for anything in your whole life."

"Yes, well. My father informed me that I was going into computer science like he did unless I wanted to pay my own way to college. And sure, I got a good job in tech and made a lot of money and bought a lot of things, but I've never been happier since quitting that job, unless you count spending these past couple of days with you two." He pauses, swallows hard. "I guess what I'm saying is, Claire, I want our daughter to have a better life than I've had."

Mom starts crying and a couple seconds later Dad joins in. "Hey, hey, you know that's contagious, right?" I joke, as a few tears of my own stream down my cheeks. It's weird seeing my parents together and extra weird watching them cry.

"I'm sorry." My dad blots at his eyes. "I didn't mean to upset everyone."

"You didn't," I say. "Don't apologize for . . . caring."

"I do care," Dad says. "I hope you know that."

"I do," I reply. "It's just going to take some getting used to."

While I'm in Netarts with Mom and Dad, the O'Riley family has a funeral in Three Rocks for Luke. Mom offers to take me back there for it, but I feel like I should stay away. When we get back to town the next day, she takes me up to the cemetery and I talk to Luke for a while, apologize for not being honest sooner, for not being a better friend and girlfriend. I meant what I said to Frannie—that her brother probably died because he thought he could save someone, not because he was distracted. But I will always regret the way I treated him, and I'll forever live with the guilt of knowing that my actions may have played a role in his death.

It's easy to feel his absence throughout the town. The flag in front of the post office flies at half-mast and the streets seem just a little quieter than they normally are at this time, the people of the town a little quicker to look away when I walk by. Fintastic has been closed for the past couple of days, but people are still showing up. Instead of coming to eat, they're bringing food and leaving it outside the front door—pot roasts, casseroles, brownies, fruit baskets. There are cards too, and flowers.

Frannie is arraigned on multiple charges of assault with a deadly weapon. Lourdes said she heard that her lawyer is going to plead temporary insanity due to the trauma of losing Luke. Frannie's being treated at an inpatient facility over in McMinnville right now. I really hope they make her see that what happened to Luke wasn't her fault.

Holden and I both plead guilty to criminal trespass and destruction of property, but since we're both first-time offenders, the judge is lenient and we end up with only probation and community service. We *are* liable for the damages to the Sea Cliff, though. Holden plans to sell his motorcycle, and he and his mom are going to move back in with his grandparents in order to be able to pay their share. My dad writes a check for part of what I owe, and my mom works out a deal with the hotel's owners for another chunk of it.

She ends up selling equity in the coffee shop to Malachi Murray, Mr. Murray's eldest son. It isn't as bad as it sounds because she is still in charge of the coffee shop, but now she has a backer who is willing to invest in things. She tells Malachi about my grandma's idea to rip out the back wall and put in a window so you can see the ocean, and he goes one better—this summer we'll be introducing brand-new patio seating at the Oregon Coast Café, sure to be a hit with tourists and locals alike. I'll also be spending this summer and next summer working as a desk clerk at the Sea Cliff Inn after it's renovated, turning over all my earnings to the Murray family. All in all, a pretty generous resolution considering the destruction we caused.

Julia comes by my house during the day on New Year's Eve.

My jaw drops a little when I see her standing there on the porch. She's wearing the same pink sweatpants she had on when I went to see her after she got out of the hospital and a fleece hoodie that I recognize from our trip to the outlet mall. "I thought you were going to DC," I say.

"Yeah, that got canceled." She twirls a lock of her hair around her index finger. "I had a long talk with my parents. After that they didn't feel comfortable letting me spend a few days by myself with Ness and her family."

"Oh. That sucks," I say. "But I'm glad you told them."

"Me too," she says. "Turns out you weren't the only one keeping secrets better off shared. And hey, they took it better than I thought. Not great—my mom spent an entire day crying—but I think they'll come around."

"Julia," I say softly. "I hope you know that has everything to do with who she is, and nothing to do with you at all."

"I hear you." She plasters a fake smile on her face, but I can tell she's hurting. "Are you going to let me in or what?"

"Yeah. I'm sorry. I'm an idiot." I hold the door for her.

She steps into the living room. "Oh, you guys got a tree this year!" She scoots around the corner of the sofa and reaches out to touch one of the branches. A reindeer ornament I made in third grade out of varnished clothespins dangles from the end. "It's so cool. I wish my parents would let us have a real tree someday."

"But you guys always put up that huge artificial tree, with all the matching ornaments," I say. "It's so pretty. It looks like something you'd see in a magazine."

"Yeah." Julia tosses her hair. "But it's not real, you know. Your tree has personality." She glances around the living room, from the tree to the mismatched sofas to Betsy stretched out in her plaid dog bed. "Your *house* has personality."

Betsy makes a soft woofing sound, as if to agree. "It's definitely got character," I admit, wondering if maybe all my insecurities about where I live are just that—*my* insecurities.

Julia touches an ornament from the Tillamook dairy. "Hey, did you hear about Katrina Jensen?"

"No. What happened?"

"I don't know the whole story," Julia says. "I just heard that the police arrested her stepdad."

"Good," I say. Katrina and I will probably never be friends, but I still don't want anything bad to happen to her.

Mom pokes her head into the living room. "Hi, Julia! Happy holidays. Can you stay for a minute? Embry has something special for you and I promised her I'd help her out."

I raise an eyebrow at my mom. I'm not sure what she's talking about, unless she's going to take Julia up to the coffee shop when it's closed to add her official sandwich to the menu board.

"Sure, Ms. Woods." Julia is kneeling on the floor now. She's petting Betsy, who has rolled over onto her back to display her belly. "Your dog is ridiculous in the best possible ways," Julia says. "Like a big baby who never grows up."

"That's Betsy, all right." I grin.

Mom pokes her head out of her bedroom. "All right, girls. Come here."

Julia gives me a questioning look.

"I know what she's talking about, but I'm not sure what she's doing," I say.

The two of us round the corner into Mom's bedroom and I gasp in surprise. Mom has the web page I built for her linked to the Oregon Coast Café's official domain. It's up on the screen and she's added the Julia Worthington to the menu section.

I tug Julia closer to the screen. "It's your present," I tell her. "I figured since you were leaving, the town needed a way to remember you."

Julia squints at the screen. "You named a sandwich after me?" She starts laughing. "This is the best thing ever."

"It's our healthiest offering," Mom tells her. "Whole grain bread, hummus, spinach, low-fat Greek dressing."

"Oh, and it's stacked tall with lots of cheese," I add with a grin.

Julia throws her arms around my neck. "This is seriously unforgettable. Look at me—I'm on a menu with Courtney Love and River Phoenix. This is seriously big-time."

"I'm glad you like it," I say. "I'm glad I got a chance to give it to you."

Julia leans back to look me in the eye. "Yeah, about that. I miss the hell out of you. Maybe we should talk about how to be friends again."

"I'd like that," I say.

We head back into my living room, leaving Mom to fiddle around with her new website.

Julia flops down on the futon. "You would have to be honest with me," she says. "I want to know about how your mom is doing. More important, I want to know about how you're doing, even after I go away to college."

"Deal," I say, my eyes growing misty. "I don't know if I deserve a second chance, Julia. I don't know if I deserve you." I swallow hard. "You know, at one point I actually considered whether you might be the person sending me the threats, whether you could have poisoned yourself just to hurt me. There were clues that pointed to you, but I couldn't really entertain the possibility. I knew you wouldn't do that to me."

"I wouldn't." Julia shudders. "I wouldn't do that to me either. I don't ever want to feel like that again. I now carry three EpiPens with me at all times—one in my backpack, one in my glove compartment, and one in my purse. My parents even gave me a keychain EpiPen holder for Christmas."

"Good. And I'm sad that you didn't get to go see Ness, but does this mean you're done with the extreme dieting for now?" I chew on my lower lip. "I'm kind of worried about you."

"I'm done with that," Julia says. "I know I got a little carried away."

Betsy lifts herself up from her dog bed—first her back legs and then her front. She stretches and then plods over to where Julia and I are sitting on the futon. She looks hopefully at me.

"Okay, fine," I grumble.

Panting with excitement, she hops up onto the futon and splays out between Julia and me. As Julia pets her soft fur, I say, "I decided Holden was only half right about me. I pull away from people I worry are going to leave me, but not physically—emotionally. I knew you'd be hurt by what I did. It wasn't about you going away. I worried if I told you the truth it would be over for us no matter where you ended up living, so I hid it. I've always felt . . . below you, I guess. And not just you. It was the same with Luke. I hid a lot of things I felt like you guys might find . . . unacceptable, because I didn't want you guys to kick me out of your lives." I blink back tears.

"Embry. Being different, wanting different things, doesn't make you below me," Julia says. "Or Luke."

"I know," I whisper. At least I'm starting to believe that.

"I can't believe he's gone," Julia murmurs.

I swallow back a lump in my throat. "I can't believe I almost lost both of you."

"I'm still here. I'll always be here, even when I'm not, you know?" Julia pulls me into a hug. "But no more secrets, Embry Woods."

"No more secrets," I agree.

Mom and I spend New Year's Eve watching a marathon of Sexy Firefighting Models and eating ice cream. Because it's a special occasion, we let Betsy join us up on the sofa. When the clock strikes midnight and the kids of the neighborhood light off their firecrackers and bottle rockets, I pull Betsy into my lap and hold her while Mom covers her ears and sings to her.

It's basically the best New Year's Eve I've ever had.

The next day I wake up early and grab Betsy's leash to take her for a walk. I tuck my dad's camera in the pocket of my jacket—maybe I can capture the sun rising over the water.

Halfway to the beach, my phone buzzes with a text. My heart leaps into my throat until I see the sender: Holden.

Holden: New Year's present for you at our old spot. Go quick though, before the tide beats you to it.

Me: WTF is a New Year's present? Why do you keep trying to one-up me on gifts?

Holden: I'm just an ass like that. Now seriously, get down here.

Shaking my head, I tuck my phone back into my purse and head down to the beach. I'm expecting Holden at the Pot Hole, but he's actually out on the main section of the beach, bending down doing something in the sand.

Not just something. He's drawing.

There are lines everywhere—some thick, some thin, some intersecting at strange angles. There are also rocks that seem to be strategically placed. There's even a tree in the middle of the picture made out of pine boughs he must have collected from up on Puffin Hill.

"What is all this?" I ask. "Are you signaling your mother ship?"

"I told you I was experimenting with mixed media, right? So come on, you two. You're going to love this." Holden heads toward one of the wooden staircases that lead up to the mansions on Puffin Hill.

I follow him and Betsy halfway up the stairs. "Okay, stop," he says. "Turn around."

Looking down, I can clearly see the picture. A lot of kids come to the beach and draw hearts in the sand. They write things like I LUV JILL or STEVE WAS HERE. But this . . . this is art on a grand scale. The lines are fallen trees, leaves, bits of debris. The smooth pebbles he's used make up the outlines of stumps, and the trunk of the lone tree that remains standing. "It's a logging field," I say. "With one tree that somehow got missed. It's beautiful."

He rakes his hands through his hair. "I didn't tell you the whole truth about my tree fascination. I don't like painting people, so I do portraits as trees. This one is you, Embry. Because no matter how much the world throws at you, you're still standing."

"Holden." I literally gasp. "That's . . . so . . . I don't know what to say." I lift a hand to my chest, which is actually aching from the way my heart feels right now. "I love it. I love you."

"I love you too," he says. "But stay here."

He hurries back down to the beach. While he's making his way down the steps, I pull Dad's camera from my pocket and take several shots of the beach. As I'm flipping back through the gallery, it hits me this would make an amazing postcard or greeting card.

Holden grabs a stick and adds something to the bottom of the picture: WILL YOU BE MY GIRLFRIEND?

I laugh. Betsy barks. Holden takes the stairs back to where I'm standing two at a time. "Now, no pressure," he says. "But let me know if the tide washes everything away and you need me to rewrite it."

"Yes, I'll be your girlfriend," I tell him.

We share a long kiss on the stairs while Betsy paces back and forth on the step below us, her tail slapping repeatedly into my legs as she barks excitedly at seagulls.

As the three of us head back to the beach, I nudge Holden. "Check this out." I show him the photos I took of his artwork on my dad's camera.

"Wow, that looks incredible," he says. "I can't believe I made that."

"I know you don't want to be an Etsy mogul, but this is the kind of thing you could put on postcards and greeting cards and sell online. No worries about expensive postage either."

"You will not rest until you commodify my art, will you?" Holden nudges me in the ribs.

"I'm just saying, I wish everyone could feel the way I felt when I saw that." I hop from the bottom of the stairs back onto the sand. "What's the harm in trying? You need money to pay off your debt to the Murrays. The world needs more beautiful things."

"Oh, does it?" Holden pulls me close, holds my face in his hands. "I only need one beautiful thing."

By my side, Betsy whines in protest.

"Whatever, two beautiful things." Holden reaches down, picks up my one-hundred-pound dog, and spins her around in a circle, her paws flailing every which way. She's so surprised, she doesn't even make a sound.

"My turn," I say.

Holden sets Betsy down and spins me in a circle. The sky has gone from purple to pink in preparation for sunrise. It's just a blur of pastels with the occasional splotch of gray and white as seagulls fly by. I feel . . . free.

"Now your turn!" I do my absolute best to lift Holden, but I succeed in getting him only like two inches off the ground before we both collapse onto the sand. Lifting myself to my knees, I take Betsy off her leash, my mouth widening into a grin as she gallops through the shallow surf. Yanking off our socks and boots, Holden and I chase her up and down the beach. I squeal as the frigid ocean laps at my ankles.

Above our heads, the silvery imprint of last night's moon is still stamped on the sky as the sun begins to peek over the horizon. It's a new day, a new year. I don't know what the future will bring, but for the first time in a long time, I feel strong enough to face it.

ACKNOWLEDGMENTS

All the love and gratitude to my friends and family, and to my amazing agent, Jennifer Laughran. Thank you for putting up with my mood swings and occasional long, ranty, middle-of-the-night emails.

I am lucky to work with a fabulous team at HarperTeen, including Karen Chaplin, Bria Ragin, Rosemary Brosnan, and countless other people who are nice enough to make my books look all shiny and perfect. You are my heroes.

Thanks to my beta-readers: Philip Siegel, Marcy Beller Paul, María Pilar Albárran Ruiz, and Christina Ahn Hickey. Thanks to the Apocalypsies, the YA Valentines, and all the super-awesome book bloggers who manage to balance being supportive with keeping it real. I love you guys.

And as always, thanks to my readers. This is my tenth traditionally published novel and I kind of can't believe that. Ten books—look what you helped me do! Truly, you are magical.